section roads

by

Mike Murphey

Section Roads
First Edition

A Border Affair, from Charles Badger Clark's book of poetry *Sun & Saddle Leather*, is used courtesy of The South Dakota Historical Foundation.

Poem, "The Merry Month of Mayhem" from *Rhymes for the Irreverent*, 2006 edition, published by the Yip Harburg Foundation and The Freedom from Religion Foundation.
Courtesy of the Estate of E.Y. Harburg and Glocca Morra Music LLC.

Acorn Editor: Laura Taylor

Cover design by Damonza

Book interior formatted by Debra Cranfield Kennedy

ISBN—Hardcover 978-1-947392-51-9
ISBN—Paperback 978-1-947392-50-2

Section Roads is dedicated to Nancy,

who makes our wonderful adventure possible.

This book is also dedicated to the memory of the first one,

the one who remains forever gentle on your mind.

Love is a series of "darlings" and "dearies"
Of "honeys" and "sweeties" and sugared entreaties
Of moonings and swoonings, and cooings and billings
All tempered of course by occasional killings

The Merry Month of Mayhem
—E.Y. Harburg

prologue

June 2009

Little towns don't forget.

"You've made a mistake," Hezekiah Boyd said. "You don't want me at your reunion."

Was it already that time again? Forty years. Four decades since he'd put that dusty blotch of a town behind him. He'd been back on only a handful of occasions, coming and going anonymously when his mother's stubbornness compelled him.

"Well, you're on my list," the woman said.

She'd identified herself as Anna Mae Wallace. Hezekiah didn't remember an Anna Mae among the people he'd known in Arthur, New Mexico.

He stood at a wall of windows overlooking the Cochran Islands and the ocean far below. Computer software money had built this mansion, clinging to a steep mountain forest of fir, cedar and a tangle of arbutus with its bright red shedding bark. When his bank account finally warranted such a splurge, he'd fled to the greenest, wettest place he could find. He loved standing before sheets of floor-to-ceiling glass, perched at the northwest corner of North America, considering the other-worldly contrast between British Columbia's magnificent Desolation Sound and the genuine desolation of New Mexico's high plains, where he'd spent the first eighteen years of his life.

"Ma'am, I don't know how you got my name . . ."

"Says right here Hezekiah Boyd. Didn't you go to—"

"Yes, I attended Arthur High School. Forgive me, though, I don't remember you."

"Well, you wouldn't," she said. "I moved here a few years ago. I'm just helping the committee."

"Okay. Melissa Stanton is still there, right? I'm sure she's smack in the middle of all this reunion stuff."

"You mean Melissa Painter," Anna Mae corrected. "Yes. She's the committee head."

"Your list says Boyd?"

"Hezekiah Boyd. Class of 1969."

He found the wake of a sailboat motoring through Thulin Passage far below him. "They let the 'Hezekiah' part confuse them. You go ask Melissa and Darrel Jensen if they wanted Buddy to attend their reunion."

"You're not Hezekiah Boyd?" Anna Mae sounded confused.

"Yes, I am. Forty years ago, though, everybody called me Buddy."

"Why wouldn't Buddy be welcome at the reunion?" she asked with a bit of snip in her voice.

Hezekiah disconnected the call.

He couldn't bring himself to tell a stranger that on October 30, 1966, Buddy Boyd shot and killed a girl named Christy Hammond.

chapter one

The Reunion
July 2009
Thursday

"You can take the call on this phone, Mr. Molloy."

Arthur, New Mexico Country Club's banquet director pointed at a clunky throwback from an earlier decade sitting on a desk in a darkened office. "The caller says it's urgent."

The flight bearing Cullen and his girlfriend Lori Summerlin from Spokane, Washington, to Lubbock, Texas, had arrived late and they'd scrambled to make the reunion's opening reception on time. Cullen frowned and told Lori, "I'm sorry, kid. I hate to send you in there by yourself..."

Lori touched his arm and kissed his cheek. "I'm a big girl, Cullen. I've arrested bikers. I've even shot people. I don't think I'll be intimidated by a bunch of folks I don't know at a high school reunion."

"Thank you," Cullen said to the former police detective. "I don't know what this is about. But I'm sure it won't take long."

Alone in the office, Cullen didn't bother switching on the desk lamp.

"Hello. This is Cullen Molloy."

"Cullen. I'm so glad I reached you. It's been so long, the cell number I have for you isn't good anymore."

"LuAnn? Wow, what a pleasant surprise. Is . . . has something happened to Buddy?"

The other voice hesitated. "I'm not really sure how to answer that."

"Well, what's—"

"His mother," LuAnn said. "They called earlier today. She's had another stroke and they don't expect . . . He took a puddle jumper from Campbell River into Seattle. He'll arrive in Lubbock tomorrow morning. I'm worried about him. I know about the reunion, so I knew you'd be there. I'm going to ask something that might be difficult."

"Sure," Cullen said. "Anything."

"I'm afraid he'll sneak in there, deal with his mom, and sneak back out without you or Shelby seeing him. I'll give you his flight number. Can you meet him in Lubbock?"

Guilt swept over Cullen in a wave. This man who had meant so much to him deserved better. Although they sporadically talked by phone, he and Buddy hadn't faced each other in almost a decade. Cullen felt gratitude and affection for Buddy. Cullen had been selfish. Followed the line of least resistance. He'd ensconced himself in Spokane, deflected Buddy's summer invitations to British Columbia with excuses, and bailed on his obligations as a friend.

"Is Buddy okay?" he asked again. "Besides his mother, I mean."

"No," LuAnn said. "Hezekiah is okay. But Buddy is not."

"I . . . I don't understand." Shadows filed past the office's windows, more reunion participants arriving.

"You know, of course," LuAnn said, "that Buddy always signed corporate papers Hezekiah Boyd."

"Well, he had to. That's his legal—"

"After you left, he asked that no one, not even me, call him Buddy anymore. He wants to be Hezekiah."

"I still don't . . ."

"Cullen," LuAnn said, her voice trembling, "I admire and respect Hezekiah Boyd more than you can imagine. But Buddy is who I love. And I'm afraid if this goes on much longer, Buddy will just fade away. You of all people *must* understand what a tragedy that would be."

"Oh, my God," Cullen said. "I thought he'd almost let Christy's death go."

"When you were with us, yes. He was so close. But then . . . I don't know. It's like he thinks Buddy doesn't deserve . . . I just don't know. I understand you'll be busy with the reunion, and I'm sure he'll ignore the whole thing. But I think being around you and Shelby might help if you can—"

"Don't worry, LuAnn," Cullen said. "I'll meet him at the airport. We'll find Buddy."

= = =¦¦= = =

"Those breasts can't possibly be real," Corinne Snodgrass said.

Shelby Blaine drank deeply from her wine glass, following the nod of Corinne's head across the Arthur Country Club auditorium, past streamers of crepe paper, hand-lettered banners proclaiming the Class of 1969, along with a cheesy cardboard galaxy of stars, moons and planets wrapped with aluminum foil. There at the punch bowl, a swan among a host of balding, overweight ducklings, stood Hannelore Summerlin. Her hair unblemished ebony, her face unlined, her eyes crystal blue with a hint of steel. She wore a pale aqua dress plunging at the neckline. Nestling there, a striking turquoise pendant dangled a curving feather fashioned of silver.

"Why not?" Shelby asked. "She's, what, maybe forty, forty-five years old? When I was forty, I still had tits like that."

"Oh, Shelby," Corinne said. "You can be so crude."

"Tits? 'Tits' is crude? This from the girl who explained to me what a hand job was when we were in the ninth grade."

"I most certainly did not!"

"You did! I received most of my early sexual education from your stories about Billy Bob's favorite parking spot."

"I did no such thing."

Shelby laughed.

"Remember that I kept a journal? I showed some of you at the slumber party just before graduation? You all begged me to burn it."

"So?" Corinne elevated her chin in a display of righteousness.

"I can show you exact quotes if you want me to."

Corinne cocked her chin a little higher. "Billy Bob and I were weak then. We've been redeemed, praise Jesus. And I don't appreciate coarseness."

They smiled, dipping their heads in greeting as two more vaguely familiar faces set below thinning hair, waved from across the room. Like most of Arthur High School's class of 1969, Shelby had fled Arthur in pursuit of a career. Corrine and Billy Bob were among the handful who had chosen to stay.

"But doesn't it bother you?" Corinne asked. "That woman, I mean. After all, you and Cullen . . . Everybody assumed—"

"Everybody except us." Shelby laughed. "If we'd stayed together, especially when we were young, we would have lost each other forever."

"Oh, you don't know that. Look at Billy Bob and me."

"Yes, I do know it. If that had happened, it would have driven such a wedge between us. Cullen is a wonderful friend. If he's found someone who makes him happy, I'm all for it."

"What about you, though? You'll be old and alone."

"I don't require someone to complete me," Shelby answered. "I like my life. I don't feel old." Despite her assurances to Corinne, though, Shelby took another glance at the woman by the punchbowl. *Well, shit.*

"And those are not real," Corinne added.

"What do you wanna bet?" Shelby asked.

"I'll bet you a dollar."

"Oh, come on. That's not a bet." Shelby stopped the passing waiter, exchanging her empty wine glass for a full one. "Bets involve risk. If we're betting, the wager has to be something that challenges your comfort level."

"All right," Corinne said. "If I win, you come to church Sunday."

"Deal. And if I win . . ."

She paused in thought, bringing the glass to her lips.

"I have to what?"

"Say 'fuck'. Before this evening is over, right here during the reception, say 'fuck'. Say it clearly and say it loud."

Corinne's outraged response was sidetracked as Helen Wallace and Jill Bates ran to them. Grabbing their hands, they performed a little stutter step while reciting a duet of lies concerning how everyone looked, how much everyone had missed everyone. Being polite, Shelby and Corinne lied back.

"The only reason I will accept this bet," Corinne said once Helen and Jill departed in pursuit of other quarry, "is because you need the influence of church. Even *you* won't walk up to someone you don't know and ask if she had her boobs done."

"Okay," Shelby said. "Let's shake on it. I'll remind you that your Christian beliefs compel you to keep your word. We have entered into a binding agreement here."

Corinne solemnly crossed her heart with the index finger of her right hand, then extended the same hand. They shared one exaggerated shake.

"You forget," Shelby said, "how well I know Cullen. He's mentioned several times that fondling a hunk of silicone is a mood-killer."

"I hate to break it to you," Corrine said, "but men become a good deal less discriminating the older they get."

"Only one way to find out," Shelby said, offering Corinne a wink.

She headed toward the punch bowl, navigating a sea of facelifts and sucked-in stomachs.

"Shelby! Shelby! No! Don't you dare . . ." Corinne called frantically.

Shelby negotiated Barry Westbrook's girth as she performed the greeting ritual before approaching this woman who surveyed the reunion landscape with a serene smile.

"Hello . . . Hannelore?" Shelby said, extending her hand. "We haven't met, but I've heard so much about you. I'm Shelby Blaine. Cullen has . . ."

Polite curiosity was supplanted with the glow of a radiant smile.

"Please, call me Lori. Cullen speaks of you often," she said with warmth Shelby took as genuine. Particularly when Lori added with the arch of one eyebrow, "Maybe a little *too* often."

Shelby had wondered how this meeting would go. Through their phone conversations and correspondence during the past three years, Cullen had gradually introduced this woman as a significant presence in his life. A month ago, he'd carefully worked into conversation that he'd be bringing a *date* to the reunion.

"Lori?" Shelby asked, taking the offered hand.

"Yes. Only my mother calls me by my full name."

"But I love it. Hannelore is so lyrical . . ."

Before Shelby could continue, Corinne reached her side, a little out of breath.

"I am soooo sorry, Miss . . . Miss . . . Please forgive Shelby. I don't know why she gets this way. Sometimes, I think she was born without any kind of a filter on that mouth of hers. Especially when she's been into the wine. She has no business asking about your . . . your . . ."

Lori raised her brows. A mischievous smile tugged at her lips. Corinne's eyes bobbed from Lori's face to her cleavage. Shelby shielded her face with one hand, then split open two fingers so she could peek through.

"My . . . what?" Lori asked.

"Oh, my sweet Lord," Corinne gasped, now switching her alternating glances from Shelby to Lori's cleavage. "You didn't ask her."

"My boobs?" Lori said, feigning outrage although she couldn't suppress a betraying smile. "The two of you were discussing my boobs?"

"Breasts," Corinne said automatically, then gasped one more time, adding, "No. No. Of course, not . . ."

"We had a bet," Shelby said.

“Aaaaaghhh,” wailed Corinne, throwing back her head, covering her face with both hands.

“Let me guess. Someone is questioning my . . . authenticity?”

“That’s about the size of it,” Shelby said, then started laughing again at the unintended double entendre.

“Aaaaaghhh,” Corinne repeated as she turned a full circle.

“Are you sure there’s a bet?” Lori asked. “The two of you didn’t just cook this up so you could come over here and cop a feel?”

“Wha . . . wha . . . why, of course not!” Corinne stammered. “I only made a casual observation that your . . . you are . . . very . . . gifted . . .”

“She thinks your tits are hot,” Shelby said.

“Shelby Blaine! I do not! I never said any such—”

“You don’t think my tits are hot?” Lori asked with a frown.

“No . . . yes . . . I . . .” Corinne stammered. “I think they are very . . . um . . . I’m sorry. I didn’t mean to imply . . .”

“What’s the bet?” Lori asked.

“If I lose, I go to church.”

“Oh, my. And if Corinne loses?”

“She has to say ‘fuck’ . . . loudly.”

Lori nodded. “Only one way to resolve this.” She glanced around the room, then held her arms wide. “Go ahead.”

Shelby arched her brows.

Corinne tuned her indignation up one more notch. “Shelby, don’t you dare!”

“Hey, you’re the skeptic. You go first.”

“I will do no such thing. Shelby, what’s wrong with you?”

“Then, you forfeit.”

“I . . . what?”

"You forfeit the bet. You lose. What do you think, Lori?"

"I guess I agree," Lori said. "I'm offering verification, and you declined. So, yeah, Corrine, you forfeit."

"Why me? Why don't *you* forfeit, Shelby? You didn't go either."

"Lori," Shelby asked, "are your breasts real?"

"Yes."

"I'll take her word for it."

"So, I think it's back to you." Lori smiled at Corinne.

"I will not touch another woman's—"

"Fine," Shelby said, "then pay up."

"I will not—"

"You promised. If you don't, you'll be breaking a sacred vow."

"Oh, Shelby," Corinne said, checking around the room as more people entered, "please don't make me."

"Hey, I didn't force you into this," Shelby said. She noticed Billy Bob approached behind Corrine, glad-handing as he came. "And remember, it must be loud enough to be heard."

"No, no, I can't—"

"I heard you say that word about a thousand times when we were kids." Shelby prodded Corinne with her index finger. "So, loosen up. You'll find it liberating."

"Oh, Shelby, I . . ."

The buzz of conversation grew louder by the second. Shelby took another quick glance at Billy Bob, then whispered, "Corinne, you are such a wimp."

Three things happened simultaneously.

Billy Bob stepped within an arm's-length of Corinne, Melissa Painter blew twice into a microphone, calling for the crowd's attention, and just as the conversation dimmed, Corinne said, "Fuck!"

Lori displayed a delighted sort of amazement. Shelby tried to hide her giggles behind the palm of her hand. Dozens of heads turned, offering various displays of shock. And Billy Bob said, "Goddammit, Corinne, you told me you weren't gonna drink tonight."

= = = ¦ ¦ = = =

"I should have known better," Corinne lamented a few minutes later. "Shelby, you've been getting me in trouble since the seventh grade. Leading me down the path. How come it's always me, instead of you, who gets caught?"

"Because she's smarter than to fall for that shit." Billy Bob laughed.

They had explained the bet. Billy Bob ogled Lori with wiggling eyebrows. "It's a shame Corinne forfeited. I'd be willing to take her turn."

"Sorry," Lori said. "That train done left the station."

"So where is Cullen?" Shelby asked. "I saw him earlier. Where'd he disappear to?"

"He got a phone call. He'll be . . . there he is."

Shelby recognized Cullen's thick silver hair and hoped the others hadn't noticed her quick intake of breath. Cullen Molloy stood six feet tall, still proportioned to his height. He'd developed the daily workout habit that warded off the overhanging midriff so many of their male classmates sported now. His grey eyes bore crinkles around their edges—evidence that an overly serious person had finally learned to smile. While he clearly wasn't a young man, Shelby couldn't believe he and she, come October, would be fifty-eight. She loved that he carried himself with a confidence absent when they were teen-agers.

A hundred memories struck her. Only during the past few years had she realized that every male she'd granted entry into her life had been measured against the bar set by an awkward, persistent boy, who insinuated his way into her heart when they were thirteen years old.

Diplomatically, Cullen gave Lori a squeeze and a peck on the lips before he turned to Shelby, wrapping her with his hug. "Shelby, Shelby. Three years is too long. Why haven't you come to see us?"

Shelby glanced to Lori, apologizing with her eyes. "Life, Cullen. Just . . . life."

He pulled her to him again and whispered, "Things will get interesting. I got a call from Buddy's assistant. His mom is ill. He's flying down tomorrow."

Shelby slipped from his embrace. "You don't think he'll attend any of the activities?"

"If I have anything to say about it, he will," Cullen said. "He needs our help. It's time everybody put all that behind them. And it's time *you* told him."

"Cullen," Shelby whispered, "that's a secret we will take to our graves. You promised me."

chapter two

September 1963

Shelby Blaine, a resilient little girl, had a strategy for dealing with the cruelty of seventh grade. She didn't expect kindness or generosity. But she would not retreat. She would make a place for herself in this new school, as she had the others. She would find girls who were friends and allies. Those girls just didn't know it yet.

Shelby stood next to the principal's secretary in an empty hallway, staring through an open door at her new math teacher. His back was turned as he wrote an equation on the chalkboard. Her late enrollment already set her apart. Once she crossed into the room, everyone would make their judgments.

She memorized what little of the class layout she could see through the doorway—a few front row desks, an unobstructed path to the teacher's desk. She shifted her books under her arm, removed her glasses with her free hand, took a deep breath, and entered.

She stood in profile to the class, face cast down, shifting her weight from one foot to the other as Mr. Hinkley held a whispered conference with the secretary.

"Class, please welcome Shelby . . . Blaine," he announced. "She comes here from Boulder, Colorado."

Reminding herself not to squint, Shelby cast her gaze quickly toward the mass of blurred lumps to whom she was being introduced, then cast her face down again.

"Take any seat," Mr. Hinkley told her.

Before she removed her glasses in the hallway, Shelby had calculated the distance to an empty desk in the front row. Head still bowed, she sat.

Shelby's auburn curls spilled long over her shoulders. She'd mastered the art of slumping a little, leaning forward so her hair shielded the view of her face. She opened her text, leaned, and slipped on her glasses.

When the bell rang, while everyone else bolted, Shelby deftly returned the glasses to her pocket. She made a show of deliberately closing her book, reaching under the desk to get the others, then stacking them with care. Mr. Hinkley headed into the hallway to monitor the bedlam between classes. Shelby thought she was alone.

"Do . . . do you need any help finding your next class?"

Shelby reacted with a start, found the boy standing just behind her, and caught herself squinting.

"You scared me. I didn't know anyone was still here."

"I'm sorry," Cullen Molloy said. "Do you know where your next class is?"

"Thanks, but I'll find it. You don't want to be late."

"Okay." He turned, but lingered another moment, then added, "Shelby is a cool name."

"Shelby is a dumb name," she countered.

He took another step toward the door, then stopped again.

"What?" she demanded with a full-on squint.

"You shouldn't feel bad about wearing your glasses," he said.

"I mean, I got my glasses this summer, and I don't like them very much. Lots of kids wear glasses, though. You're . . . you're pretty. No one will—"

"Oh, yeah?"

She bent her head, again hiding behind the mask of her curls. She slipped on her glasses, waited a beat, then raised her hands to either side of her head, fingers bent like claws. She thrust her face forward with a little leap toward Cullen, teeth bared and snarled, "Aaaahhhh!"

Cullen jumped. He saw black, thick-rimmed goggles, their fat lenses filled with green globes magnified to the size of quarters.

"Holy crap . . ." he gasped before catching himself.

She stared at him, until enormous eyelids tipped with caterpillar-like lashes blinked the spheres away.

"Um . . ." he stammered.

"What? Aren't you going to tell me it's not so bad? That people will get used to it. When they know me better, they won't notice at all? That I'm being too hard on myself?"

Cullen stood, mouth open, shaking his head. Finally, he shrugged. "God, no. . . . What are you gonna do?"

Shelby squinted again, then began to laugh, the sound rich and infectious. Soon, Cullen laughed along with her.

Finally, she managed, "If you think of something, please let me know."

= = = ¦ ¦ = = =

A few weeks passed before Shelby finally trusted Cullen. If not for his persistence, she probably would have ignored him as she did other boys.

Shelby's father moved with his job as a small-college history professor every few years, so she'd been through this new school thing three times already. She'd developed a strategy. She would do her best to hide her glasses for a couple of weeks, search out a group of girls whom she thought might be potential friends—other band girls were her best bet—and win them over with her personality before revealing the awful truth.

Once she had allies, the first couple of months would still be a test. That's when stares, jokes and jabs were the worst. *Four eyes, coke bottles, bug-eyed geek, goggle girl, cyclops. What happened to the plastic nose that goes with those glasses? Where's the cane and the dog?* She'd suffer quietly, hope her new friends would defend her. Simply weather the storm. When the novelty wore off, most kids would grow bored with the taunts and she'd be just another girl—although not one in whom the boys were interested.

Those first two weeks, though, would be a challenge. She sat at the front of each classroom, sneaking her glasses onto her face when absolutely necessary.

She'd bump through hallways between classes, sometimes waiting for the rush to ease so she arrived at her destination right before or—too often—just after the tardy bell.

In classes they shared, this boy usually hung back.

"Stick close to me," he said. "I'll get you there."

Shelby appreciated the help, but not the attention. She didn't need a boy complicating her strategy. Worst of all, this boy sat next to her during band. They both played saxophone and he held second chair. After listening to Shelby play, their band director, Mr. Bullard, assigned her third chair, although she knew she was capable of being the lead saxophonist. Being first at anything, though, drew attention. Right now, that was the last thing Shelby wanted.

Band was difficult because the chairs formed concentric half-circles, director at the center. Saxophones looked directly across to clarinets. Trumpets were behind the clarinets, and trombones behind them. As a result, thirty or forty kids looked right at Shelby. So, at night she memorized her music.

On Wednesday of the second week, Shelby, following close at Cullen's elbow—not so close, though, that anyone would think they were walking together—entered the band room, unpacked her instrument and made her way carefully to her chair, avoiding collisions with the vague shapes rushing around her. Filing sideways through her row, though, her stomach fell as she saw an indistinct white square on each stand. She sat, wetted her reed, and waited.

Shelby held her breath each time Mr. Bullard ordered the next selection. She squinted fiercely at the clock as a minute hand she could not quite see plodded toward the end of the hour. She thought she'd survived until Mr. Bullard said, "I think we've got enough time to try the new piece. Everyone, find *Fingle's Cave*. This is a difficult selection, so we won't spend much time with it. I just want to see what you can do. This was written by Mendelssohn in the early 1800's, but you'll recognize it from the cartoon."

He directed them to bar thirty-two, then instructed the saxophones and clarinets to play a familiar melody line that accompanied a hopping, indestructible mynah bird through a series of Warner Brothers cartoons any 1960's kid with a television set would know.

Shelby mimed playing her horn under cover of the others.

The disaster occurred when Deidra, seated two places to her right, couldn't find some of the notes. Mr. Bullard rapped his music stand. "This will be a good sight-reading exercise. We'll start with the saxophones."

First chair Troy Fuller flawlessly played the melody line. Cullen was next. That he took his time was obvious to Shelby as she begged silently for the bell.

"Work on your armature, Mr. Molloy, and your tempo," Mr. Bullard said. "Now, Miss Blaine."

Shelby hung her head. She reached her hand to her pocket.

"Owwwwwww!" screamed Cullen. He jumped from his chair, knocking over his music stand and Shelby's as well. Every eye fixed on him as he hopped, shaking his pants leg, swatting at his thigh.

"What's wrong?" Mr. Bullard demanded, slapping his baton on his director's stand in a futile attempt to quiet the tide of laughter accompanying Cullen's antics.

"A . . . bee . . . I think," Cullen said. "I got stung. On my leg."

"A bee?" Mr. Bullard's tone dripped suspicion.

The bell rang.

Two minutes later, only Cullen and Shelby remained as they gathered the spilled sheets of music.

"How did you know?" Shelby asked.

He glanced at her. "Your music was upside down."

= = = ¦¦ = = =

Cullen hoisted his saxophone case onto a band-room storage shelf. He placed Shelby's instrument next to it. The shrill clang of the second bell told them they were late. The emptiness of the surplus barracks building smelled of institutional floor cleaner and valve oil. Mr. Bullard had left as soon as the bell rang, hurrying to the high school band room across the street.

"Come on," Cullen said, "I'll walk with you to the gym. Who's your home room teacher?"

"Woodson."

"Oooh, that's not good. Her class sits right in the middle, starting with the bottom row."

"I don't wanna go," Shelby said. "How big a deal is it if I miss?"

Fourth period, just before lunch, served as home room for seventh graders. The class was basically a study hall. Most school-wide assemblies were held during fourth period so kids new to the junior high format wouldn't miss other classes.

Cullen stared at Shelby, knowing she couldn't see fine details of his face—like exactly where his eyes were directed—and thought how pretty she was.

"Depends. A lot of teachers don't take attendance with everybody in the bleachers."

"I'm going to stay here then," Shelby said. "If Mrs. Woodson asks me why I didn't show up, I'll say I got lost. Then when she asks how I could get lost, I'll show her my glasses. I'll say I don't want anyone to see how I really look. Then she'll feel sorry for me, give me a lecture about not caring what other people think. Then she'll get all distracted, asking me how I'm succeeding in class without seeing things. The glasses are good for getting me off the hook—a couple of times, anyway."

Cullen decided he would stay, too.

After an awkward silence, he said, "I don't think Shelby's a dumb name."

"What?"

"That first day, you told me Shelby is a dumb name. I think it's cool."

"I wish I had a normal name, like Sally or Jane or something."

"Why?"

She sighed. "Pretty girls can get away with odd names. But if you're not pretty, you just want people to leave you alone. An odd name attracts attention."

Cullen's mouth fell open.

"Shelby, you're the prettiest girl in the seventh grade."

"No, I'm not. And you don't have to say things like that. I'm okay with not being pretty."

Another awkward silence.

"You do have to, sooner or later," Cullen finally said. "Wear your glasses, I mean."

"Yeah, I know. But I need another week or so for some of the band girls to get to know me. Then it won't be so hard . . ."

Her voice reverberated in the cavernous room. They'd resumed their seats in the deserted saxophone section.

"What happened to your eyes?"

"I was born prematurely so I was in an incubator. Doctors say high oxygen levels messed them up."

"Wow. Can't they do anything?"

"In a few years they can do some kind of surgery and maybe I can wear contact lenses. There's new kinds of contacts coming out."

"My mom says I can get contacts in a couple of years," Cullen said. "I hate my glasses. They make me look dorky."

Shelby replaced her glasses. Her pupils bloomed to fill thick lenses.

"Take 'em off," she told him.

He did. She looked at him straight ahead, then leaned left

and right viewing his profile. "Yeah, they do make you look dorky, a little bit. Be happy they aren't like mine, though."

"Yeah. But, geeze, lots of people have stuff that's wrong with them."

"Okay, what's wrong with you?" she demanded. "And your glasses don't count. If I had your glasses, I'd be thrilled."

"I don't smile much," Cullen said, "because I've got ugly teeth."

"Lemme see. Big grin."

He bared his teeth.

"Yup. Those front teeth have yellow stains. Why don't you brush 'em?"

Cullen closed his mouth. "I do brush them. Sometimes three or four times a day. The stain won't come off."

Shelby removed her glasses, once again becoming the most entrancing creature Cullen had ever seen. "Have a dentist clean them."

"Won't work. My dentist says it's permanent. He says he could cap them when I'm older. My mom says no. She says we won't grind down perfectly good teeth."

"Yeah," Shelby nodded, "it's pretty amazing sometimes what moms aren't able to see. How'd you get stained teeth?"

"The water here. If you lived in this dumb town when your permanent teeth were developing, and you drank the water all that time, you could get these stains. The water has a lot of um . . . fluoride. That's what they say. If you get the stains, your teeth are like iron. I've never had any cavities. My dentist says I probably never will."

"You're sure it's not because you smoke?"

"No, I don't smoke! What, you think I'm some kind of hood?"

"My mom smokes, and she's not a hood. Could be you

smoke. Could be you just made up this fluoride stuff, so people won't know you're secretly a nicotine fiend. I don't like that my mom smokes. I don't wanna hang around with a nicotine fiend. Which is what you'll become if you're already smoking."

"If I smoked, especially enough to be a fiend," Cullen protested, "people could smell it on my breath."

"Lean over here and breathe."

"No. I might have . . . halitosis or something."

"Hey, if I'm gonna be your friend, I have to know."

Cullen smiled, at first offering the timid, lips-closed expression he normally allowed himself, then remembered she couldn't see details. So, the grin overtook his face. "You're gonna be my friend?"

"I'm thinking about it. But lean over here. I need to smell your breath."

He leaned. She leaned too, brushing her lips against his—the scant hint of Cullen's first kiss.

Cullen jumped away, mouth agape.

"Nope," Shelby said. "You don't smoke."

chapter three

The Reunion
July 2009
Friday

Cullen sat outside the security station at Lubbock Preston Smith International Airport, observing the flow of arriving passengers trickle towards luggage and freedom. As the trickle grew into a stream, Cullen spotted the shining head of Hezekiah Boyd bobbing above the crowd.

Despite years separating them from their last meeting, Cullen easily recognized Buddy. Although he'd shaved his head in a gesture of surrender to encroaching baldness, the sharp nose, the cleft chin, the chiseled cheekbones marked Buddy like a bar code.

Eyes hidden behind sunglasses, Cullen could not tell whether his friend stared absently or scanned the faces around him with apprehension. Whichever the case, the man took no notice of Cullen as he walked past. Cullen waited a moment, then moved into the stream.

"Hezekiah," Cullen called.

The figure ahead of him stopped.

"Buddy," Cullen said a little louder.

His friend turned. "Cullen!" Buddy hugged him, then separated himself so he could push the sunglasses to his forehead. "I don't know why I'm even surprised."

"LuAnn called," Cullen said. "Told me about your mom. She's worried about you. She thought you might need someone."

"And you drove all this way, just like that?"

"Shelby, too. Along with another friend of mine. They're with my car."

They walked toward a baggage recovery area consisting of a series of conveyor belts emerging from a portal that disgorged luggage. These belts snaked around before disappearing through an identical portal along the wall. An obnoxious beep squawked, warning people to stand back lest they be sucked into the netherworld of baggage.

"LuAnn called you yesterday?" Buddy asked. "How'd she know you were here?"

"The reunion. She gets all the mail, doesn't she?"

"Sure. She's a great secretary. Of course, I can't call her that anymore. She's a great executive assistant."

"An executive assistant who lives with you in a mansion overlooking an ocean? When are you going to admit she's more than that?"

Buddy deflected the question. "I may be in British Columbia half the year, but I've still got a company to run."

Cullen clasped a hand to his friend's shoulder. "So, your mom . . ."

"Mom died early this morning," Buddy said. "I took the first flight available, but I couldn't get here soon enough. I wanted to be with her when . . . even though she wouldn't have known."

"I'm so sorry. LuAnn just told me she was ill, and you were on your way."

"Like they say, it's sad, but it's a blessing." Buddy offered a mirthless laugh. "She hadn't known who I was for at least three years. She always said she wouldn't want to live that way. That's what everybody says, though, don't they? Never expecting it'll be them lying there oblivious to the world."

"We came to see if you needed anything."

"You shouldn't have," Buddy said. "I've got a rental. And it's not like I don't know the way."

"I didn't want you just to drive off by yourself. You shouldn't do this alone. Shelby's anxious to see you. If we didn't catch you here, we were afraid you'd sneak in and out."

They stood facing each other like boulders parting the waters of a rushing stream as a throng of strangers hurried around them.

"I tried to get Mom to move, you know." Buddy checked on luggage emerging from the hole in the wall. "Back when she could make decisions. I took her on vacations, showed her the world. I wanted her to live in Phoenix where she'd be close, and I could see her every day. But she wouldn't. She made me promise to let her stay at home. So, I hired live-in caretakers."

Buddy reached toward a bag moving along the belt. "One more besides this one," he said. "It looks the same."

"I used to see her when I'd visit—when my dad was still alive," Cullen said. "She told me she'd never leave. She said moving away would just be letting the assholes win. Those were her very words."

"Yeah," Buddy said. "Because I ran away, she felt like she had to stay and prove something."

"Come on, Buddy. You didn't run away any more than I did. Or Shelby did. There was nothing for any of us here. No kind of life for anyone who wanted something more than farming or pumping gas or teaching school in a little town. You would have left even if . . ."

Cullen stopped there. He didn't say it. He never said it.

"Even if I hadn't killed her?" Buddy completed the sentence.

"Even if the *accident* never happened."

"Half this town still calls it murder," Buddy said. "They think I should be getting out of prison about now."

"Fuck 'em," Cullen said. "Fuck 'em all. The judge didn't call it murder."

"The judge didn't call it an accident, either."

"But *you* know. And that's what matters. Especially after all these years. I think you'd be surprised at how many people would like to see you. You should stop by some of the reunion activities tonight or tomorrow. You could come with us."

Buddy shook his head. "If I showed up, Darrel and Melissa would shit a brick."

"The same brick? Or would they each have their own?"

Now, Buddy's laugh sounded genuine.

"Like I said," Cullen continued. "Fuck 'em. Nobody anointed them as anything. They're just two people who never mustered the ambition or courage to leave." He put his arm around Buddy's broad shoulders.

"Even the day after it happened, all I doubted was whether you did it at all."

"Oh, I did," Hezekiah said. "You don't know how many times I still wish I could believe I didn't. You've got to stand up and accept responsibility, though. That's what a man does."

"Even if the man is only sixteen years old? I know the person you are, Buddy. Don't ever forget that."

chapter four

October 1965

Cullen didn't pretend to be a tough guy. Mostly he just tried to keep his head down and get along. Some things couldn't be ignored, though. So, here he was, Thursday night, after a ninth-grade football game, behind the bleachers, fists up, waiting for Ricky Nellis to take the first swing.

Ricky and a couple of other wannabe hoods had been under the band section, pinching the girls' butts through the cracks of the bleachers, or poking smaller boys with sticks, guffawing each time someone squealed. Sitting next to Cullen, Shelby Blaine had given a startled jump. "Owww!"

With one motion she stood, turned and dumped the soda Cullen had bought her onto the culprits below.

"Shit!" Cullen heard someone sputter. He saw Ricky and his two buddies scramble out the end of the bleachers. Shelby waved her empty cup at them.

"Are you okay?" Cullen asked, not sure what had happened.

"One of those assholes pinched my butt, so I poured my pop on 'em," Shelby said.

Cullen peered around her. Ricky and his pals had disappeared into the sparse crowd. Football was a big deal in this part of the world, but worship services were mostly reserved for high school Friday nights. Here, junior high cheerleaders encouraged a small gathering of parents, the band, and a handful of students.

"Do you want me . . ." he started.

Shelby sat and put her hand on his shoulder. "Don't worry about it. They're just jerks."

She smiled.

When Shelby smiled, Cullen didn't even see her glasses.

= = = ¦¦ = = =

Cullen and Shelby joined other band members trooping from the bleachers toward the band room. Parents waited in a parking lot across the street.

Cullen walked with Shelby toward her father's car. As they passed through black shade of cottonwood trees, they paused long enough for Shelby to bless his cheek with a thrilling kiss. His smile fled, though, as a voice carried through the darkness.

". . . you'd think with those glasses she could at least see well enough to hit his lips . . ."

A small chorus of derisive laughter followed Ricky's witticism.

Cullen put down his saxophone case, taking two quick steps toward Ricky before Shelby grabbed his arm.

"Cullen, don't. I don't care what a moron like that says."

Cullen heard a car horn honk over his shoulder.

"It's my dad," Shelby said. "I've gotta go. Please, ignore them. Please? Call me tomorrow, okay?"

Cullen watched Shelby all the way to her dad's car. He answered her wave, then turned to face his adversaries. They were gone.

Cullen rode a motorcycle, a little 90cc Honda he'd campaigned and pestered over for so long, his father had finally relented. Shelby's parents forbade her to ride with him. His bike sat between the band room and the football stands alongside a few others.

The football field was a deserted dome of light. A bright tent of illumination glowed over the tattered patch of grass with strictly defined shadows for walls. As Cullen strapped his saxophone to the motorcycle's rear seat with bungee cords, he saw three figures emerge from the night, their features obscured by the glare behind them.

"There he is," one of them said.

"Hey, Molloy!" another called as he advanced on Cullen.

"That's a freaky girl you hang out with," said Ricky.

"Shut up, Nellis," Cullen ordered.

"Or, what?"

"Or," Cullen heard himself say, "I'll kick your ass."

"Ooooohhh," said another shadow.

"Uh oh," chorused the third with a little laugh.

"The only way I'd let her close," Ricky sneered, "is if she took off her glasses and kissed my dick."

Cullen peeled away his band sweater, balled his fists, dropped into the kind of fighter's stance he saw Muhammad Ali employ on TV. He began circling Ricky. Thin and wiry, his adversary stood half a head taller than Cullen.

"You gonna fight, or you gonna dance?" Ricky taunted as he cocked his right arm, faking a punch, then aimed a kick at Cullen's groin.

Without realizing where his reaction came from, Cullen dropped his left arm to block the kick, then leaped before Ricky could regain his balance. He wrapped his right arm around Ricky's head and squeezed with a headlock straight out of Big Time Wrestling. When Ricky bucked, Cullen clamped down harder, extending his lower body for leverage.

And that was pretty much the extent of the fight. Ricky grunted and whined as he tried to escape Cullen's grasp. When he flailed at Cullen with his fists, Cullen exerted more pressure, the knuckles of his left hand digging into Ricky's temple.

Ricky's companions stood by, at first offering suggestions like, "C'mon, Ricky, kick him in the nuts." Or "Hit 'im. Hit 'im."

As the headlock remained and Ricky's whining intensified, they shifted to, "Hey, Cullen. Let him go. You're gonna hurt him!"

On one hand, Cullen thought that was kind of the point. But his heart wasn't into *really* hurting anyone. So, he eased his hold, letting Ricky squirt away.

Ricky stood for a moment, hands on knees, breathing hard. Then he scrambled up with a squeal and took two wild swings, both of which Cullen dodged. The second lunge again left Ricky off balance. Cullen restored the headlock.

"I let you go because I thought you were done," Cullen grunted, then glimpsed a figure striding toward them from the main buildings. As the man passed through an island of light, one of Ricky's companions warned, "Jesus, it's Anderson."

"That's enough!" came a shout as the teacher continued toward them.

Ricky's companions melted away. Cullen released Ricky for a second time. He raised his hands, signaling his compliance with the order, his attention on Mr. Anderson. And Ricky hit him. A looping right caught Cullen flush. His canine tooth punched a neat hole through his upper lip. Blood gushed down his chin and onto his white shirt. Cullen rocked backward. Ricky smirked.

"I said that's enough!" Mr. Anderson barked, grabbing Ricky's shoulder. He turned Ricky and, seeing he was unmarked, said, "Both of you in Mr. Kendrick's office Monday morning. Nellis, you get out of here. Go!"

Ricky slunk after his friends.

Mr. Anderson assessed Cullen's injury. "You're bleeding like a stuck pig. Did he break your nose?"

Only now did Cullen see a red triangle of blood marking the front of his shirt.

"No." Cullen took inventory. Nothing really hurt. "I think he just cut my lip."

"Lemme see."

Mr. Anderson produced a small flashlight, withdrew a handkerchief and swiped at Cullen's face.

"Naaah. Won't need stitches. Poked a hole right through your lip, though. It'll stop bleeding in a minute. Can you get home okay?"

"Yes, sir."

"Then scram. And don't forget Monday morning."

Cullen trudged to his motorcycle. He leaned there a moment, ruing his gullibility—letting Ricky sucker punch him.

He heard voices. Before he could get the motorcycle key from his pocket, a knot of six boys led by Darrel Jensen marched around the corner.

"Where's the fight?"

Cullen turned away and played at adjusting the bungee cords holding his saxophone case.

"Fight's over," he said.

"You?" demanded Darrel. "Who'd you fight? Some other band bozo?"

Cullen could feel Darrel close behind him. He caught an odor of beer.

"Ricky Nellis," Cullen felt Darrel's hand clamp onto his shoulder and spin him around.

Darrel looked at the blood on Cullen's face, then at the dark stain marking his shirt. A couple of other boys laughed. Not Darrel. He pointed a finger at Cullen. "You goddamn pussy! You let a wimp like Ricky Nellis . . . I oughta' beat your ass just for being such a pussy!"

Cullen and Daryl locked stares. What could Cullen do? He couldn't protest. He couldn't say he'd won, that Ricky had only sneaked one punch at the end. This crowd wouldn't believe him. And he'd sound whiney for making an excuse. If he didn't say or do something, though, the story all over school would be that Ricky had beaten him up.

He simply didn't have the will, though, to fight Darrel.

"Leave him alone, Jensen," a new voice rumbled from the blackness.

The six turned to confront their challenger. Their body language shifted to supplication, though, as the figure accompanying the voice took form.

"And get the hell off my motorcycle!"

As Darrel initiated his effort to humiliate Cullen, one of his cohorts had stepped astride Cullen's bike where he sat, smiling a challenge. Another of the boys leaned onto a larger motorcycle parked nearby.

When the voice barked, they both scurried like rats seeking shadows.

The dark outline took on distinct features as the boy emerged. The width of his shoulders became defined. His thighs stretched his jeans tight. His face materialized with a soft hint of stubble peppering a square jaw. A strip of tape placed at an angle above his left eye did not quite cover threads of four stitches closing a game-inflicted cut.

As a fifteen-year-old, Buddy Boyd's childhood was already being sacrificed to a man's body. Cullen knew Buddy only as a nodding acquaintance in the hallways. Although they shared an English class, Cullen sat towards the front, Buddy in back.

"What's it to you, Buddy?" Darrel asked with a tone that questioned his enthusiasm for the challenge.

Buddy studied Cullen's face and shirt.

"You guys did this?" Buddy turned, balling his fists.

"We didn't do shit to him," Darrel said. "He let himself get beat up by Ricky Nellis."

"I didn't get beat up," Cullen said quietly.

Darrel grunted, mustered a glare at Buddy, then jerked his head toward the darkness. Buddy and Cullen were alone.

"I didn't get beat up," Cullen repeated, humiliation washing over him in waves.

Buddy bent to take a close look at Cullen's lip.

"Well, maybe not, but you look beat up. Why'd you fight Ricky?"

"That asshole said some things about Shelby, so I—"

"Shelby? She's the one with the glasses, right?"

"Yeah . . ." Cullen said warily, wondering if he would have to defend Shelby's honor yet again.

"She helps me with math sometimes," Buddy said. "I think she's cool."

"He didn't beat me up," a relieved Cullen said one more time. "I had him in a headlock the whole fight. He was practically crying. I was afraid I was hurting him, so I let him go."

Buddy laughed. "You fought him, but you didn't want to hurt him?"

"I . . . I mean, really hurt him. Like brain damage or something."

"What do you weigh? A hundred thirty pounds? I don't think brain damage was imminent."

Imminent? Not a word Cullen expected from a football player. He gave Buddy a reappraising look. "Anyway, Mr. Anderson told us to stop. So, I did. That's when Ricky sucker-punched me. He only hit me once the whole fight."

"I think you might not be cut out for this fighting deal," Buddy said. "My advice is just figure out how to get along with people."

"How do you get along with assholes like Darrel Jensen?"

"Yeah. Darrel's a real prick. He's big, but he got his ass kicked in football drills, so he quit the team. Why do you care what he thinks, anyway?"

Cullen sighed. Behind them, he heard the clank of a heavy switch and the field lights went dark.

"Because of what he'll say, what everyone *else* will think."

"You know the truth, though, right?"

"That's easy for you to say," Cullen said with a note of anger. "You're a football player. People leave you alone. Try being in the band. Our world's different."

"Hey, wait a minute. You know how many jerks are on the football team? You think anyone makes it easy? There's a half dozen guys big as me who want to knock my dick in the dirt because I don't hang with them, do the stupid crap they do. Every game, they're just waiting for me to screw up, so they can have an excuse to kick the snot out of me at practice. And no one would tell them not to."

"So, what would you do if they insulted *your* girlfriend?"

Buddy looked at him sideways. "Shelby is your girlfriend?"

"Well . . . yeah."

"She ask you to fight Ricky?"

"No. She would never—"

"Then don't blame her. If someone really hurt a friend of mine, I'd do something about it. But if my friend was able to deal with it, I wouldn't make my life more complicated by getting beat up."

"I didn't get beat up!"

"Whatever. Like I said, I know Shelby a little bit. I think she's pretty comfortable with who she is. What's she gonna say when she hears about this?"

Cullen sighed again. "She'll be pretty pissed off."

"At Ricky or at you?"

Cullen fell silent for a moment. "Mostly me. She'll say it was stupid."

"So, tell her you're sorry and just live with what people think. Couple of weeks, everyone will have found someone else to rag on, anyway."

= = = ¦ ¦ = = =

Three years earlier, the Arthur School District leveled a block of houses across the street to build a new high school, a rambling single story of red brick and sleek architectural lines. Seventh, eighth and ninth-graders inherited the old high school—a grim WPA-era edifice of two floors, brick now faded to a mottled brown. Classrooms admitted light through floor-to-ceiling windows, most frozen shut by the passage of time. Hallways were dark tunnels with oak floors polished by so many feet over so many years, they shone like mirrors where the ceiling lights touched them.

Wednesday following the fight, Shelby found Cullen, head

down, trodding somberly along this gloomy path to the clang of lockers and a buzz of conversation. He'd been right. Shelby had been angry. Not now, though. Now she worried. Some of the jocks and hoods were ridiculing Cullen, and he was taking it hard.

She caught up with him, slipping her arm through his.

"You okay?"

Before he answered, assistant principal Cosgrove, said, "Molloy, you better separate yourself from Miss Blaine there, or I'm gonna twist that arm right off."

Shelby made a point of holding both hands high as a demonstration that the separation was complete.

"Stupid rule," she said. "If you weren't already in trouble, I'd kiss you right on the lips and see what Cosgrove would do then."

Cullen smiled his first smile all week.

"On the lips?"

"Come see me after school. I'll show you."

"Can't," he said, slipping back into his funk. "I'm grounded because of the fight."

"Speaking of the fight, I came out of geometry this afternoon, and heard Ricky talking to some guys—including that jerk, Darrel. When he saw me he said, 'Hey goggle girl, I kicked your boyfriend's ass,' Darrel and his guys were laughing."

Cullen's head drooped a little lower.

"I started to say something, but Buddy Boyd was right behind me. You know what he did?"

"What?" Cullen mumbled.

"He said, 'Ricky, Shelby is my friend. You call her that again, and we will have a conversation that won't end well for you. And that's not what I heard happened. I heard you were crying like a little girl when Cullen let you go. Then you sucker punched him when Anderson showed up.' Ricky turned about as pale as he could get."

"Yeah?" Cullen asked. "What did Darrel say?"

"Not a word." Shelby smiled. "Buddy was looking pretty mean."

chapter five

July 2009
Friday

Waiting as Cullen searched for Buddy, Shelby and Lori shared the back seat of Cullen's rental. Both nursed a hint of a hangover. Being honest with herself, Shelby felt a little intimidated. She wanted to like Lori. Lord knows Cullen had made some bad judgments concerning love and commitment over his life. The biggest part of Shelby wanted him to find something that would work.

That other little sliver of her that would always love Cullen Molloy felt insecure, selfish.

Shelby had come to this reunion with no expectations. She was more than comfortable with her independence. After her second attempt at marriage disintegrated during her early forties, she carefully considered her options. She could go through the whole weary process of searching for some man bright, industrious and funny enough to hold her interest, who understood her career was just as important as his, who would not be initially attracted by her outgoing, slightly flirtatious nature, then try and change her once he had staked his claim.

Or, she could embrace her seclusion and content herself with sleepovers.

Though Shelby loved time spent with friends, she feared neither silence nor solitude. She liked dogs, cats and horses. Her dream had always been a place in the mountains, bordered by a river, with winter snow, summer sun and room for all the animals she wanted.

Without anyone's help, she'd made that happen.

She'd been named a division supervisor at New Mexico's Bureau of Land Management a few years earlier. She made a good living while building a generous pension. She'd invested well.

Her second divorce had been amiable. When they sold the Santa Fe house, they'd split the profit, each taking with them the assets they'd brought to the marriage. She couldn't count on being that lucky again, though, could she?

At one time, Cullen might have made her reconsider. The last forty years of their lives, though, seemed an ongoing series of near misses, as if their fates ran along those unvarying section roads that defined rural New Mexico. They were never far apart. They could see each other coming and going. But they couldn't hit the intersection at the same time.

Cullen had told her about Lori, about his infatuation with this woman a dozen years his junior. Shelby knew Cullen needed a meaningful relationship more than she did. So, she came to the reunion anxious to see him, content with her understanding that this would be one more fleeting glimpse of a past that teased them and a future holding different destinations.

= = = ¦ ¦ = = =

Lori and Shelby sat lost in their own thoughts. Lori hated the awkwardness. Thankfully, Shelby broke the stalemate.

"Um . . . I'm sorry about the whole, you know, boob thing last night," she said. "Sometimes I really am too forward. Having a couple of glasses of wine didn't help."

Lori laughed. "Hey, I thought it was funny."

"Mostly I wanted Corinne to loosen up," Shelby said. "She's fun when she backs off her whole born-again Republican thing and remembers who she was when we were kids. I thought my odds of winning the bet were pretty good. Knowing Cullen, I'm sure you're just about perfect."

"Hardly. You mean he hasn't told you I only have one nipple?"

"One . . . what?" Shelby stammered. "Why would you think he . . .?"

"I get the feeling there's not a lot you two don't talk about. And the one nipple thing is kind of how we got together."

Lori smiled, closed her eyes, leaned back and waited.

"Okay, I'm sorry if it's not any of my business," Shelby said after a long moment, "but you can't say something like that, then just leave me hanging."

Lori grinned. "I'm sure he told you I was a Spokane cop."

"Yes, but that's as detailed as he got. He didn't say anything about anyone's nipples."

"Well, Spokane suffers some long-standing public relations issues regarding police force and community. And the city council periodically forms committees to talk about it. Cullen, being a semi-wealthy, semi-retired, civic-minded attorney, gets recruited onto committees. I was assigned as a police representative. So, we got to know each other a little there. Then I got shot—in the left breast. Took my nipple right off. I shot the other guy, but still . . ."

"Oh, my God!" Shelby gasped. "You got shot?"

"Yes. Cullen came to visit me at the hospital—"

"You got shot?"

"Yes, and, see, I was something of a controversial figure within the department, so the higher-ups decided I should retire on a disability—"

"You got shot!"

"Yeah, apparently some men believe a woman needs both nipples to function as a detective . . ."

"I'm so sorry," Shelby said. "Oh, my God, Lori. They shot you!"

"Yes, they did. I needed an attorney, so I asked Cullen. He said we could fight it but the settlement they were offering was good, and did I really want to go through a lawsuit where everyone in town would be talking about my nipples? And Cullen didn't mind that I only had one, so we started dating."

"I never knew anyone who got shot. Are you okay?"

"I'm fine. It happened three years ago. I could get it fixed. My nipple, I mean. I just haven't gotten around to it."

"I . . . I feel so bad. I was feeling kind of . . . jealous . . . and it's dumb and I hate that . . . and now . . . you got shot!"

"But you've got to admit," Lori said, "I'll bet the one-nipple thing makes you feel a little better."

"Um . . . well . . . yes. Strangely, it does."

= = = ¦ ¦ = = =

July 2009
Friday

"I'll ride with Buddy," Shelby whispered. "Do you mind? It'll give us a chance to talk."

"No, I think that's a good idea." Cullen lifted his eyebrows, which Shelby dismissed with a wave.

Hezekiah stood a little apart from them at the Enterprise counter. They'd been through the greeting rituals. A hug for Shelby, which she returned with a kiss to his cheek. A polite, interested handshake with Lori.

Cullen and Lori left them and began an hour-long drive through the agricultural blight of West Texas.

"So, what's the deal with Buddy?" Lori asked. "I know you worked together a long time ago, but you really haven't talked much about him."

They drove along a paved road—an impossibly straight line heading north. Deep green alfalfa fields alternated with stubby rows of cotton and weedy, untilled soil bank every few miles forming a pattern replicating itself off into a horizontal infinity. Heat waves shimmered along the pavement. From the soil bank, dust and debris climbed columns of rising, swirling air.

At the age of five, Cullen came to believe these thermal dust devils were pathways for souls fleeing to heaven. He believed this because on the summer day his grandmother was buried at a rural cemetery with brown grass and a few gnarled, wind-battered elms, one of these dust devils sprang from an uncultivated field across the road and as it grew—sucking dirt and paper and tumbleweeds along—passed over the mounded red earth marking the new grave. A spurt of dust leaped from the mound, painting a segment of the great undulating pillar a pale rosy shade. This pink apparition climbed as the thermal moved across the cemetery, finally disappearing into a hot, whitish-blue, eastern New Mexico sky.

Dust devils always made Cullen think of the people he loved who were no longer alive. His mother and father rested with his grandmother at that same cemetery.

Cullen had a ready description when his friends asked him about his home town. Arthur, New Mexico, along with hard-scrabble oil patch towns like Hobbs, Artesia, Midland and Odessa, was located on a high plane called *Llano Estacado* which, Cullen originally speculated, was Spanish for something like *really windy dry flat place.*

Occupying Eastern New Mexico and Northwest Texas, the region is characterized by hot blustery summers and even colder blustery winters. The wet part of the Llano received barely twenty inches of rain during a good year. “Arthur,” Cullen would note, “is in the dry part.”

Bleak as they might be, the Hobbses, Odessas and Artesias of the world were at least plopped down atop semi-vast underground puddles of oil. Not Arthur. Not a drop. If tumbleweeds had been a cash crop, though, the homesteaders would have prospered.

Arthur and Arthur County were named for Chester A. Arthur, America’s twenty-first president. Researching a junior high school history assignment, the most compelling facts Cullen found about him were that Arthur was America’s fifth fattest president and owned eighty pairs of pants.

The community of eight thousand—at an elevation of four thousand feet above sea level—had nothing geographical, like a river or a canyon or an oasis, to warrant its location.

Arthur just *was*.

The flat monotony spread in every direction. “Given a clear day,” Cullen was fond of saying, “you could climb a six-foot stepladder and see the earth curve.”

He often puzzled over the pioneers’ judgment. Certainly, more attractive locations waited further west. He supposed the settlers might have been tired and stopped to rest, thinking they would wait for a good rain to replenish their water supplies before they moved on. And when the livestock had all died of thirst, they were stuck.

Still, despite this hardship, there grew a civilization defined geographically by dirt roads that formed the borders of all those perfectly square six hundred and forty-acre sections of land claimed by early twentieth century homesteaders.

As Cullen composed his answer to Lori's query about Buddy, he thought of those section roads, and all the ways straight lines and straight laces had twisted the paths of this small group of friends.

"I told you about Christy Hammond, didn't I?" Cullen answered. "The girl who was shot to death our sophomore year?"

Lori gave a little gasp. "That was Buddy? Oh, no. And he went to jail?"

"Juvenile detention. He pled guilty to manslaughter. They kept him until his eighteenth birthday. They took him away in November of 1966. He came back May of 1969."

"At least he got to come back."

Cullen gave a rueful laugh and shook his head.

"No, that was part of the punishment. A lot of people thought he should have been charged with murder. They thought he should have been sent away for life. When the judge didn't agree, half the town was furious at the injustice of it all. Christy's uncle is a lawyer. He convinced juvenile court authorities to make Buddy finish high school here as a condition of his release."

"But why would they—"

"It was their last shot at punishing him," Cullen said. "They had a few weeks to give him hell when they knew he couldn't fight back."

chapter six

July 2009
The Reunion
Friday

Shelby towed one of Buddy's bags as she followed him to the rental counter. He pulled a matching bag and shouldered a computer case. Shelby watched from a bench while he went through the paperwork process.

"Do you want full or partial coverage?" the rental agent asked. She was maybe twenty-three. The nameplate clipped to her snazzy rental car vest said Peyton.

"I don't want any coverage," Buddy said.

"We're giving you an almost-new automobile," Peyton said. Her smile did not match her tone of voice. "You have to be covered."

"I am covered. The credit card I'm using provides rental coverage."

"Limited coverage." Peyton's smile faltered.

"Give me an example." Hezekiah said.

"Of what?"

"Of the limitations."

"Hail damage."

"It hasn't rained here in months."

"Fire damage."

"While I'm driving, or while the car is sitting by itself?"

Her smile faded completely. "Does it matter?"

Shelby smiled as the transformation took place. Buddy was back.

"Yes," Buddy said. "If the car catches fire while I'm driving, I'm assuming the fire would be the result of a catastrophic accident, probably fatal, and I wouldn't really care if the car's covered or not."

"Sssir . . ." Peyton hissed.

Buddy raised a finger and pointed toward a video camera above the service desk. A slightly scary semblance of the smile restored itself.

"I don't want insurance."

"Fine." The smile persisted. "Will anyone else be driving the vehicle?"

"No, I'm alone."

"You are not alone." Peyton nodded toward Shelby. "That woman walked up with you. She has a bag that matches yours."

Buddy looked over his shoulder. Shelby smiled and waved.

"Never saw her before."

"Sssir . . ."

"I'll be the only driver, I promise."

The smile disappeared again. Peyton took a deep breath, as if gathering herself. She tried the smile once more and this time it stuck. "Will you return the car full or empty?"

"How could I return it empty? I'd have to run out of gas to do that."

"Are you enjoying yourself, sir?"

"I'm sorry. I know they make you ask all this stuff, because the company makes as much on insurance and extra driver fees and gas as they do from the rental fees. I'm just being . . ."

"An asshole?"

"Yes, ma'am," said Buddy with a straight face.

"Well, at least we agree on one thing."

= = = ¦¦ = = =

"You were kind of mean to her." Shelby laughed as they walked toward an outside kiosk. "She's only doing her job."

"I know. I can't help myself, though. Her job is to extort money by trying to frighten me. I cut her off before she got to the possibilities that the car could be stolen or eaten by wolves."

"Eaten by wolves?"

"Well, the tires, anyway."

Buddy handed the contract to a tall African-American man, who seemed about Peyton's age. His name tag read LaMarcus.

LaMarcus gave the contract a cursory look. "Hezekiah?"

"I know. My dad wanted it. It's a Jewish name."

Then Buddy pointed at the name tag. "LaMarcus?"

"Yeah. My mom. It's a Black thing. In high school, they just called me Buddy."

Buddy grinned. "Me, too."

LaMarcus took a quick glance at the contract. Shelby guessed he wondered if Buddy was kidding.

"We have a high school friend whose name is Cullen," Buddy said.

"Cullen?"

"Yeah. His mom. It's an Irish thing."

"What'd they call him?"

"They called him Cullen. He kinda' got screwed, because Buddy was already taken."

"Hey," said LaMarcus, "do you realize you declined the insurance coverage?"

= = = ¦¦ = = =

About five miles from Arthur, Cullen turned off the main highway onto a road with a wide sweeping curve that appeared to arc around grain elevators, the first visible signs of civilization ahead.

"This is the short cut," Cullen explained when Lori asked where he was going. "This way we can avoid downtown."

"Why don't we want to go through downtown?"

"This way we miss the traffic lights."

"Right. Both of them."

Cullen laughed. "Everybody who lives over by the university takes this road when they're driving from Lubbock. Always have for as long as I can remember. I guess I'm not sure what the reasoning is."

"Maybe it's the novelty of driving on a road that curves," Lori suggested.

Cullen slowed a little, respecting the long, gentle bend. He saw a dot emerge in the distance. The dot gradually became a man wearing a Hawaiian shirt splashed with yellow and orange. Cullen slowed more as details materialized. The shirt was buttoned at the collar. A knit Rasta hat, woven with greens, reds and yellows, covered the man's head. Dreadlocks hung from under the hat. The Caucasian man wore a pair of beige cargo shorts, black socks under sandals. In his left hand he held a face mask, snorkel and swim fins. With his right, he held aloft a sign that said *Blue Hole?* Something that might have been a joint was balanced behind his right ear. A duffle bag sat at his feet.

Rolling slower, Cullen glanced over his shoulder. "You know, I think that might be Weard."

"I think that might be an understatement," Lori said. "So why are we stopping?"

"It is Weard! I don't believe it."

"We don't have to verify it, for heaven's sake."

Cullen tromped the brakes and put the car into reverse. He steered carefully and rolled down the passenger side window.

Cullen leaned across the driver's seat, bending a little over Lori's lap so he could see the man's face. The man put both his hands on the window sill and stooped to meet Cullen's gaze. His expression didn't change. With a voice void of surprise or enthusiasm, he said, "Hi, Cullen."

Cullen jumped from the car with open arms and embraced the man, who awkwardly returned his hug. He included a few gentle pats of Cullen's back.

"What are you doing here?" Cullen asked him.

The man stepped away from the hug and offered Cullen a suspicious look. "I'm taking the shortcut." He assessed Lori for a moment and added, "You aren't cops, are you?"

"No, it's me. You know I'm not a cop."

"She's a cop." He pointed at Lori.

"No. She's Lori. She only *used* to be a cop."

Casually as he could, the man put his sign under his arm, reached to his ear and palmed the joint. "Cause if you're cops, then I'm sick. I have a prescription."

"We aren't cops, so you can be well," Cullen said. "What's with the snorkel?"

The man seemed puzzled. He pocketed the joint, held his sign so it faced him, then gave a nod of recognition. "Dude, I'm going to Santa Rosa. They got this really strange lake they call the Blue Hole. There's no other water anywhere. Just this little round lake. It's blue, and it's bottomless. Or that's what they say. They say it goes down forever. But that can't be true. If that was true, the hole would go all the way through and water would run out the other side."

"I've seen the Blue Hole," Cullen said. "I think the whole bottomless thing is, like, a local legend."

"See, that's what I think, too. So, I'm going to prove it."

Lori opened her door. "So, clearly you two know each other."

Cullen smiled. "Hannelore, please meet one of the most interesting men you'll ever know. He's the only CIA agent ever to hail from Arthur, New Mexico. Weard Ward. Weard, this is the lovely Hannelore Summerlin."

"Retired, not exactly an agent," Weard corrected. His voice remained void of inflection. "But I worked there."

Lori cautiously extended her hand. "I apologize for Cullen if he's said anything . . . impolite."

Weard frowned, his eyes shifting back and forth as if he'd missed something.

Cullen laughed. "She thinks I'm calling you weird."

"No. That's my name. Weard. W-E-A-R-D. My middle name, actually. It's English. It means *guard.* My first name is William. Nobody calls me that anymore, though."

"William Weard Ward?" Lori asked.

He nodded. "I know. I was pissed off about it for a long time, but my parents didn't think anyone would find out."

"So why are you here?" Cullen asked again. "This isn't on the way to Santa Rosa from anywhere."

Weard looked at the grain elevators.

"This is Arthur, isn't it?"

"Yeah," said Cullen. "Um . . . we're here for the reunion. Is that why you're here?"

"Yeah. Yeah, I think so." Weard frowned. "I would have graduated a couple years before you did, though. Why are *you* here?" A vein in his temple throbbed. "What year is it?" he asked with closed eyes.

"It's 2009."

"Well, shit. I'm late."

= = = ¦¦ = = =

As they talked, a couple of cars came along behind them. Rather than honk at the car blocking a lane of traffic, friendly drivers slowed, offered waves, then pulled around going on their way. The third stopped behind Cullen's vehicle. Buddy and Shelby got out.

Together, they walked curiously toward this roadside gathering centered on an odd man wearing a Hawaiian shirt, until Buddy stopped, waved, and said, "That's Weard!"

"It is!" Shelby said. "Weard, um . . . Billy. Billy Ward! I haven't seen you since . . ."

Following the instant of recognition, they'd hurried their steps. Before she could finish her thought, Shelby embraced him.

"Hi, Shelby," said Weard, tolerating the hug. "Nobody calls me Billy anymore. I'm Weard. Hi, Buddy."

Buddy clapped Weard's shoulder.

"In school, though," Shelby said, "they tormented you with that name."

"Yeah. But someone gave me some advice once."

Buddy smiled. "Attaboy," he said.

They exchanged fist bumps.

"Are you here for the reunion?" Shelby asked.

"No. I'm late."

= = = ¦ ¦ = = =

April 1966

Shelby and Cullen sat under the shade of an ancient elm that would have been stately if not for eastern New Mexico gales. Over the decades, wind bent and sculpted the tree into a gnarled caricature. Its branches reached hard to the southeast as if fleeing in the opposite direction.

Only a light breeze wafted by on this late April afternoon of their ninth-grade year. As Buddy predicted, the stigma of the fight had been mostly forgotten and no longer haunted Cullen. Except when Cullen read smirking aspersions cast toward him by Darrel's gang. But Darrel had a new target, and Billy Ward inadvertently took the heat off Cullen.

Sitting here, mingling their sack lunches, Cullen had inched his hand to Shelby's. Between chips and bites of her sandwich, she voluntarily returned it to his grasp.

Across the street separating the junior high school complex from the high school, they saw a small, thin boy with pale skin and haunted eyes walking toward them under the weight of a backpack.

"Oh, man, there's Billy," Shelby said, her voice tinged with sympathy.

As he grew closer, Billy displayed the look of a troubled soul grimly awaiting the next assault on his dignity. Sure enough, somewhere from shadows cast by the old two-story school building came a sing-song voice, accompanied by a chorus of laughter. "Hey, there's Weard. Hey, Weard-O! Yeah, we're talking to you!"

Cullen saw Billy cringe.

"I hate them," Shelby said, her voice cold with anger. "I hate them all." Then she called, "Hey, Billy!"

Billy slowed.

Shelby waved him over. He froze for a moment. At first, Cullen thought he would flee. Billy took a cautious step toward them, then seemed to decide something.

Shelby's welcoming smile glowed below green orbs magnified by her glasses. Cullen felt undecided about the invitation. He'd finally sunk below the radar. Under Buddy's protection, the assholes were mostly leaving Shelby alone, too. An association with Billy Ward wouldn't be advantageous to either of them.

"They're jerks," Shelby said. "Come sit with us."

Billy sluffed off his backpack, letting it fall. "Hi, Shelby. Hi, Cullen."

Cullen nodded. He thought about asking Billy why he walked to the junior high school during lunch period, but he knew the answer. Billy was a year younger than the ninth graders. High school kids either shunned or bullied him.

Cullen didn't know what to say. Ever since fourth grade, like everyone else, he'd regarded Billy as different. Not bad. Not obnoxious. Just different. Billy fell asleep during class. He didn't get jokes. On the rare occasion he did talk, the subject was math or rockets or dinosaurs or rocks. In fifth grade, he spoke Russian, for God's sake. Spent a whole month answering every question in Russian.

So, once they got beyond, "Hi," Cullen simply had nothing else to say. Not Shelby, though. Shelby got right to the point.

"Okay, Billy, what's all this 'weird' stuff?"

Billy sighed.

"My name is Weard," he said sorrowfully. "And now they know."

"What's weird about Billy?" Cullen asked.

"No. My middle name is Weard."

"So . . . what is it?"

"Weard. W-E-A-R-D. It's English. It means guard."

"Why did your parents do that to you?" Cullen asked.

"Because they had to." Billy plucked a handful of grass and threw it above his shoulder, as if testing the wind. "My dad's middle name is Weard. My grandfather's, great grandfather's, and on and on. They had to, or else they'd get disinherited or something. You guys wouldn't understand."

The cruelest thing about it, Cullen thought, was that Weard *was* weird. He'd been promoted to their fourth-grade class from third at mid-semester. He got perfect marks, though he seldom participated—never answered questions or offered opinions—unless a teacher made him. During sixth grade, he added Chinese to his linguistic repertoire. When asked a history question one day, Billy answered with these strange chirping sounds and everyone laughed. Except Mrs. Butler, who thought she was being mocked. When she demanded what Billy thought he was doing, Billy appeared startled. "Uh . . . oh, I forgot."

"Forgot what?" Mrs. Butler asked.

"Um . . . my brain was just . . . thinking in Chinese, and I forgot."

Everyone laughed again.

Mrs. Butler sent Billy to the principal's office where they determined he really *was* speaking Chinese. The next week, they advanced him to seventh grade.

"You're wrong," said Shelby. "I understand."

Billy gave her a skeptical *Oh yeah?* look.

"My name is Shelby. They named me after my uncle. People tease Cullen, because Cullen is an odd name."

"So, how'd everyone find out? About your middle name, I mean," asked Cullen.

Again, Cullen thought Billy would leave. Instead, he sighed. "Every year, my Mom goes to the school office and the superintendent's office. She orders them to keep my file secret."

"At least your folks understand," Shelby said.

"I guess my dad went through all this when he was a kid. He's a big guy, though. He would just beat people up. I think he thinks that's what I should do, too, but . . ."

He made a show of flexing his skinny arms, displaying an absence of any discernible bicep.

". . . what can I do?"

"So, what happened? About your name?"

"You know Jackie Palmer at the high school? He's a junior. His mom works in the principal's office. Well, she saw my file, and told Jackie's dad. Jackie heard her, then he came to school and told everyone."

"Oh, man . . ." Shelby said.

"So now my mom says she's gonna sue the school, Jackie's saying if his mom gets fired, he's gonna pound me . . . and everyone calls me Weard."

Shelby withdrew her hand from Cullen's, reaching to take both Billy's smaller hands with her own.

“Tell your mom she can’t sue anyone. Tell her she has to let it go—or else they’ll never stop.”

Billy seemed surprised at Shelby’s touch, though he didn’t pull his hands away.

“I don’t know. She’s pretty mad.”

“When I was in . . . um . . . third grade, I think,” Shelby said, “a bunch of kids started calling me all kinds of names because of my glasses. Well, they’ve always called me names, but this was an organized kind of thing. And my mom wanted to get involved. My dad told her if she made any kind of formal fuss, things would just get worse for me. He said I had to learn to deal with other kids.”

“So, they left you hanging there on your own?”

“I found out later my dad handled it through back channels. He contacted two or three of the other dads and told them he’d kick their butts if their kids didn’t shape up. The point is, Billy, if your mom makes this a big production, they’ll never leave you alone.”

Billy shook his head. His face crumbled a little more. “I know. My dad said the same thing.”

“The thing about you, Billy, is you’re smart,” Cullen said. “You should use your brain to deal with this. That’s how you fight them. Just know you’re smarter.”

“Wear it.”

The deep voice coming from the other side of the twisted elm startled them.

Billy flinched, jerked his hands from Shelby’s.

Cullen craned his neck and found Buddy Boyd towering over them. Billy might have fled, Cullen thought, except his backpack was too heavy for a quick exit.

"Hey, Cullen, hey, Shelby." Buddy nodded a greeting at Billy.

"Buddy, how long have you been there?" Cullen asked.

"Not long. I wasn't spying or anything. I saw you guys here, and I wanted to ask Shelby something about geometry. I heard what you guys were talking about while I was walking over."

"Do you know Billy?"

"I've seen him around."

Buddy bent over, extending his hand. Billy rose to shake it.

"What did you mean, wear it?" Shelby asked.

"His middle name. Stop hiding it. Put it out there. *Insist* that teachers call you Weard. Be proud of it. Sign your name that way. Anyway, that's what I'd do. Like I told Cullen, the jerks have a short attention span. If they think they aren't getting to you, they'll get bored and find someone else to pick on."

"Or," Shelby said, smiling at Buddy, "you could beat them up. After all, you're a big strong football player." She made a show of taking off her glasses, smiling and batting her eyelashes. Cullen saw Buddy's double take at seeing Shelby without her glasses. He wasn't sure how he felt about that.

"Naaah." Buddy laughed. "I don't like fighting. You ever hit anyone? I mean seriously doubled your fist and smacked someone's head? It's not like the movies. Hitting someone really hurts. I don't recommend it. Hang in there, Billy. Cullen's right. You're smart. Handle it the smart way."

Billy frowned. "I know how to build a bomb. If you know where I can get some C-4, I could blow up Jackie's car."

Buddy laughed. "There you go. Just be sure he's not parked next to me when you do it."

"What did you want to ask me?" Shelby asked Buddy. Cullen was relieved she'd put her glasses back on. "About math?"

"It'll keep. See you guys later."

As Buddy walked away, Cullen felt Billy's stare. He glanced suspiciously from Cullen to Shelby. "Why are you doing this?"

"Doing what?"

"Being nice to me."

Shelby grinned, pointed at her eyes, magnified behind her glasses. "You and me, we're freaks. Freaks gotta stick together. It's kind of an obligation we have."

Billy pointed to Cullen. "What about him? He's not a freak."

Cullen felt a little insulted. "Wait a minute, you can't—"

But Shelby put her arm around Cullen's shoulders. "He's kind of an honorary freak. Believe me, there's a hidden freak inside him. I know."

"And I have ugly teeth," Cullen added.

chapter seven

May 1966

Cullen fidgeted under a porch light glow, took a deep breath and pushed the doorbell on a Sunday evening. The ninth-grade school year had ended two days ago. Today, he'd fulfilled his obligation to the Methodists and suffered through his mother's stiffly formal Sunday dinner. Finally, summer felt real.

He'd been almost giddy with anticipation all afternoon. Three glorious months! Of course, the last two weeks or so would be consumed with apprehension over facing the intimidating world of high school. But tonight, that reality was eons distant for a fifteen-year-old boy calling on his girlfriend. Her father served as a more immediate reality, and the sound of heavy approaching footsteps was more than enough to de-giddify Cullen.

"You again?" Jack Blaine said as he opened the door.

"Daddy, don't!" came a disembodied protest.

"Hello, Mr. Blaine," Cullen said, attempting a smile that failed.

"You didn't bring that motorcycle, did you?" Shelby's father asked.

"Mother! Go make him stop!"

Mr. Blaine was a forbidding man with heavy brows folding

over his eyes in a way that made everything he said seem an accusation. The rest of his facial features offered no relief. He had a squarish, chiseled countenance. His nose would have been sharp had it not been broken—maybe a couple of times, Cullen guessed, from the way it sort of laid on its side that way. Shelby's father worked as a history professor at Eastern State University, the sole cultural saving grace of Arthur. Though his hairline betrayed him, he stood trim and broad shouldered—a presence plenty intimidating for a skinny kid.

"No, sir," Cullen said, swallowing hard. "I got my driver's license last week. So, I—"

Mr. Blaine peered around Cullen to his driveway.

"Holy sh . . . What is that?"

Cullen looked at the ground. He couldn't bring himself to claim the pink 1956 Nash Rambler parked next to Mr. Blaine's bathtub Porsche.

"My dad won't let me drive any of our other—" Cullen began.

"Annie, come here!" Mr. Blaine called over his shoulder. "You won't believe this!"

"Daddy . . .!"

Shelby's mother stepped through the door, squeezing her husband's arm.

"Jackson Blaine," she said, her scolding tone offset by a smile, "stop this right now. You leave Cullen alone. You're embarrassing your daughter, and you know you're doing it on purpose."

Mr. Blaine gave a snort. "I am not trying to—"

"You are so!" called the voice. "Now stop!"

Mr. Blaine harrumphed and retreated.

"Please, Cullen, come in," Ann Blaine said. "Shelby will be ready in just a minute."

Cullen followed Mrs. Blaine to a sitting room, where she motioned him to a chair laden with pillows. Uncertain about pillow protocol, Cullen perched himself on the chair's front edge.

Shelby's mom was so pretty, she didn't look like *anyone's* mother, Cullen thought. And without her glasses, Shelby was her mother's clone. Same auburn hair. Same golden skin. Same chameleon eyes that could shift from an understated hazel to an impossible green.

Mrs. Blaine was always nice.

"I don't think he likes me very much," Cullen said, swiping at perspiration he felt beading on his brow.

"Oh . . . yes, he does, Cullen. He really does. He and I both appreciate that you've been Shelby's friend—that you were so kind when we moved here. But . . ."

Cullen heard a qualifier coming. He shifted his attention from the polished wood floor to Mrs. Blaine's earnest expression.

". . . but," she continued carefully, "you two aren't in seventh grade anymore."

Her arched brows suggested . . . something . . . Cullen hoped not what he suspected. He felt heat rise through his neck.

"And in my experience," Ann Blaine continued, "it's difficult for fathers to encourage any boy who is involved when his daughter starts to . . . date."

She lent a scary inflection to that last word.

"Oh . . . geeze . . . no. No, Mrs. Blaine," Cullen stammered. "We would . . . I mean, I wouldn't . . . well, I would never . . ."

Now his face had gone scarlet, and he was short of breath.

Mrs. Blaine smiled. She withdrew a pack of cigarettes from a pocket of her skirt and tapped one into her hand. She used a lighter on the end table to summon a flame, inhaled deeply, pushing smoke out the side of her mouth, away from Cullen's chair.

"Be careful, Cullen," she said. "Don't make promises you might not be able to keep."

Cullen's mind became a blur of forbidden images. He dabbed again at his forehead, thinking of increasingly passionate kisses with which he and Shelby had been experimenting. He flashed to several afternoons earlier when they'd found themselves retrieving their saxophones from the deserted band room after school. He'd turned her shoulders to him. She'd eagerly met his kiss, slipping her tongue past his lips, tickling his tongue with a few light brushes.

The tongue thing was new.

Cullen had timidly initiated the experiment several days before. She'd pulled away, seeming a little surprised. Her expression had remained serious, though—sort of determined, Cullen thought—as she'd reengaged, this time urging his tongue to come on over. Cullen found the experience almost unbearably erotic. He'd felt somewhat reluctant to return to the scene of that crime, although Shelby clearly remained interested.

These were not things he could dwell on sitting here with her mother, though. He considered making a run for it. Absent that option, he felt a compelling need to apologize about something . . . anything.

"My car is pink."

Mrs. Blaine made an unsuccessful attempt to suppress a laugh. "Are you trying to tell me something, Cullen?"

The suspected context of their conversation occurred to him.

"Oh, no!" he said. "I'm not . . . no . . . it's not like I picked the color. My dad . . . but he's not . . . Oh, man. I told you because he says . . ." He stopped.

Mrs. Blaine laughed. "He says what, Cullen?"

"He . . . he says I can only drive the pink car . . . because then I won't be able to get away with anything—when I'm driving, I mean. Because it's pink, see? Everyone will know it's . . . our car."

"I'll be sure to tell Shelby's father," she said. "That will make him feel better."

"Mother, please," came a quiet admonition. A relieved Cullen saw Shelby, wearing jeans with a green blouse that buttoned up the front hanging loosely at her waist.

"Is everything okay?" her mother asked her.

"Yes," Shelby said, rolling her eyes behind the thick lenses of her glasses.

"Come on, Cullen," she said. "Let's go."

Cullen followed Shelby outside as her father's voice wafted omniscient. "One hour is plenty of time to go get a coke! One hour!"

"And a half! It's summer!" Shelby countered, banging the door closed before the negotiation could continue.

"Hurry and let's go," Shelby urged him. "My parents are just so . . . so . . ."

As Cullen backed carefully out of the driveway, she continued. "I'm sorry to keep you waiting. I'm sorry you had to sit with my mother."

"I like your mother."

"Yeah, *right*," she said. "They both can be *so* embarrassing."

They reached a stop sign at the corner of Shelby's block. As Cullen came to a careful halt, he looked first left, then right. He found she had closed the gap. She placed her hands on his cheeks and kissed him, her tongue failing to respect the boundaries.

"Wow," Cullen said, smiling at her.

"There are no cars." She returned his smile. "We can go now."

Cullen was glad he'd gotten his contact lenses a couple of months before. He thought trying to French kiss with two pairs of glasses involved could invite some sort of optical disaster.

As they drove, she snuggled close.

"Your mom was a little strange tonight," Cullen said.

"Oh, gawd." Shelby groaned. "What did she say?"

"Nothing, really. Not . . . directly, I mean. But I got the feeling she thinks I'm . . . that we're . . . And I mean, what can I say? I can't just tell her we're not, because that might not be what she was talking about. How stupid would that sound?"

"Oh, that's what she was talking about, all right," Shelby said. "It's not your fault, though. It's because of these."

Cullen did not dare speak.

Shelby answered his nervous silence. "Are you trying to tell me you haven't noticed?"

Cullen could think of no tactful response. "Um . . ." He concentrated on white dividing lines as they disappeared below the headlights.

"My boobs!" she said with exasperation.

He glanced quickly, eyes wandering over the green blouse. "Um . . ." He jerked his attention back to the roadway, praying he hadn't compounded his sins by veering across the center line.

"A few months ago, I woke up one day and none of my bras fit. So, we got new ones. Now, they don't fit again."

"Um . . . they don't?"

"No. They bind, they pinch . . . and last year, when I got tired of wearing one I could just . . . take a break, you know? No one noticed . . ." She looked suspiciously at Cullen. ". . . did you?"

"Me? What . . . no . . . I mean . . ."

"But now my mom won't let me out of the house without a bra. It's why I'm wearing this blouse loose, instead of tucking it in. If I tuck it in, I look like I've got a camel under my shirt." She giggled. "The two-humped kind."

Cullen relaxed a little.

He slowed at the intersection of West Eighteenth and South Avenue I, careful not to extend the Nash's front bumper past the stop sign. He made a show of looking both ways, then activated his left turn signal.

Again, on his glance to the right, Shelby kissed him. This time her tongue settled in like it owned the place. Cullen set his emergency brake, shifted into neutral and put his arms around her. When they disengaged, Shelby removed her glasses. They held each other's gaze. To their left, where a persistent turn signal urged them, lay town, the drag, drive-ins and the latest rock n' roll from radio station KOMA in far-away Oklahoma City. To their right along the section roads, amid miles of dark empty prairie, lay perdition.

Cullen switched the turn signal to the right.

= = = ¦ ¦ = = =

He drove along a labyrinth of black section roads, his hands still carefully affixed at two and ten, with Shelby tucked tightly by his side in that simpler era before bucket seats and floor-mounted gear shifts.

Cullen felt the steering wheel become slick, his mouth ashen. He experienced a charge, like plugging into an outlet, each time

Shelby turned to kiss his cheek. Mostly, they remained silent, each studying the gloom beyond jiggling headlight beams as the Nash jarred over a hard, washboard surface created by the passage of heavy farm trucks.

These section roads were unvarying in their path, straight as a gunshot, with perfectly perpendicular intersections every mile. Cullen drove to the first juncture and took a left. Next, he turned right then left again, searching for any place to pull over. Section roads, though, are not scenic. They don't come with rest stops. Barbed wire fences border each side. Soft red sandy shoulders extend only a couple of yards from taut strands of wire. The roadbed itself was wide enough for oncoming pickups to pass each other if they did so carefully. If bigger farm trucks became involved, someone would need to back up.

Thankfully, they encountered no traffic. Cullen didn't know what he'd do if confronted by a set of headlights. Probably just go home and turn himself in, because certainly, whoever it was would see the pink car and report directly to Cullen's father, so they could collect the reward.

One more intersection, one more turn—Cullen had no idea where they were now—produced a miracle. Off to the right stood a windmill amidst a copse of scrub oaks with a rutted one-lane path curling past a cattle guard framed by two fence posts.

Cullen slowed, his voice husky. "Um . . . we could stop here and . . . rest. Before we head back, I mean."

"Yeah, okay," Shelby whispered.

Cullen considered driving straight across the cattle guard, then thought better of it. Ultimate disaster would be getting stuck in sand while trying to turn around somewhere over there by the windmill. So, he decided to back in, which would also make their escape easier when the posse showed up. Making a ninety-degree reverse turn through a narrow space between fence posts was, he discovered, a lot more complicated than maneuvering around cones at the high school parking lot. The process became a roughly twelve-point exercise—inching back, cranking the wheel hard one way without benefit of power steering, inching forward, muscling it around the other direction—still nearly scraping the fencepost.

Finally, they were docked.

Cullen cut the engine and cranked down the drivers' side window. Shelby slid to the passenger door, beckoning him to follow. She held her arms open, offering an embrace he accepted with total disregard for awkward parental admonishments, Methodist Youth Fellowship discussions concerning a *courageous choice of chastity,* not to mention the looming specter of Shelby's father.

They melted into their kiss—this one sparking as none had sparked before. Finally, Shelby gently urged Cullen away.

"Just a minute," she said. "I'm taking off these stupid glasses."

Cullen watched as green orbs became emerald stars. She ran her hands through a silky halo of dark hair, retreated to the crook between the door and front seat, then invited him again.

Cullen did not come to her this time, though.

A strawberry moon rose over his left shoulder. Its light reflected off the windshield bathed Shelby's face with an ethereal glow. Without the mask of glasses, her eyes were electric. Her face held an expression somewhere between innocent lust and wonder.

During all the years of his being, during all they shared with each other as both children and adults, during their estrangements and reconciliations and the myriad men and women who would intersect or divide their lives, Cullen would remember this moment above all others—simply the most beautiful sight he would ever behold.

"Cullen," Shelby whispered. "What's wrong?"

"You're so . . . so . . . beautiful. But that's not even the right word. I don't know if there is a word . . ."

"The way you're looking at me, I really do feel pretty. I've never—"

"Oh, God, Shelby, you are so incredible, and you don't even know it."

She urged him into another deep kiss. He felt a soft crush of breasts against his chest.

From the perspective of adulthood, Cullen edited this script. According to his polished, rewritten version, they held each other and, unwilling to compromise that convergence of space, time and innocence, rearranged themselves and drove home.

That's not what happened, though.

The kiss rekindled the lust, giving it the wherewithal to kick wonder and awe in the ass.

Cullen released his embrace. His hands dropped to the green blouse. He cautiously found the top button. When his gaze fell to the task, so did hers. He undid the button, then checked for her reaction. Her eyes didn't exactly tell him yes, but neither did they say no.

They both watched as he engaged the next button. It came undone, exposing a deep valley. Cullen dared one more button, glancing anxiously for a warning before leaning to her for another kiss.

While her eyes might be undeclared, Shelby's tongue told him everything was just fine.

Now he spread the shirt wide, bound by only two more

buttons. Cullen moved his fingers to the top edge of her bra. He pushed gently as his hand slipped inside.

She sucked in a breath.

"Oh, my God," Cullen whispered.

Then he realized he had a problem. He tried to think of a subtle, maybe even suave way of doing this. But he couldn't. And it hurt. He gave an involuntary grimace.

"Cullen, are you okay?"

He squirmed. "I . . . um . . . there's . . . I . . . I'm bent."

"Bent?"

"Yeah. And it's . . . painful."

"It . . . oh . . ."

She began to giggle.

Cullen squirmed a little more.

"Well, fix it."

He leaned tall against his seat, reached inside his pants and adjusted himself.

"Oh, that's so much better," he said

Still smiling, Shelby glanced down at her open blouse. "So . . . what do you think?"

"Oh, God, Shelby. They're . . . wow."

"They're getting huge," she said with a note of helplessness. "Every morning when I get up, I pray I can still see my feet."

"No." He parted the green shirt a little more, placing a hand on each one. "They're perfect. Nothing's too big or too . . . anything."

"But what if they just keep going? My last set of bras lasted three months. Do you know how embarrassing it is to borrow a bra from your mother, so you can go on a date?"

Cullen yanked his hands away as if he'd touched a hot stove. "Your . . . your mother?"

"Yeah. And it's kind of a *mother* bra, if you know what I mean. She wouldn't give me one of the sexy ones."

"Your mother?"

"I could take it off."

"NO! Um . . . She'd know if you . . . I mean, it's *her* bra and everything."

"How's she gonna know? She's not James Bond. It's not like she gave me a bra with a hidden microphone."

"I don't know, Shelby. It just seems . . . strange. I don't know if I can . . . I think she'll just . . . you know . . . *know*. Maybe things are going a little . . . maybe we should . . ."

"I'm the one who's supposed to say all that," Shelby said with an amused smile that abruptly died. "Oh, my God. You don't think I'm, like, a nympho or anything?"

"A nympho? I don't . . . of course, not."

"But I didn't tell you to stop, did I? I was going to take off my shirt, show you . . . everything. And I liked it when you touched . . ."

Shelby pulled her blouse closed. "Turn away. Don't look. I'm buttoning up now."

Cullen slid back behind the wheel, focusing out the driver's side window.

"Okay." Shelby sat on her side of the car.

Cullen wasn't sure what had just happened. He *was* sure, though, that, in only a matter of minutes, his life had become a lot more complicated.

chapter eight

July 2009
The Reunion
Friday

"So, will you hang around for some reunion activities?" Cullen asked Weard.

"I don't know, since it's the wrong one and all. I'm kind of anxious to clear up this whole bottomless thing in Santa Rosa."

"Bottomless? In Santa Rosa?" Shelby asked.

"No, it's not what you think." Cullen laughed, and nodded at the mask and swim fins. "Weard, I don't think a few days' delay—"

"But it's fraudulent, man. You said so yourself. They're like, perpetrating a tourism con. And little kids. It's like Santa Claus. Man, don't get me started on Santa Claus . . . okay, yeah, I'll hang out a couple of days."

"You got anywhere to stay?" asked Buddy.

Weard thought a moment. "I'll head to Santa Rosa."

"No," Buddy said. "You can stay with me. At my mom's house. She died, and the place is empty. I have to go through her stuff and—"

"Died? Yeah. We should go through stuff. Find out who did it."

"Um . . . no one did it. She was just old. She'd been sick a long time."

"I'll make some calls," Weard said.

"Well, okay. For now, come with me and Shelby. We can talk about it."

= = = ¦ ¦ = = =

"So, what's the deal with Weard?" Lori asked. "Why's he so . . . strange? He sounds like . . . um . . ."

Cullen checked over his shoulder and pulled onto the pavement.

"Like he's a little fried?"

"Like he's . . .disconnected. Does he smoke a lot of pot?"

"I wouldn't be surprised. He had a rough time when we were kids."

"Why did he say he *should have graduated*? Didn't he finish high school?"

"Not really. He was too smart. He skipped three grades that I know of, and then sometime during my junior year the CIA came and got him."

"Came and got him?" Lori's amused smile betrayed her disbelief.

"Weard is crazy-out-of-sight-off-the-boards smart. Like a savant. You know, guys who have some specific incredible mental ability but don't function well in society? Weard was always kind of on the edge of that *functioning in society* thing. He had this bizarre facility for language, though. You'd be having a conversation with him, and out of the blue, he'd be speaking Russian or Chinese or Swahili or Vietnamese. And he wouldn't even realize it."

"How'd the CIA get involved?"

"I guess language skills are a high CIA recruitment priority." They passed the grain elevators, and Buddy turned left ahead of them. "They're always looking for specialists in a given language or set of languages, so they were intrigued by a kid who spoke them all. I think they sent him to some East Coast university for a year and then, as soon as he turned eighteen, they put him on the payroll."

"That was the Vietnam era."

"Yep. I've talked with him about it a couple times when I'd run into him. A bizarre situation, like this one today, where he just appears. He spent some time in Vietnam and Cambodia, and probably even China during the seventies. And then from what I can gather, he woke up one day and the language ability was gone. So, they put him in some other kind of program."

= = = ¦ ¦ = = =

A parallel couplet of one-way streets bisected Arthur, snaking through town and forming a two-mile elongated *S*. Only two traffic lights interrupted one-ways on each side of the compact area around the courthouse square officially designated as downtown. Every other intersection deferred to this route, creating an ideal cruising track for high school students practicing their deification of the internal combustion engine. The drag mutated into highways at either end of town. One route headed west to Roswell and its economy obsessed with mythical aliens, the other striking east toward Amarillo, a bastion of a West Texas culture that worshiped God, oil and high school football.

Kids had been making the drag around that endless loop since their parents came home from World War II, Cullen supposed. Apart from late-night excursions on section roads, the drag served as the principal means of entertainment during his high school years. And when—following the initial reunion reception last night—he, Lori and Shelby made their way back to one of Arthur's two motels, Cullen witnessed a faithful observation of that same ritual. Only the cars and the music had changed.

As Buddy disappeared around one of the two turns, Cullen steered toward a small building that might be described as a hovel anywhere else. The forties-era hamburger stand formed a simple rectangle, maybe twenty feet across the front and thirty feet from front to back, exactly as he recalled from his earliest memories. The white paint had grown dingy. Two sliding walk-up service windows looked out from opposite ends of its face. A broad sign above the windows declared in a flowing script, *Pat's Twin Cronnies*. A menu was painted on the front wall. Seating consisted of a lone, battered picnic table, which occupied a space in the dirt parking lot.

"What's a cronnie?" Lori asked as Cullen shut off the engine.

"It's supposed to be c-r-o-n-i-e-s, with one *n*. But they misspelled it. Crony. It's like a 1920's word for pal or buddy. Like a *chum*. Legend has it that the guy who opened this place after the war had twin daughters who couldn't stand each other. So, he put them in that box and made them work together every day after school and weekends. The sign served as a reminder that they needed to get along."

"How'd that work out?"

"I think about two years into it one of them assaulted the other with a hatchet."

They waited behind a pair of Hispanic men clad in overalls, work boots and straw hats. Black hair matted with sweat curled below their hats. The skin of their hands resting along the small service window shelf displayed cracks and calluses.

"And they haven't corrected the spelling after all this time?" Lori asked.

"Nope. Not much changes here unless it absolutely has to."

"Nos dan dos tacoburgers y dos batidos, por favor," said one of the men.

"¿Desea que las papas fritas o los aros de cebolla?" came the response from inside.

"Uno de cada uno."

"Está bien. A cinco minutos."

Cullen smiled at the rapid, flowing lilt of Spanish.

The two men stood aside so Cullen could place his order.

"Two cherry limes."

A blond-haired, teenage girl used a soda and soft drink fountain, circa 1947, to mix a blend of liquids into plastic cups. She added a half a lime to each. Cullen handed one of the scarlet mixtures to Lori.

"Actually, I guess some things do change," he said.

"Yeah?"

"Those two guys," he said, gesturing to the Mexicans. "Back during the sixties, you wouldn't have heard people speaking Spanish to order anything. And you wouldn't have found a blond high school girl who could understand them."

Lori regarded him with a skeptical tilt of her head.

"What's so strange about Spanish being spoken in New Mexico?"

"*Eastern* New Mexico. And I'll remind you, West Texas is only twenty-five miles that way." He pointed toward the grain elevators.

"From kindergarten through sixth grade, I can recall kids from only one Hispanic family as classmates. The other Mexican kids attended grade school across the tracks. So, when we were all funneled into one junior high school, the integration was awkward to say the least. Lots of anger and suspicion among kids, and school policy was skewed to encourage Hispanic students to drop out."

"For example?" Lori challenged.

"Speaking Spanish on the junior high school campus was grounds for suspension or even expulsion."

"Oh, come on . . ."

"Absolutely true." Cullen drew an X with his index finger over his heart.

As a former police detective, Lori had considerably more conservative leanings than Cullen. Throughout their relationship they shared lively disagreements over political philosophies, although each had since mostly given up trying to convert the other.

"How could they possibly have justified—"

"The 1960's. Civil Rights movements took place somewhere else. Arthur's black population was, roughly, zero. Caesar Chavez and his farm workers movement was still years away. Nobody had to justify anything."

"Well, a child needs to speak English to function in society." Lori said.

"They already *did* speak English. Every one of them. They were bilingual, yet most Anglos here smugly considered Spanish-speakers intellectual inferiors, even though they spoke two languages while the rest of us spoke only one."

Cullen sipped his cherry lime, frowned, and stirred the drink with his straw.

"They were forbidden to speak another language, because teachers and administrators couldn't understand what the Mexican kids were saying. They worried those kids might be talking about *them*."

"In New Mexico?" Lori's tone accused Cullen of allowing his liberal bias to twist his memory.

"*Eastern* New Mexico. What's so hard to believe? We still have idiots running around demanding the same thing for the same reason. *This is By God 'Murica, and everybody should talk By God English!* Most of the world is multilingual, while Americans are not."

"That is a typical liberal oversimplification."

"I'll tell you something else that changed." Cullen took another sip and made a sour face. "That girl may speak Spanish, but she doesn't know shit about making a cherry-lime. This is awful."

"You're changing the subject."

Cullen laughed. "Okay. And you're a borderline Nazi who—"

Lori winked. "Yeah. But I'm a borderline Nazi with a great set of knockers. Real ones, I might add for the benefit of any other of your old girlfriends who might want to know."

"Well, there is that, kiddo," Cullen conceded.

"So . . ." Lori asked, "Do you wanna fuck?"

Cullen grinned. "Oh, you silver-tongued temptress."

= = = ¦ ¦ = = =

"You do realize," Lori said, "that you're still in love with her?"

Cullen lay with Lori, two pillows under his head, the back of his hand lightly grazing the puckered and scarred indentation where, eventually, she said, a replacement nipple would appear. She'd asked him about his preferences. *"There's no law that says nipples have to match. I always thought my nipples were sort of boring. What about different colors? Maybe a blue one?"*

Lori propped herself on an elbow, her fingers making lazy circles across his chest.

Standing along the highway earlier that day, Shelby had put on a pair of sunglasses. Lori felt Cullen momentarily disappear within himself. As he returned to the moment, she wasn't quite quick enough to conceal the tiniest worried frown.

"I guess I wouldn't deny that," Cullen said with a sigh. "It's not what you think, though. If we'd ever really thought we could make things work without driving each other crazy—or killing something important to us both—we'd have done it a long time ago."

"Should I be concerned?" Lori hoped her smile would hint she was teasing, knowing her tone hinted she was not.

"Hannalore," he said, "we've been together, what? Three years now? It's taken a long time for me to accept that you're real. You're young . . ."

"Younger."

". . . and beautiful. You're smart. You're tough. You're an incredible lover. You could have your pick of men any time you enter a room. Yet you choose me. Now, it's taken me a while to trust your choice. I do believe it, though. And I want it. One of the things that makes me think this will work is that you're secure enough in yourself—in us—to allow me my relationship with Shelby. Because she *is* very important to me."

"She was your first, wasn't she?"

"My first love? Yes."

"And your first lover." Lori made it a statement.

"Oh, we fooled around a lot when we were kids. But no. Back then, we never did the deed."

Lori gave him an incredulous look.

"Honest to God," he said.

"Why in the world not?"

"Me, mostly. I was a very . . . romantic kid, I guess. I was a victim of MYF—that's Methodist Youth Fellowship. The pastor's wife gave these talks on Sunday evenings about the wonderful knowledge that, on your wedding night, you were sharing this special treasure no one else could ever have. I bought into it. The morality. The romanticism. Along with a healthy dose of guilt dispensed by my mother. The pastor's wife never said anything about feeling each other up, though. So, we groped a lot."

"God," Lori said, "I lost my virginity when I was like, a junior in high school. I can't imagine that you two didn't . . ."

"Oh, there were a couple of times we came pretty close."

= = = ¦¦ = = =

September 1966

"If you're going outside," Shelby's mother said, "you have to wear your sunglasses."

Shelby had answered the door, anxious to see Cullen. She drew him into the entryway, checked quickly over her shoulder, then kissed him.

"Shelby!" This time, her mother's tone scolded.

"Mother!" Shelby scolded right back.

Mrs. Blaine pursed her lips. "I wouldn't let your father see you do that if I were you."

Shelby directed Cullen outside to the porch, where he glanced carefully both ways before kissing her again.

"God, I missed you," he said.

Shelby and her mom had been in Albuquerque for the past two weeks, where Shelby underwent surgical procedures that allowed her to wear a new kind of contact lens.

The front door opened behind them. Cullen's heart stopped. He was sure Shelby's dad would be standing there with a machete. Thankfully, Shelby's mother reappeared, wielding only a pair of sunglasses.

"Um . . . hello, Mrs. Blaine," Cullen said. "I was just . . . I was . . ."

"Uh, huh. Shelby, you do not go outside without these. You know what the doctor said."

"I'm not outside. I'm on the porch. In the shade."

"Take them."

Shelby shoved the sunglasses onto her face.

"That's better."

"I'm in the shade!" Shelby called as her mom retreated inside. "I can't see, because it's too dark!"

"You have to wear sunglasses now?" Cullen asked as Shelby pulled the door closed.

"For a couple of weeks. The surgery left me sensitive to sunlight. It'll take time for them to adjust."

She slipped the sunglasses to the end of her nose and opened those beautiful eyes wide.

"You can see my contacts if you look close," she said. "They feel weird still, like you said yours did at first. But the doctor says I'll get used to them pretty quick. Right now, I'm a little blinky."

"So . . ." Cullen said tentatively, "no more glasses?"

"Only when I'm by myself. I don't ever want anyone to see me like that again."

"Or when you're alone with me. I don't mind your glasses . . ."

"Absolutely not with you." Shelby sat on the hanging porch swing, patting the space next to her. "Especially for you, I want to be pretty."

"I've known you were pretty from the first minute I saw you."

Shelby tucked her arm into his as he sat.

"So what movie are we seeing tonight?"

"The Ghost and Mr. Chicken. Don Knotts."

Shelby leaned her head onto his shoulder and they looked across her front lawn to the Nash. "You know, if you didn't bring the pink car," she said, "we could go to the drive-in instead."

"Oh, geeze, I don't think my folks would let me see that movie. It's supposed to be . . . um . . ."

"Really sexy." Shelby reduced her voice to a whisper. "Corinne said she and Billy Bob went a couple of nights ago. She said there's a scene with boobs, nipples and everything."

"You're kidding. Nipples? In a movie?"

"That's what Corinne said."

Despite residual guilt hanging over their mystical June journey along the section roads, the pink Nash had found its way to that same windmill several more times this summer.

Although Shelby still expressed concerns about her potential nymphomania, she rarely said no once the Nash was on its way, unbidden, like a salmon instinctively swimming upstream to the spawning grounds. In daylight, Cullen knew this terrible temptation should be resisted. He knew Shelby should shine radiant, her purity preserved until some distant, theoretical time when they would be married.

But come the darkness, with the Nash finding its way, he could not escape his baser self. During the last couple of journeys—before Shelby left for her surgery—her breasts had become familiar territory. He'd seen them in their entirety, nuzzled them, kissed them. And he certainly had no objection to seeing different breasts. On the other hand, alone in the light of day with only his guilt to guide him, he realized breasts were moral kryptonite.

"I . . . I don't know," he said. "You've been gone . . . and maybe, maybe we should just go see Don Knotts."

"Okay, sure. If they make you drive the pink car."

= = = ¦¦ = = =

"Where's the Nash?" asked Mr. Blaine.

A sedate boxy-looking Mercury Comet, hiding Ford's 289 engine that would nearly get the car's front wheels off the ground if Cullen really floored it, sat at the curb.

"Um . . . broken," Cullen said.

He had fully intended to bring the Nash. He hadn't even explored an alternative. When Cullen entered the garage earlier that evening, though, he stepped into a sticky ooze. He found a spreading black puddle, as if his little pink car had been stabbed. His father said something about piston rings and head gaskets, then declared the Nash critically injured. There would be no attempt at resuscitation.

"Hmmmmmph," said Mr. Blaine. "I'll tell her you're here."

Shelby appeared wearing the infamous green shirt. Her auburn hair spilled over her shoulders. Her eyes shone like jewels. Her magnificence had begun to scare Cullen. Until now, Shelby's true beauty had been their secret. Without her glasses, though, everyone would know.

"Be home when the movie's over!" Mr. Blaine called as they left.

"We might get a coke after," Shelby bartered. The front door closed on her father's counter-offer.

"You got the green car!" Shelby said. "I didn't think you would!"

"Well . . ." Cullen said, once again laid low by the siren song of boobs, "I knew you wanted to go to the drive-in."

Just a little lie, he reasoned. They could grieve over the Nash later.

= = = ¦¦ = = =

Blow-Up, starred David Hemmings and Vanessa Redgrave. Shelby and Cullen both gasped a little when Vanessa bared her breasts to Hemmings, although her back was to the camera, so boobs were only implied.

"Wow," said Cullen. "That's pretty sexy."

"Just wait," Shelby said. "Corinne told me."

The best part came when Hemmings and not one, but two starlets shared a love scene.

"Okay, okay, here," Shelby said.

There they were! Two pairs, nipples and all.

"Oh, my God!" Cullen said.

"Corinne said you have to watch really close. The one on the right . . ."

Unmistakable! A flash of black pubic hair that must have consumed a full second of the ninety-minute film.

= = = ¦¦ = = =

They didn't wait for the credits. As soon as the actors were clothed, Cullen and Shelby discovered the Mercury knew its way to the windmill just as well as the Nash did.

Upon their arrival, Shelby's shirt and bra seemed to melt of their own accord. Cullen was nuzzling her when she said, "Why did you get to see two sets of boobs and all I saw was the backside of a naked guy."

Cullen regarded Shelby with uncertainty. The thought had never occurred to him. "You mean you'd really want to see some guy's . . . um . . .?"

"Well . . . yeah. What's the difference, me curious about dicks, you curious about boobs?"

Cullen was a little shocked. He took a few moments to formulate an answer. "Penises and boobs are . . . not . . . congruous . . ."

"Congruous?" Shelby laughed. "This isn't geometry."

"No, I mean, breasts are beautiful. And they're not . . . down there. They're not . . . you know."

"Pussies?" Shelby suggested.

Cullen wasn't ignorant of vaginas. Parker Calder's dad had a deck of cards hidden in the back of a bedroom closet that showed naked women assuming all sorts of contortions that laid the facts wide open. This was not a bit of anatomy he'd ever consciously associated with Shelby, though. She wasn't the same sort of creature as those pasteboard women who could be shuffled and dealt.

"You don't want to see me?" Shelby asked tentatively.

"Um . . . you mean you'd want to see . . . me?"

Shelby's eyes grew wide. She offered the slightest nod.

Cullen's mouth became so dry, he couldn't swallow.

Shelby finally broke the silence. "Okay, we both go on three, all right?"

Cullen nodded a fearful agreement.

"One," she said.

"Two," he answered.

They both said, "Three."

Jeans were unzipped and shoved down.

"Oh, my God," Shelby whispered. "Does that . . . hurt?"

"Um . . . sometimes."

Cullen found the vague outline of what lay below a lustrous patch of fur. As he remained focused on that mysterious, forbidding portal, Cullen experienced a wave of pure carnal lust against which the Methodist Youth Fellowship didn't stand a chance.

Then, inexplicably, an old wringer washing machine that sat on his grandmother's front porch when he was three or four years old came to mind. The wringer washer, an electrified tub that sloshed clothes back and forth, was topped with a set of rubber rollers clamped tightly together. Wet laundry was fed through the rollers and squeezed flat to expel most of the water.

Originally, the wringers were operated by hand cranks. By the time Cullen came along, they, too, were powered by an electric motor. His grandmother warned him against getting too close. She said if he did, the wringers would catch his fingers and yank his arm off, or grab his hair, then squash his head.

For a four-year-old, these possibilities were both frightening and compelling.

Would it really? And how close would he have to get?

He learned that the wringer washing machine came equipped with a demon that had a gravelly, persistent voice attempting to lure him every time his grandmother switched on this killer appliance. "Come closer, little boy. Touch it. Just once. It'll be fuuuuuunnnnnnn! Heh, heh, heh . . ."

On this night, out along the section roads, Cullen discovered that same demon resided in vaginas.

= = = ¦ ¦ = = =

Cullen and Shelby stared at each other for what seemed like a century or so.

Finally, Shelby broke the silence.

"Um . . . what now?"

"I think," Cullen said, ". . . either we take off our pants, or we go home."

"Okay, which?"

Cullen couldn't look away. "Maybe pants are . . . overrated?"

"Okay," Shelby said. "You go, then."

"Um . . . why me?"

"Because if I take off my pants, I'd be naked, and I can't just be naked. I'd have to put on my shirt first. But you're still wearing your shirt, so you could sort of skootch your pants down."

"And you think we should?"

"If you do."

"Well, okay. If you're sure."

He slid from behind the steering wheel, kicking off his penny loafers. He lifted his butt, then wiggled his jeans and underwear away. Shelby extended a tentative hand that hovered like a ghost in the dark.

Until Cullen said, "Oh, shit. There's a car!"

"What? Where?"

Headlights probed along the section road back towards town, jittering up and down along the washboard surface, and coming fast.

"Oh, my God," Shelby gasped. "What do we do?"

Cullen yanked at his jeans. He had one foot remaining in his underwear and one out, so it bunched at his crotch.

"Hurry. Put on your clothes!"

"Where's my bra? I can't find my bra!"

"Forget your bra, just get your shirt! And zip up your jeans."

"What if the cops make us get out of the car? I can't get out without my bra!"

"There, on the floor. Put it on, put it on. I'll hook it."

"Hooking a bra takes you forever."

She put the bra around her waist with the cups behind her, hooked it, then tugged it around. She calculated the car's progress as she slipped her arms through the straps. The Mercury's windows fogged as they contorted and fumbled in a desperate race against the headlights.

With the lights charging on and on, Cullen's pants were zipped, but his underwear remained semi-unaccounted for. Shelby had almost finished buttoning her shirt.

"Your buttons are crooked!" said Cullen. "The top button's not . . ."

"I've got to fix my pants first."

The headlight beams painted the cattle guard. Cullen and Shelby ducked, barely breathing, and waited beneath the dashboard for the knock on the window. After a couple of seconds, Cullen dared to peek through the steering wheel. He saw tail lights, floating off across the prairie.

Cullen leaned back and took deep breaths. "It's . . .it's okay," he whispered.

Shelby exhaled, rose and realigned her buttons.

Cullen considered taking off his pants again to reorganize but realized he'd fallen victim to panic. He didn't want her to see him on a waning tide.

Finally, when he could hear over his pounding heart, he said,

"I think that might have been a sign."

"Yeah," Shelby said. "And if we don't leave now, I'll be late getting home."

Cullen eased the car through ruts toward the section road when Shelby kissed him. The Mercury scraped a fence post along the full length of the passenger door as they crossed the cattle guard.

= = = ¦ ¦ = = =

"So, you can't take me to the movies?"

Disappointment registered in Shelby's voice as hallway traffic flowed around them.

"Or anywhere else for at least a month," Cullen said. "I'm grounded. My dad's furious about the car. I can't go anywhere on weekends, except for band stuff, and I have to come home right after. I can't drive. I'm not supposed to call anyone—that's why I didn't call you yesterday—but I don't think that one will last. And I'll be working weekends at some of the rental houses until he decides I've paid off the cost of repairs."

"How did you explain hitting the fencepost?"

"I didn't. I told him we parked at the movies and when we came out it was like that."

"Then how did he blame you?"

"I'm not a very good liar, so I don't think he believed me. He said if that's what happened, I should have called him and the police to make a report for insurance. He said I should have known better than to drive away without calling anyone."

chapter nine

Friday October 28, 1966

"You'll be there?" Kevin Quinn demanded.

"No . . . I . . . you guys go ahead," Buddy said, hoping Kevin would let him off this particular hook.

"Look, I don't care how good you are," Kevin said. "This is a *team,* remember? You, Andrews and Franklin are pissant sophomores. You gotta be in the house."

The implication of Buddy's performance earlier that night against Artesia was clear. Jack Saddler—a senior tailback who had complained to his buddies about this *sophomore punk* pilfering his playing time—would be seeing a lot of the bench.

Atresia had pounded Arthur 45-18, but Buddy rushed for 123 yards. Exhausted, Buddy stripped to his shorts and sat slumped against his locker, assessing his bruises. A subtle perfume of sweat and Flex-All hung in the air.

That's when Kevin walked down the row where sophomores were billeted. "Boyd, Andrews, Franklin. I need you up front."

Judd Andrews, a lineman, and defensive back Ray Franklin were peeling off pads on either side of Buddy. A subtle grimace crossed both faces. Buddy read their minds—*what do they want with us now?*

"How about we catch you after we shower?" Buddy replied.

"How about you get your asses out here right now."

Piss off! rested on Buddy's lips. Before tonight's game, though, his father had taken him aside and talked about *team*.

Buddy appreciated that his dad wasn't one of the overbearing fathers who lived vicariously through his son's athletic achievements. He encouraged Buddy to follow his own path. Whatever Buddy chose, though, his dad wanted him to be good at it. Because Mr. Boyd had played minor league baseball before becoming a civil engineer, he knew athletic talent and intellectual talent when he saw it. Mr. Boyd told Buddy that he possessed both.

Buddy, though, was a loner. Getting along with people—being one of the guys—was fine, just not a priority. Many of his junior high teammates mistook his distance and quiet confidence for conceit. Because he was big, tough and usually non-confrontational, though, they grudgingly granted him his space.

High School football proved more complicated.

"You've got a shot at playing college ball," his father told him after watching his son's performance off the bench earlier that season. "If that's what you want, then try a little harder to be more of a team guy. If it's not what you want, then that's okay. Live your life to meet your own expectations and fulfillment. Not for someone else."

Buddy liked that he was good at football. But he hated football psychology. The message got drilled into them every day: Football is everything. The subtle suggestion that, if you're not a good football player, you're not a worthwhile human being. He understood the absurdity of that premise. And if a fundamental philosophy of the coaching staff was fraudulent, what else were these adults lying about? How much worse might it be at the college level?

He trusted his dad, though. And knowing his dad, the assertion that Buddy "had a chance" to play college ball was likely an understatement. Football could mean a scholarship to the kind of university where his quiet intellect wouldn't mark him as an eccentric goofball who didn't fit any of the molds.

So maybe he would give this *being one of the guys* thing a try.

= = = ¦¦ = = =

Saturday, Oct. 29, 1966

"You three hide inside," Kevin said. "We'll bring the girls. Don't do anything until we're almost there. Then one of you jump across the doorway. The others make spooky noises, maybe walk by a window. We'll scare the shit out of them."

Buddy, Judd and Ray exchanged incredulous glances.

"Why?" Buddy asked.

Kevin poked Buddy's chest. "Because it'll be funny. You've gotta be one of the densest—"

"What's going to make it funny?" Buddy asked, thinking that if Kevin poked him again the quarterback would have trouble throwing with a broken finger.

"Jesus Christ, Boyd. Don't you get anything? Just do it."

So, three sophomores waited in a ramshackle house—at least a decade deserted—which sat at the end of a rutted red-dirt driveway along a section road three miles from town.

On the hovel's windward wall, tumbleweeds had piled to window height. The porch overhang sagged precariously as a center pillar had buckled. A settling foundation had jammed the front door halfway open. What remained of any window glass lay in shards on uneven floors.

Brown, withering corn stalks filled fields to either side of a narrow drive snaking a good fifty yards from the section road. The tall stalks created a sense of encroaching walls, and a cold breeze rustled their dry leaves, as if something crept through the corn. A sliver of moon hung low where the corn gave way to a plowed field, the loose soil tilled into long red mounds and deep, soft furrows.

"Man, this is bullshit," Judd said. He held the sheet he was supposed to wear.

Buddy could see Judd's breath as his words hung in the cold October air.

"It's creepy is what it is," Ray said. "What was that? Did you guys hear that?"

The old house creaked and groaned as wind threaded its way through cracked walls. The floorboards complained each time they took a step or shifted their weight.

"It's dangerous," Buddy said. "Just stay here. I sure wouldn't go walking around inside."

"Don't worry, man," said Ray. "This is as inside as I'm gonna get."

"Get down," said Judd. "I think they're here."

A knife-like glow stabbed along the corn, then swept toward the house before blinking off. The muffled sound of four doors slamming shut drifted toward them.

"All right," Buddy said, pulling his sheet over his head and adjusting the eye cutouts so he could see, "we might as well get this stupid shit over with."

Looking as if they were refugees from a Klan meeting, the three boys waited. Judd pressed his back to the wall inside the front door. Ray stood next to what had once been a picture window. Buddy stepped a few paces back into the concealing shadows. A vague group of figures shuffled carefully along the driveway, illuminated dimly by the new moon.

"... c'mon, guys, let's don't," a shaky female voice said. "Who cares about some stupid old house? Let's just go back to the car, okay?"

"Hey, we're already here," answered a male voice, probably Kevin's. "You've gotta see where they found the body. Phil said you can still see blood stains."

Moving together like a disjoined caterpillar, the group continued its slow advance. The mass resolved itself into seven figures—three tall, four shorter. Kevin, Jim and Preston Vantz—a senior defensive linemen who'd lost his starting job to Judd—were the tall ones. The other four were girls.

"None of that's true," came a more assertive female voice. "If anyone had died here, we would have heard about it."

"Happened a long time ago," Preston said. "A farmer murdered his wife with an axe."

"Please, guys," another shaky female voice said, "that place looks dangerous."

"Let's at least get close enough to look through a window." Buddy recognized Jim's deep voice.

"I'm staying right here. I'm not going any further."

"If you're that scared, Melissa," Kevin said, "just go wait at the car."

"As long as someone comes with me ..."

Two figures stopped. Five crept forward. One girl—Buddy was not sure who—clung to Kevin's arm as they moved almost in lockstep. Buddy recognized Christy Hammond. A junior with a reputation as a free spirit and a fun date, she'd separated herself a little from the others.

Buddy edged deeper into shadow as the group stopped about five yards short of the porch.

"Christy," hissed Kevin, "go look through the big window."

"You go look through the damn window," Christy said.

"Who cares about some stupid . . ." came the tremulous voice. "Let's—"

With a piercing yell, Ray gave a frenzied wave of his arms and leapt across the window.

The girl clinging to Kevin screamed. As she tried to run, her feet tangled, and she fell, dragging a startled Kevin with her. Following Ray's lead, Judd initiated a jump across the doorway, flapping his arms in an attempt at spookiness. His eyeholes shifted during mid-leap, though. He cracked his head on the door frame.

Buddy saw Kevin and the mystery girl fall. His attention, though, remained riveted to Christy as she reached into her purse. She withdrew an object that reflected a dull sparkle of moonlight, then . . . a flash of fire.

Bang!

"My God, she's shooting at us!" Buddy yelled as he dove to the floor. He rolled, tangling himself in his sheet. He spotted Ray, prone, a dark stain spreading onto the sheet at his head.

Judd scrambled through the window. Buddy heard a heavy thud as Judd fell to the porch. Buddy crawled toward Ray when he saw Christy swing her gun toward the spot where Judd had fallen.

"No!" he yelled. "No! Don't—"

Another flash of flame. Another sharp pop. Still fighting with his sheet, Buddy stumbled outside where Judd, silhouetted against the moon, lurched through plowed furrows.

Christy ran a half dozen steps, took a classic firing stance—a slight crouch, both hands on the pistol, arms extended. She fired twice more before Buddy reached her.

"Christy, goddammit, stop!" he yelled and leaped. He wrapped his arms around her as they fell, twisting her body so the gun was caught between them. He kept his arms draped tightly around her, squeezing as hard as he could until she gave a gasp, then seemed to relax.

"Christy, listen to me!" Buddy said. "You shot Ray. He's bleeding. You might have shot Judd, too. We just wanted to scare you. We weren't gonna hurt anybody. Put the gun down, so we can help them."

Christy's body heaved with what Buddy first thought were sobs.

"I'm letting you go now," he said. "Give me the gun."

He released his grip. When she pushed away from him and rolled to a sitting position, though, he saw she was laughing. *Why would she laugh about shooting Ray?*

To his horror, as her whole body was gripped by a spasm of glee, she leveled the pistol at his chest.

"Buddy, you dummy . . ." she wheezed, and pulled the trigger.

Flame spat from the barrel. Buddy cringed, his hands raised to fend off a bullet. He felt the smack of something against the front of his jacket.

". . . they're blanks," she gasped, trying to catch her breath. "I didn't shoot anyone."

In an absolute panic, Buddy patted at his chest. He probed for blood or holes, finding only a burned and discolored spot.

"But . . . Ray . . . he's bleeding . . ."

"Hey, man," Ray said from behind him, "I split my head open when I ran into the door. I might need some stitches"

"What about Judd?" Buddy asked.

"I think," Christy said through another spasm of laughter, "I think he's . . . he's probably still running."

Kevin lay face down, hands covering his head. He'd apparently been scrambling toward the corn on his belly while Christy was shooting. Quickly, the quarterback stood, dusting himself off.

"Christy," Buddy repeated, "give me your gun."

"No way. It's my uncle's. He'd kill me if I lost it. I have to put it back before he knows it's gone. What's the big deal? You guys brought us here to scare us. So, I decided to scare you. You can't take a joke?"

"Yeah, Boyd," Kevin said. "You were terrified. I'm surprised you didn't piss yourself."

Buddy stood and took a step toward Kevin.

"You were on the ground covering your head because you thought it was so funny?" he asked, voice sharp with anger.

"Fuck you. And yeah, seeing you guys running around like idiots was funny. Anyone who heard those little pops would know the bullets were fake."

Buddy clenched his jaw tight.

Christy tried to suppress her giggles.

"Take us back to town," one of the other girls demanded.

"Yeah, we're coming," Kevin said.

"Hey, wait a minute," Buddy said. "Ray needs to get to an emergency room, and I need help looking for Judd."

"You've got your own car, you take him," Kevin snorted. "That fuckin' Judd is probably halfway to town already. Fuckin' coward."

The group withdrew. Buddy heard car doors slam shut, then a dome of light moved away, the retreating car hidden by the corn.

= = = ¦ ¦ = = =

Buddy waited at the emergency room while first Ray's parents, then Judd's, came to deal with their injured sons. Three stitches closed a gash above Ray's eye. He would be fine. Judd wasn't so lucky. Buddy and Ray had found him sitting at a ditch on the far side of the ghost house field. He'd waved at their car as they approached.

"Buddy?" he called, peering through the glare of headlights. "Man, am I glad to see you guys. I thought you might be . . . is everyone okay? Did that crazy bitch kill anyone?"

"No, man," Buddy said. "Those bullets were fake. Ray's got a pretty bad cut, though. I'm taking him to the emergency room."

"You gotta take me, too," Judd said. "I did something to my knee running through that damned field. It's burning like crazy."

Buddy stayed long enough after Judd's parents arrived to overhear the ER doc's quick summation of Judd's injury.

"I don't know," the doctor said. "There's a lot of swelling, and we need that to go down before I can get a better idea. X-rays don't show anything. At worst, it could be a damaged ligament. Or something as simple as a meniscus tear. In any case, it'll be a while before he can play football."

Buddy's anger simmered as he drove towards home along the snaking one-way where cruisers were making their endless loop. He directed his anger at Christy—although he did admit the whole thing would have been funny if no one had gotten hurt. So, he shifted his focus to Kevin. Kevin had forced Judd to be there. Kevin should be held accountable.

Things wouldn't have escalated, though, if Buddy hadn't seen them standing by Kevin's car at Pat's. Kevin and Christy were laughing, draped over each other, wobbling a little.

Buddy would have just driven by had Kevin not seen him. Kevin pointed, which set off another round of guffaws and knee slaps. Buddy took a right at the next intersection, rounded the block, and stopped behind Kevin's car.

"Hey, Buddy!" Kevin called. "You ever find your little friend? Or is he someplace in Texas by now?"

Christy shook with laughter, clamped a hand over the top half of her face and stomped her foot.

Buddy waited for her laughter to subside. "Christy, I thought you should know Judd hurt his knee trying to get away. He can't play for a few weeks. Maybe longer."

Christy stopped laughing. She tried to stand straight, wobbled again, and leaned against Kevin's car.

"He's hurt?" she said.

"They don't know how bad yet."

Kevin clapped Preston's shoulder. "Seems like you've got your starting job back."

That remark pushed Buddy beyond his limits. He took a quick step forward, grabbing Kevin's shoulder, spinning the taller boy to face him. Kevin shoved and threw a fist, his swing wild. Buddy dropped low, almost into a squat, and drove his body upwards. His uppercut caught Kevin flush at the bottom of his jaw. Kevin's head snapped back. He collapsed against his car.

Caught in a surrealistic glow of a flashing neon sign, Kevin struggled to stand. Buddy, whose anger still burned, raised his fist again. Preston grabbed him from behind.

"That's enough, Buddy," the lineman whispered.

Buddy found Christy, who wore an expression of horror, suddenly seeming cold sober. He pointed an accusing finger. "I hope someday, someone shows you how scary it is to stare down the barrel of a gun and think you're going to get shot."

= = = ¦ ¦ = = =

Sunday, Oct. 30, 1966

"Here, man. This is the gun she used."

The pistol was old and small—almost dainty. It didn't seem something that would frighten anyone, but it had scared the living piss out of Buddy last night. Kevin had wrapped it in a dish towel to keep it out of sight.

As music blared, the room tilted a little. Buddy held a plastic cup in one hand and steadied himself with the other. "What's in this?"

Kevin said, "Southern Comfort. You know, Janis Joplin drinks it."

"What's the red stuff?"

"Cranberry juice. Pretty smooth, huh?"

Buddy took another sip. "Reminds me of cough syrup."

"They've got beer if you'd rather have that."

"It sure seemed bigger last night." Buddy noticed his voice was a little slurry. He'd have to focus more when he talked.

"Well, fuck, man, she shot at us. Looked like a fuckin' cannon," Kevin said. He had a bruised and swollen jaw. He and a couple other seniors had tracked Buddy down earlier, threatening reprisals.

"Coach will bench you for sucker punching me," Kevin said.

They'd put it behind them, though, if Buddy would *help them get even* with Christy.

Kevin offered the gun. "Push that little button there by the top sight."

Buddy took the gun from the towel and did as instructed. The barrel and cylinder swung away from the handle and trigger. An extractor popped five bullets onto the kitchen floor.

Kevin bent to retrieve them, then handed them to Buddy. "Put those in your pocket. Here's what Christy used."

He produced what looked like a .22 shell casing. Rather than a conical lead tip, a blunted wad of cardboard packing protruded from the brass casing.

"So, what am I supposed to do with this?" Buddy asked.

"She's in her uncle's office, changing the music. Stereo's there, but it's wired to those speakers." Kevin pointed at a closed door in the nearest wall of the old mansion's entry hall where maybe thirty kids danced and drank.

"Hide the gun under your jacket. When Christy comes out, point it at her and shoot."

"She'll know it's a fake bullet," Buddy protested. "She did the same thing to us last night."

"No, man. Someone pulls a gun on you, I bet you don't think that fast. I bet she'll shit. We've gotta get even with her. She's telling everybody how we screamed and ran away."

"I don't know. This seems really dumb."

Kevin poked his finger at Buddy's face. "Just do it, or you're off the team."

= = = ¦ ¦ = = =

Buddy felt the little pistol against his belly. He'd put it under his belt when Kevin handed him another cup of the Southern Comfort cocktail. He took a sip, then attempted to analyze these strange sensations. He floated a little—no, not all of him floated. Just his brain. His thoughts seemed to be emanating from a point about a foot above his head.

He found the sensation pleasant enough, although he couldn't close his eyes longer than a few seconds before his brain told him he was beginning to tumble. Then when he opened them, the room seemed to be coasting to a halt following a slow rotation on its axis.

Only a few minutes before, Buddy had retreated into a half-bath to which Kevin had gestured. He'd reluctantly slid the blank shell into the revolver.

He faced the mirror and said to his reflection, "Just get this shit over with." He remembered Judd, grimacing with pain at the emergency room. "She deserves this."

Buddy returned to the entry hall, placed his drink on an end table beside a couch where two couples sat among a pile of beer cans. As the office door opened, he gripped the gun beneath his jacket, his finger slipping through its trigger guard. Christy saw him and displayed an expression of scornful amusement. As he withdrew the pistol, the wash of sound from the stereo speakers went silent.

"How funny do you think it is now?" he asked as he pulled the trigger.

She registered no fear. She only smirked, as if she knew . . .

BANG!

Her smirk contorted to shock. Blood welled from her chest. She stumbled backward into the office.

Buddy froze. He vaguely perceived shouts and panic around him. The room tilted almost ninety degrees before righting itself. When his brain allowed him movement, he sank to his knees, staring at a closed door. Then his head rang, like it did when he made violent helmet-to-helmet contact on the football field, and he felt himself fade.

chapter ten

July 2009
The Reunion
Friday

Lori fell onto the pillows, still breathing hard, enjoying the afterglow, Cullen smiling down at her.

"Not bad for an old man, huh?" he asked. "Twice in . . ." He glanced at the clock beside them. ". . . an hour."

Lori touched his chest.

He kissed her.

"Forgive me," she said with an apologetic smile, "but I'm so curious. After you and Shelby went that far, why didn't things continue to . . . progress?"

Cullen traced a line with his fingers, starting at her forehead, over her nose and between her breasts.

"We took different directions, and our paths didn't converge again under that set of circumstances until a decade later."

= = = ¦ ¦ = = =

Arthur
November 1978

"Cullen!"

Twenty-eight-year-old Shelby Blaine's enthusiastic smile

greeted him through an old-fashioned screen door that creaked against its spring when she slipped open a hook-and-eye latch. "What a surprise! I've been looking forward to seeing you and Lisa at the reunion next summer! And here you are!"

She embraced him. He responded by putting his right hand behind her head, wrapping her thick, dark hair with his fingers, pulling her face to his shoulder. He still hadn't spoken a full two minutes later when she pushed away, searching his eyes. "Cullen, what's wrong?"

He shrugged, offered a weak smile. "Everything."

"Wow. A lot must have happened in five years. Do you have any specifics?"

"Lisa and I are separated. We're trying, but I don't see how we can put it back together. My job kind of sucks. And I'm standing on your doorstep, the very last place I should be."

"I see," Shelby said, taken aback by Cullen's despair. "Do you . . . do you want to come inside?"

Shelby lived alone at a rented farmhouse on the outskirts of Arthur with a host of pets. The house and outbuildings were a ramshackle set of structures typical of post-World War II construction. Pinkish-orange stucco faded in spots to a mottled grey, streaked with water stains, covered the house. The scene, especially during late fall with leaves fallen and gardens gone to seed, mimicked a grim monochromatic etching.

A barn and pump house, which had a fragile look to them, along with a smaller wooden shed leaning hard away from prevailing winds, sat among a half dozen scraggly trees, all clustered around a windmill, which reminded Cullen of *their* windmill.

Inside, though, Cullen found Shelby's imprint everywhere. The colors were bright, the rooms alive with a . . . what? A spirit that *was* her. Cullen sensed the allure the minute he entered. While his conscience begged him to go, he wanted to be there more than any other place he could think of.

He felt her presence behind him.

"You're divorced," he said to the wall.

"Yep."

"What happened?"

"After two years we kind of realized neither of us was all that much into it, so we cut our losses."

"Just like that?"

"Mostly my idea. I mean, Rick would have hung on for a long time, I think. I knew it would only hurt us a lot more in the long run, though. I've come to understand I'm a solitary person. I don't think I'm willing to bend my life to somebody else. Some of my friends say that makes me selfish. I think it makes me realistic." After a long moment, she asked, "So what's with you and Lisa?"

Cullen sighed, acutely aware she'd stepped closer.

"It's complicated." He continued to address the wall. "Things kind of fell apart when we moved to California. I hate the East Bay. So does she. We've both made a lot of mistakes. We've both . . . I don't know how to say it. I think she loves me, but . . . she doesn't really like me anymore. Does that make any sense?"

Shelby chuckled, the sound rueful. "More sense than you could possibly realize."

He felt her hand on his shoulder.

"God, I've missed you," she said. "Not so much the day-to-day presence . . . but the . . . soul of your friendship, kind of like a friendly ghost—a knowledge that no matter how far away you might be, or where ever your life takes you, you're still with me.

When I was married, I missed thinking of you without feeling guilty, because you were *the first one*. That's how Rick put it. You remember the last time we saw each other? That time five years ago when we were with Lisa and Rick? I never heard the end of it. He couldn't accept that I have people who are a part of my foundation, relationships I treasure, without feeling threatened. Then, I saw the look on Lisa's face. I knew we wouldn't be allowed our bond anymore."

"I . . . I don't think I can be here, Shelby," Cullen said. "Your house, I mean. I think we need to find some neutral ground. Can we have dinner somewhere? Without causing a scandal?"

"Certainly, two old friends can have dinner, can't they?" she asked.

They drove to the Overbite Bar, which had added a kitchen and served a passable steak. They drank margaritas made with not enough tequila, followed by a disappointing wine. Neither noticed, though, as they sorted through the past decade.

"So, what's the deal with your job?" Shelby asked. "I thought you liked being a lawyer."

"I don't know if anyone really *likes* being a lawyer. Not the first ten years, anyway. The hours are longer than you can imagine. I tried being a public defender. God, talk about a thankless task. Then I joined a firm. And I hate the politics. We had a merger with a whole new set of partners, who put me on a business law track—acquisitions, taking companies public, tax stuff. That's why I'm here. I'm coming back from St. Louis where I was doing some . . . Shit, I'm depressed just talking about it. Anyway, since I have a weekend, I flew into Lubbock so I could drive over and see my folks."

"And me?"

"No. I *swore* to myself I wouldn't see you."

"Have our lives changed so much?" Shelby asked softly. She slid her hand across the table, put it on his. Cullen was lost.

Back at Shelby's house, they slowly undressed each other, like nomads returning to distant and familiar territory. Shelby gave him a wry smile. "The one I never actually made love with is the one I liked best."

Unabashed and stunning, she stood before him, then led him to her bedroom.

"Do you realize," he said, "this is the first time we've actually seen each other naked? I mean, I guess we've seen all the parts, but never all at once."

"You're gorgeous," Shelby said.

"No, I'm not. I'm just another guy. Always have been. You, though, remain the most exquisite woman I've ever imagined."

"You know, I hear compliments like that from guys now. Not that I do *this* a lot. With guys coming on to me, I mean. I remember a time, though, when you were the only boy who saw me that way. You made it possible for me to . . . keep faith. You kept me from giving up on myself. I'll always love you for that."

Shelby had never spoken *that* word to him before. He ached to answer her. He couldn't be sure, though, given this emotionally-sexually charged moment, that he would be telling her the truth, or just telling her something he wished could be true. His marriage had taught him, at least, what a difficult person he could be. He could be quick to anger, resentful, incredibly selfish. Shelby would be patient to a point. She would tolerate him for a year, maybe two. Shelby wasn't Lisa, though. Shelby wasn't a long-suffering, aspiring martyr.

So, he drew her onto the bed . . . and his attempt to make love to her failed miserably.

"It's okay," she said. "It happens."

"I guess my line is, but *not to me*. Which is true, though terribly trite. I'm sorry. Please don't think this is any reflection on you. My God, I've fantasized this moment so often . . ."

"Cullen, I have never known anyone so manipulated by guilt. Your parents must have really done a number on you."

"Not my parents. My mom. We ate guilt for breakfast at our house. And don't forget the MYF."

"That's why you never pressured me to *do it* when we were kids, isn't it?" Shelby said.

"I pressured you plenty to fool around."

"Didn't take all that much, if you'll recall."

"But no, I wasn't going to put my dick in anyone until I'd married them. I don't know that any moral ethic drove my behavior. Mostly just an absolute fear of the wrath my mom would rain down on me if I got anyone pregnant."

Shelby remained quiet for a few moments. Then, she asked, "So you and Lisa didn't . . ."

"We did. Not before the wedding was a few weeks away. What about you and Rick?"

"Oh, yes."

They lay curled together, both staring at the ceiling for a long, blank interlude before Cullen whispered, "My dream as a kid was a distant day when we'd marry. We'd make love on our wedding night. Afterwards, I'd ask, *was it your first time?* Knowing the answer would be yes."

Silent tears tracked along her cheeks and into the halo of thick auburn hair spread on her pillow. They lay together for nearly an hour before Cullen dressed. Shelby wore an oversized t-shirt as she stood with him on her porch, bathed by the light of a rising moon.

"So, I'll see you next summer at the reunion?" she asked.

Cullen shook his head. "Shelby, I can't do this. I think I have to stay away."

= = = ¦ ¦ = = =

August 1979

Cullen's office phone rang. Struggling through the morass of an initial draft for a merger agreement, he resented the distraction.

"Molloy," he snapped, expecting some junior attorney or paralegal with a question to an answer they could have found by doing their own research.

"Hello, Molloy. This is Blaine."

"Shelby!" A smile spread over his face.

"You didn't come to the reunion," she said.

"I told you I wouldn't."

"I know. You didn't miss a lot. Half of the people were preening and posturing, trying to impress everyone with their success. Everyone else was mostly interested in drinking and replaying old football games."

"So, were you impressed?" Cullen asked.

"I hate to say it, but a lot of the popular kids have become fabulously successful. I think I detest them all over again."

"You're fabulously successful," Cullen argued.

"I'm a supervisor at a government agency."

"Hey, the BLM is a big deal. Making someone as young as

you a department manager is a bigger deal. Now if you could just escape from Arthur . . ."

"I am. That's why I called. They're relocating me to Santa Fe next month."

"Oh, man, Shelby, that's wonderful," he said, rotating his chair to find the view from his office window. "You'll love it there."

"Yeah. I actually think I can afford that place in the country we talked about when we were kids. Maybe a little bit of land with a stream or a pond or something."

Cullen sighed. While Shelby was making her dream come true, he felt as if his life had ground to a halt. "That's magnificent."

"And you?"

"The divorce papers have been filed. I've reached a dead end here at the firm. I guess I could go out on my own, but God, I can't imagine starting over."

"Um . . . that's another reason I called. I talked with Buddy—"

"Buddy was at the reunion?" Cullen was shocked.

"No, he wasn't. Being there made me think of him, though, so I called. He's the biggest success of all."

"Yeah. Computer software."

"He mentioned he needs someone to come to Phoenix and help him take his company public."

"Yeah?"

"He asked if I thought you might be interested."

chapter eleven

The Reunion
July 2009
Friday

Freshly showered from his noon-time exercise with Lori, Cullen walked to the motel lobby. He found Shelby at the breakfast nook, drinking coffee as she scanned a painfully thin copy of the Arthur News-Journal.

Cullen sat across the table from her, and without preamble, said, "Guy walks into a bar with his alligator and asks, *do you serve lawyers here?* Bartender says, *Yes, of course we do!* The guy says, *Okay, I'll have a beer for myself, and a lawyer for my alligator.*"

Shelby's shoulders shook as she did her best not to laugh out loud. "Cullen, stop it."

"I'm a lawyer, so I can tell that joke," he said.

"Just stop!" The giggles grew louder.

"Guy walks into a bar, says, It was terrible. I was stranded on an island with Adolph Hitler, Joseph Stalin and a lawyer, and my gun only had two bullets left. Bartender says, Oh, my God! What did you do? Guy says, I shot the lawyer twice."

Now Shelby couldn't contain herself. The people around them stared.

"Stop with the lawyer jokes." She turned away and made a point of focusing on her coffee.

"Okay." He gave her a moment to recover. "Blind guy walks into a bar, orders a drink and says, *Hey! Does anyone wanna hear a blonde joke?* The woman next to him taps his shoulder. She says, *Listen mister, I'm a bodybuilder, five foot nine of pure muscle, and I'm blonde. The bouncer over there, he's a martial arts expert. His hands are registered as lethal weapons! He's blond, too! And our bartender, she's six foot two, a roller derby star. She's blonde! So, do you still wanna tell that blonde joke?* Blind guy says, *Well, not if I have to explain it three times.*"

Shelby leapt to her feet and sprinted through the restroom door, mercifully, only a few steps away.

She emerged dabbing the front of her blouse with paper towels.

"You made me squirt coffee out my nose."

They shared laughter, followed by awkward silence.

"I've missed you so much, Cullen," Shelby finally said. "When we were kids, we laughed like this all the time."

"Oh," Cullen said with a little edge to his voice, "not *all* the time." He immediately wished he hadn't.

Shelby's smile faded. "No, not always."

"I'm sorry, Shelby. I don't know why I said that. I've missed you, too. And I love hearing you laugh."

The silence settled between them until Shelby asked, "Does it bother you that Buddy's here?"

"No," Cullen answered. Too quickly. "Buddy's a good man. I owe him a lot. Does . . . does it bother you about Lori?"

"Yes, a little. I like her, though. It's . . . we can't ever seem to time things right, can we?"

Cullen said nothing, just melted into those beautiful green eyes.

Shelby broke the spell.

"So, I was waiting to see if you guys wanted to grab a late

lunch. I convinced Buddy and Weard to join us. I thought we'd try the steakhouse. Have a nice meal."

"Buddy said he'd come?"

"Well, sort of. Anyway, he didn't say he wouldn't. I think you'll have to do a little more convincing when we get to his mom's house. Weard was almost excited about it."

"Weard probably won't remember by the time we get there."

"Yeah, he was kind of fading in and out."

= = = ¦ ¦ = = =

The Overbite Steakhouse had improved itself by at least a star and a half since the last time Cullen dined there.

"You'd think by now they would have changed the name," Shelby said.

"No, they're past that." Cullen examined a dark room with its long, oak bar and an awkward arrangement of booths and tables. "At first, the name sounded funny, a little bit gross in an inadvertent sort of way. Now, it's quirky. It's been around long enough to become a part of local culture."

"Still a little gross," said Weard as he pulled a set of sunglasses from a pocket of his Hawaiian shirt. Weard wasn't wearing his Rasta hat, so his dreadlocks fell to his shoulders. And, since the joint was obscured by Weard's hair, the others hadn't noticed it resting just behind his ear. When he pushed his sunglasses on, though, the doobie became dislodged. Weard bent casually and picked it up.

"You might not want to go waving that around," whispered Buddy as the restaurant hostess approached.

"Shit." He palmed the joint.

"Five, please," Shelby said. "Maybe something in back?"

Anonymous seating was Buddy's condition for joining them. He wanted to call as little attention to himself as possible. Shelby and Cullen argued that his shaved head would keep most people from recognizing him after forty years.

"So, what's with the name of this place?" Lori asked as she settled next to Cullen. "The Overbite Steakhouse?"

"Well, ask a waitress or the chef, and they'll tell you it's a joke. They'll tell you a group of dentists used to own it. It's not true, though."

"It's not?"

"No," said Shelby. "The original name of this place was The Overbite Tavern, founded 1975 or so by a guy named Randle Overbite. This was the first place you could get a beer in Arthur. I think. Anyway, it's the first place Cullen and I ever drank in this town."

"Arthur County was dry," Cullen explained. "Prohibition may have ended constitutionally in 1933, but not here. The good citizens of Arthur County voted to remain dry. That lasted until the mid-seventies. This is the Bible Belt. When we were kids, community leaders didn't trust people to police their own morality."

"Folks drove twenty miles down the road to Curtis County for their booze," Buddy told her. "I made that run a couple of times. Not these guys, though. Cullen didn't drink."

"Didn't drink?" Lori said. She knew Cullen dearly enjoyed three fingers of Woodford Reserve bourbon most evenings.

"Oh, I think Shelby, Corinne and some of the other band girls might have gotten into their parents' liquor cabinets on a couple of occasions," Cullen said. "But not me. Not until right at the end of our senior year."

= = = ¦¦ = = =

"What's with the old guy staring at us?" Lori whispered as their food arrived. "He hasn't taken his attention off us since we sat down."

A row of booths lined the wall behind them. At their round table, Shelby sat to Lori's right, her back against a wall next to the service entrance. Buddy sat next to her, facing across the table toward Lori and Cullen. Weard's back was to the room.

Cullen followed Lori's line of sight. An elderly man glowered their way as he spoke into a cell phone. "He's just talking on the phone," Cullen said.

"No, she's right." Weard concentrated on cutting his steak into inch-square pieces. "That old guy's been all over us since we walked in."

"What old guy?" Buddy raised a hand as a place mark in his conversation with Shelby.

Cullen tried again to steer the discussion a different direction. "What are you talking about, Weard? Your back is to the room. You can't even see—"

"I see everything. It's a curse. The CIA, man. They fucked me up."

Lori grinned. "Okay. Don't turn around. Tell us what the waitress is doing."

"The blonde or the redhead?" Weard raised a chunk of steak on his fork for inspection.

"I don't see a redhead," said Shelby.

"She just went into the kitchen. The blonde is taking an order from two guys sitting over by the door. She's a little peevish because the short guy's hitting on her."

Cullen found the blonde, rolling her eyes, avoiding the leer of a short, chubby twenty-something. Cullen's scan of the room returned him to the elderly man no longer on the phone. He conducted an agitated conversation with the woman seated opposite him. His attention alternated between their table and his companion.

"He's probably someone's dad who recognizes us as kids he used to know," Cullen said.

"No," Weard said as he probed his baked potato with a steak knife. "He knows who we are. That's Damon Hammond. The woman probably works for him."

Buddy gave a sharp gasp. "My God, Weard, I think you're right. I knew this was a mistake."

"Ignore him, Buddy," Shelby said. "You have every right to be here."

Their meal continued under a cloud, though. While both Cullen and Shelby made attempts to redirect their table's attention to nostalgia, the threads of conversation lacked the strength to sustain themselves.

When the old man finally stood, he took a couple of shambling steps toward them. His companion—a fortyish brunette clad in business attire—tugged at his sleeve.

"Damon, no!" Cullen heard her plead.

He sloughed her off and continued toward them, his face fixed with a scowl. Buddy stood slowly. When Hammond was half a dozen steps from them, he extended his right arm, aiming a boney index finger like a gun.

"Murderer!" he said, his voice low and mean. "Murderer! How dare you come back here to mock me—mock the memory of my niece this way. If I was a younger man, I'd thrash you. My niece still has friends here. You're not welcome."

Outwardly calm, Buddy said nothing.

Cullen stood. Lori placed a cautionary hand on his arm. A new voice intruded.

"I don't fuckin' believe it," came a growl from behind the redheaded waitress, who had been drawn by the tension radiating from the back of the dining room. "It *is* you."

Cullen had been so intent on Buddy and Hammond, he hadn't seen Darrel Jensen arrive.

"Darrel, what do you want here?" Cullen asked.

Darrel ignored him. As Hammond stepped away, Darrel filled the space vacated by the old man.

"You've got some fucking nerve showing your face here, especially with our reunion," Darrel said, bunching his fists.

"Darrel, you moron," said Shelby. "Buddy is here because his mother passed away. There's no way you don't know that."

Despite his beer gut, Darrel Jensen remained formidable. Cullen felt momentarily concerned. Buddy, though, was no longer the business executive who wore his wealth and success with a comfortable self-deprecation. Suddenly, he'd transformed into every bit the six-foot four-inch slab of granite he'd been when Hammond and this community sent him into exile. As Darrel raised his challenge, Buddy seemed to expand his presence, like a cobra flaring its hood.

"Believe me, Darrel," Buddy said in a chilling tone, "you, of all people, don't want to do this."

Darrel took a step back. Cullen could see the artery throbbing along his neck.

"What do you want, Darrel?" Cullen said. "What's the point?"

"He doesn't belong here," Darrel said, holding his stare. "He shouldn't be here. He should be in prison."

The room fell quiet, the attention of patrons and staff now fully engaged. Shifting into cop mode, Lori stood and stepped into Darrel's space. Cullen touched her shoulder. "Just go away. Leave us alone," he told Darrel. "Nobody's doing anything to—"

"I want that man removed," Hammond said as if giving an order.

"So, Hammond calls and you still come running, Darrel?" Buddy said. "You're not a cop anymore, and I'm not on any kind of probation. I can fight my own battles." He reached to pull Cullen aside.

Darrel took a step back. Lori placed a hand on Buddy's chest. And that's when Weard said, "Holy shit, Darrel. You could harvest that nose hair and knit a sweater, man."

Weard leaned backwards along the table, one hand holding a fork and the other a breadstick. He craned his neck so he stared directly into Darrel Jensen's nostrils.

"Who the fuck are . . . Billy? Billy Ward?"

"Don't call me that, man. Nobody calls me that anymore. My name is Weard. You call me Billy again and . . . well . . . there's five ways I could kill you with this breadstick."

He thrust the breadstick. Darrel jumped back.

"What is this guy doing here?" Darrel demanded of Cullen. "He's a certified lunatic."

Weard stood, holding the breadstick high like a dagger.

"He . . . he . . . the CIA fried his brain," Darrel announced to the entire room.

Weard faced Darrel again. Now, he gripped two breadsticks.

"Five ways, man," Weard said.

Darrel conducted a quick survey of witnesses, then pointed

his finger at Buddy. "He better stay the fuck away from the reunion. You hear me?"

Darrel escorted Damon Hammond away.

An embarrassed silence ensued for a few seconds after the door closed behind them.

Shelby broke the spell. "Weard, can you really kill someone with a breadstick?"

Weard seemed confused for a moment, then studied the sesame seeds on his weapons.

"You know, I think I probably can."

= = = ¦¦ = = =

They finished their meal in silence. Cullen considered suggesting dessert despite stares and whispers—just to prove some kind of point, he supposed—but Buddy clearly wanted to leave.

They exited the restaurant into the afternoon heat. As Cullen unlocked his car doors a police cruiser rolled into the parking lot, blocking both Cullen's and Buddy's rentals. A hatless man wearing a uniform got out. A metal tag on his shirt pocket said *Phillips*.

"Howdy," he said offering a pleasant smile. "Were you folks done with lunch?"

Cullen estimated Phillips at mid-thirties. A big man, tall as Buddy, broad-chested with trim hips. His size made the pistol on his creaky leather utility belt seem delicate. He had a deeply tanned face and arms. The top half of his forehead—below a shock of black hair—glowed stark white. Before anyone could answer, Phillips ducked into his car, grabbed a baseball cap bearing a badge logo and *Arthur PD*, and a clipboard.

“What can we do for you, Officer?” Cullen asked, hoping the joint wasn’t still tucked behind Weard’s left ear. There it was, though. Not quite covered by dreadlocks.

“Is one of you . . .” Phillips glanced at his clipboard. “. . . William Ward?”

“No, man,” said Weard, “I’m not that anymore. I’m Weard.”

“Um . . .” said the officer, “I beg your pardon, sir?”

Cullen intervened.

“He’s not trying to be difficult, Officer,” Cullen said. “His name is Weard . . .”

“How weird could it be?” the policeman asked.

“No,” Cullen said. “It really is Weard.”

“You mean like an alias?”

“No,” Shelby said, putting her arm around Weard’s shoulder, “like a middle name. His full name is William Weard Ward . . .”

“It’s English, it means ‘guard’.”

“. . . but he doesn’t like the William part anymore.”

“Oh . . . okay, Mr. um . . . Ward. We received a complaint a few minutes ago that you threatened someone and brandished a weapon.”

“Brandished?” Cullen laughed. “I wouldn’t think Darrel Jensen even knew what a word like *brandished* means.”

Phillips couldn’t conceal a smile. “Mr. Jensen used to be a police officer. Brandished is sort of a police report word, so that’s where he learned it. Mr. Ward, did you brandish a weapon.”

“Well . . . yes. Yes, I did.”

“He brandished a bread stick,” Lori said.

“A . . . breadstick? Are you sure? Because I had the impression he had a gun or a knife.”

“No,” said Shelby. “Just a breadstick . . .”

“Two of them,” Weard interjected.

". . . ask anyone inside."

"The hard-toasted kind," Weard added.

"Okay . . ." Phillips consulted his clipboard again. "Mr. Jensen said you threatened to kill him with it."

The heat shimmered from the black hood of the police car in waves, providing an ethereal background as Phillips loomed in the noonday sun.

"That's not what Weard said at all," Lori said. "He made a general statement about potential lethality of the . . . the breadstick."

"Ma'am," Phillips said, "are you a lawyer?"

"God, no. I'm a retired police officer."

"I'm the lawyer," said Cullen.

"Are you Mr. Ward's lawyer?"

"He doesn't need a lawyer," Lori said. "It was a breadstick."

"Deadly in knowledgeable hands," said Weard as he leaned against Shelby's car.

"You're not helping yourself here," Lori said.

"How do you kill someone with a breadstick?" Phillips asked.

"It involves bodily orifices and lingering infection."

"So, if a person got . . . treatment in a timely fashion . . .?"

"Nah," said Weard. "You stick a breadstick up someone's . . . whatever, there might be some bruising, but unless you make him leave it there for a few days, he'll probably be all right. It's a breadstick, you know?"

"Officer, if a threat was implied," Cullen said, "it was very broadly implied. And Mr. Jensen made threats of his own."

Phillips turned his attention to Buddy, who stood beside the open door of his rental car.

"Are you Mr. Boyd? Buddy Boyd?"

"My name," the answer terse, "is Hezekiah."

"And you're here attending your high school reunion?"

"No. My mother passed away. I'm here to deal with her house and belongings. I have no interest in any reunion."

"When will the service be?"

"There will be no service. My mother didn't want to be memorialized here or buried here."

"Well, sir, I'm sorry for your loss. I'm sorry your mother didn't like Arthur. At the same time, I'll ask that you stay away from any reunion activities."

"I *was* staying away. Nobody would have known anything about me being here if Damon Hammond and Darrel Jensen hadn't caused a scene."

"On what basis are you telling Mr. Boyd to stay away?" Cullen asked, irritation conveyed through his tone.

"Nothing official," Phillips said, tilting the ball cap back on his head. "I'm just asking a favor."

"If Darrel Jensen would mind his own damn business and leave us alone," said Shelby, joining Lori, "the issue never would have come up."

"Yes, ma'am. I don't doubt that." Phillips tossed his clipboard onto the front passenger seat, and had his right leg extended through his car door when he paused.

"Mr. . . . um . . . Weard, is that a marijuana cigarette behind your ear?"

Weard touched his hair. The joint disappeared. "I'm sick," he said.

Phillips eased out of the car again. He approached Weard, waving Cullen over.

"If you *are* Mr. Ward's attorney, I think he's in need of legal advice."

Weard frowned.

Cullen said, "Okay . . ."

"You should advise your client that we are standing within twenty-five feet of a restaurant entrance. New Mexico law prohibits smoking within twenty-five feet of an entry to a public establishment. Now, not having examined the cigarette he palmed a minute ago, I can conclude only that it appeared to be a tobacco product. Your client should walk to that trash receptacle right over there . . ." He pointed at a plastic garbage can. ". . . and shred said tobacco product. If he will, I won't investigate further."

"Thank you, Officer. I'm sure Weard will be happy to comply. Won't you, Weard?"

Weard stood over the trash can, where he tore the joint into tiny pieces, appearing even more despondent than usual.

chapter twelve

The Reunion
Saturday
July 2009

"So what kind of reception will we get after the thing with Darrel yesterday?" Shelby asked, gliding into the motel lobby.

Cullen felt temporarily derailed by Shelby and Lori's attire. Lori wore a blue dress that opened down the front, secured by a narrow sash wrapping her waist. A simple gold chain circled her neck.

Shelby wore a green flowing dress with a scooped neckline. She'd borrowed Lori's turquoise and silver necklace, which added depth to the green of her eyes.

"Nobody will be doing anything tonight but admiring the two of you," Cullen said. "You going to drive over with us, Shelby?"

"No. I'm taking my car. I have to pick up my date."

"Your date?"

"I'm going to Buddy's and get Weard. He said he'd go with me."

= = = ¦ ¦ = = =

Buddy offered a polite nod when his friends dropped Weard off following the dance. After the restaurant confrontation, Cullen sensed Buddy's withdrawal into Hezekiah as plainly as if he'd pulled closed a curtain.

"Did you know this man is a dancing fool?" Shelby asked Buddy, patting Weard's shoulder.

"Yeah," said Cullen. "He drew a lot of attention with his kilt."

That, at least, drew the hint of a smile from Buddy.

"We came to get you," Shelby said. "We're hungry. We're going to Pat's and have grease. Please come with us."

"No, guys. I'd better stay here," Buddy said. "I don't want to cause any more trouble than I already have. I'll catch a plane out early tomorrow. I'll hire someone to deal with this house and Mom's stuff."

"Buddy," Cullen said, "people are asking about you. They heard about your mom. A lot of them would like to see you. Let's make the drag once or twice and then stop at Pat's, like old times. Please. Let us help."

"What if Darrel shows up?" Buddy asked.

"Fuck Darrel," Shelby said.

= = = ¦ ¦ = = =

Weard declined their invitation.

"I'm a little run down. I think I'll stay home and... recharge."

"Just don't smoke in the house," Buddy said.

They took Shelby's car. Cullen and Lori shared the rear seat as they drove three loops of the one-ways. Scattered among caravans of high schoolers cruising on a warm summer night were a smattering of representatives from the class of '69, guided by sweet memories of carefree July evenings forty years earlier. As a car slowed beside them. Shelby recognized Angela Kowalski, who frantically motioned for Shelby to lower her window.

"Hey, Shelby," Angela called, "Judy and Jim have asked everyone to their house . . ." Angela interrupted herself with a delighted gasp. ". . . is that Buddy? Buddy Boyd? Look, everyone, there's Buddy!"

Buddy gave a tentative wave and tried to sink from sight. A car horn honked. To Buddy's right, he encountered the grinning face of Ray Franklin. Buddy hesitated, then lowered both the window and a four decade-long barrier.

"Buddy!" Ray yelled. "You gotta' come over. Cullen told us you were in town. We aren't gonna let you leave without having a beer."

"I told you, Buddy," Cullen said. "People want to see you. It's time you put the past where it belongs."

= = = ¦¦ = = =

Judy and Jim Callison's home was part of a new development near the university. Cullen's group walked onto a brightly lighted backyard deck where a dozen people gathered around an impromptu spread of alcohol, dips and chips.

Cullen braced himself for their reaction to the tall, bald man being ushered somewhat reticently on Shelby's arm. Puzzled expressions marked faces as each person sought some spark of recognition. The last time any of these people had seen Buddy, he had a full head of thick black hair and a haunted look of oppressive guilt.

"Buddy!" shouted Judd Andrews, extending his hand. His smile slipped away as he added, "I'm sorry about your mom."

Buddy welcomed each greeting politely, almost as if Christy Hammond's death was new and it wouldn't do for him to appear celebratory under the circumstances. As the evening wore on, though, Buddy's sharp edges softened. Cullen felt Christy's ghost retreating as old friends asked questions about Buddy's well-publicized computer software success.

"After my Vietnam tour, I got involved with some early Army computer stuff," Buddy explained to a knot of his football pals and their wives. "I got so interested that I re-enlisted."

"Wasn't that taking a pretty big chance?" Judd asked. "I mean, they could have sent you back into combat."

"No, I'd screwed up my knee, so I got the assignment I wanted. Then I used my GI Bill money for college and focused on learning code to write software. Of course, Bill Gates hit the big jackpot by developing an operating system for personal computers. Then our products took advantage of that market."

"So how rich are you?" Billy Bob asked with a grin.

"William Robert Snodgrass!" said Corinne as she slugged her husband's arm. "That is not the kind of question polite people ask."

"That's right," Shelby said. "You don't ask someone how rich they are. You ask their friends. How about it, Cullen? How rich is Buddy?"

Cullen smiled behind a sip from a bottle of Pacifico. "Richer than me, that's for sure."

"Okay," Billy Bob asked Shelby, "How rich is Cullen? He worked for Buddy, what, ten years? I read, I think it was right after our twentieth high school reunion—when he left and headed off to the Caribbean—that Cullen had a lot of stock options."

Shelby and Cullen exchanged a long glance.

"I . . . don't know, Billy Bob," Shelby said. "But I'm sure Cullen is rich enough."

The party gathered momentum as more people arrived. Cullen watched with satisfaction as, little by little, Hezekiah retreated, and Buddy laughed with these people whom he'd not seen since high school. Each time the back gate rattled, Cullen held his breath, hoping Darrel wouldn't show up.

Finally, a knock accompanied the rattle.

"Come on in," Judy Callison called into the darkness. "Reach over to get the latch."

The gate opened. Officer Phillips and a second uniformed policeman made their way across the deck and said something into Buddy's ear. Buddy turned to Cullen, shook his head with an aura of resignation and sadness, as Phillips took his arm and guided him back through the gate.

= = = ¦ ¦ = = =

"Why did you arrest Hezekiah Boyd?" Cullen demanded of Gerald Burke, Arthur's chief of police.

"We need to ask him some questions," Burke said.

Cullen, Lori and Shelby found Weard seated in the police department reception area when they followed Phillips' squad car to the police station.

"Questions about what?" Cullen demanded.

"Who are you?" Burke asked.

"Cullen Molloy. I'm Mr. Boyd's attorney, and I want to see him now."

Burke snorted. "Attorney, huh? We're investigating a homicide We have information that Mr. Boyd argued with our victim earlier today. An incident took place at the Overbite Steakhouse. Threats were made."

They'd just seen Darrel at the dance. *So*, Cullen concluded, his heart accelerating, *Damon Hammond is dead?*

"My client didn't argue with anyone," Cullen said. "I've got four witnesses, including myself, who can attest to that."

"Damon Hammond is dead?" Lori asked.

"Who are you?"

"This is Hannalore Summerlin," Cullen said. "She's a former detective with the Spokane, Washington Police Department."

"Big deal."

"She works for me as an investigator," Cullen added. "My client and Mr. Hammond didn't exchange a single word. The only argument was initiated by one of your former employees, Darrel Jensen. Darrel did his best to pick a fight with Mr. Boyd, who didn't respond."

Burke shook his head at the mention of Darrel. "So, who made the threats?"

"That's immaterial . . ." Cullen began.

Weard waved. "Me," he said from his chair. "But I didn't threaten old man Hammond. I threatened Darrel. With a breadstick."

"A breadstick?" Burke looked over his shoulder at Officer Phillips, who shrugged.

"Why are you wearing a skirt?" Burke asked Weard.

Weard scowled. "I'm not talking, man. Even if you waterboard me, I'm not saying a word."

"He attended the reunion dance," Lori told Burke. "His kilt is the only formal wear he has with him."

"And why is he here?" Cullen asked the police chief.

"Until right now, I didn't know," Burke said. "He showed up earlier. Sat on that chair. Said he refused to talk to anyone. Who is he?"

"He's Weard . . . um . . . Billy Ward. Weard is his middle name. Not a judgement," Shelby said.

"It's English," Weard said. "It means guard."

"So back to my original question," Cullen said. "Why are you holding Mr. Boyd?"

Burke summoned Cullen and Lori through a swinging gate behind the reception counter, and into an interview room complete with two-way mirror and a metal table with a ring for handcuffs and shackles welded to its center. He didn't close the door.

"Well, despite your witnesses," Burke said, "Mr. Hammond apparently felt threatened. Said he wanted to file a complaint. Said the man who killed his niece was in town and he—Mr. Hammond—feared for his life."

"When was Hammond's body discovered?" Lori asked.

"Ma'am, I can't . . ."

"Oh, come on," Lori said. "How many people have been murdered in Arthur today, anyway?"

"We got there about ten p.m.," Burke said.

"Is my client under arrest?" Cullen asked.

"Well . . . The officers might have been a little over-zealous when they read him his rights," Burke said.

"Then release him so I can take him home."

"Like I said, we have some questions . . ."

"Which he won't answer until after I've had a chance to talk with him."

"He hasn't asked for an attorney," Burke countered.

"Go tell him I'm here."

Ten minutes later, Buddy stood with his friends on the sidewalk.

They squeezed into Shelby's sedan.

"Thanks, Cullen," he said, "I—"

Cullen held up a warning hand.

"Don't say anything. We'll talk when we get to your mom's."

On the short drive, Shelby made a couple of attempts at expressions of concern, including a question about what the police had asked. Cullen emphasized his order of silence. When they arrived at Buddy's house, Cullen asked Buddy to wait in the back bedroom.

"Why can't we talk?" Shelby asked.

"I don't want Buddy making any secret confessions if he's feeling guilty. If he did say anything incriminating, you might find yourselves in an unfair position. You might feel you have to perjure yourself to protect him."

"Buddy's not guilty of anything," Shelby protested.

"And you know that how?" Lori asked.

"Oh, please, Lori. You really think he could have done this?"

"Doesn't matter what anyone thinks," Cullen responded. "Whether he did it or not, my job is to see that the police and prosecutors must prove every little thing—without any help from Buddy."

= = = ¦ ¦ = = =

"Did they ask you if you killed him?" Cullen said.

"Yes."

They gathered in the bedroom Buddy's mom had used as an office. Cullen and Lori stood. Buddy sat on the edge of a small desk.

"And they said you were under arrest?"

"At first, they did."

"Okay. Do you have any cash?"

"Cash?"

"In your wallet," Cullen said. "Do you have any money?"

Buddy seemed puzzled as he reached to his hip.

"Give me a dollar," Cullen said.

Buddy riffled through the bills. "I don't have a dollar. Smallest I've got is a five."

"That'll work," Cullen said, pocketing the five. "You've just hired me. If this thing goes any farther, we'll find a high-powered defense attorney. We'll start looking for someone on Monday. Right now, though, you'll have to settle for me. Lori, to be sure we've got all the confidentiality bases covered," Cullen added, "I'm officially hiring you as my investigator."

"Okay," Lori said, "what's my cut?"

"Your cut?"

"Of the five dollars. I need to know how much to set aside for taxes."

= = = ¦ ¦ = = =

When they returned to the living room, Cullen directed Shelby, Weard and Lori to the couch. Buddy stood.

"Weard," Cullen asked, "why were you at the police station?"

"I had a vision, man. I was on the porch, looking at the moon. I saw old man Hammond lying down somewhere. And . . . and I knew trouble was coming. So, I went to help Buddy."

"A vision?" Lori asked.

"How long have you had visions?" Cullen said.

"Ever since the CIA sent me to that drug program."

"The CIA put you in drug rehab?" Shelby asked.

"No, man, they didn't want me to *stop* taking drugs." Weard tugged at his kilt which was riding up. "They wanted me to start. I keep telling you, the CIA fucked me up."

Cullen closed his eyes and rubbed his forehead.

"Look," Buddy finally said, his voice flat, unemotional, "I was here from the time we got home from the restaurant until we went out this evening. They can't prove something I didn't do. I appreciate your concern. Right now, though, I'll be in the bathroom. I didn't want to go at the police station."

With Buddy absent, Shelby appealed to Cullen again. "Surely you don't think he could have . . ."

"As I said earlier, what we think doesn't matter. There's a process we have to follow here or else—"

They turned as Buddy emerged from the hallway, his face ashen. His calm stoicism had dissolved. He wobbled and reached to the doorframe for support. Cullen took his arm, fearing he might pass out.

"What?" Cullen asked.

"There's . . . there's a gun.," Buddy said.

Cullen felt a tremor run through him.

"In a cabinet under the sink. And . . . I think it's the same gun I shot Christy with."

Cullen guided Buddy to the couch.

Shelby started into the hallway, but Lori intervened. "Don't go back there."

"Why . . ."

"Just don't," Cullen said. "You and Weard stay together out front while Buddy, Lori and I talk."

= = = ¦¦ = = =

"The last time I touched that gun was forty-three years ago," Buddy said.

He sat on the couch, head in hands.

"And you don't know what happened to it after you were sentenced when you were a kid?" Lori asked.

"No idea. They sure didn't give it me."

"Okay," Lori said, "this is important. Have you fired a gun in the last forty-eight hours?"

"No!"

"You're sure?"

"Of course, I'm sure."

"Okay. We're calling the police."

"I didn't do anything," Buddy said, his voice a ragged whisper. "I only wanted to take care of my mom. This *can't* be happening again."

= = = ¦ ¦ = = =

They stood on Buddy's front porch when Chief Burke arrived at the head of a procession of police cars.

"Where's the gun?" he asked.

"Show me your warrant," Cullen said.

Burke produced an official-looking paper, which Cullen read carefully. "All you're allowed to seize are guns and ammunition. The pistol's in the cabinet under the bathroom sink. Through that hallway there."

"Do you have any other weapons?" Burke asked Buddy.

Buddy started to answer, but Cullen cut him off.

"No, he doesn't. And please address any questions you have through me."

"So, what was your beef with Hammond?" Burke asked.

The group had shifted to the living room as officers

conducted their search. Buddy glanced at Cullen, who nodded.

"I didn't have one. Not anymore. I put that part of my life behind me a long time ago."

"You killed his niece?"

"Yes. October of 1966."

"Why would Hammond be afraid of you now?"

Buddy sighed. "I don't know. I've had no contact with the man since I joined the army, May of 1969."

Phillips returned. "We didn't find anything more," he said. "Just the gun."

"No ammunition?"

"Only what was in the pistol—three live rounds and two empty shells. The gun's been fired recently. This thing's an antique."

Phillips produced a Ziplock bag containing a small silver pistol with pearl grips.

"Twenty-two caliber," Phillips continued. "You break it open like a double barrel shotgun to load and extract the shells.

Burke showed Buddy the bag.

"This your gun?"

"No, it's not."

"But you've seen it before."

Buddy trembled. "Yes. I think it's the same gun that killed Christy Hammond."

"Buddy," Cullen admonished, "don't jump to conclusions. How can you possibly know . . ."

He fixed Cullen with a defeated stare. "Some things, you can't forget."

= = = ¦ ¦ = = =

"So how did that gun get here?" Buddy asked Cullen and Lori.

The police had gone. Cullen gathered everyone together. The living room ceiling fan pushed air around as the heat of the day lingered.

"If it is the murder weapon," Cullen said, "the only time it could have been planted was after police took you to the station."

"Unless," Lori said, "someone planted it much earlier, while Weard was taking a nap."

"I was in the second bedroom going through Mom's financial records." Buddy said.

"So, you would have heard anyone come inside?"

"Well, maybe not. If they were quiet."

"Weard, where were you napping?" Cullen asked.

"Right here." Weared pointed to the couch. "No way could anyone have gotten by me."

"Even if you were asleep?" Lori asked.

"No. In the CIA they teach us—"

"Weard," Lori said gently, "I'm sorry. But when we first met you, out on the highway? You thought you were in Santa Rosa."

"No, man. That was a whole different thing. Stuff has really cleared up since I've been around you guys."

Weard scooched around on the overstuffed couch with its flowered upholstery pattern.

Lori turned away. "Weard, if you're wearing a kilt, don't be quite so . . . open. It's very unladylike."

Shelby giggled, poking Weard with her elbow.

"Oh, yeah." Weard snapped his knees together. "Sorry, man."

"When you had your vision and went off to the police station," Cullen asked Weard, "did you lock up when you left?"

"Um . . ."

"That's a pretty big chance for a killer to take," Lori said. "Sneaking in here with a murder weapon, not knowing if police were watching the place, or when someone might be getting home."

"You still think I might have done this, don't you?" Buddy asked her.

Lori smiled. "Buddy, I think you are a good guy dealing with some very difficult things right now. I *hope* you didn't sneak over and shoot poor Mr. Hammond."

"I didn't."

"Good to know. Keep in mind, though, that's what they all say."

chapter thirteen

July 2009
SUNDAY MORNING

"No gunshot residue," Cullen said to Arthur County's District Attorney, Clifton Gladly. "You don't have a case."

Cullen, Buddy and Lori sat at Buddy's kitchen table grouped around Cullen's cell phone, which he'd set on speaker mode.

Gladly gave a metallic little grunt. "There *was* gunshot residue."

"What was the particulate count?" Lori asked.

Gladly paused a long moment before saying, "We had a particulate count of . . . ah . . . three hundred on the hands."

"Three hundred is only background noise," Lori said. "Residue is everywhere. In a gun-toting little town like Arthur, I'll bet both you and I would test 300 just from saying hello to the right person. You need a count of 2,000 plus before you can—"

"We've suffered the murder of a prominent member of this community," Gladly said. "We found a gun, probably the murder weapon, in your client's possession. Given the history between your client and our victim, Boyd is our primary suspect."

"You do understand, don't you," Cullen said, "that Buddy Boyd is a very smart man? He's made a whole lot of money.

Don't you think he's bright enough not to murder someone then bring the gun home and put it under his bathroom sink? Isn't it obvious someone is trying to frame him?"

"My question," Gladly said, "is how someone would get possession of that gun in the first place? It's supposed to be stored in an old evidence file. I've got people looking, and you know what? They haven't found it yet. So maybe it's not there. And maybe someone as rich as Mr. Boyd could have bribed someone to steal and destroy a box of old evidence. Except maybe he kept the gun as a souvenir. And maybe he's smart enough to make it *look* like someone's framing him."

"He wanted a memento of an act that has haunted him the rest of his life?" Cullen said. "That's beyond crazy."

"In any case, I'll wait for ballistics and fingerprints," Gladly said.

"So, will you re-arrest Buddy or not?"

Gladly sighed.

"Not at the moment. But I don't want him going anywhere. If he leaves, I *will* arrest him, and you can be sure that under those circumstances no judge will grant him bail."

= = = ¦¦ = = =

Sunday, Oct. 30, 1966

"It was just a stupid joke!" a sobbing, quailing Kevin Quinn told the detective. "We didn't mean for . . . this was Christy's idea, for God sake. Christy made a fool of Buddy the night before, scaring him with that gun. Then," Kevin pointed, "this jerk who thinks he's such hot shit tracked her down and got in her face about it in front of everyone. She was pissed, man. She wasn't gonna let it go. Christy was like that. She didn't put up with stuff from anyone."

"So, you're saying this whole set-up was her idea?" the detective asked.

Buddy sat, one wrist handcuffed to a chair, amid a smoke-filled office space crammed too full of desks and filing cabinets. Kevin and Jim Hardesty sat together at another desk. Uncuffed.

Despite the cuffs, Buddy pressed a towel filled with ice to his head where someone had hit him. He couldn't remember that part of it.

"Yeah, she wanted to scare him again," Kevin said, his voice a quivering whine. "Tell him we were getting even with her for what she did. Then make him think he'd really shot her, with fake blood and everything."

"If it had turned out to be only a joke," the detective said, "what did you think would happen with a room full of kids there? Didn't it occur to you that someone would call us?"

"No," James said. "Christy said she'd wait until Buddy panicked, then she'd get up and make him look like an idiot again. Everyone was drinking and fooling around, so who would call the cops? Just to be sure, she said she left an extension off the hook upstairs. The nearest pay phone is blocks away, so even if somebody did call you guys, everyone would have time to leave."

The policeman regarded Jim with disdain, crossed his arms and spoke to Kevin. "The gun you handed this guy was loaded with blanks?"

"Only one. When Buddy opened the gun all the real bullets fell out. I gave him the blank. But it was a blank!"

The police chief, who sat on a creaky wooden office chair, had already tried questioning Buddy. Now, he tried again, He swiveled his chair and rolled himself to within a foot of Buddy's face. "You got nothing to say about any of this?"

"My head hurts, and I'm having trouble focusing," Buddy said. "I don't want to say anything until my dad gets here. There are parts I don't remember."

The chief snorted and swiveled to face Kevin when the door to the office opened. The scene froze. Nobody moved a muscle except Buddy, who jiggled his wrist against the bite of the handcuffs.

"Chief Jackson," said Damon Hammond with a tight, angry voice, "please remove everyone except this . . . this . . ." He made a backhanded gesture toward Buddy. ". . . hooligan from the room now."

"Well, Damon, we've got to—" Jackson began.

Hammond roared, "Now!"

Buddy estimated he sat alone more than an hour, pressing the towel to his head, trying to understand what had happened, replaying over and over the bark of the gun, the spurt of red from Christy's chest and a thud that registered when something hit his head.

= = = ¦ ¦ = = =

Wednesday, November 2, 1966

"My niece's death is neither an accident nor a joke!" Hammond shouted from the witness stand. "He threatened her the night before! A half-a-dozen witnesses heard him! This miscreant should be treated as an adult. He is guilty of murder!"

An early crowd had gathered as a community reacted to the

careless killing of one of its children. They were disappointed, though, when a bailiff unlocked the courtroom entrance only long enough to tell them this hearing would remain closed since the person in custody was a juvenile.

Buddy found he couldn't face his accuser. He stared at the court stenographer, instead, as her hands silently recorded each spoken word. Before his attorney could rise and object to Hammond's demands, Judge Eldon Whitfield spoke.

"Damon, I understand you are distraught. I understand you've lost your niece. But I'm not sending this boy to prison for thirty years. He's sixteen. He, too, is clearly upset."

"Your Honor," said defense attorney Thurmond Sanders, "Buddy is more than upset. He's mortified. This was a horrible, tragic accident. Buddy's life will never be the same."

"He at least *has* a life, doesn't he!" Hammond shouted.

From behind Buddy's seat, he heard his mother sob and his dad's intake of breath.

"Damon," Whitfield said firmly, "you asked to be heard. I've let you have your say, but that's enough. And I'm sorry, Mr. Sanders, this *was* more than an accident."

Whitfield pointed the handle of his gavel at Buddy.

"I'll remind everyone that we have a confession. We have the events of the night before—a threat—that witnesses, including Buddy, agree on. Not only did he behave recklessly at the party, he was drinking. Alcohol undoubtedly contributed to this tragedy. I'm sorry, Damon. We've known each other a long time. I must point out, though, alcohol was being provided to minors in your home. We have others, including the victim, who helped create an atmosphere where such a thing could happen."

For a moment, Buddy felt a flicker of hope. The instant he

felt it, though, his conscience assailed him. Christy was dead.

I deserve this.

"I can't treat this as just an unfortunate incident and send everyone home," Whitfield said. "An element of anger and retribution *was* present. Being drunk is no excuse, not in my book. Doesn't matter who provided the liquor. You still chose to drink. So, here's what we'll do. Buddy, I want you to stand up."

Buddy stood with quivering knees, hands folded in supplication at his waist, face raised to the judge. He felt his father's hand on his shoulder.

"Now you folks can contest this if you want," Whitfield said. "Drag things out. I think your attorney will advise you, though, this is the best deal you can hope for. Buddy, I order that you be remanded to the juvenile detention facility in Springer until your eighteenth birthday. I will require that you maintain your studies and behave yourself while you're there. When you turn eighteen, you will reappear before me. At that point, I'll decide whether to reopen the issue of incarceration as an adult on charges of manslaughter.

"You've made a grave mistake. Your life is at a crossroads here. What happens now is mostly up to you," Whitfield concluded.

= = = ¦¦ = = =

Friday, November 18, 1966

"Shelby, *please* tell me," Cullen said. "What did I do wrong?"

They sat in the Mercury, but not at the windmill. The Mercury had wanted to go there, but Shelby said no. Instead, they sat at Pat's, facing the drag as their classmates executed the eternal loop defining Arthur Saturday nights.

"Please, Cullen, can't we just get a coke like we told my dad we were going to?"

Although Cullen had been freed from his incarceration a couple of weeks ago, Buddy's tragedy intervened. This was the first Saturday night he and Shelby could see each other in weeks.

Just as well they hadn't chosen the section roads tonight, he thought as he watched traffic flow by. A bitter north wind blew. Tiny ice crystals swirled and sparkled as they caught the reflection of street lights. Getting stuck in the boondocks during a snowstorm would probably earn him a sentence worse than Judge Whitfield had given Buddy.

Cullen had been a little surprised when Shelby said yes to going out.

During the term of their forced separation, she'd become distant at school. She switched from alto to tenor sax, so they didn't sit together any longer. Mrs. Wilbanks' seating chart for English put Shelby near the doorway. He sat half-way back along the windows. She no longer waited for him to walk to Algebra. And after Algebra, where he sat just ahead of her, she gave him something of a perfunctory farewell each day before rushing off to join Corinne and several other band girls for lunch.

When the band played at a couple of home football games during his banishment, Cullen's dad insisted he drive straight home. He'd tried to steal a few moments with Shelby, but she made an excuse about not making Corinne wait.

Shelby, who made a point of sitting all the way over by the passenger door, sighed. "What makes you think you did anything wrong, Cullen?"

"Because everything's different. All semester, in the little bit of time we've been able to spend together, you act like I'm . . . I don't know . . . some kind of nuisance. I don't know what happened. If I screwed up, then tell me and I'll fix it."

She stared through the passenger side window. Cullen turned off the radio. The weather took its toll as, with each lap of the drag, traffic thinned.

"You didn't do anything." She wouldn't face him.

"Then what's—"

"I'm upset about Buddy," she said, exasperation in her voice. "I can't imagine what he must be going through. And you should be worried, too. He's our friend."

"Shelby, I do care about Buddy. But there's nothing I can do about it. I can't believe Buddy killed Christy. He said he did, though. So, he had to go away. I'm . . . I'm a whole lot more worried about us."

Tears dabbed Shelby's cheeks.

"You've been a good friend," she said, her voice husky with emotion. "There's just . . . just a lot of stuff going on right now. I . . . I can't . . . be with you like before."

"But . . . I love you, Shelby."

The words were out of his mouth before he was sure he'd even said them. Had he actually spoken them aloud? Or was it only what he wished he could say? Now her tears rolled freely, single streams, as she took a breath, opened her mouth, then seemed incapable of speech.

Cullen's thoughts became a kaleidoscope of emotion: anguish, fear, regret, hope—then drifting toward anger. Finally, he spoke through a mouth so dry his voice sounded like a rasping whisper.

"I wish you'd never gotten that operation, Shelby. I wish you still wore your glasses. That operation changed everything about you."

Shelby covered her face and began to sob. Finally, she said, "I want to go home, Cullen. Please take me home."

= = = ¦¦ = = =

During the next week, Shelby wouldn't speak to Cullen. She avoided him during their shared classes, then practically fled into the hallways. Cullen couldn't help noticing that her distance seemed to convey sadness rather than anger.

And on Friday, she left.

"Hey, Billy, was Shelby in first period today?"

"No," Billy Ward answered. Though two years younger than Cullen and Shelby, Billy was now officially a junior. He shared a first-period typing class with Shelby. "I didn't see her before school. Usually she gets there early, and we talk a little bit."

"Has she seemed . . . different to you lately? Upset about something. Or maybe, just mad at me?"

"Yeah. She's been like, preoccupied, you know? But she hasn't said anything about being mad at you."

After band practice, Cullen stopped Corinne as she put away her clarinet.

"Is Shelby sick today?"

"I don't know. I haven't heard anything from her."

"Is she mad at me?"

"I don't know if she is, but I am. I think you acted like a real jerk."

Cullen was taken aback.

"What did I do? No one will tell me what I did."

"I don't know exactly. I only know you really hurt her. She wouldn't tell me. She cried when I asked her about it."

By Wednesday, Cullen could stand the uncertainty no longer. Shelby remained absent. None of her friends seemed to know any details. When Corinne called her, she was told only that Shelby would miss school for a while.

Cullen sat by his bedroom phone that evening, manufacturing the courage to call. His hand hovered over the receiver a half dozen times before he could finally take the dare. Twice he dialed four of the five numbers before hanging up. Finally, he decided he would wait three rings. If she didn't answer . . .

The phone was picked up immediately.

"Hello."

Shelby's dad.

Cullen's first impulse was to hang up.

After an awkward moment of silence, Mr. Blaine said, "Hello? Is someone there?"

"Um . . . yeah, it's me, Mr. Blaine. Cullen. Can I talk to Shelby?"

"No." One word. Followed by a dial tone.

Shelby did not return the next week, either. No one knew why. Corinne told him curtly she was worried.

On the first Saturday of December, Cullen rang her door bell, offering a prayer that either Shelby or her mom would face him. But prayers weren't being answered that day.

Mr. Blaine offered only a silent, hostile stare.

"I . . . I'm just worried about Shelby," Cullen offered, his tone meek with apology.

"Yeah, I'll bet."

"Is she okay?"

"No, Cullen. She's not. She's not here. There were some . . . complications. Related to her surgery." As he spoke, Mr. Blaine seemed to struggle to keep his anger in check. "She'll be gone for a while."

Cullen remembered his last words to Shelby. *I wish you'd never gotten the operation, Shelby. I wish you still wore your glasses.*

"I'm so sorry. I didn't mean to—"

"Yeah, well, I guess you should have behaved a little more responsibly, shouldn't you?"

"Please, Mr. Blaine. Can I call her?"

"No, you can't. And when she comes home, don't come around here. Never again. Is that clear?"

Guilt weighed on Cullen like an anchor.

"Can you please tell her I'm sorry?" he said.

"You're sorry?" Mr. Blaine shook his head with disgust. He closed the door.

chapter fourteen

July 2009
Sunday Afternoon

"Jesus, it's the cops!"

Weard had been peering through a crack between curtains covering the front window while the others talked in the kitchen.

"If you want to run for it," Weard whispered to Buddy, "I can make a call. How do you feel about South America?"

A knock sounded.

"I'm not running anywhere."

Buddy met Chief Burke and Officer Phillips at the door and invited them inside.

"Are you here to arrest my client?" Cullen asked.

"That's a little complicated." Burke glanced over his shoulder to check on Weard, who lurked his most ominous lurk.

"So, you didn't find his fingerprints," Cullen said.

"Um . . . actually we did."

As Burke directed his attention to Cullen, Weard tiptoed to the wall near the front door and resumed his stance.

"I already told you I'm sure I held the gun," Buddy said. "But that was forty-three years ago."

Weard shuffled a few steps to his right. When Burke checked on him again, Weard pointed two fingers at his own eyes, then directed the fingers to first Burke and then Phillips.

"The problem is . . . the problem is . . . What is that Weard guy doing?"

Cullen shrugged. "Weard, will you please go to the kitchen?"

Weard offered an elaborate wink. "Gotcha."

He made a show of ignoring the officers as he left.

"That guy's nuts," said Phillips.

Cullen noticed the officer drop his hand to the pistol at his hip. "A little," Cullen conceded. "You were saying, Chief Burke?"

"The full autopsy won't be conducted until tomorrow. Preliminary findings show Damon Hammond was shot three times."

"First of all," Cullen said, "Mr. Boyd has already given you a plausible explanation as to why the gun found here would have his fingerprints. Second, why would my client be so stupid as to shoot Hammond, fail to wipe his fingerprints then bring the gun here, and finally, turn it over to you? I can't imagine you've had time to get ballistics results. You can't yet prove the pistol found here is the one that killed Hammond."

"We'll get ballistics tests back tomorrow, as well. We're getting a rush on them. What I've been trying to say is that we verified a second set of prints."

"Well, there you go," Cullen said. "Buddy held the gun forty-three years ago. Someone else found it and used it to kill Hammond yesterday evening."

"We recognize that possibility."

Burke nodded to Phillips, who walked to the kitchen. "Miss Blaine, you have the right to remain silent. You have . . ."

"I . . . I think," Shelby said, her confusion apparent, "I'd like to speak to an attorney."

= = = ¦¦ = = =

Cullen recovered from his shock sufficiently to say, "Chief Burke, you need to give me a few minutes to talk with my client."

"Talk with Mr. Boyd all you want. We're taking Miss Blaine with us."

"Shelby is also my client," Cullen said.

Burke smiled, shook his head, and heaved a sigh. "Is that correct, Miss Blaine? Does Mr. Molloy represent you, as well?"

Cullen offered an almost imperceptible nod.

"Yes, he does."

"Okay. We'll wait outside."

"Not necessary," said Cullen. "Lori, come with us."

"Can you do this?" Shelby asked as Cullen closed the office/bedroom behind them. "Represent both me and Buddy, I mean."

"No, not in the long run. But for the moment I'm going to. I don't trust anyone else around here with your best interest. Why? Do you want someone else?"

"No, Cullen. Of course, not."

"So, pay me. A retainer makes this legitimate."

"I'll have to get my checkbook . . ."

"A dollar," he said.

"I have a dollar in my purse."

"Lori, please loan Shelby a dollar."

"It's a good thing you made a lot of money when you worked for Buddy," Lori said, "because you sure work cheap when it comes to criminal representation."

She handed a dollar to Shelby.

Shelby passed the dollar to Cullen.

"Okay," Cullen said, repeating the message he'd given Buddy, "I am your attorney. Lori is my investigator. We are bound to hold anything you say in confidence. Okay?"

Shelby nodded.

"First," Lori said, "tell us how the police would have a record of your fingerprints for comparison."

"That's easy. Several years ago, the President visited the Governor of New Mexico. The Secret Service took all our fingerprints. Some data base or another would—"

"Okay. How did your prints get on the gun?" Cullen asked. "And don't tell me you don't have any idea, because at some point you touched it. That print is yours. There's no other interpretation."

Shelby sighed.

"How long do fingerprints last?" she asked.

"Why does that matter?" Lori replied.

"Because, just like Buddy, I held the pistol that night in 1966."

Cullen took a moment to process what she had said.

"Wait, you're saying you were there? And . . . the gun?"

"Cullen, I didn't want you to know any of this," Shelby said, after glancing reluctantly at Lori. "The night twenty years ago, when I told you about my pregnancy, I wanted to tell you everything. You were so hurt, though . . ."

"Well, you have to tell me now, or else they'll charge you with murder."

"Whoa, whoa," said Lori. "Pregnancy?"

"Yes," Shelby said. "But on the night Christy was shot, I didn't know it yet."

= = = ¦¦ = = =

October 30, 1966

Shelby wasn't sure whether she should be scared or thrilled. She'd never attended a party featuring alcohol. Seemed like she was trying lots of new things lately. Maybe it was all too much, too fast. She'd spent her whole life being the freak, though, the one people pointed at or whispered about. The one who didn't get invited. Not anymore. Now, Cullen assured her, she was pretty. So, she wanted to be a little reckless. She'd let her conscience sort things out later.

This crowd consisted of maybe thirty kids, mostly juniors and seniors, milling around the entry hall and kitchen of Damon Hammond's home. Hammond lived with his niece Christy on the edge of Arthur's city limits, occupying Arthur County's only three-story house.

The 1920's era structure had been built on the pretense of a southern manor. A Greek Revival edifice displayed four massive columns extending to an overhang above the second floor. Smaller columns from the second floor supported the base of a narrow third floor porch, a low iron fence shaping boundaries of a widow's walk accessed by a set of French doors.

A first-floor veranda spanned the house's main entry, complete with rocking chairs and low tables. The lord of the manor could sit and sip a mint julip while surveying his domain.

Shelby had seen this house—set back from the roadway among a grove of elms—each time she passed along the paved road that served as an unofficial demarcation between town and country. Everyone regarded the place as regal, although from a distance, Shelby realized, you couldn't see the decline that had set in. The asphalt surface of a long curving driveway was cracked and buckling from the thrust of tree roots.

The veranda floor boards sagged dangerously. Elaborate metal sconces flanking the main entry showed rust. One hung an inch away from the wall, suspended by a set of electrical wires. Cracks spidering through the exterior stucco coating displayed putty and paint repairs.

Except for the elaborate entry hall, the exterior seemed no more than a facade hiding a warren of small rooms, dated furniture and worn rugs. Shelby had expected an elegant center stairway, flaring at the bottom and leading to a second-floor walkway, like in *Gone With The Wind*. But the stairs were way off against an exterior wall where they ascended into shadows.

To the rear of this room a kitchen with a swinging door featuring a little porthole-like window provided much amusement. Kids came and went—some of them a little wobbly—holding beer cans or sipping at something red from clear plastic cups They laughed at the push-or-pull confusion caused by the swinging door. Music blared from stereo speakers positioned on the walls around the entry hall.

Cullen, of course, wasn't there. Although he'd been freed from his father's detention decree, Cullen wouldn't attend a party that included alcohol. He'd be hurt to know she would. But Shelby didn't want to miss this. She'd heard rumors about the fake shooting and fight the night before. She wanted to see that Buddy was okay. When she and Corinne arrived, she'd found Buddy standing among a huddle of the football guys over at a far corner near a closed door. He wasn't there now.

She couldn't stop thinking about Buddy. Except when she

thought about Cullen. She found herself re-evaluating her feelings for the boy who had become her best friend, and that seemed so . . . deceitful. For four years, Cullen had been her rock. He'd stubbornly made an effort to know her when no other boy bothered.

But Cullen wasn't Buddy.

She needed to remind Buddy she was still here. She wouldn't have a conversation. She wouldn't hang around. She'd just say hi, then walk right out the door with Corinne. Very cool. Very . . . Lauren Bacall.

Last summer, she and Cullen saw a movie called *Harper* with Paul Newman, whom Shelby considered the sexiest man alive, and Lauren Bacall. Cullen said Shelby reminded him of Lauren. Her voice, the way she turned sometimes, looking over her shoulder with her hair covering part of her face and *laughing with her eyes*. Cullen said those kinds of things.

She took a deep breath, as if doing so could banish Cullen from her conscience.

She held a can of Coors someone had given her a few minutes ago. When she dared a sip, Corinne said, "Shelby! You go home smelling like beer, your mom's going to know!"

"We'll get gum," Shelby said.

"Come on, Shelby, let's leave. We shouldn't be here. We don't really know any of these people. None of them talk to us at school."

"And they never will if all we do is go to band practice. Here. At least, taste it."

She held the beer can under Corinne's nose.

"It smells awful," Corinne said.

"Just taste it."

"No."

"Oh, Corinne, you are such a wimp."

"I am not!" She tilted the can to her lips. "Eeeeeewwwww. Tastes worse than it smells. Okay, let's go now."

"We just got here!"

"Shelby, I don't know how I let you talk me into this. But you said *we'll only take a look*. We've done that. We've consumed alcohol. Now, let's go."

"I wanted to say hi to Buddy. I can't find him."

"He probably had the good sense to leave. Let's go, Shelby. If my folks find out I was here, I'll be grounded forever!"

Shelby sighed. The noise grew louder. More people arrived. Maybe Corinne was right.

"Okay," she said reluctantly, "Let's go."

"Good. We have to buy some gum."

A hand clasped Shelby's shoulder. Darrel Jensen. He held a cup of the amber liquid and weaved a little.

"My, oh my, Miss Shelby! Is that you? When did you get so hot! Come over here. Have a drink with me!"

"Sorry, Darrel." Shelby shrugged free of his grip. "We're just leaving."

"So, where's your dweeb boyfriend?" Darrel asked. "You stepping out on him? Good thing he's not here tonight, because I'm feeling rowdy. I'm looking to kick someone's ass."

Shelby started to say something caustic in Cullen's defense, when well beyond Darrel's shoulder, she saw Buddy standing in profile and looking toward an open doorway.

"If you want to get into it with someone," Shelby said, her voice dripping venom, "there's Buddy. He doesn't like you much. Or are you not feeling *that* rowdy?"

"What, you think I'm afraid of—"

Buddy seemed to be saying something as he pointed at whomever he addressed. The music faded.

BANG!

The noise jolted the crowd into a split second of silence. During that fraction of an instant, Shelby's brain registered a thin column of smoke curling from Buddy's outstretched hand.

Absolute pandemonium!

Screams left the air heavy with a stink of fear. Surfing along the top of an unintelligible clamor were snippets of words forming themselves as horrible declarations. *He shot her! He's got a gun, he's got a gun!*

A coursing river of shoulders, arms and torsos swept Shelby along. Still, she managed to keep Buddy in sight as he sank to his knees. Shelby felt rather than saw a doorframe pass by her. She reached at the smooth wood, trying to hold her place despite the torrent carrying her along. She lacked the strength. She found herself outside, tangled among bodies on the grass. Hands grabbed and shoved as the flailing mass tried to find its feet and flee.

"Shelby! Shelby!"

Corinne's hand found her.

"Shelby, we have to go! We have to go!"

= = = ¦¦ = = =

2009
Sunday Afternoon

"You never told me you were there," Cullen said.

"Most of the kids didn't tell *anyone* they were there until everything came out during the police investigation," Shelby said. "I guess they got the answers they wanted before getting around to Corinne and me. Anyway, our folks never knew."

"Why did everyone run? Why didn't someone help Christy?"

Shelby's expression clouded. "If you'll remember, the news reports said the bullet sliced through her aorta. They said she died within minutes."

"You didn't know that at the time," Cullen said.

"You have to remember how scared everyone was. At least those of us who didn't know it was supposed to be a joke. The only phone nearby was in the house. Buddy had a gun, so nobody was about to go back. Kevin and the other football jerks, who knew about the joke, thought Christy was fine."

"Forgive me here, folks," Lori said, "but I'm still a little stuck on this pregnant thing. You're telling me the two of you have a child somewhere?"

= = = ¦ ¦ = = =

October 30, 1966

"Shelby, Shelby, get up!" Corinne said, "We've got to leave. My dad will kill me if he finds out I'm here. The police are coming . . ."

Shelby's head rang. "Why would Buddy shoot anyone?" she asked.

"I don't know. We've got to go!"

"I have to see if Buddy's okay."

"Shelby, no! Buddy's got a gun! I've gotta get my dad's car out of here."

"Go! Just go. I'll see about Buddy and walk home. I'll cut

across the back field, and I'm practically there."

She escaped Corinne's grasp, then climbed onto the porch. The terror and flight took place behind her now. She peered carefully inside. Blaring music contradicted the stillness. Her attention went first to Buddy's inert form. She couldn't find Christy.

Shelby knelt and whispered Buddy's name. He groaned. She saw a swelling bruise across the side of his face. He was breathing, though. She saw no other sign of injury.

Buddy groaned again and rolled slowly onto his back.

A gun lay beside him. She had to hide it! She picked it up. A siren wailed. Through a window, she saw flashing blue and red lights racing through the distance.

"Oh, my God! I'm holding the gun! And the police are coming. With ambulances. For Buddy . . ."

She dropped the pistol and ran.

= = = ¦¦ = = =

July 2009
Sunday Afternoon

"Why in the world would you pick up the gun?" Lori asked.

"Because I was a high school sophomore, who panicked and did something stupid."

"What about it?" Cullen asked Lori. "Would fingerprints last that long?"

"Sure, if the pistol was put in something like a plastic bag and kept from moisture."

"There's no way to fake a fingerprint?" Shelby asked.

"Only in movies. So, you guys are parents, huh? Shoot, you

could be grandparents by now."

"I didn't have a baby," Shelby told her. "I miscarried late and nearly died myself."

"And it wasn't *our* baby," Cullen said quietly.

"So, who—"

Shelby and Cullen exchanged a glance. The pain on Shelby's features revealed her lingering anguish.

"Oh . . . no," Lori said. "Don't tell me . . . not Buddy?"

chapter fifteen

July 1989
Twenty-Year Reunion

"Do you think it's still there?" Shelby asked.

"The windmill?"

"Yeah, the cattle guard, the trees, the windmill? The moon?"

"Well, I'm pretty sure the moon's still there," Cullen grinned. "But we're thirty-eight years old. How would we explain things to your dad if we got arrested for necking out in the sticks?"

When Shelby's dad answered Cullen's knock earlier that evening, his greeting had been chilly.

"I'm not even sure I know how to get there anymore," Cullen said.

"Oh, yes, you do," Shelby said as she laughed.

The band played Buddy Holly's *True Love Ways,* and Cullen held her impossibly close as they swayed on the country club dance floor. The only light came via the glitter of a disco ball rotating above them. Shelby felt a contentment she could not describe.

"The Corvette you're driving isn't pink, so no one will call your dad and tell him what you're up to."

"No, but Hertz will ground me for a month if I scrape the

quarter panel on the fence post. It's one of the paragraphs in really fine print at the bottom of the rental car agreement."

Cullen had grown distinguished as he neared forty. The random grey strands woven through his jet- black hair caught the rotating shafts of light with subtle glints. While a lot of the other men were in suits and ties, Cullen wore a navy sport jacket over a pale blue dress shirt open at the collar. More than the way he looked, though, Shelby sensed an ease about him, a comfort with himself that was something new.

She found the attraction almost unbearable.

The beauty of this moment faded as Shelby felt a shove from behind. They staggered backward. Cullen barely managed to keep them from falling.

"Oh, shit, I'm sorry," slurred Melissa Painter. "Darrel, you've got to watch where we're going."

"Hey, you were the one driving," Darrel said with a harsh guffaw. "I'm just heading wherever you take me. But now that we're here, I think we should trade off."

Darrel gave Shelby the same hungry look so many other men had offered this evening. "How about it, Shelby? You guys wanna swap? Swapping can be fun, can't it, Melissa?"

Melissa erupted into a drunken giggle and slapped Darrel's chest.

"Oh, Darrel, you behave!"

The song ended. The band launched into *Mony, Mony.* Darrel gave a yell that reverberated through the room, breaking into sloppy, grinding contortions. The staid old country club ballroom bounced and jived with men and women clumsily pretending to be eighteen.

"Come on, Cullen," Shelby said. "Let's get out of here."

= = = ¦¦ = = =

"So, why'd you rent a Corvette?" She looked at a floor-mounted gear shift separating bucket seats.

"Oh, just posturing, I guess," Cullen said as he backed from his parking space. "Showing off. Want everyone to know how successful I am."

"Buddy's company is doing well, huh?" Shelby asked.

"Not Buddy anymore," Cullen said. "He prefers Hezekiah. And yes, we're doing okay. Nothing like what's about to happen, though."

They followed the highway that entered Arthur from Fort Sumner, got onto the one-way that took them past the misspelled Pat's Twin Cronnies and Dub's Drive-In.

"Oh?" She put her hand on the driver's-side backrest, then dropped it lightly onto Cullen's shoulder, her fingers caressing the back of his neck.

"Yeah. I'm breaking about a dozen federal laws and SEC regulations. If you tell anyone, I'll probably go to prison. We're making an acquisition. If I were you, I'd buy some stock between now and September."

Shelby had looked forward to this weekend for months—not so much the reunion as seeing Cullen. Maybe the time was finally right. They'd shared a half dozen phone calls this past year as Shelby's ongoing relationship with a career staffer in the New Mexico State Legislature suffered its death throes. Her second marriage had ended three years earlier. And Cullen had given no indication he was encumbered by a serious relationship.

"No," he'd said when she'd finally asked a couple of weeks ago. "The last woman I dated with any regularity drifted away about six months ago. Just sort of disappeared. But then I haven't been very available. I've been working pretty much seven days a week on . . . a project. I can hardly blame her. Actually, things at work are getting under control. I was thinking of giving her a call this weekend."

"Um . . . could you do me a favor?" Shelby asked, looking absently out the window of her Santa Fe office.

"What's that?"

"Don't. Call her, I mean. At least until after the reunion?"

Cullen exited the drag onto South Avenue I, heading along the street leading to the four-way stop and the turn leading to the section road leading to the cattle guard, the windmill and the moon.

Cullen did remember the way, after all. Their little grove of trees still stood. As Corvette headlights swung across the cattle guard, Cullen stopped.

"What's wrong? You having second thoughts? Are visions of the Methodist Youth Fellowship dancing through your head?"

"No. I'm worried about this car," Cullen said. "Corvettes ride pretty low. They aren't made for off-roading."

"Come on, Cullen. It's a rental."

They bumped over the cattle guard. Shelby watched him wince as the Corvette's chassis scraped metal bars. The road had worn to deep ruts. Cullen carefully drove off to the side, so they wouldn't be high-centered. When they reached the turnout, Cullen stopped and opened his door.

"Let me check that it's not too sandy before I turn around."

When he returned, Shelby was laughing.

"What?"

"When we were kids, you weren't anywhere near this patient."

He pulled her to him, the kiss electric. She felt his hands slide from her shoulders to her breasts. She put her arms around his neck and her satisfied, "Mmmmmmm," became "Ow!"

Cullen backed away with a start.

"What did I do?" he asked.

"Nothing." Shelby rubbed her ribs. "I just ran into the damn gear shift knob. I never thought I'd say this, but I miss the Nash."

Cullen laughed as Shelby leaned against the passenger side door. Her hand slid to the V of her blouse. She tugged at the folds of cloth. The laughter stopped as Cullen's mouth fell open.

Slow and tantalizing, Shelby pulled the blouse open wider, then slipped it off her shoulders. The garment fell to her waist. Her sheer bra, the palest shade of green, concealed nothing.

Shelby smiled.

Cullen stared.

"Well," she finally whispered. "Aren't you going to say anything?"

"Um . . ." he managed, "you're . . . my God, Shelby, you are the most beautiful woman I've ever . . . and . . . and . . ."

"And what, Cullen?" She added a note of mischief.

His face broke into a broad grin. "That's not your mother's bra, is it?"

Shelby laughed, summoning him with open arms. Cullen did his best to lean across the gearshift.

"Um . . . maybe we should use the back seat," Shelby said.

"It's a Corvette. There isn't a back seat."

"Okay. We're adults. Let's get a hotel room."

"Where?" Cullen asked. "We go to either of the two motels in Arthur, or even Clovis, it'll be all over town tomorrow morning."

"You still worried what your mom will do if you get me pregnant?"

"No. I guess I'm assuming *you're* worried enough about what would happen if you get pregnant that you've already taken precautions."

"You mean you don't have a rubber in your wallet?" Shelby asked, feigning shock. "You're assuming the woman will take care of this?"

"I haven't ever had a rubber in my wallet. I think that's more a Darrel kind of thing. And I'm perfectly willing to take responsibility for precautions if I'd only known the woman would be hot to trot."

"Is that what I am?"

"Sounds better than horny," Cullen said.

"You're trying to tell me you didn't assume—"

"I didn't assume, Shelby. I hoped."

"So where will we do this?" she asked. "I'm not going to lose my Cullen-virginity fighting with the gear shift in the front seat of a Corvette."

"We could drive to Roswell."

"Cullen, that's ninety miles both ways. And what will you tell your mother about why you didn't come home tonight?"

"I'll tell her I was making love with the most extraordinary woman I've ever known."

"What about the guilt she worked so hard—"

"I've been in therapy, I'm impervious to guilt."

"Mmmmmmm." Her smile turned wicked. "That raises all kinds of possibilities."

"How about your house?" Cullen asked.

"My house? Are you kidding?"

"Your old room? The one you snuck out of after the prom? I'll bet we could sneak in."

“Do you have any idea,” she said, “what my dad would do if he caught us in bed together?”

“Yeah. Your mom could handle it, but . . . he still doesn’t like me, does he?”

Diplomatically, Shelby ignored his question.

“Well,” he said, “I did remember to bring a blanket. Two of them, actually.”

“Oh, Cullen,” Shelby said, “on the ground? Here? I . . . I don’t think I . . . what about snakes, and . . . and prairie dogs.”

“Prairie dogs? The worst a prairie dog could do is stand at the edge of his hole and watch.”

“That’s what I mean. I don’t think I can deal with all those beady little eyes.”

Cullen grinned. “Have you ever noticed how long a Corvette hood is?”

“We’re going to do it on the hood of a Corvette? Really?”

“Just take a look.”

They stood at the front of the car, Cullen behind her, cupping her breasts through her sheer bra.

“You have to admit,” Cullen said, “it’s kind of phallic.”

She turned within his embrace and kissed him.

“Get the blankets.”

= = = ¦ ¦ = = =

When they were done, they reclined against the windshield, one blanket beneath their naked bodies, the other covering them. Shelby nestled into Cullen’s arms as they gazed into a sky strewn with stars.

She kissed him. “Mi amore, mi corazon.”

"My love, my heart," he said. "You still remember?"

"How could I forget the most perfect day we ever spent together?" she asked.

"Look there," Cullen said. "Do you see it? That's a satellite."

Shelby found the rapid little moon streaking through the heavens. "It's going so fast."

"It's a Russian satellite."

"How would you know?"

"Because it's tracking north to south. Most Russian space launches involve a polar orbit, because that puts most of the satellite's path over the USSR land mass. U.S. satellites track west-east."

"You're such a smart man." She smiled and kissed him.

"So why . . ." he asked after a few minutes, "why is your dad still pissed at me? Your mom likes me. I'm successful. I've got plenty of money. I haven't committed any felonies. What did I do?"

Shelby's smile faded. She took Cullen's hands. "I swore I would tell you this before . . . but, dammit, I wanted us to finally have . . . this moment. Please understand that?"

Cullen felt a chill. He'd already been wondering how they were going to work out the living arrangements. He wouldn't ask her to leave her career and join him in Phoenix. He *could* leave his job and go to Santa Fe. He'd made enough to be more than comfortable. He could probably find some interesting work there. Not government or politics, though.

This renewed fantasy of a shared future developed the tiniest crack with those words: *Please understand.*

"Cullen, there's something I have to tell you."

A cloud passed, casting Shelby's face into shadow. The chill deepened with her silence. The cloud drifted on.

"When . . . when we were sophomores, when I was so . . . mean after you were grounded for wrecking your dad's car . . . and then I went away . . . I'm so sorry . . ." Her voice trembled.

Cullen put his hand under her chin, turning her face to his.

"You had the eye complications. You were upset and scared. I didn't understand then, so I said that awful thing about wishing you still had to wear your glasses."

"That didn't hurt me," she said softly. "You only said that because you didn't . . . You couldn't understand because you didn't know the truth. I . . . I was pregnant. My parents sent me away to have the baby."

Cullen felt confusion bordering on pain. He'd been jerked back from the most beautiful hope for a life together to the depths of misunderstanding.

He took a deep breath. Finding words took a few moments. "Pregnant?" he finally whispered. "But . . . but we didn't . . ."

Shelby's face crumbled.

Cullen knew whatever response she'd hoped for, this wasn't it.

"No, Cullen. We didn't."

= = = ¦¦ = = =

Cullen felt everything stop.

A moment before, the blankets had been warm, leaves on twisted trees rustled like parchment. Grey, flat clouds sailed gently across the moon. Shelby's breathing filled the distance between them, and Cullen's heart beat a rhythm reflecting the exquisite consummation of something that had tempted them for twenty-five years.

"Pregnant?" he heard himself whisper. "But . . . but we didn't . . ."

"No, Cullen. We didn't."

Then, nothing. Only a stillness so absolute, Cullen feared the universe itself had come to a standstill. He found himself occupying a single frame of a movie that had jammed before the unrelenting glare of a projector's white-hot bulb. The world melted into a nonsensical smudge of light and color.

Finally, a leaf stirred, a cricket chirped, and the film began to roll again. Shelby stood, her back to him, stepping into her clothes. He slid off the hood and did the same. She waited with the car separating them, still facing away, her arms crossing her chest as if to warm herself.

Cullen walked around the car to embrace her. They stood in silence for a moment, her face buried in his chest. He rested his chin lightly on her head, smelling honey and cherries. Finally, she withdrew from his arms and reached for his hand.

"Wow," he said. "I . . . what happened?"

She offered a rueful laugh. "What usually happens, I guess."

"But . . . when?"

"Those weeks at the start of school when you were grounded. I just got . . . I don't know. You weren't around, and suddenly . . . for the first time in my life, other boys noticed me. Those things we had done together were so . . . exciting . . . so wonderfully forbidden. I . . . I thought that's how it would be with someone else, too."

"So how many times did you—?"

"Oh, just the once." She raised her face to the stars. "Lucky me. I hit a jackpot the very first time I placed a bet."

For the most fleeting of moments, Cullen fearfully braced

himself for anger. But he could find within himself only a bottomless regret. And sorrow. A foolish gullibility.

"How could I have not known?" he wondered aloud. "It never occurred to me."

"No one knew. Not Corinne. Not . . . him. Only my parents. I'm sure there was some speculation, some gossip, and I'm a little surprised you never heard anything like that. But everyone seemed to accept the story about my eyes and . . ."

Her voice trailed away. A cloud passed. They heard the yip of a coyote.

"What about the baby?"

"I put off telling my folks for as long as I possibly could," Shelby said. "I . . . I lost the baby. A girl. With all the complications, I . . . That's why I was away so long."

Cullen felt his hands trembling. Guilt and doubt cloaked her with an aura Cullen could see just as clearly as the moon sitting on her shoulder.

"You can't think you were responsible for your baby's death. You can't punish yourself that way."

"I know. I've told myself the same thing for a long time now."

A silence descended over them. Cullen felt sure they were both thinking how to confront the next question.

Finally, he sighed. "Who . . . who was he?"

Shelby withdrew her hand.

"I've never told anyone."

"No one? Not even the father?

"Not even the father."

"What about your folks?"

"Nope. My dad tried to make me say who. But I just wouldn't. So—"

"So, he came to his own conclusion," Cullen nodded, finally understanding Mr. Blaine's anger.

"I told him it *wasn't* you. I'm not sure he's ever believed me."

"I can't imagine the strength of will it must have taken, keeping that secret from your parents."

"The mistake was mine," Shelby said. "I couldn't punish someone else. But not telling my folks wasn't the hardest part. The hardest part was not telling you. And not just then. I've wanted to tell you a dozen times. But I just couldn't."

"Why?"

"Because I'm selfish. Even in the seventh grade, I felt I could count on you above anyone else. If I *really* needed something, I knew you'd find a way. I needed you so badly . . . I knew how much you would be hurt, though. I was afraid you'd hate me."

Cullen put his arm around her. The world came back into focus. The injured boy needed to cede the stage. Before the boy retreated, though, Cullen had to know.

"Why did it happen? How did it happen?"

"If you'd asked that question the day after, I wouldn't have had an answer. But over the years, I think I've put most of it together."

She looked at him for permission to continue, which he granted with a nod.

"You were out of the picture for a month and that happened right when . . . well, you know what we were doing, how things were progressing. I guess I was absolutely overcome with an . . . erotic curiosity you made seem so innocent and easy for me.

"I had a secret crush on this guy, and with you not around I guess I made myself available. I'm not blaming him for anything. He didn't make me do anything. I wasn't entirely sure I *wanted* to do it, but the point came when *you* would always say something funny, or something weird would happen, and we'd stop. I guess maybe I expected everyone would be like that, especially him. We didn't quit, though. After, at school and stuff, he was nice to me, just like he'd always been. He didn't avoid me or talk about me. It was like nothing happened, though. I was . . . I didn't understand."

During her explanation, a veil of mystery lifted.

"Buddy," he whispered.

Tears appeared on Shelby's cheeks.

"You can't tell him," she pleaded.

"*You* should, though."

"I . . . I might have, once. But everything was happening with Christy and the shooting, and nothing I was going through seemed important. You can see why I couldn't let anyone know it was Buddy. How much worse would that have made everything for him?"

Cullen straightened and walked into darkness. Sand shifted under his feet. A wind gusted from nowhere. He heard the rustle of tumbleweeds, and the slightest hum from the barbed wire stretched taut between posts along the section road.

He'd had this conversation before—been on the receiving end of confessions of infidelity. In one case, he'd tried to get past it, tried to make a relationship continue. But the effort only extended the pain, inflated the animosity. Was this different? They had been children. How could he be sure, though?

He wouldn't put himself through that again, couldn't subject Shelby to the anger he feared waited in the weeds.

He felt Shelby's presence behind him. She folded herself around his arms and chest, resting her head against the back of his shoulder.

"I'm so sorry," she whispered.

"Hey, we were kids. It's not any more complicated than that. In an hour, or a day, I'll be able to set all the confusion and . . . and self-pity aside. But you've got to give me a moment . . . Shelby, please understand. There are two people *I've* always felt I could count on. You and Buddy . . ." He caught himself. "I . . . I know neither of you meant to hurt anyone."

They walked hand-in-hand to the Corvette. Cullen eased over the cattle guard. They drove to Shelby's house, sharing awkward small talk. A light in the front room burned, just like when they were kids.

"He's still waiting up for you."

"He's my dad. He worries about me."

"Tell him . . ." Cullen said, "tell him I'm sorry. I misjudged him. All he did was care about his little girl."

Cullen opened the passenger-side door for Shelby.

"So, what happens now? To us, I mean?" She slipped her hand into his as they stood there.

"Shelby, I . . . I don't know. I've been working for Buddy for ten years. The things he hired me to do have been done. I dotted the i's and crossed the t's on this acquisition thing last week. I've made enough money, and . . ."

"And now this." She sighed, leaning into him. "Please don't let this be the reason you do something rash."

". . . I've been considering this off-the-wall thing. A guy bought some old sailing ships, and he's outfitting them to be small cruise ships in the Caribbean. He needs some legal help. A partner, maybe."

"Sounds pretty exotic," she said. "If you'd been seriously considering it, though, you'd have told me already."

He didn't tell her that until a few minutes ago, he'd decided to turn down the offer.

"I think . . . maybe I need to get away from everything for a while. So far, my choices have been . . . safe. I think . . . I think I need to run away and join the circus at least once in my life."

He felt her shoulders quiver.

"You could come with me," he whispered.

She put her hands on his chest and made a space between them. "There was a time when I guess I was like most girls. I wanted someone to . . . to make me whole. I've had several chances at commitment, and each time, I find myself concluding that I'm okay. After my second divorce, I kind of decided that would be it. I've got a career I like. I'm good at what I do. I've got friends.

"I know for a while you and I would be fabulous together. Cullen, I can't tell you how much I respect who you are, what you've accomplished. But I'm not sure I trust the . . . passion. The fire we'd build would be very hot, I know. If it burned itself out, though, where would we be?"

She paused a moment, and when he started to reply, she put a finger to his lips. "If you wanted to try my world, I'd take the chance. But I don't think I'm a circus kind of girl."

"Is this why it's taken us so long?" he asked. "To share *that* moment?"

Shelby nodded. "I think it's because of something you said when we were kids. You remember? You said you didn't want us to go all the way because on our wedding night, you wanted to ask me if it was my first time, knowing the answer would be yes. After Buddy, I knew whenever we shared ourselves completely, I wouldn't be able to lie to you. I didn't know what I would say, but I knew I couldn't lie."

Cullen felt a hollowness he doubted could ever be filled again.

"So, ask me."

He looked at her with a sad smile. "That horse is a little bit out of the barn, don't you think?"

"Please, Cullen, ask me. Please?"

He sighed and whispered, "Shelby, was it your first time?"

She peered so deep within him, he felt she must know every one of his secrets. "No, Cullen, my love. But it's the first time I ever wished it *was* the first time."

He could not turn away from the most beautiful face he'd ever known. Neither could he speak. And in his silence, he knew Shelby had found his answer.

Shelby kissed him, then said, "Let me know how things go in the Caribbean."

"You do know," he said, "that I love you. I always have."

"I know, and that's the irony of it all. It's like we're on separate trains running along parallel tracks. We're so close and, somehow, we keep missing each other."

Cullen smiled a sorrowful smile and kissed her forehead. "I suppose," he said, "that's better than a train wreck."

chapter sixteen

Sunday, 2009

"You have got to be kidding me," Lori said. "How much worse can this get?"

"Worse?" Shelby asked.

"Look, Shelby, your ongoing friendship with Buddy over the years provided a *grasping-at-straws* kind of motive for killing Damon Hammond. That motive just got a lot more plausible. You and Buddy were closer than anyone has suspected. When they question Buddy about all this, they'll ask about your relationship. If either of you try to hide this, a decent prosecuting attorney will eat you alive."

"Buddy doesn't know. So how would they find out?"

"Believe me, if they charge you with murder, they'll dig up everything about you. You can't take that chance."

"Um . . . are you serious about the whole confidentiality thing?" Shelby asked.

"Of course," said Cullen.

"Then there's something else you probably should know."

"Okay."

"Something strange is going on here," Shelby said, "because when I shot Damon Hammond last night, I was very careful to wipe the gun afterwards. I even went to the kitchen and found some Windex."

= = = ¦¦ = = =

Lori recovered first.

"You shot Damon Hammond?" she gasped.

"Not on purpose." Even as she said it, Shelby realized her story would inspire skepticism among some folks.

"You killed Damon Hammond?" Cullen finally found his voice.

"I don't think so. I only shot his foot."

Cullen's face drained of color.

"You'll have to bear with me a little," Shelby continued. "It's complicated."

Cullen sank onto the bed. "Well, I certainly hope so."

"I drove to Hammond's house during the dance, because I was pissed off about the thing at the restaurant. See, my dad knew Hammond, because he'd done some research for one of Hammond's lawsuits. I thought I'd try and appeal to his better nature, even though I suspected he didn't have one."

"So, instead, you shot him?" Lori asked.

"I think he was already dead. He didn't seem to be breathing, and he had this little hole on the side of his head. So, I sort of assumed . . ."

Cullen's chin collapsed onto his chest. He held his forehead in his hand.

"I would have called someone, except I'd picked up the gun . . .."

"You find a guy lying there with a hole in his head," Cullen said, "and naturally, you pick up the gun. Like you didn't learn your lesson the first time?"

"I had to handle it, because it looked just like the gun from all those years ago. I was worried Buddy *might* have killed him. So, I wiped it down, to be sure."

"That's when you accidently shot him?" Lori asked, her voice laced with sarcasm.

Shelby knew no other course than to plow ahead. "I was cleaning the trigger."

"Oh, my good Lord," Cullen said. Now he fell back, winding up prone on the mattress. The headboard thumped against the wall.

"Triggers get fingerprints, too, don't they? I was just being thorough."

"The gun went off?" Lori said.

"Yessssss."

"You shot him where?"

"His left foot."

"But he was already dead."

"If he was alive, I would have expected him to jump up and down a little, or at least say ouch!"

"And then . . ." Lori asked.

"I left."

"No one saw you?"

"I don't think so. The house sits way back on that huge lot. No one else was there."

"Buddy wasn't there?" Cullen asked.

"No."

Cullen contemplated the ceiling.

Lori paced for a moment, her heels clicking on hardwood floor.

"So, if you accidentally shoot someone who's already dead,"

Shelby said, "how bad can it be? I mean, can't forensics people tell something about the order in which someone was shot?"

"Yes, they can," Lori said. "But forensics will not reveal which shooter shot his head, and which one shot his foot."

"Oh," Shelby said with a frown. "So, I could be in a little bit of trouble here, couldn't I?"

= = = ¦ ¦ = = =

"I'm sorry, Chief Burke," Cullen said. "I don't believe it's in Miss Blaine's interest to speak with you at this point."

Burke pushed up from the couch where he and Officer Phillips had been waiting.

"Then you understand that we are taking her in?"

Cullen heard Shelby gasp.

"The reason Miss Blaine's prints are on the gun is the same as Mr. Boyd's. She touched it, all right, but like Mr. Boyd, that was October of 1966."

"Certainly, you can understand how I might be a little doubtful," Burke said as he nodded to Phillips. "There's no way of knowing when any of those prints were deposited."

Phillips reached for his handcuffs.

"That's not exactly true, Chief Burke," Lori said, positioning herself between Shelby and Phillips. "A couple of processes have been developed for determining the age of a print."

Phillips gave a short laugh.

"These methods," Lori continued, "map chemical composition of the prints with a sub micrometer resolution and look at how the compounds move. You see, most of the material deposited by a fingerprint initially is in the ridges of the pattern. Over time, it diffuses into the valleys. Smaller molecules move faster, heavier ones slower, but all can be modeled with a standard function for molecular diffusion."

"Um . . . okay," Burke said.

"All we need is an imaging mass spectrometer, and I think we can easily prove the prints are all too old to have been deposited during the time frame of Mr. Hammond's murder."

"We don't have one of those."

"You can probably rent time on one. Maybe Albuquerque or Denver?"

"Sounds expensive," Burke grumbled.

"Very." Lori smiled.

"Well, fortunately, we have more than just the print," Burke said. "We have a witness. So, if you'll allow Officer Phillips to proceed . . ."

= = = ¦¦ = = =

July 2009
The Reunion
Saturday Evening

Aggie Smoot had been a snoop and a gossip for eighty-three of her eighty-five years. She couldn't speak coherently enough to tattle on her older siblings until she was two, and she regretted the lost opportunities. Beyond that point, though, her siblings could get away with nothing.

Aggie did her best over the decades to keep up with technology. She owned a pair of good binoculars by the time she was eight. She spent World War II scouring Arthur for Nazi sympathizers. Soon after the war, she bought a surplus parabolic microphone and spent evenings seated atop her house, eavesdropping on the conversations and arguments of her neighbors. She kept copious notes regarding her observations.

As decades passed, she purchased all manner of cameras and recording devices.

She might have made a career as a private investigator, except she couldn't resist telling people what she'd learned. Being first to reveal a tidbit, seeing a look of greedy surprise cross the faces of her confidants as they plotted their opportunity to pass the information along, provided her immense satisfaction.

So, it wasn't unusual that Aggie would be seated in the darkness of her upstairs bedroom on the evening Damon Hammond was shot, her windows open as she watched the big house across the field through her night vision binoculars, earbuds inserted for her parabolic microphone, notebook at her side.

One reason Aggie bought a house in Arthur's new west-side development was the clear view her bedroom window offered of the huge house across the road. The comings and goings of rich folks were always a subject of a small town's interest.

She made careful journal notations of the activity that evening. With her night vision goggles she had an unobstructed view of anyone entering the front door. Tall windows looking into the entry hall were blocked by interior darkness and half-closed curtains, so she couldn't see enough to know precisely what happened. Each time an instantaneous flash of light momentarily whited out her goggles, though, she arrived at only one conclusion. The flare indicated the muzzle flash of a firearm.

= = = ¦¦ = = =

The late-shift dispatch officer alerted Chief Burke just after nine p.m. on Saturday. "Sorry to bother you at home, Chief, but we've received reports of gunfire at the Hammond place."

"Well, get someone over there."

"Okay, I wanted to check first. The reports are from Aggie Smoot. I know we've stopped taking Aggie's calls, but we *did* dispatch an officer to a dispute involving Hammond and a Hezekiah Boyd earlier this afternoon. So, I thought—"

Burke sighed. "You did the right thing. I'll go take a look."

When Hammond didn't answer his doorbell a half hour later, Burke and Officer Phillips exchanged a worried glance. Phillips drew his sidearm. Burke twisted the doorknob and cautiously entered. Although darkness prevailed, they could distinguish a figure lying on the couch along the east wall.

"Mr. Hammond?" Burke called. "Mr. Hammond, are you all right?"

He wasn't.

= = = ¦¦ = = =

July 2009
Sunday Afternoon

"She's their witness?" Lori asked dubiously as she and Cullen watched a gnarled little woman walk alongside Chief Burke with a determined stride.

"Good afternoon, Miss Smoot," Cullen said.

Aggie regarded him carefully. "I know you," she said. "You're the kid with that pink car, used to go to the boondocks with those girls. Drove right by my house. I called your father about that."

"Yes, ma'am. I'm sure he appreciated it . . . Um . . . Chief Burke, can we get on with this?"

"We're waiting for the District Attorney. He wants to be here when . . . ah, here he is. Cullen Molloy, this is Clifton Gladly. Mr. Molloy is representing Miss Blaine."

"Yes, we've spoken by phone. But I thought you were representing Mr. Boyd."

"Sort of a temporary thing," Cullen said. "We'll sort it out."

Gladly hadn't dressed for the occasion. He wore jeans and an untucked collared shirt. Whatever attempt he'd made at combing his hair did not address undisciplined wisps waving from the back of his head. Glasses made him look studious.

"Sorry to keep you folks waiting. I've been over at the crime scene and . . ." He stopped when he saw Aggie Smoot. ". . . and . . . Chief Burke, may I speak with you for a moment?"

Cullen watched Burke follow the DA a short distance away where they spoke in urgent whispers. Gladly seemed annoyed. Burke winced a few times as Gladly made his point. Burke followed with a response, prompting Gladly to produce a couple winces of his own.

They took a moment to calm themselves before returning.

"If you'll follow us," Burke said.

They trooped toward a small observation room, featuring a two-way mirror. Phillips waited until they were situated, then withdrew, reappearing as he beckoned four women to follow. Shelby stood as the third woman from the left.

"All right, Miz Smoot," said Chief Burke, "is one of these women the person you saw enter Damon Hammond's home yesterday evening."

"Yes, sir," Aggie answered without hesitation.

"Which one?"

"Third one from the left."

"Thank you. That will be all for now."

"Just one moment, Chief," Cullen said. "I'd like to ask Miss Smoot a couple of questions."

Gladly nodded his assent.

"Miss Smoot, you don't know the third woman to the left, do you?"

"No. If she's one of them here for the reunion, though, I could check my journals if you need me to."

"No, that's all right. What about the first woman? Do you know her?"

"Raylene Tuttle. Used to be Raylene Stark, but she divorced Ronnie because he was tomcattin' around. Then she took up with Lionel Tuttle back when Lionel and Charlene were—"

"Thank you. The second woman. Do you know who she is?"

"Not by name. I see her at the Safeway sometimes on Wednesdays."

"And the woman to the far right?"

"Alva Henson. She lives south of Elida. She's a widow woman."

"Thanks." Cullen smiled at Clifton Gladly.

Officer Phillips escorted Aggie away as Gladly fumed.

"Mr. Gladly," Cullen said, "I think you have a problem with your lineup."

Gladly spread his arms with exasperation and glared at Burke, who said, "Well, goddammit, it's pert-near impossible to find anyone around here who Aggie Smoot doesn't know something about, especially at this hour of a Sunday afternoon."

= = = ¦ ¦ = = =

Darrel Jensen entered the office area of the Arthur Police Department from the back hallway. He found the room deserted except for Homer Ridley, who pecked at a computer keyboard. Darrel was halfway towards the lobby door when someone called to him.

"Darrel, what are you doing here?"

Darrel saw Randy Phillips.

"Oh, I was downtown and thought I'd drop a hunting picture off for Cantwell. I left it over on his desk."

Phillips didn't respond.

"Heard there's been an arrest in the Hammond murder," Darrel said.

"Yep. Can't talk about it, though."

"Oh, come on, Phillips. It's me! Just because I'm retired doesn't mean you guys have to treat me like a civilian. I'm an old pro at this stuff. I'm guessing old Mr. Hammond made Buddy Boyd mad yesterday afternoon . . ."

"Made an arrest. Wasn't Boyd."

Darrel's mind raced as he tried to process the statement.

"Not . . . not Boyd?" he asked. "But I thought . . ."

A door opened and Darrel faced Aggie Smoot.

Aggie stopped, stared at Darrel, then extended a boney index finger at the tip of a stringy, age-spotted arm.

"There's another one!" she said.

"Ma'am?" Phillips asked.

Darrel squinted at Aggie.

"Him," she said, her finger unwavering. "And don't you try to deny it, Darrel Jensen!"

Darrel's mouth gaped open. "Miz Smoot?"

"Deny what?" Phillips asked.

"He was another one I saw go inside right before the gunshot."

Phillips crossed his arms and blocked Darrel's path.

"Hey, I don't know what she's talking about! I was at the reunion dance all evening. A hundred people saw me."

"How'd you know the time frame concerning the gunshot Miz Smoot is talking about? How'd you know that happened during the dance?"

"I . . . I . . ." Darrel waved toward Aggie. "Why are you listening to this crazy old coot, anyway? She's been making up stories for years."

"So, what were you doing at Hammond's?" Phillips asked Darrel. "You and Shelby Blaine decided to get together and kill him?"

"Shelby Blaine?" Darrel looked puzzled. "She wasn't . . . um . . ."

"Wasn't what?" When Darrel didn't answer, Phillips turned to Aggie. "Why didn't you tell us there were two of them, Miz Smoot?"

"You didn't ask."

"So, the two of them went inside—?"

"They weren't together. Darrel came and left. The Blaine woman was later."

"Who fired the shots?"

Aggie opened her purse, withdrew a handkerchief, and wiped around her mouth. "Both did as far as I could tell."

"Darrel Jensen," Phillips said, "I'm arresting you for the murder of Damon Hammond. You have the right—"

"I want a lawyer!"

"Isn't gonna be anyone available on a Sunday." Phillips frowned. "We'll get you a bond hearing by at least Tuesday morning."

The door from the hallway room opened. Clifton Gladly walked through, followed by Shelby, Cullen and Chief Burke.

"Him!" Darrel shouted. "He's a lawyer!"

Cullen stopped, looked over his shoulder at Gladly, then back to Darrel.

"Me?" Cullen asked.

"I damn sure don't want the DA to represent me!" Darrel said.

"What?" Gladly asked.

"I just arrested Darrel here for the murder of Damon Hammond," Phillips said. "Miz Smoot says Darrel was there and shot him before Miss Blaine got there and shot him."

Gladly's chin fell to his chest. He took a deep breath, then said to Chief Burke, "You people are idiots."

Cullen winked at Shelby, then said to Darrel, "I can't represent you. I represent Shelby and Buddy. They've also been charged with killing Hammond. So that would be a conflict of interest."

"Why isn't it a conflict for you to represent the both of them?" Darrel demanded.

"Well . . ."

"So," Darrel said, "you'll be a little bit more conflicted, is all."

Burke and Gladly both glared at Phillips.

"What?" he asked. "What did I do?"

"So," Gladly asked Aggie, "they didn't shoot him together?"

"Not as I could tell."

"Mr. Jensen was there first?"

"Yep. Come skulking, lookin' all around like he didn't want anyone to see him. Went inside and FLASH! Then, he left."

"How much later did Miss Blaine get there?"

"Maybe forty-five minutes or so."

"So, are you gonna represent me or not?" Darrel demanded of Cullen.

Cullen gave Gladly a shrug and a questioning glance.

"Oh, hell, why not?" Gladly asked. "This thing's already so fu . . . um . . . screwed up. We'll get him someone else tomorrow."

"Why are you doing this?" Lori whispered as they followed Darrel toward the interrogation rooms.

"Because something doesn't make sense here, and Darrel may have information that will help Shelby. Otherwise, I wouldn't piss on Darrel Jensen if he was on fire."

chapter seventeen

April 1967

"Cullen, phone's for you!"

"Okay, Mom, I got it. You can hang up now."

Cullen waited for the distinctive click of an extension being returned to its cradle.

"Hello?"

He was greeted by a moment of silence, then heard her wonderful low voice.

"Hi, Cullen. I . . . I'm home. I was . . . hoping you'd call."

He'd wanted to. He'd thought of calling a half dozen times after Corinne told him Shelby had returned. But he didn't know how to handle it. For one thing, he was still a little angry that she hadn't even written. For another, Carol Scott. They'd been dating for weeks. And finally, he considered Shelby's father, who'd made it clear he didn't want Cullen Molloy to ever bother his daughter again.

Cullen knew what he should say at this moment—what he really wanted to say. "I'm so glad to hear your voice. I've been worried about you. I can't wait to see you."

Instead, "I called every week you were gone until your dad ordered me not to."

"I know." She sounded defeated. "And I'm sorry. I should have—"

"Even if you couldn't call me, you could have written a letter or a postcard, letting me know what happened, whether you were all right. Your mom told me there were complications. But your dad . . .well, after a couple of months I just stopped trying."

"I was really . . . sick for a while. I couldn't . . . I should have written. I know."

There followed a silence until Cullen finally asked, "So when will you be back at school?"

"Monday. They wanted me to stay home for a week. I'm fine, though. Um . . . I was wondering if you'd take me to a movie Friday?"

"I don't think your dad would approve."

"My mom talked to him. He'd let me go if—"

"I can't this weekend, Shelby. I've kind of been dating Carol Scott. There's a dance. I already asked her."

"Yeah, Corinne told me you'd been seeing Carol. I understand. I guess I'll see you at school Monday. Goodbye, Cullen."

= = = ¦¦ = = =

"I thought we were going to the dance?"

"I can't go now," Carol said. "That bitch Lindsey will be there with Mark. She wants to make me look like a fool."

"I thought you didn't care about Mark anymore."

"I don't, but them being there together is just, like, throwing it in my face, you know? We can go see a movie instead."

Arthur County's courthouse was a four-story reddish blonde

brick edifice. Built as a Works Projects Administration development in the 1930's, the building aspired to Roman architecture and stood at the center of a square that was the heart of Arthur's modest downtown. The two one-ways formed north-south borders of the square. Commercial buildings—three banks, two drugstores, a barbershop, the post office, the police station, a Sprouse-Ritz and a Woolworth's, a western wear shop, a hardware store and several clothing stores—faced the courthouse on four sides.

At the northeast corner of this commercial center stood the Palace Theatre, a single-screen movie house that, during the 1960's, changed features like clockwork each Wednesday and Saturday evening.

The theatre entry was at a forty-five-degree angle to the street, leaving a stand-alone ticket booth tucked under an overhang where people crowded to escape wind and cold while waiting for the next show.

Glass doors opened onto a red-carpeted lobby on each side of the box office. Popcorn and soda machines, along with candy displays, a jar of giant dill pickles and a dozen withered wieners turning slowly on heated rollers emitted a conglomeration of odors that captured the incoming crowd. Cullen had never seen anyone order a hot dog. He suspected they only replaced a weenie when it wrinkled like a raisin and took on a greenish tinge.

Entries to the theater itself were a pair of wide curving, sloping walkways at each end of the concessions counter. These walkways started under bright light, then faded to darkness as they curved to a pair of aisles dividing seating into three sections. Steep stairways off each curve led to a notorious balcony. Couples seen climbing those stairs became the subject of much speculation at school. Since most of the high school movie-going crowd would be at the dance on this particular night, Cullen considered asking Carol if she wanted to climb the balcony stairs.

Cullen eased into one of the angled parking spots along a wide sidewalk which separated the courthouse square from the one-ways. He took Carol's hand, and they jaywalked to the ticket booth. A waiting crowd huddled under the overhang to escape a raw April wind. Cullen and Carol squeezed among them.

As they waited Cullen glanced across the crowd and found Shelby with her mother. He shifted positions, blocking Carol's view and putting a fat man between him and Shelby's line of sight.

He peeked around the fat man.

Shelby seemed tired, her face downcast, her complexion pale. What struck Cullen most—what scared him—was an aura of defeat, of surrender that draped her like a shroud. Something so foreign to Shelby Blaine, Cullen could hardly process it. The Shelby he knew glowed with delight or defiance. But not now.

Yes, she had hurt him. Yes, he still felt angry. She'd made no effort to explain anything. At that moment, though, only the grip of Carol's hand kept him from running to Shelby, begging forgiveness for whatever he might have done to damage her and their relationship.

Shelby's mother said something. Shelby smiled, took her mom's arm, and walked into the lobby. Cullen breathed a sigh of relief. He urged Carol toward the auditorium.

"Aren't we getting popcorn?" Carol asked.

"Um . . . let's get our seats first. I'll come back."

They passed the balcony stairs. Cullen didn't even consider them. No way could he go up there with Shelby and her mom below. He chose the very last row of seats.

"You don't want to try a little closer?" Carol asked.

"Sitting too close makes everyone so huge, you know? And it's bad for your neck."

They watched a newsreel and the start of previews. Finally, when he felt sure Shelby and her mom would be settled, Cullen went for refreshments.

He walked along the curving ramp into light, eyes cast down as he worried about Shelby.

"Hello, Cullen." Mrs. Blaine leaned against the wall, her arms crossed.

Cullen opened his mouth but found no words.

"It's okay, Cullen," Mrs. Blaine said. "I know you didn't do this purposely. We didn't expect you to be here. Shelby thought you and Carol would be at the dance."

"We . . . um . . . we were, but . . ."

Shelby's mom raised her hand, then forced a smile. "Shelby has been through a very difficult time. I know, or I think, anyway, that the way things have occurred have not been . . . fair to you. You're both young. You are at a complex time of life. Being your age isn't easy. I'm not so old I can't remember that. You make other friends, other commitments; it's the way these things usually go. One favor I would ask . . . please . . . don't be unkind. I don't know if Shelby could take it. Not from you."

"Oh, Mrs. Blaine," Cullen said, "I would never deliberately hurt her. I would never . . ."

Mrs. Blaine held up her hand again.

"Thank you, Cullen. We're sitting opposite where you are. When the movie's over, we'll leave quickly if you and Carol could give us a few minutes before you go?"

= = = ¦¦ = = =

April 1969

"Um . . . hi, Mrs. Blaine, I don't suppose Shelby's home?"

"No, Cullen. She's not."

"She's probably out with Doug, huh?"

"Cullen, I'm sorry, Shelby isn't . . ."

Cullen sighed into the phone. He wasn't sure why he'd called. Of course, Shelby was with Doug Hoskins. Saturday night. No way would Shelby be home.

"Okay."

"I'll tell her you called."

"No. No, Mrs. Blaine. That's all right. I shouldn't be bothering her. I just . . . we don't talk anymore. I . . . I just miss her, I guess."

"Where's Carol?"

"Oh, we haven't been dating for a while now. I'm not really seeing anyone. I mean, I sometimes have a date, but, you know, not like . . . not like . . ."

"I understand. Just because Shelby and Douglas have been going together doesn't mean the two of you can't be friends. I think she misses you, too. With only a month before you graduate, I hate to see you leave this unresolved. I know things happen. I also know how close you two have been. I think you'll both regret it if you don't find some way to at least talk. So . . . so, Cullen, you hang in there, okay?"

Cullen disconnected the call, wondering at Mrs. Blaine's last comment. Could it be possible she was rooting for him? Didn't matter, though, did it? Shelby always made up her own mind.

At the start of senior year, they had been friendly. But as Shelby and Doug's relationship became more serious, the distance between them grew. Weeks passed. Cullen found he could no longer be indifferent to Shelby's new relationship. He wavered between regret and anger.

Cullen considered his Friday night options. He knew some band guys had gotten a keg and were heading to the dry alkali lake bed by the Arch highway. Shelby and Doug might be there, though. Some of Darrel's crowd would probably crash it.

So, he would drive and think. He made one loop of the drag, waved at a few friends, avoided others. After he made the U-turn past the university for this second lap, he went left at the Sinclair station, left again by the Senior Center, past the airport, past the golf course, onto the first of two sharp turns that would take him through the tiny town of Floyd, then to Melrose and beyond.

He wished he could just keep going. Six weeks from now, he *would* keep going. Not east but west, to Roswell, then through the Hondo Pass and Ruidoso, the Lincoln National Forest, down to Tularosa, and White Sands. Then Las Cruces. A different life—a whole different identity if he wanted. No one would know him. Shelby Blaine would just be . . . someone who lived in the past. None of this would matter. All the answers would be there. New friends. Another Shelby? Someone. He would find her.

He hoped.

And he might have kept going tonight except, five miles past Floyd, the Mercury ran out of gas.

"Shit. Shit, shit, shit. Double shit!"

The Mercury coasted to a stop along a barren ribbon of two-lane pavement. Cullen stepped into a black silence that hovered for a minute before the prairie forgave his intrusion. Crickets began to sing. Mesquite bushes rustled as night creatures resumed their business. A couple of coyotes yipped. When Cullen took a few steps toward the barbed-wire fence bordering the roadway, a dozen quail bolted from a growth of prickly pears with a furious whirr of feathers.

Cullen opened the Mercury's trunk. The interior bulb by the left side tail light cast a dim glow, revealing tools Cullen's dad always carried along with an empty tin gas can.

Floyd's lone gas station would be long since closed for the night. His only option was hiking a section road intersecting the pavement to find a farmhouse where he could either use a phone or borrow some gas.

He'd walked a half-mile towards Floyd when he reached a hard-pan roadway on a perpendicular to the left. He saw dim lights glowing a mile distant.

"Nah, I cain't hep ya," said the man who answered his knock. He was fiftyish, tall and lean in bib overalls, a sweat-stained tee-shirt under the shoulder straps of the bibs, and a tanned face offset by a stark pale forehead marking the line of his John Deere cap.

"If the car was here, I could siphon you a gallon. But the missus is in Clovis to see her sister. All I got is dissel. The truck and equipment all run on dissel."

Cullen understood the translation to be "diesel."

"I don't suppose your rig could run on dissel, could it?"

"No, sir, I don't think so."

"I'd give you a ride except I'm babysittin' a cow 'bout to drop her calf, and I cain't leave. We don't have a phone."

Shit, shit shit, Cullen thought.

"Do you know whether anyone else close by might . . ."

"Well, sir, the Martins live a couple more sections up this road. But I couldn't tell you if they're on the place tonight.

Weekends they might be at Melrose playin' forty-two."

Cullen decided he wouldn't chance the Martins. Toting his empty gas can, he trudged back toward pavement and what small semblance of hope it might represent.

As he neared the highway he found a glow of headlights off toward Fort Sumner. The vehicle coming fast. He had to cover a hundred more yards to reach the highway. With the gas can pounding against his leg, he ran for all he was worth. He reached the fence line just in time to raise the can high as the car flashed past.

He thought they hadn't seen him until brake lights flared about fifty yards down the road. As the car began backing toward him, he bent to catch his breath.

It reversed past him, leaving him painted by headlights. He squinted as a disembodied voice called, "Is that your car back there?"

"Yes, sir," Cullen answered, raising the gas can as evidence of his plight.

A passenger side door opened. A tall, wide-shouldered silhouette emerged.

"Cullen?"

"Buddy?" Cullen said to the headlights. "Is that you?"

= = = ¦¦ = = =

"Dad, I can run Cullen by a gas station, then back to his car," Buddy said.

Harold Boyd snorted. "Sorry, Cullen, but the best we can do is drop you at your house. It's late and Buddy will go straight home. How would it look your first night back, running around at all hours?"

"Dad, I won't—"

Harold Boyd exited the car, leaving Buddy's mom alone inside.

"Let me spell it out for you, Buddy," Mr. Boyd said. "They released you from Springer a week before your eighteenth birthday and made you come back here for one reason. Damon Hammond wants you to screw up. I will remind you that Judge Whitfield will hold a hearing after your birthday to determine what happens. He can still send you to prison. You can't give them any excuses. The only time you'll set foot outside our house between now and then is when you're at school. This is your whole future we're talking about. I'm sorry, Cullen, we'll just drop you at home."

"That's okay, Mr. Boyd," Cullen said. "I appreciate the lift."

He and Buddy got into the back seat.

Mrs. Boyd offered a patient smile. "Hi, Cullen. What are you doing out here this time of night?"

"Just . . . driving," Cullen replied.

They rode in silence. There was no 'boy' left of Buddy. He'd grown an inch taller during the thirty months he'd been gone. He'd grown harder, too. While his shoulders, arms and hands radiated a raw kind of power, his face was gaunt, eyes wary. Even at rest, Cullen sensed an almost electric tension humming through him. His right hand resting atop the door's armrest clenched to a fist.

Though Cullen did his best not to stare, his attention kept drifting to Buddy. Eventually, Buddy caught one of Cullen's uncertain glances and offered a grim smile.

"Um . . . are you okay?" Cullen asked with a tentative semi-whisper.

Buddy shrugged.

"So . . . so how was it?"

Buddy gave a mirthless chuckle. "Not something I'd recommend."

Buddy might have been asleep when they drove through town, negotiating sparse traffic along the one-way toward the university.

So, Buddy didn't see Shelby Blaine exiting the movie theater, her face bright with laughter as Doug Hoskins embraced her.

But Cullen did.

chapter eighteen

May 1969

During his first week home, mostly, Buddy was a curiosity—an object of whispers and stares. None of his peers had known anyone who'd killed someone before. Accounts of what happened the night Christy Hammond died had been embellished with thirty months of gossip and imagination.

Kevin Quinn and the other senior football players, who orchestrated the event, were two years removed from high school. Kevin and a couple of others had gone off to junior colleges, perpetuating the fiction that they had some athletic future beyond dusty, Friday night football fields. The others had melded into the day-to-day reality of life and a realization that whatever they made of themselves would be made amid the heat and wind and stifling uniformity of Arthur, New Mexico.

Looking back, Cullen could never escape the irony. Buddy was the only one among them who had an opportunity for football to take him to a better place. That future, though, was sacrificed to jealousies, insecurities, meanness, and a stupid joke—a fate of tragic proportions had all of this befallen anyone lacking the raw determination and resilience of Buddy Boyd.

= = = ¦ ¦ = = =

The uneasy peace collapsed at the end of Friday lunch hour.

Shelby waited at the high school's main entrance for Doug and their daily drive to a sandwich shop near the university.

As she lingered, Cullen stepped through the front doors. Their eyes met. Cullen had avoided Shelby for weeks. She'd grown tired of his act. He was the one who hadn't wanted to see her when she'd returned. He was the one who chose skanky Carol. So, what was she supposed to do? Doug had asked her out and she found she liked Doug a lot. *He'd* been there for her as she put the last year behind her. Not Cullen.

Cullen quickened his step. His avoidance made her angry.

"Hi, Cullen," she said pointedly.

Cullen stopped.

"My mom said you called."

"Um . . . yeah. I did."

"Why, Cullen? Why would you call me?"

His expression drifted from what might have been anger, to a kind of blankness, to some sort of surrender. "I miss you, Shelby. I just miss you."

She'd been formulating some sharp response that would lend a satisfactory finality to this scene, but it died as she watched him hurry away. Doug slipped beside her and took her hand. "Hey, beautiful, you ready for lunch?"

They were returning, walking across the big parking lot in front of the gym when she noticed a solitary figure seated at a picnic table in a shady space separating the gym and main building.

Buddy, a brown paper bag and a can of Dr. Pepper before him, held half a sandwich and a paperback book. He made a point of ignoring the world around him.

"Hmmph, Buddy Boyd," Doug said, shaking his head. "Why would he come here? I mean, if you'd shot someone, would you come back?"

"They made him," Shelby said, trying to keep the catch from her voice.

"Who made him?"

"The judge."

"Oh, yeah, I heard something about that. Like until he's eighteen, right? I hope they send him to prison."

Shelby stopped. "Why would you want that?"

"Well, he killed Christy. You kill someone, you should spend more than a couple of years at some reform school."

"It was an accident." Shelby didn't try to disguise the anger in her voice.

"Oh, gee, Shelby, I'm sorry. You . . . you were kind of his friend, weren't you? I forgot. I didn't know him much. I . . . he was just this jock and I didn't—"

"He's a nice guy. He was nice to me when a lot of other people weren't."

"Hey, I shouldn't have said what I said. I hope he's . . ."

They were about twenty yards from Buddy now. A flurry of movement caught Shelby's attention. A group of five senior boys led by Darrel Jensen, stood within a few feet of the table. Shelby saw Darrel's mouth move, but she couldn't hear his words. She drifted closer.

". . . I said, how you doin,' *killer*?" Darrel repeated, biting hard on that last word.

Buddy's attention didn't waver from the book as he said, "Go piss up a rope, Darrel."

"You wanna make me, *killer*. "Again, the ugly emphasis.

Buddy stared at his book.

Darrel grabbed the end of the table, jerking upwards. Sandwich, soda and paper sack bounced to the ground. The movement knocked the paperback from Buddy's hand. Now Shelby could see the venom. Now she was afraid—afraid Buddy might kill Darrel.

Darrel read the warning, too. He took a quick step back.

When Buddy didn't rise from his seat, though, Darrel gathered himself.

"Do something, *killer*. What, you only fight with girls? You goddamn pussy . . ."

About twenty people clustered around them.

"Get him, Darrel," said someone from the edge of the crowd.

"Beat his ass," said someone else.

"Who's the pussy?" came a voice Shelby knew.

Cullen pushed his way forward. "You know he can't fight back. Only a coward would push someone who can't fight back, Darrel."

Buddy stood. "Cullen, don't."

Cullen stepped between Buddy and Darrel.

"What, you want some of this, Cullen?" Darrel sneered. "You call me a coward and think you can walk away?"

Jackie Handler, a tall, skinny kid, one of Darrel's cohorts, crowded Cullen.

"Punch him, Jackie!" came a call from Darrel's cadre.

Jackie threw a long, looping blow with nothing behind it. His fist smacked off Cullen's cheek.

Cullen would tell Shelby later that he felt stunned for a moment—not from the blow, but from its lack of effect. Little more than a slap. Cullen's last physical confrontation with anyone had been the ninth-grade fight. It wasn't like he'd practiced, or anything. He said he reacted without knowing where the response came from. He threw a short left jab to Jackie's exposed cheek, standing the boy straight, then, with his feet firmly planted and his shoulder behind the blow, drove his right into Jackie's chest.

Air from Jackie's lungs expelled with a whoosh. He collapsed.

Cullen's moment of glory was short lived. Darrel was all over him. When he staggered dazed into a half turn from a shot to his temple, the blows fell upon his back and kidneys.

Shouts urged Darrel on.

Shelby's instinct was to help Cullen, somehow place herself between him and Darrel. She was diverted, though, when Buddy leapt over the table.

With Cullen down, futilely raising his hands to parry Darrel's blows, Shelby ran to Buddy, instead. She grabbed him around his waist from behind and said urgently, "You can't do this, Buddy. You can't. Just leave. Go. Now! I'll help Cullen. They'll send you away forever if you . . ."

Buddy didn't go. But neither did he fight. At that moment, three teachers converged, pulling Darrel off Cullen, tending to Jackie who was still breathless and writhing.

Once order was restored, Mr. Danford, a PE teacher, pointed at Buddy and said, "What did you have to do with this, Boyd? What did you do here?"

"He did nothing!" Shelby screamed, inches from Danford's face. "He did nothing! Darrel threatened him and insulted him! He would have forced him to fight if Cullen hadn't—"

"Nobody asked you, young lady!" Danford snapped. Then to Buddy, "You're lucky we don't call the police. Now, everybody get to class. Jenson, you and Handler go to the office. Molloy, you'd better see the nurse first." As the crowd drifted apart, Danford shouted, "Graduation is three weeks away! Anything like this happens again, there will be suspensions. You can take F's for the classes you don't complete, then finish your requirements this summer. How'd you like that?"

Cullen rose painfully, his nose bleeding. one eye swelling shut. He grimaced as he couldn't quite manage to stand straight.

"Can you get to the nurse by yourself?" Danford asked. "Or do you need help?"

"Give me a minute," Cullen wheezed. "I'll be fine."

Danford snorted, then left Cullen with Buddy and Shelby. Doug stood an awkward distance away.

"Um . . . Shelby," said Doug. "We're gonna be tardy if . . ."

Cullen leaned, hands braced on his knees. He wouldn't look at her.

"Okay." Her voice quavered.

As she left, she heard Buddy say, "Goddamn, Cullen, what the hell were you thinking? I told you in the ninth grade you weren't any good at this fighting shit."

= = = ¦ ¦ = = =

Cullen felt like he'd been hit by a truck. He took a deep breath, wincing as pain streaked along the line of one of his ribs.

"Yeah, in retrospect, maybe I could have handled things better."

"Can you walk okay? Here, let's get you to the nurse's office."

Cullen rubbed his nose and his hand came away bloody.

"No, Buddy," he said. "You have to stay away from me. You can't have people thinking you were a part of this. Darrel was . . .

was deliberately provoking you. You get tied to this at all, you could end up in prison."

= = = ¦ ¦ = = =

"You probably have a bruised rib. Your right kidney is likely bruised as well," the nurse told Cullen. "Your nose isn't broken, but that eye is almost shut. Get some ice, and a cold pack for your rib and kidney, too. If there's any blood in your urine, go to the emergency room."

The nurse's phone rang as Cullen painfully put one arm and then the other through the sleeves of his shirt.

"Yes, okay. Cullen, they want you at the principal's office."

Cullen found Principal Roger McGowan and Police Chief Duard Jackson waiting for him, along with Darrel and Darrel's father.

"This is crazy," Mr. Jensen was saying. "Since when do police get involved when boys . . ."

He paused when he saw Cullen's battered face and his painful walk.

". . . get in a fight," he continued a little more quietly.

"Because there's more to it than just a fight," said Jackson. "In a few weeks, these kids will be adults. We could bring assault charges here. Some kids I've talked to say your boy was trying to provoke Boyd. The stakes are pretty high for Buddy Boyd."

"I didn't provoke anyone," Darrel said with a little whine. "Boyd was who—"

"Buddy didn't do or say anything, Darrel, and you know it," Cullen said.

Darrel glared.

"Why'd you beat Cullen so badly?" McGowan said to Darrel. "He's no match for you."

"I was just protecting Jackie. Cullen attacked him. Practically knocked him out."

"Jackie threw the first punch," Cullen said. "All I did was defend myself."

"Doesn't look like you did it very well," McGowan said.

"We've got a lot of conflicting stories here," Jackson said. "But I'll tell you what, Darrel. I lean toward believing Cullen a lot more than I believe you. Now here's what will happen. Between now and graduation there will be no more incidents, or there will be arrests. You two will keep as far away from each other as you can. And," he said as he stared hard at Darrel, "Buddy Boyd is off limits. You have any idea what it's like where he's been the past two-and-a-half years, Darrel? You're damn lucky Cullen got in his way today. You push Buddy Boyd, he's liable to kill you. I'm not kidding."

Mr. Jensen grabbed Darrel by the elbow and hauled him away.

"I called your dad," McGowan told Cullen.

"Cullen," Jackson said, "if you hadn't thrown a punch, I'd be arresting Darrel Jensen. But basically, it's your word against his as to how this whole thing happened. I'll put the fear of God into Darrel, and I hope he'll leave you alone. Once you guys graduate, though, I'd watch out for him if I were you."

"A week after I graduate," Cullen said, "I'm going to Las Cruces. I'm already enrolled for summer session at New Mexico State. I don't think I'll be coming back." He thought of Shelby. "I can't wait to leave here."

= = = ¦¦ = = =

July 2009
Sunday Evening

Arms folded, stares fixed, Cullen and Darrel faced each other across a metal interrogation desk. Darrel practiced his most intimidating scowl as he waited for Cullen to speak. Cullen matched him glare for glare.

"You sure they aren't listening?" Darrel finally asked, nodding at the two-way mirror.

"You tell me," Cullen said. "You worked here. Did you eavesdrop on attorney-client conferences?"

"Fuck," said Darrel under his breath.

Seated beside Cullen, Lori said, "I'll go read the riot act to Clifton Gladly."

When she'd gone, Darrel said, "Okay, Cullen, how are you gonna get me out of this . . ."

Cullen shook his head. "Wait a minute, Darrel. I haven't decided to represent you."

"Why not?" Darrel demanded as Lori re-entered and took her seat.

"Because I don't like you. Because from eighth grade on, you did your best to make my life miserable. Because of how you treated Buddy when you knew he couldn't fight back. Because you beat me bloody and destroyed the last few weeks of my senior year. Because you're a coward and a bully. You want me to continue?"

"We were kids. That's just how it was. This is now."

Although Darrel still blustered, Cullen saw the fear. No cop or ex-cop wanted any part of jail. Arthur's criminal activity was sort of a generational thing. Some of the young thugs he'd share a holding cell with over the weekend might be sons or nephews of men whom Darrel had bullied when he was a member of the Arthur police force.

And Cullen needed some details to protect Shelby.

"First, I want a retainer."

Lori rolled her eyes.

"How much?"

"How much you got?"

"I got a hundred twenty dollars, but they have my wallet."

"Lori," Cullen said, "would you . . ."

She smiled and left the room.

"So, what's going—"

"Not until you've officially hired me, Darrel. Client/attorney confidentiality doesn't kick in until then. And, by the way, that confidentiality extends to Lori, who is my investigator. We'll find you another attorney tomorrow."

"So, I'm paying you a hundred twenty dollars to represent me until tomorrow?"

"You could always stay here a couple of nights for free."

Lori returned.

Darrell paid.

"So," Cullen said, "what's the hold Damon Hammond has on you?"

"Wait a minute. How about getting me released?"

"First, I need information. You answer my questions now, and I'll refund sixty bucks."

"And you can't tell anybody what I tell you now?"

"Nope. No one."

= = = ¦¦ = = =

Darrel calculated what he could get away with. What should he omit? The series of events leading to the shooting of Damon Hammond started with Damon's call from the restaurant Saturday, ordering Darrel to confront Buddy Boyd.

"I can't do that stuff anymore, Mr. Hammond," Darrel had told him. "I haven't been a cop for years. I know you've got someone currently on the police force. Use him."

"People take vacations. My man is out of town. So, it's your job."

"If I'm a cop and there's a fight, the other guy gets arrested. That's not how it is anymore. They'd probably arrest both of us."

"Fine. Do it. I'll put up bail."

"I . . ."

Hammond twisted the knife. "I still have the documents. There's no statute of limitations on murder."

"It was a car accident," Darrel snapped. "I can implicate you, too."

Hammond's laugh crackled through the phone.

"You've got the same problem you've always had—credibility. Also, I'll remind you, as a bank board member I might suggest we take a harder look at some of the farm loans this fall."

Darrel's son eked out a living on a farm with leased acreage a few miles west of Arthur. Loans were the lifeblood of small farms. So, Darrel had reluctantly gone to the restaurant, though he was far angrier with Damon Hammond than with Buddy. Then, that lunatic Weard Ward got involved and, *shit, the CIA . . .*

Darrel had withdrawn and called the police station, hoping

he'd reach Clinton Funkhauser, one of the few remaining officers who had gotten along with Darrel. Clinton wasn't available, though, so they'd dispatched Phillips who had let Boyd, Ward and the others off the hook.

Later Saturday afternoon, Hammond called again. "I trust that Mr. Boyd is incarcerated?"

"No," said Darrel. "I tried."

"You didn't try hard enough."

= = = ¦ ¦ = = =

Darrel took a deep breath, put his elbows on the interrogation table, then leaned closer

"With Hammond, it's never just one thing." Darrel spoke in a gravelly voice elevated barely above a whisper. Then, he sighed. "It starts small. You think he's doing you a big favor. Then it builds and builds until you're trapped. Here's the funny thing. For me, it started with Buddy Boyd. You remember our senior year when I kicked your ass?"

He said it conversationally, without any hint of apology or remorse. Although Cullen felt disgust and anger rising, he replied with a nod.

"Hammond gave me fifty bucks to fight Buddy. I never liked Buddy. I don't know how Hammond knew that, but that's what happened. Then you got in the way. After we graduated, I finished at the police academy."

"Why'd you need his help?" Cullen asked.

"I was pretty low on the totem pole in my class. Then, right after I finished, I was celebrating with some of the guys. One of them had some grass and—"

"Failing the piss test should have finished you for good," Lori said.

"Hammond pulled some strings. When I retired, I thought I was through with him. The old bastard has been forcing me to do his dirty work for thirty-five years. When he called me today, something just snapped."

Cullen leaned forward. "So, you went to Hammond's house . . ."

"Yeah. I told everyone at the dance I was going to the bathroom. Most people were drinking quite a bit, so I figured no one would miss me for twenty minutes. I was gonna have it out with him. Threaten him . . . anyway, when I got there, he was asleep on the couch, lights turned off. The gun and the gloves were on his desk. Like a gift."

"What happened then?"

"I shot him. I left the pistol there."

The room fell silent. Darrel waited. Finally, he said, "So, what do we do now?"

"You just shot him, in cold blood, while he slept?" Cullen finally managed.

"Yeah," Darrel said. "All he had was cold blood. He was the worst, most conniving, manipulating old bastard—if you knew the whole story . . ."

He stopped abruptly.

"There's more?"

"I'm not saying anything else."

"What made you think you could get away with it?" Lori asked.

"Buddy. With Buddy here, and the restaurant scene . . . plus, Hammond claimed Buddy's prints were on the gun. I didn't see how that could be possible after all these years, but it didn't matter. I figured Buddy would get the blame."

"So, you hid the gun at Buddy's house to frame him for murder," Cullen said.

"No. I left the gun at Hammond's."

He paused and seemed to consider his next statement before he added, "Your girlfriend must have taken the gun to Buddy's."

"You mean Shelby?"

"Aggie Smoot says Shelby was there after me."

Cullen's thoughts raced. Had Shelby lied? If she had, why? For a moment, he'd lost his train of thought.

"So now get me out of here!" Darrel demanded.

Cullen drummed his fingers on the metal table and took a deep breath.

He'd despised Darrel Jensen for decades. He looked at this puffing, strutting, balding asshole, who had done so much to humiliate and hurt him. He indulged himself for one long satisfying moment with a fantasy that he could walk from this room and name Darrel as the killer. Make a deal with Clifton Gladly, maybe. Darrel Jensen for an agreement not to prosecute Shelby or Buddy.

Instead, he said, "You do nothing. You say nothing. Admit nothing. Don't lie about anything, just don't answer."

"How's that supposed to work?" Darrel said. "It'll only convince them I'm guilty."

Cullen gave a rueful smile. "Well, don't lose sight of the fact that you are. But unless you do or say something really stupid—which as we both know is a fair possibility—they can't do anything."

Darrel's expression told Cullen the man suspected some sort of treachery.

"Listen, Darrel. They have no physical evidence connecting

you to the crime. The fingerprints they *did* find can be explained away. They have a questionable witness, who watched you enter the house and a few minutes later saw what she presumed was a muzzle flash. She heard nothing. And here's the real jackpot. You're the third person they've arrested tonight for murdering Damon Hammond. The most incompetent defense attorney you find will be able to build a case for reasonable doubt, because even the police can't decide who they think is guilty."

= = = ¦ ¦ = = =

They exited the interview room to find Shelby seated at one of the desks. She chatted with Aggie Smoot and held Aggie's night vision apparatus. Gladly, Burke and Phillips listened.

"What are you doing?" Cullen asked Shelby.

"Miss Smoot is showing me how this thing works. I asked Chief Burke to turn off the lights, so I can see what it looks like. He won't do it, though. He thinks I'll escape."

"Can we talk to Darrel now?" Gladly asked Cullen.

"You can try, but he won't answer your questions."

"Then Chief Burke will jail both him and Miss Blaine."

"Oh, come on," Cullen said, "what's the point? You've arrested both of them. You don't have any direct evidence of which one might have done it. You think one of them will be dumb enough to solve your dilemma by running away? Just send them home. I'll be sure whomever you finally decide on shows up for arraignment."

Gladly took Burke aside. They conferred amid hisses and snorts, pausing occasionally to direct their gazes at either Shelby or Darrel. Red-faced, both men finally returned.

"Miz Smoot," Chief Burke said, "you told us you saw three

flashes. Who fired the gun twice? Miss Blaine, or Darrel?"

Aggie scowled at Cullen. "You're not gonna' let 'em go, are you?"

"Which one," Burke repeated through clenched teeth, "fired twice?"

Aggie harrumphed. "Neither."

"You said you saw three flashes."

"I saw the other flash right after that Melissa Painter woman snuck in there."

Chief Burke paled and leaned heavily on the desk.

Gladly said to the ceiling, "Oh, my merciful Lord. You're saying there was another one?"

Aggie shrugged.

"Before we go any further," Gladly said, his voice dripping sarcasm, "did anyone *else* stop by to shoot Mr. Hammond yesterday evening?"

A phone rang.

Officer Phillips answered.

"A big homely woman, bless her heart, got there last," Aggie answered. "Wore a funny hat and a plaid skirt. I didn't recognize her. I don't think she shot him, though."

Cullen thought someone would have to restrain Chief Burke when Phillips interrupted.

"Um… Chief? That was the coroner. They still haven't finished the autopsy, but he says the preliminary shows Hammond was shot three times—head, chest, and left foot."

"The foot?"

"One other thing," Phillips added. "He said Hammond had a carrot lodged in his sinus cavity."

"Oh, God," Cullen and Lori said simultaneously.

"What?" demanded Gladly as he turned on them.

"Phillips!" yelled Burke. "Get Melissa Painter and Weard Ward! Now!"

"Just pick them up!" Gladly called after him. "For Christ's sake, don't arrest any more of them!"

= = = ¦¦ = = =

Ultimately, nobody went to jail that night.

Cullen agreed to represent both Weard and Melissa temporarily, cautioning them to say nothing. Melissa, obviously drunk, claimed no memory of shooting Damon Hammond when she gave Cullen her dollar.

"I would've snuck out when the cops showed up," Weard told Cullen during their private conference, "but I knew they had you and Shelby. I figured you had a plan."

"What were you possibly thinking when you stuck a carrot in Hammond's nose?" Cullen asked.

"I didn't do that." Weard said with a broad wink.

"I'm your attorney," sighed Cullen. "I must hold anything you tell me in confidence. You gave me a dollar, remember?"

Weard had borrowed the dollar from Officer Phillips. Darrel watched the transaction and objected. "A dollar! A fucking dollar? You charged me a hundred and twenty. How's that fair?"

"I like Weard," said Cullen. "I don't like you."

Weard noticed his reflection in the two-way mirror over Cullen's shoulder. "You think I should get some of that Grecian Formula stuff? My dreads are almost white, man."

"Why did you stick a carrot up Damon Hammond's nose?"

Cullen repeated.

"To throw them off, man."

"How would . . . Weard, a half dozen people heard you threaten Darrel Jenson with a breadstick."

"Right." He offered another wink. "That's why I used a carrot with Hammond."

"Were you trying to kill him?"

"No. I was only going to threaten him, tell him to leave Buddy alone. There was no premeditation, man. I acted on an irresistible impulse when I saw him lying there asleep."

"What do you know about *irresistible impulse*?" asked Cullen.

"The CIA, man. They taught us all kinds of stuff about criminal defense strategies, in case we got caught."

"Did you bring the carrot with you?"

"Well, yeah."

"That pretty much demonstrates premeditation," Cullen said.

"No, no. It'll still work. I'll just have to say something like, I only wanted to embarrass him. Like, how funny would it be at the emergency room for some guy to walk in with a carrot up his nose?"

Cullen had no response to that.

"I had to do it, Cullen. Old man Hammond was coming after Buddy again. I couldn't let that happen."

chapter nineteen

July 2009
Monday Morning

Cullen herded his troop of murder suspects toward a long dark pew in an empty third-floor courtroom at the Arthur County Courthouse. They were a silent group at eight a.m. Cullen sat between Lori and Shelby, Buddy to Shelby's left, Weard, Melissa, then Darrel, who had refused to sit by Weard.

Only Darrel broke the silence as they waited. "I think I need a different lawyer."

"I think so, too," Cullen told him. "But you might wait and see what happens when Clifton Gladly gets here."

Gladly arrived at ten after eight, pointed at Cullen, and said, "Let's walk to my office. The rest of you wait here."

As Cullen stepped through the doorway, he turned to offer a confident nod to his clients, and the realization hit him.

My God, it's the same courtroom.

= = = ¦¦ = = =

May 1969

Cullen sat behind the rail separating the gallery from the

defendant's table, his father next to him. The facial swelling had eased, blacks and purples had begun their transition to a mottled yellow. His ribs still ached, but nothing like the first couple of days.

Cullen faced the back of Buddy's head, who sat with Scott Vineyard, a young attorney new to Arthur. Mr. Boyd flanked Buddy on the other side. Buddy's mom sat near Cullen.

Across the aisle, District Attorney Morris Stone studied a file folder spread open before him. The only person behind Stone was Hammond. He wore a grey three-piece suit over a white shirt, a pale blue silk tie knotted perfectly at his throat. Gold cufflinks caught a glint of light cast by a series of thick, white globes suspended from fifteen-foot ceilings.

Hammond's lips were a grim slit. He turned toward the defense table. Finding Cullen, Hammond's expression morphed to one of pure malice.

The old courtroom was a cavern decorated with dark woods and darker expressions of various court personnel, setting the somber, silent tone of a place where grave decisions were made, harsh fates dealt.

The absolute quiet as they waited was broken only by the sound of the swinging door behind them whooshing open, then shutting, joined by a gentle tapping of shoes on polished wood as someone else arrived.

Cullen did not turn to find out who. His mouth had gone dry, and he needed to cough. He feared, though, the bailiff might reprimand him for disturbing the gloom. Knowing he shouldn't cough only made the urge more intense until he felt some foreign presence—like maybe a large, hairy spider with sticky feet—tromping around down there. And this creature would not leave of its own accord.

He experimented with a slight, close-mouthed attempt at clearing his throat. A gentle little *ahem* to shoo away the spider. The sound reverberated like thunder.

Cullen bowed his head as he waited for the bailiff to take him away. The creature began a little eight-footed tap dance on Cullen's uvula. He sought solace by swallowing, but now his mouth was so dry his swallower could barely function.

Finally, he could stand it no longer. With a great effort of will, he fought the wheezing gaaaack working its way up from his toes. Miraculously, though, just as the explosion occurred, Judge Eldon Whitfield burst through a door from his chambers with a flourish of robes and a haste, lending the impression of a man late for several more important appointments.

Cullen's cough was lost amid the ruckus. He indulged himself with another.

"Allrisebeseated," droned the bailiff.

The assembly popped up like bread from a toaster, then sat back down.

"Hezekiah Boyd," the judge said. He donned a pair of half glasses, rounded at the bottom, flat along their upper frames and peered over them. "You last appeared before this court in November of 1966. We are here to reach a decision concerning your future. You turned eighteen yesterday?"

Scott Vineyard stood, gripping Buddy's arm, directing him to stand as well.

"That is correct, Your Honor," Vineyard said.

"All right, Mr. Vineyard. Have your say."

"Your Honor," the young attorney replied, directing Buddy to sit again, "Mr. Boyd remains profoundly regretful of his role in events that resulted in Christy Hammond's death. This was not a calculated murder. This was not a scheme formulated by Buddy. This was an elaborate practical joke aimed at Buddy, masterminded by the victim, herself. Buddy doesn't seek to minimize his role. But it *was* an accident. The statements of other boys involved, taken the night of Buddy's arrest, make that clear. Buddy has already paid a heavy price for his mistake. He lost his junior and senior years of high school. He lost a promising athletic career. This young woman's death will haunt him all his life. He's *been* punished. He has been productive and cooperative during his time at the Springer Correctional Facility. He maintained excellent grades. There is no record of his causing trouble there. He's not a criminal by any means."

"Mr. Stone?" Whitfield swiveled his chair.

"Yes, Your Honor. Unfortunately, Christy Hammond doesn't have the option of getting on with *her* life. And I don't know where Mr. Vineyard found any evidence that Christy orchestrated this event."

A whispered exchange took place between Buddy and his attorney.

Whitfield waited. "Mr. Vineyard?"

"Your Honor, the victim wore a device to simulate a bleeding gunshot wound. Buddy tells me that, at the police station, Kevin Quinn said specifically the whole scenario was Christy Hammond's idea."

"Your Honor," Stone said, "no recording or transcription of those initial interviews can be found. The officers who were present have only a vague recollection of who said what. Regardless of Christy's role, I think it's more than appropriate for Mr. Boyd to serve an additional prison term which would reflect, at minimum, a sentence appropriate to manslaughter."

Judge Whitfield shuffled through a sheaf of papers, adjusted his reading glasses. "Says here, Buddy, you were involved in a fight at school last week?"

"No, sir."

"Your Honor," Vineyard said, "Buddy had absolutely no part in the fight. I have asked two witnesses to be here today. They will testify under oath that Buddy did nothing to instigate any incident. A boy named Darrel Jensen attempted to goad Buddy. When a fight finally did break out, Buddy did not take part."

With Vineyard's reference to *two witnesses*, Cullen knew who had entered the courtroom behind him.

Whitfield toyed with his gavel. "Well, I could take a few days—check on these missing statements. I think I already understand what happened, though. So, I'll rule now. Buddy has been truthful about his role. He hasn't tried to place blame. As far as I can tell, he's done what I've asked . . ."

Cullen's hope soared as the judge paused, then plunged as Whitfield added the qualifier.

". . . but, as Mr. Stone stated, Christy Hammond doesn't have the option of getting on with her life. Here's what *your* options are, Buddy. I don't think anybody's best interest is served by your presence in Arthur. I only see turmoil ahead, because we have a certain degree of community outrage at work. So, one way or another, you'll leave here. You can either serve a five-year term at the state penitentiary, and unless you really screw up, you'll probably do two years at most . . ."

Cullen heard Buddy's mother try to suppress a sob. Someone else whispered, "Oh, no."

". . . or tomorrow, you can enlist in the army. If you serve a two-year tour of duty, and serve honorably, I will have your juvenile record expunged. You can be free and clear of this tragedy and this community. By all accounts, you are a talented young man. I hate to see talent squandered."

Buddy's dad stood and put his hand on Buddy's shoulder.

"Your Honor," Buddy said with a steady voice, "I'll take the army."

Buddy's mom cried softly.

Damon Hammond cast a malevolent, lingering glare at all parties before he left the courtroom. As Cullen turned, he found Shelby seated in the last pew between her mother and father. Tears marked Shelby's cheeks. Her mother nodded slightly.

Cullen felt a hand on his arm.

"They wouldn't let me talk to you before," Buddy told him. "They told me it would look like we planned what happened with the fight. I owe you big time, Cullen. What you did for me took guts. You kept me out of prison. Because in another couple of seconds, I was going to take Darrel Jensen apart."

Cullen nodded. His breathing turned ragged. When he could speak, he said, "Buddy, they're sending you to Vietnam."

Buddy nodded gravely. "I know."

= = = ¦ ¦ = = =

July 2009
Monday

Gladly's office seemed straight out of a Perry Mason set. Immense walnut desk, the wall behind it lined with floor-to-ceiling bookshelves stuffed with legal tomes. The other walls, though, remarkably free of clutter for a prosecutor's office. Only a couple of framed diplomas proving Arthur County's District Attorney had, in fact, graduated from law school and was a member of the bar.

Two overstuffed brown leather chairs faced each other next to a window. Gladly directed Cullen to one, choosing the other for himself.

"So," Cullen said, "what will you do? I think you'll have a lot of difficulty convicting *anyone* of murder. The only evidence that any of them were there at all is testimony of a witness, whom everyone in town knows has spun any number of wildly unbelievable tales."

Gladly rested his elbows on the fat leather armrests, steepled his fingers over his nose and mouth, appearing both contemplative and pissed off.

"We have ballistics results from the pistol we recovered at the Boyd residence," Gladly said presently. "Autopsy results still aren't complete, but they used the bullet from Hammond's foot for comparison."

"And . . ." Cullen asked.

"It is the weapon that shot Hammond . . ."

"In the foot," Cullen emphasized.

"Do you have any doubt the other two bullets will match as well?"

Cullen shrugged. As he and Lori had discussed, none of this made sense. Shelby was the third shooter. Shelby wiped the gun clean. Buddy insisted he hadn't gone anywhere near Hammond's place on Saturday. So how did both sets of prints mysteriously reappear when the gun showed up in Buddy's bathroom?

Cullen had grilled them during the wee hours Sunday morning. *Did Shelby find the gun before Buddy did?* They insisted she hadn't. Why would they lie? If Shelby took care enough to clean it meticulously at the murder scene, why wouldn't she do the same if she'd found it at Buddy's house?

"This is the gun with the fingerprints?" Cullen asked Gladly.

Gladly rubbed his face with the back of his fists.

"It *is* the gun we recovered at the Boyd, residence, yes," he said, although he mumbled a little when he said it.

"Beg pardon?" Cullen asked.

Gladly repeated, "It's the gun we recovered at—"

"That's not what I asked," Cullen said, his heart leaping. *Could it be possible?*

Gladly sighed.

"The fingerprints are no longer . . . um . . . I'm not sure . . ."

"Don't tell me police were so careless handling it that they smudged the prints." Cullen grinned.

Gladly did not respond.

"Must I remind you about rules of discovery?" Cullen prodded. He tried not to sound gleeful.

"The prints are gone," Gladly said. "Someone wiped the gun clean."

"Creating a significant issue with chain of evidence," Cullen said. "Some unknown wiper with access to a police evidence room? What about a serial number?"

"Guns manufactured before 1968 weren't required to have serial numbers, so a lot of them don't," Gladly said. "Especially antique guns."

"This gun is an antique?"

"Yes. That's why we're confident it's the same gun. There aren't many like it—an H&R Smith Wesson .22 top break revolver, manufactured sometime around 1907. And it's the gun found at the Boyd residence."

"The one with fingerprints?" Cullen asked.

"Yesssssss."

"But you lost the fingerprints?"

Gladly scowled.

"Buddy said it was the same gun he used the night Christy Hammond died," Cullen said. "Have you done a ballistics comparison with the slug removed from Christy's body?"

"No."

"Why not?"

"Because . . . because after all these years, Chief Burke can't locate the bullet."

"So, if you're right, and this is the same gun that killed Damon Hammond, and Buddy's right that it's the gun that killed Christy, you have another problem. How did a gun held as evidence since 1966 escape custody?"

"We're looking into it."

"And you are honestly telling me, given this train wreck of an investigation, you still intend to charge one or more of my clients with a crime?"

"All of them!" snapped Gladly. "Something's going on here! Some kind of conspiracy or . . . or I don't know what. I'm considering charging Mr. Boyd, Miss Blaine, Melissa Painter and Darrel Jenson with at least attempted murder."

"You've got four potential killers and three gunshots."

"I'll charge one as a co-conspirator."

"What about Weard Ward?" Cullen asked.

"Him, I don't know. If I can't figure out anything better, I'll charge him with the mutilation of a corpse!"

chapter twenty

July 1999
Thirty-Year Reunion

"Cullen," Shelby gasped. "You said you wouldn't be here."

A tanned Cullen Molloy, striking in a multicolored shirt open at the collar, a pair of white linen pants and soft blue-leather boat shoes stood at the steps of the Arthur Country Club for Thursday night's reception.

Shelby had caught sight of him through the window at her table. She rushed to greet him with a kiss.

Cullen grinned and swung her around a full circle.

She saw a tiny gold stud glinting from the lobe of his left ear. "Cullen, you have an earring."

"Guilty. I suppose I should take it out, being in Arthur and all. But every time I do, the damn hole heals over."

"So . . . is this earring a sailing kind of thing?"

"Yeah, to the extent that getting my ear pierced involved a lot of rum."

"You told me you couldn't make it," Shelby said.

"Well, our boat sank."

"What?"

"One of our boats hit a rock, and it sank. There aren't many rocks in the Caribbean, but our captain found one. Right when that happened, we were figuring out there's a reason why most cruise ships are humongous floating cities. Turns out economy of scale is very important to the cruising industry. Making money with a fleet of beautiful but intimate little sailing ships is tough. Then our boat sank, so no one will insure us. The company went tits up, and I was free this weekend after all. Thirty years. How could I miss that?"

Shelby took both his hands, stepping back to look at him. "I wanted to do a cruise with you guys, I really did. Seems like over the course of six or seven years I would've, but things came up."

He shrugged.

"I did actually book one, "she said. "I know you said to call you and you'd get me a deal. I just booked it, though, to surprise you. Then when I looked closer at the package, the information said it was a *swingers'* cruise. And if that's what I think it is . . . well . . ."

Cullen laughed. "It's what you think it is, all right. We did several swingers cruises, gay cruises, transvestite cruises."

"You went on a swingers' cruise?"

"There's sort of a management responsibility . . ." He grinned.

"I guess I'm . . . I'm shocked."

"Every life needs a little debauchery," he said. "God knows mine did. There are no straight lines in the Caribbean. We did a Presbyterian cruise, too, if that makes you feel any better."

She felt an old familiar longing when she heard Michael clear his throat.

Shelby turned and took Michael by the elbow.

"Cullen Molloy, this is Michael Finnerty."

"Nice to meet you," Michael said, extending his hand.

Cullen responded in kind as Shelby said with a sorrowful look that only Cullen detected, "Michael was nice enough to accompany me and meet all these people I've been telling him about."

= = = ¦ ¦ = = =

July 2009
Monday Night

"Weard, are you sure . . .?" Cullen asked nervously as he and Lori crouched by narrow stairs that led to the back door of Hammond's house while Weard fiddled with the lock.

They'd parked a car in a nearby housing development. Shelby and Buddy waited in a second car, watching for signs of police—or anyone else, for that matter—entering the estate through its main gate.

Weard, Cullen and Lori had hiked down a couple of alleys, then crossed the section road near a barbed wire fence running along the back of Hammond's property. This clandestine intrusion onto the murder scene was born that morning as they'd gathered at Buddy's house, puzzling over the disappearing fingerprints.

"I swear to you on anything you want me to swear on," Shelby said, "I wiped the gun clean at Hammond's house and never touched it again."

"Cullen," Buddy said, "you *know* me. We worked together ten years. We shared some highly stressful situations with millions of dollars at stake. There were times when a little lie here or there would have made things a lot simpler. You know I did my best to be honest. I hope you can believe me now when I say the only time I touched that gun was forty-three years ago."

Cullen raised a hand of warning.

"You've already all said too much. Let's not forget, the three of you could still be charged with crimes and could be forced to testify against each other. So, let's don't go into any details of what happened at Hammond's house Saturday night."

"Some of us may know things the others don't," Shelby protested. "If we put everything together, it might make sense . . ."

"You've given me your stories individually. I'm the clearinghouse for details. All that really matters is they've got some huge evidence problems."

"I'd feel better," Lori said, "if I could look at the crime scene."

"Good luck with that," Cullen said. "They won't give us access until they've finished investigating. As screwed up as this police department is, I'm not sure that will be any time soon."

"You just made my point," Lori said. "We've got the Keystone Cops here. Who knows what they're missing or misinterpreting. Shelby is entirely correct. Something doesn't make sense."

"They have to tell us what they found," Cullen said.

"Theoretically, yes," Lori said. "But given your limited experience with criminal defense, you might be a little naïve. You've no way of knowing what they might withhold. Don't forget, as a police detective, I spent a lot of time working the other side of that equation."

"You mean you cheated?" Shelby asked.

"I wouldn't say 'cheated.' I would say we were careful with how we played our half of the chess match. And don't ever forget, defense attorneys are scum."

She kissed Cullen's cheek.

= = = ¦ ¦ = = =

Eight hours later, darkness having overtaken the scene, Cullen stood at the back of Hammond's house wearing latex gloves. He rationalized that he had plenty of money and wasn't really doing much lawyer stuff anymore, so being disbarred for breaking and entering at a crime scene wouldn't be the end of the world.

Lori took his hand, offering a reassuring squeeze. Weard bent over the lock, the door rattled a couple of times and swung wide.

"No alarm," Weard said. "We're good."

"What if Aggie Smoot is out there with her night vision goggles?" Cullen whispered.

"The view she has is of the front of the house," Lori said.

"What if she's sneaking around that big field somewhere?"

"She must be well into her eighties. I suspect she is fairly sneaking-impaired."

"If she causes any trouble," Weard said cryptically, "I'll call someone." He slipped inside.

"Do you think he really means it when he says things like that?" Lori asked.

Cullen had never been in the Hammond house. Its back door opened onto a hallway, extending the structure's full length. He saw a staircase at each end of the long hall. Directly across from the rear entrance was the kitchen.

A couple of closed doors provided access to other rooms.

Walking in a tight little knot, they shuffled through the kitchen and into the main entry hall. This room occupied at least a third of the ground floor. Furniture was configured in several different seating areas.

"Where was he?" Lori asked Weard.

Weard pointed to a heavy sofa set among a cluster of matching chairs.

Lori knelt to inspect the sofa.

"Okay," she said. "Here's the first problem. Where's the blood?"

Cullen knelt beside her.

"This spot right here." He pointed at a half-dollar-sized stain on a pillow set against one arm of the couch. "You can't tell color in the dark, but isn't that blood?"

"Hammond was shot three times—once in the temple," Lori said. "This couch should be soaked. Weard, did you see a lot of blood when you were here that night?"

"Like I told you," Weard said. "I thought he was asleep. Although, come to think of it, he *was* pretty calm when I stuck the carrot up his nose."

"According to Aggie Smoot," Lori said, "Weard was the last one here. Blood should have been everywhere."

"A .22 caliber pistol is a little gun," Cullen said. "So, there shouldn't have been exit wounds? Could that minimize the bleeding?"

"Maybe," Lori said. "Depends on the ammunition. I can understand the chest wound and foot wound not bleeding, because Melissa, according to Aggie Smoot, got here first and apparently fired the initial shot. If that shot was fatal, the other two wounds wouldn't have bled much. But the head wound should have been a gusher."

"Would they have turned the sofa cushions over?"

They flipped the cushions, finding nothing.

"You didn't see the gun when you got here with your carrot?" Lori asked Weard.

"No, man, and I looked around, too. For hidden cameras or alarms or stuff."

“And you didn’t find anything else unusual?” Cullen asked.

“Yeah, I did,” Weard said, pointing at the door to Hammond’s office. “That room there. The office.”

“What about it?” Lori asked.

“It’s too small, man. It’s too small.”

Lori and Cullen exchanged a puzzled glance.

“You mean it’s too small for an office?” Cullen asked.

Cullen thought Weard’s deadpan expression might have betrayed just a hint of impatience when he said, “Offices come in all sizes, Cullen. How could something be too small for an office? As long you get a little desk and . . . okay. You’re confused. Sorry for flying off the handle like that.”

Weard closed his eyes, took several deep breaths. He said, “Ooooohhhmmmm.”

Several seconds ticked by.

“Okay. I’m in control again. What I meant to say is, the inside of that room is too small for the outside.”

Lori offered a skeptical look and opened the door.

“See what I mean?”

“Um . . . actually, no.”

They followed her inside.

Weard shut the door behind them. “We can use lights. There’s no windows.”

Cullen found the switch.

“Now you see,” Weard said.

Cullen and Lori exchanged another glance. Cullen observed a room with a polished wood floor. A desk was centered in the generous space. Matching wainscoting covered three walls. A second door behind the desk was a mirror image of the door by which they had entered. Cullen stepped around the desk and opened this second door a crack. A slice of light stabbed into the hallway that ran along the back of the house. The fourth wall consisted of floor-to-ceiling shelves full of books.

"I'm sorry, Weard," Cullen said. "This looks like a normal room to me. How can you tell the inside is too small for the outside?"

"Oh, shit. I keep forgetting. It's the CIA, man. I . . . notice stuff. I can't help it. This room is about two feet smaller than it should be."

"You mean, two feet deeper? Two feet narrower?" Lori asked.

"Now that's the real question, isn't it?" Weard's face went blank, his expression empty.

Cullen would have been worried, except Weard remained upright. After about a minute, his internal light winked on again.

"That wall," he said, pointing to the floor-to-ceiling shelves, "should be about thirty inches that way."

He put his face a finger's width from the shelves and worked his way along the room's entire length.

"Okay." He stepped to a shelf, which contained a set of encyclopedias, removed the first volume and reached into the empty space.

Cullen heard a muffled *snick.* a set of shelves swung away, revealing a dark space behind.

"Hidden room," Weard said. "Probably where the clues are."

Cullen swung the bank of shelves wide, revealing a space about two feet deep that extended the width of the office. Inside to his left he found more shelves, leaving just enough space for a person to squeeze sideways. Files, photographs, old cassette tapes and various ledgers populated these shelves. To his right, the cavity was empty, save for a stack of cartons. He found a light switch. A forty-watt bulb hanging by a single wire from the ceiling cast a pale, yellow glow swallowed by shadows at each end of the cavity.

Lori stepped around Cullen and directed her flashlight toward the stack of cartons.

"Those," she said, "are evidence storage boxes."

She slid into the cavity, took a box from the pile, and brought it to Hammond's desk.

"See what it says here?" she asked Cullen. She pointed at a printed space that looked something like the slip in old library books where each borrower signed a name, along with a stamp for dates of withdrawal and return.

"This record is supposed to maintain the chain of evidence," she said, "and old evidence shouldn't be in the hands of a private citizen."

"Hammond's an attorney," Cullen observed.

"Doesn't matter. To look at the contents of the box, Hammond would sign for it like anyone else. He certainly couldn't remove it from evidence storage and keep it."

Cullen peered closely at the label Lori indicated.

It included a number that would match the transcription of whatever court proceedings occurred, along with a date charges were filed, defendant's name, victim's name, the date the investigation opened, and the date of the case's disposition.

This carton apparently contained evidence relating to embezzlement of funds from The Arthur National Bank. A charge had been brought against Willard Zed—the name meant nothing to Cullen—during January of 1978. Zed was found guilty at trial six months later. The box contained financial records and a couple of tape recordings.

"What about the other cartons?" Cullen asked.

Lori entered the narrow walkway. Cullen crowded in behind her. He followed her flashlight beam as it played over the other four containers. Cullen had not done enough trial work during his corporate law career to be familiar with disposal of criminal evidence. "Maybe after so many years you can request stuff from old cases."

"No," Lori said. "If there's anything valuable unclaimed by heirs, those things might eventually be auctioned off. But everything else, including weapons, is supposed to be destroyed if the boxes are old enough . . ." She focused her light at the bottom carton. "Look here."

The name on the carton read: *Christy Hammond.*

Only two names appeared on the check-out list. One, Cullen did not recognize. That person looked through the box in 1996. The second, though, was a hasty signature scrawled three separate times. Darrel Jensen had accessed the box during 1976, 1978 and 1981.

= = = ¦¦ = = =

"We've been here too long, man," Weard called from outside the hidden space.

"He's right," Lori agreed. "We should leave."

They withdrew the Christy Hammond box from the bottom of the stack. When Cullen stooped to get it, he felt surprise at how light it was. The others were weighted with heavy files.

He passed the carton to Weard, then quickly inspected the other end of the hidden space, sorting through files and tapes stacked along narrow shelves.

"This all could be blackmail material," he said to Lori. "Stuff Hammond had on other people. If that's so, clearly there'd be no shortage of folks around here who wouldn't mind seeing him dead. We should take a closer look—"

"No," Lori said. "We have to go. We don't want the Arthur police making any more arrests this evening."

"Okay. But we have to see the Christy Hammond evidence."

"I agree," Lori said. "Not here, though. We'll take it with us."

Okay, thought Cullen. Breaking and entering compounded by burglary. Why not?

Lori made one last inspection around the couch, scanning the wall behind it. She craned her neck toward the ceiling.

"Cullen, Weard," she whispered, "stand right behind me. Block the view from those windows behind us so I can use my flashlight."

"What?" asked Cullen.

The light flicked. Its narrow beam played along the seam where wall and ceiling met.

"That dark spot," Lori said, letting her light linger for a moment.

She crept to a row of windows looking out on the front porch.

"There," she said, pointing to a pane at the top of one window.

Cullen saw a neat hole, about the size of a .22 round. Lori traced a path from this hole to the spot at the ceiling with her finger.

"I'll bet it's a bullet hole," she said. "The slug was either removed, or it's stuck up there in the plaster."

"That could have happened any time."

"Could have," Lori said. "But it could also mean somebody

fired a fourth shot Saturday. Someone stood on the front porch and fired through the window."

They slipped outside, across the field and along the alleys. Weard carried the evidence carton. When they reached their car, Cullen called Shelby. "We're good. Meet you at Buddy's place."

"All those hidden files in Hammond's secret compartment could be important if this thing ever goes to trial," Cullen told Lori as they drove. "Since all they have is a shaky witness and a little bit of circumstantial evidence. With those blackmail files, we could construct a fortress of reasonable doubt. We could create dozens of viable suspects."

"Who's to say they're blackmail files?" Lori asked.

"Who's to say they aren't?"

They rode silently for several minutes before Lori asked carefully, "Are you forgetting that we actually have four guilty people—guilty of *something,* I mean?"

"Not our concern," Cullen said. "Our concern is forcing the DA to prove what he believes happened. I don't think he can."

Through the rear-view mirror, Weard appeared to be napping. Cullen signaled for Lori to lean closer and said more quietly, "Look, we don't know for sure if Darrel or Melissa shot Hammond first. One of them, though, is the killer. And believe me, if that's all there was to it, I wouldn't lift a finger to help. I'd be more than happy to let Darrel burn. But he's one of the herd, so he gets the benefit of whatever reasonable doubt defense we create for Shelby and Weard."

"What about cutting him loose and trying to prove he *was* the first shooter?" Lori said.

"The defense doesn't have to prove anything. We only need to create enough confusion, and that's a lot easier than building a case against Darrel."

"Has he gotten his own attorney yet?"

"No. He was so thrilled I kept him out of jail, he wants me to keep representing him."

"But you can't," Lori said.

"If things move anywhere beyond a preliminary hearing, I won't represent anyone. My last criminal trial experience was way back when I worked for a public defender's office. Shelby or Buddy will need someone a lot more competent than me. But for now, I'm representing everyone. Especially Darrel. We have more questions to ask."

chapter twenty-one

July 2009
Monday night

As Weard placed the carton on the kitchen table, Buddy felt his chest constrict.

He and Shelby had spent an awkward time alone together, cruising Shelby's old neighborhood and looking for any sign of police or anyone else who might approach Hammond's house while the others were inside.

When Shelby rode with him from Lubbock, her conversation had been funny and breezy. This evening, though, she seemed distant. Probably worried, he thought, about their legal predicament.

They waited in silence until the others arrived. Weard placed the evidence carton on the kitchen table. Buddy saw Christy's name.

"Where did that come from, and why did you bring it here?" he asked Cullen.

"This is the official evidence storage carton related to Christy Hammond's death. We found it hidden behind Hammond's bookcases. We think Hammond had Darrel steal it from police storage sometime after 1996. That's the last time anyone went through the proper procedure to view it."

"Why, then?" Lori asked. "Why would anybody care about this case in 1996? And who is . . ." She peered closely at the name scrawled on the carton. "... I can't even make out this signature. Cullen, can you read it?"

"The name is Charles LaVelle," Buddy said. "A private investigator. I hired him to find out more than what I knew about Christy."

"Why 1996?" Cullen asked. "What happened to make you—"

"You quit, is what happened," Buddy said, pointing an accusing finger at Cullen.

Memories settled on Buddy's shoulders like a weight.

"If there's a date next to the signature, you'll notice it's probably sometime early November? Halloween of 1996 was the thirtieth anniversary of Christy's ... death."

"Okaaaaay," Cullen said, elongating the word to encourage further explanation.

"That night—her death—has always haunted me. I've talked to psychiatrists, priests, bartenders, even a psychic, searching for some way to set it aside. I've had many a ... *crisis of conscience* I guess you'd call it ... over the years. And that was one of them. You know this, Cullen. We talked about it many times."

He stood, walked to the counter by the sink and poured himself coffee at least twelve hours old, hoping to quell his growing anger.

"I was considering," he continued, his back to them as he confronted the blackness beyond the window, "establishing a fund, some kind of endowment, to honor her and benefit the community. And I really knew nothing about her—her interests, her causes. God, she was only seventeen."

He faced them. "I know what you're going to say. You and others have told me a hundred times. She wasn't an innocent. She put everything in motion out of ... I don't know ... petty meanness, I guess. I know all that. I've rationalized it. I think . . . I hope, anyway . . . I've come to terms of some sort. But I still pulled that trigger."

A vein on the side of his bald head throbbed visibly.

"So. 1996. I wanted to throw money at it, see if that would appease my conscience. I hired LaVelle and sent him here to talk with people who knew her. See what might be appropriate as a large, anonymous endowment in her name. I don't know why he looked at evidence related to her death. He was a thorough, scrupulous man, so I guess he wanted to be sure he earned the fee I paid him. He called me and said he needed to talk as soon as he got back to Phoenix. Indicated he'd found something interesting. But he . . . he died in a car wreck driving back. One more blot on my conscience."

Buddy locked his gaze on Cullen.

"If *you* hadn't been off running around the Caribbean, if you'd stayed with our company, I would have asked you, and you would have made me see the pointlessness . . . the futility. Charles LaVelle might still be alive. You quit, though. And you've never told me why. We were a good team. I still needed you. What did I do?"

Buddy heard Shelby's intake of breath.

"Did Mr. LaVelle find anything?" Cullen wouldn't let Buddy divert him. "Did he offer any insight into Christy Hammond?"

"He mailed a partial report before he left Arthur. It said she was a self-involved, greedy, manipulative narcissist. An unflattering description probably fitting half the teenagers in America. Most of them grow out of it. Most of them find their way. Christy never got the chance."

"You already paid them, Buddy," Cullen said. "You paid them with thirty months of your life. You paid them with your college scholarship and football career. You paid them with a tour in Vietnam. You don't owe the Hammonds or Arthur or anyone else another dime."

Buddy leaned onto the table between Shelby and Lori. His voice took on more of an edge.

"You talk as if all that's a great price," he said. "To a fifty-eight-year-old man, thirty months is an instant of time, a distant memory of little consequence. I probably got every bit as good an education at Springer as I would have at Arthur High School and covering a much broader range of subjects—hard life experiences that made me see very clearly what I did not want to be.

"Football? Maybe I would have gotten a scholarship somewhere, probably some little school where I'd waste four years on a mediocre education. Football wasn't something worth devoting my life to. As for Vietnam, you'll notice I re-enlisted after my first tour? I used the Army for a specialized education, to learn all I could, leading to the company that has made me—and to a lesser extent you, Cullen—a wealthy man. More importantly, the company gave real meaning to my life."

"Why don't you ever talk about Vietnam?" Cullen countered. "You and I have told each other things we wouldn't share with anyone else. You can't make me think Vietnam was easy for you. I know you're not a coward. Were you some kind of hero?"

Buddy scowled. "The heroes all died in that senseless war. And to quote Forrest Gump, *that's all I have to say about that*." He gripped Cullen's arm. "So, what about you? Why did you leave the company out of the blue? Was it just about the money? You got the big payoff from the merger—take the money and run? Or did I do something wrong?"

Cullen's face dissolved to a brief expression of pain before he composed himself. "Buddy, that's not my judgment to make."

"That isn't an answer!" Buddy yelled. He pounded his fist into the table. "And my name is Hezakiah!"

= = = ¦¦ = = =

Shelby felt the tears. She stood and shouted, "Stop it, both of you!" She had to leave before they saw her cry. In the moment she wheeled and walked away, she registered the bewilderment on Buddy's face and an unspoken apology in Cullen's expression.

Lori hurried after her, put an arm around her shoulders as they sat on the couch. "I'm sorry, Shelby. Cullen wouldn't purposely hurt you. He loves you."

"Yeah," Shelby said through her tears, "but the hell of it is, he loves you, too. And you got shot. In your stupid nipple. How could I ever compete with that?"

Lori leaned her forehead against Shelby's and hugged her.

= = = ¦¦ = = =

When Lori and Shelby returned, Cullen kissed Shelby's forehead as apology, then took Lori aside for a whispered conversation.

"I don't want to upset Buddy even more," he said, "but this LaVelle thing might build Gladly's case. He already suggested that a man as wealthy and smart as Buddy might have bribed someone to steal the gun from the evidence box. If a record remains of LaVelle's connection, well, that could be bad."

"I'll check on it," Lori said. "With any luck, their clerical staff will be as incompetent as the rest of this mob."

When they finished this conversation, the others waited with expectant expressions concerning what came next.

"We took the risk of removing this box from Damon Hammond's house," Lori said. "Now I suppose we should see what's inside."

Weard sat on the countertop. Shelby took a chair by the outside door. Cullen and Buddy were separated by silence and the width of the kitchen table.

"I have no interest," Buddy said. "This is all old news. If you think there's something that might help any of you defend yourselves, have at it. But I'll be outside."

"Who wants to do the honors?" Lori asked.

Cullen removed the lid.

"Okay," Lori said, "here's the clothing Christy was wearing."

She removed a long-sleeved blouse, underwear, a skirt, a pair of shoes, all marked with once red stains now faded toward black. The stains were not of an even color, though. They found a strap-like device with a protruding wire connecting to a small round tube and a plunger that would fit a person's hand.

"This is the stage device that releases a red liquid to simulate blood. Christy would have had it under her shirt, with a wire running down her sleeve and the plunger in her hand. When Buddy pulled the trigger, she'd push the plunger so a red stain would spread across her chest."

As Cullen studied the device, something didn't seem right about the scenario Lori had just constructed. He was still formulating his thoughts when Lori said, "The gun isn't here, obviously, but the bullet is. And the spent cartridge."

She withdrew two small plastic envelopes. They were identified as evidence and bore several dates and signatures.

"What about an autopsy report?" Cullen asked. The fake-blood device still nagged at him.

"I don't see a formal report. There's simply a statement from a medical examiner: *The victim died as the result of a single gunshot fired at close range. The bullet severed the aorta. The result of such an injury would be death in a matter of seconds.* Wow. They could never get away with something like this now."

"You mean an autopsy report should be more detailed?" Shelby asked.

"Absolutely."

Lori pawed through the box a little more. "I don't see a ballistics report. Or fingerprint results."

She withdrew a thin sheaf of papers stapled together.

"These, I guess, are supposed to be transcripts of the interviews with Buddy and other witnesses, but there's very little here. It's like they barely investigated."

"Of course," Cullen cautioned, "we don't know what might have been lost or destroyed after the carton was removed from police custody. All of that stuff might have existed at one time."

"Or it might not," Lori said, offering one more piece of paper. "This is a letter from Damon Hammond to Chief of Police Duard Jackson, dated the day after Christy's death."

She read the letter aloud.

Duard,

I wish to prevail upon both you and the district attorney not to drag this thing out any longer than is absolutely necessary. I am particularly concerned about further desecration of my niece's body. An intrusive autopsy is not warranted here and would only add to our grief. Neither should the county incur the further expense of detailed tests or reports. This is a crime for which we have a confession and several witnesses whose stories are consistent. I have no question what happened. Since the Boyd boy is not denying his guilt nor the circumstances of my niece's death, I would consider it a great favor if we would simply move ahead with a sentencing hearing next week and not impose any further emotional trauma on me and my family.

Sincerely,

Damon Hammond

"Unbelievable," Lori said.

Cullen shook his head. "Small town, unsophisticated police force that rarely dealt with murder, limited budgets and a confession? Sure, why not? Hammond had a lot of influence. Given some of those hidden files I looked at, I don't think he had any reluctance about using whatever dirt he could find to impose his will on people. If anyone could cut off an investigation, it would be him."

"Does that letter sound like Damon Hammond to you?" Shelby asked. "I mean, I didn't know Christy very well, but I heard her talking about her uncle a few times and she wasn't expressing any love for him. I remember her saying once something like, 'He thinks I'm just a nuisance, so I do everything I can to irritate him.' I remember, because I thought how awful that a person might have to live with a parent who didn't like them."

"Something else is bothering me," Cullen said, still trying to formulate his thoughts regarding the fake blood apparatus. "You're wearing this harness, right? You've got this plunger hidden in your hand, so Buddy doesn't see it. You're waiting for the gunshot, trying to push the plunger at just the right instant. Then, instead of a blank cartridge, a real bullet strikes you, causing a traumatic injury that kills you within seconds. Do you still push the plunger? Aren't you so shocked and incapacitated that you drop it, instead? Do you even have the physical ability to push it?"

"Could have been a reflex action," Weard suggested.

"Or she could have pushed it a split second early," Lori said, "in anticipation of the shot."

"Maybe she didn't push it at all," Shelby said. "Maybe the stain is all real blood."

"Yeah," Cullen said slowly. "Maybe any of those things."

He spread the blouse on the table for inspection.

"See the variation in colors here? I think the staining is a mixture of blood and something else."

Lori studied the blouse.

"Buddy . . .um, sorry, I mean, Hezekiah," she called through the screen door. "How close was Christy when you fired the gun?"

He opened the screen, then froze when he saw the blouse.

"How close?" Lori repeated gently.

"I don't know, ten feet maybe?"

"Show me."

Buddy entered, distanced himself across the kitchen about ten feet, then revised his estimate. "No, that's too far. Maybe five feet."

He closed the distance.

"And what happened?" Lori asked. "How did she react? Immediately, I mean."

Still fixated on the blouse he said, “Lori, I’m not sure I can . . .”

“Buddy, please.”

“I don’t know. As soon as I fired, I got coldcocked. I don’t remember much else until I was at the police station.”

“I hadn’t heard that before,” Cullen said. “About you getting knocked out.”

“Yeah. You remember Wilmer Hatfield? The guy was huge. A senior defensive lineman. He wasn’t in on the joke. He thought I’d keep shooting people. He slugged me.”

“But you’re sure about the distance?” Lori asked.

“She was pretty close.”

Lori bent over the blouse again. Then she fished through the box and removed the blood-stained bra. Buddy turned away.

“Cullen, Weard, Shelby, come look at this. This is where the bullet entered.” She directed them first to the blouse, then the bra. “Tell me what you see.”

“I see holes where a bullet passed through the shirt and bra before entering Christy’s body,” Cullen said.

“No, man,” Weard said. “The holes are different.”

“They *are* different,” Shelby said. “The hole in the bra is bigger, and they’re both . . . I don’t know . . . a little jagged.”

“Exactly,” said Lori. “Buddy, do you have a magnifying glass around here?”

Buddy rummaged through a kitchen drawer. He found a reading glass the circumference of a softball.

Lori used the glass, then passed it to Cullen. “Look close,” she said, “because it’s hard to notice with the discoloration of the old stains.”

“The hole, or anyway the left half of it, is jagged,” Cullen said. “And the hole isn’t perfectly round. It’s elongated.”

Shelby took the glass.

"There's a little discoloration around the jagged places," Shelby said. "Hard to see through the stain, but, here, it's easier to see on the bra. I think it's kind of brown."

"It's a burn mark," Weard deadpanned. "The jagged part was burned when the bullet passed through."

They couldn't hide their surprise.

"What?" Weard said. "The CIA. I keep telling you."

"And the hole in the bra is slightly bigger than in the blouse," Lori said. "Who handled the gun? Buddy? Please?"

He turned. "Besides me? I don't know. When Kevin showed the gun to me, he hid it in a towel. He told me it had real bullets and told me to take them out. It wasn't like guns you saw on TV. It had a clasp sort of thing at the top of the barrel. I pushed it. The barrel and cylinder swung down. I remember the bullets fell on the floor. So, I put them in my pants pocket. Then Kevin handed me this odd bullet with a real blunted nose—a blank round."

"So how did a live round get substituted for a blank?" Shelby asked.

"God, I don't know. I've asked myself that question a million times. The only thing I can think is, somehow, I mixed them up. I'd had a lot to drink so I can't really be sure what I did."

"Do you think it's possible?" Cullen asked Lori, his voice ripe with excitement.

"Possible enough for more of your reasonable doubt," she said.

"What?" Hezekiah asked.

Lori stood.

"Okay, here's the thing about blank cartridges. People think they're harmless, but they're not. They fire a wad of paper or cardboard that exits the barrel with considerable velocity.

Because they are cardboard, they often burn when they do so. People have been badly injured, even killed by blank cartridges if the gun is close enough when it's fired."

"The night when Christy pretended to be shooting everyone," Buddy said as the memory began to flow, "she shot me from about two feet away. The weather was cold, so I wore a fairly thick jacket. I noticed it had a burned spot, like somebody might have touched it with a cigarette."

"Exactly," Lori said.

"You think the blank cartridge killed Christy?" Shelby asked.

"No. I think the hunk of lead in this evidence box is what killed Christy. I think the blank cartridge is was what burned her blouse, her bra—and probably her chest. If they'd done an autopsy, I bet they would have found a burn near the entry point of the bullet."

"But that would mean . . ." Buddy said, his mouth agape.

"Yes, Buddy," Cullen said. "Someone else killed Christy Hammond."

chapter twenty-two

Monday night
July 2009

Buddy's mind raced, thoughts tripping over one another. His conscience had become so accustomed to accommodating guilt over having killed Christy, his remorse held a place in his heart like an old friend.

For forty-three years he'd never considered that Christy had not died at his hand. He knew he hadn't *meant* to kill her. Despite booze and coercion, he knew his actions were indefensible. He knew—according to the letter of the law—he hadn't been guilty of murder.

Manslaughter? Perhaps. Criminal negligence? Undoubtedly. None of that changed the fact of Christy's death, though.

Even the possibility someone else might have been involved seemed an almost obscene violation of the carefully crafted, fragile peace he'd tried to make with himself.

He'd meant it when he told Cullen that, without the punishments visited upon him by the Arthur community, by Hammond and by the Darrel Jensen's of the world, he would not be the man he'd become. At times, he'd even found a way to like that man.

"I believe," he'd explained to Cullen once during the time

they worked together, when Cullen had become as close to him as any person ever had, *"we are the sum total of our experiences and our influences—not just the good ones. All of them.*

"You've had a great deal to do with who I am," Buddy also told Cullen that night. "So did my mother and father. But so, too, did Damon Hammond, Darrel Jensen and those kids at Springer—some of them were awful. And the people who forced me to go to Vietnam, because that ordeal, hard as it was, had a profound influence. A lot of us have things we might like to change about our pasts. I think we'd change them at great peril. What could have seemed like an easier path at the time might have altered everything—and that includes good things about us as well as bad."

"Guys," he said, "I don't need to prove someone else did it. I mean, I was there. I know what I did. Whatever else might have happened, I can't deny the role I played. I don't want to escape responsibility."

"It's not that simple," Cullen said. "You, Shelby, Weard could be charged with another murder. What really happened forty-three years ago might help explain what happened to Damon Hammond on Saturday."

"And you see something here that will help Shelby or Weard should Clifton Gladly decide to prosecute one or all of us?" Buddy asked.

"Not in court. Probably nothing we've found here would be accepted as evidence at a hearing or a trial, because the chain of evidence was broken when Hammond had someone—in all likelihood Darrel—steal it. But it could convince Clifton he can't possibly win a case against any of you."

Buddy sighed. "So, what do we do?"

= = = ¦ ¦ = = =

Standing in the living room, Lori looked through the doorway into the kitchen.

"This won't work," she said. "Everybody follow me."

Lori focused on the closed door that led into a bedroom. She tested the door, swinging it inward.

"Okay, Buddy, we're in Hammond's entry hall, and this is his office door. Show me where you stood."

Buddy took a position about five feet from the doorway.

"And Shelby, you come over here and be Christy. Buddy, where was she standing?"

"Well, the office door was open . . ."

"Light on or off? Quickly!"

"Off, I think. No, the ceiling light was off. Maybe the desk lamp behind Christy was on."

"So, had Christy come into the living room? Or was she in the office?"

"Um . . . maybe just inside the office. Yeah, because I remember shadows. Not her face, though. I could see her face. She had this smirk."

"So, you aimed and fired?"

"Yes."

"Then, what?"

"Like I said, Wilmer slugged me. I was out cold."

Lori's mind recreated the layout of Hammond's house and superimposed that scene here.

"Weard," she said. "You come over here and be Wilmer."

"I'd rather not."

"Okay . . . any particular reason?"

"I never liked Wilmer. He wasn't nice. If I was to *be* him, well, it would fuck with my mind, man. If I can be me, I'll stand where ever you want."

"Sure," Lori said, then asked Buddy. "So where was Wilmer? Where should Weard stand?"

"I . . . I wasn't paying much attention to other people around me. He was somewhere off to my left."

"How close? Come on, think."

"Not too close. I had the sense when I took the gun from my belt there was this, I don't know, this bubble around me. I was sort of all by myself. I'm sure he was farther away from me than I was from Christy. At least ten feet, I guess."

"Okay. Christy steps into the doorway. You raise the gun and say something . . ."

"I said it *as* I raised the gun."

"Christy reacts with a smirk and you fire. That would take no more than a couple of seconds?"

"Yes."

"What did Christy do then?"

"I told you, I don't—"

"But you do know," Lori said, pointing to Weard. "It's going to take a few seconds for Wilmer—"

"I'm not Wilmer, man," Weard said.

"Right, sorry. It will take an instant for Weard to register what's happened. I mean, it's a gunshot, for God's sake. Then it will take him a couple more seconds to cover the ground between you and him. I'm guessing you had three to five seconds before you were knocked unconscious."

"I . . . I . . ."

"Did she fall straight down?" Lori demanded, now the cop—the interrogator. "Answer, don't think!"

"No. She staggered back."

"Where were her hands? A person suddenly faced with the prospect of being shot typically reacts by raising their hands into some kind of defensive position."

"She didn't raise her hands. But then she didn't think the gun would hurt her."

"So?"

Buddy closed his eyes and recreated the scene.

"Her left hand was at her side, closed, like a fist."

"That was the plunger to release the red liquid," Lori said. "What about her right hand?"

"A little behind her. On the doorknob. Her right hand was on the doorknob."

"She didn't fall in the doorway?" Lori pushed him.

"No. She, like, stepped back, jumped back really, and at the same time, the door closed."

"She pushed it closed."

"Yeah. She closed it."

"You didn't actually see her fall?"

"No, I guess I didn't."

Lori ordered Shelby to take a position with her hands as Buddy had described.

"If you were falling backwards," Lori asked, "how difficult is it to close the door at the same time?"

Shelby experimented by shifting her weight and holding the door knob.

"Pretty hard. I'd be pulling the door into me as I fell. I'd be in the way."

Cullen observed this demonstration with a little smile that turned to a frown as Lori posed her next question.

"Shelby, when you ran back to help Buddy, was the door to the office open or closed?"

A couple of seconds passed before Buddy seemed to register the implication.

"Closed," Shelby answered.

"What?" Buddy said. "You were there?"

Shelby nodded.

"I didn't see you," Buddy said. "Of course, I was drunk and I . . . I didn't see you."

"You didn't *notice* me," Shelby said softly. "You hadn't noticed me for weeks."

= = = ¦ ¦ = = =

A new set of images inundated Buddy's mind—snippets, bits and pieces, finer details sacrificed to the passage of time. Shelby, darkness, a blanket on grass, laughter, teasing, sweaty kisses followed by a silence that had lasted forty-three years.

= = = ¦ ¦ = = =

The tension percolated as Buddy seemed lost. Cullen cursed under his breath. Other priorities demanded their attention. They couldn't deal with this right now.

"You didn't see the shooting, though, did you?" he prompted Shelby.

"Um . . . no. No, Corinne and I were leaving. We were just at the front door when I heard a bang. I turned. I thought I saw a little wisp of smoke. Other people were blocking me. I didn't see Christy at all, or Wilmer. People were running away, and Corinne and I were sort of swept along."

Shelby wandered from the hallway and the others followed.

"Someone knocked me down in the front yard. By then most of the people were outside. I got back inside and saw Buddy lying there. The office door was shut. I checked to see if I could help him. His eyes were closed, and he was groaning. Then, I heard sirens, and I figured someone would be there to take care of him really quick. So, I left. I walked home through the alleys."

"But before you left, you picked up the gun," Lori added.

"Yes," Shelby said.

"So, the gun had your prints, along with mine," Buddy said. "That's why they arrested you, too."

Cullen motioned for Shelby and Buddy to sit.

"Now we have two questions," he said. "Who was hiding in the office to shoot Christy? And how did police find those forty-year-old fingerprints yesterday on a gun Shelby had carefully cleaned only a few hours before?"

"Aren't you concerned any more about us being forced to testify against each other?" Buddy asked Cullen.

"Buddy, this case is so screwed up, I don't think it will ever go to trial. We've got to put some pieces together here, though, so the five of us must make an agreement."

"Cullen," Lori said. "Be careful. You're treading on dangerous ground. Conflict of interest? Advising clients not to tell the truth?"

"Maybe just not *all* the truth. There's a difference. Whatever happens to me from a professional standpoint will happen. I don't need to be a lawyer anymore."

Lori frowned. "These people mean that much," she said, as if understanding for the first time.

"The three—no, the four of you in this room do. I don't care what happens to Darrel and Melissa. And I *will* trade them for the rest of you if I have to."

"You could be sent to jail yourself," Lori warned.

"Yeah, but it'll be some lawyer jail with tennis courts."

= = = ¦ ¦ = = =

"We have to put this evidence back in Hammond's secret room," Cullen told them.

"Then we'll get some anonymous person to call the police about files and boxes hidden there?" Buddy asked skeptically.

"That's right."

"They'll know it's us," Buddy said. "Only a moron would think we didn't set the whole thing up."

"Doesn't matter. There's a big difference in what they think and what they can prove."

"I can fix it, man," Weard said. "Let me make some calls. We can route a phone call all over the world. They'll never figure it out. It'll only take a couple of days to retask some satellites."

"Thanks, Weard," Cullen said, "but I don't think the plan needs to be that complicated."

Buddy and Sheila resumed their roles as lookouts while Cullen, Lori and Weard retraced their steps along the alleys. Although a couple of dogs barked from behind backyard fences, no lights chased them as they crept along. Weard handled the old door lock with ease.

Cullen knew he and Lori were thinking the same thing. They needed one more puzzle piece. As soon as they entered the old kitchen, Cullen knelt below window level and beckoned the others to join him.

"Okay, Weard, we're looking for a box, like a jewelry case only bigger. Sturdy, probably with a lock or clasp. It wasn't behind the bookcases, so we might have to search some other rooms upstairs."

"No, man," Weard said. "There's a box like that under some papers on Hammond's desk."

Smiling, Lori shook her head.

Again, wearing their latex gloves, they bumped through the dark. Once inside Hammond's office, they closed the door connecting with the living room. Cullen switched on the desk lamp. The box they sought sat beyond the narrow cone of light cast by the lamp and was exactly where Weard said it would be.

Cullen placed it under the light.

He saw a container about a foot square made of heavy, polished cherry. A brass piano hinge gleamed along a line where lid and base came together. An indentation, about four inches by two inches, was scribed about a sixteenth of an inch into the top. Cullen guessed it had probably held an engraved plaque. In front was a brass hasp made to accommodate a small padlock that wasn't there. Cullen let his hands hover over the box for a moment.

"Okay. Either we're right, or none of this makes any sense."

"Open it," Lori said.

Holding his breath, Cullen lifted the lid.

Thick green felt lined its interior. The felt flowed smoothly into a pair of impressions, each the size and shape of the antique revolver with which they were now familiar.

"Okay," Cullen said, grinning. "Put everything back. I'm going to take some pictures of those blackmail files. Then we'll go."

= = = ¦¦ = = =

"Two guns?" Buddy asked. "A pair of identical antique revolvers?"

"It's the only thing that made any sense," Cullen said. "The gun police found under the bathroom sink was not the gun Shelby left at Hammond's place. At some point after they took the gun with fingerprints into their possession, somebody switched it for the other gun."

"But why?" Buddy asked.

"Because this isn't 1966," Lori said. "This isn't a shooting of a teenage girl. No way Damon Hammond's murder will slip by without autopsies and ballistics tests. Whoever switched the guns had to know the bullets in Damon Hammond's body wouldn't match the gun with Buddy and Shelby's fingerprints."

"Neither will the gun with your fingerprints match the slug they removed from Christy's body," Cullen said.

"How do you draw that conclusion?" Shelby asked.

"The evidence box sat on some storage shelf for thirty or so years," he said. "Darrel looked at it a couple of times about ten years after the murder. The only other person to officially see it was an investigator hired by Buddy in 1996. Do you think it's a coincidence the box was never checked out again? Or that it wound up hidden at Damon Hammond's house? Or that Mr. LaVelle died?"

"No," Shelby said. "No. Somebody got nervous when Buddy's investigator took it upon himself to examine the old evidence. They thought Buddy was trying to reopen the case."

"The real murderer couldn't afford to let that happen," Lori said. "Because he knew the pistol with Buddy's prints wouldn't match the slug taken from Christy's body."

"And that person would be?" Buddy asked.

Before Lori and Cullen could answer, Weard said, "Old man Hammond."

chapter twenty-three

October 30, 1966

Damon Hammond was beyond furious. He'd forbidden Christy to have anyone in the house during his absence. Even from a mile away, though, as soon as he turned off Highway 70 onto Eighteenth Street, he could see the place was lit up like Mardi Gras.

He was scheduled to be home Monday afternoon. He'd been in Santa Fe, lobbying zoning legislation. Meetings were expected to run well into evening.

This was Halloween weekend, though, and legislative staffers wanted to get home for family trick-or-treating rituals, so they'd cut things short. Damon was on the road by seven p.m. Sunday for the four-hour drive.

The scene gained detail as Damon drew closer. He found his driveway lined with cars and had to maneuver his Lincoln carefully along the narrow track remaining. Vehicles blocked both garage doors at the carriage house, so he parked beside the smaller building. As he opened the car door to the muffled sound of the rock-n-roll music pounding inside, he knew he could tolerate his niece no longer. He'd have his assistant start looking at boarding schools on Monday.

= = = ¦¦ = = =

Damon had been saddled with his brother's daughter since she was thirteen. After her parents died in a private plane crash, Christy had no place else to go. He hadn't wanted her, felt no affection for the girl, and would have preferred to send her on her way. But the community would have judged him cruel and uncaring, thus tarnishing his image. Unacceptable.

Damon Hammond didn't want to be a president or a governor or even a mayor. He wanted to be king.

His kingdom needn't be grand.

No question he could be elected to the state legislature. Both Democrats and Republicans had already asked. There he could construct the kind of political base that could take him higher. He saw the danger, though. If he pursued a public life, sooner or later, one of many whom he had manipulated along the way might grow so desperate as to sacrifice themselves to bring him down. He doubted they could come up with any real proof. Just his word against theirs. Rumor, however, could devastate a political career.

So, why overreach?

Why not be satisfied owning the biggest house, having people seek his opinion and approval, holding sway over the life of a small town? Plus, he could make a fortune. The legal tentacles slithering from his law office touched all of Arthur's banks and brokerages, local commerce, educational and religious institutions.

Everything.

And with all of that money, he afforded anonymous vacations to parts of the world where he could indulge his personal vices without fear of discovery.

Camille, his late wife, had served as a buffer between Damon and his niece. Camille did her best to be a mom while Damon watched with indifference. When Camille succumbed to pancreatic cancer, Damon and Christy became two contentious strangers occupying a gloomy old house. Damon set rules. Christy broke them. She pushed him at every turn.

As she grew older, Hammond began to see more of himself in her. He did not regard this with any sort of *chip-off-the-old-block* pride. He considered it with a wariness that evolved toward fear. Hammond didn't bother to know many people, but he damn sure knew himself. He operated with little regard for conscience, which rendered him capable of, well, anything, he supposed. The only factor that safeguarded his enemies was his fear of consequence. And in this girl who shared his house, he saw an ever more dangerous clone.

Their argument before his departure on the Santa Fe trip elevated the contention to a new level. He'd assigned one of the older receptionists at the office to stay with her, but Christy said she'd lock the doors and not let the woman inside. Hammond sneered, telling her the woman had her own set of keys.

Christy played her trump card. "If that fat old bitch comes here," she said, her voice low, threatening, "I'll tell her you've been molesting me."

At first, Damon laughed at the absurdity of the charge.

"Good luck finding anyone who will believe you," he said.

Then the realization of his own vulnerability struck him. Any number of people might be willing to believe Christy or promote the rumor whether they believed it or not. How could he disprove such a charge? He'd understood in that moment that Christy's tantrums and threats had accelerated beyond the life drama of a normal teenager.

So, he'd relented. He'd left Christy, a high school junior, at home alone.

=== ¦¦ ===

Damon stormed toward the back door as he considered his alternatives.

If he made a scene, Christy would be livid.

Using the back hallway, he could enter his office unseen. There, he could call the police and pretend to be a neighbor upset about the noise. Officers would come, arrest most of the kids for underage drinking, and Christy would be blamed.

He considered his exit strategy. After he made the call, he would drive along the rutted dirt path covering the short distance from his carriage house to a barbed wire gate at the back of the property. There, he could take the section road bordering his land, catch an intersecting road to Highway 70, then return home shortly after police arrived. Christy could not blame him, and the incident would damage her credibility should she make accusations against him.

Groping through darkness of the windowless hallway, Damon reached the back entry to his office. The blaring music would conceal any noise he might make. He opened the door a crack.

The banker's desk lamp provided light. Its elongated green porcelain shade focused a bright spot on top of his desk. A separate sliver of illumination drew Damon's eye.

A figure stood at the office door accessing the entry hall. As his vision adjusted, Damon recognized Christy. The blaring sound from the stereo speakers faded, and Christy pulled open her door.

A boy holding a pistol met her, said something, and fired a single shot! Her hand still on the doorknob, Christy stumbled backwards and pushed the door closed. Music screamed to life again.

Damon instinctively rushed to her aid.

She cried. "I think the asshole really shot me!"

"Let me see!" Damon demanded.

Despite her fear and pain, Christy registered surprise at her uncle's presence. "Uncle Damon! What are you doing here?"

The front of Christy's white blouse, bathed now in a dark stain, showed scarlet when Damon tilted the desk lampshade toward her.

"It burns!" she cried. "It burns! Am I shot?"

If Christy was bleeding this profusely as the result of a gunshot, how was she still standing, asking questions? He glanced at his desk, noting a wood box that usually rested on a shelf behind his chair. The box, normally locked, contained a pair of matching antique pistols—a gift from a client years before. Only one pistol now rested in its felt-lined interior.

He calculated possibilities.

"Am . . . am I bleeding?" she gasped, looking at the scarlet stain spilling down her blouse as she sagged to the floor.

"If you were bleeding this much, you'd be . . ." He touched the stain. "What is this?"

"Colored water," she said. "It's a trick . . . It burns! Is there real blood?"

Damon studied the blouse. At the middle of a red stain he saw a hole, but not a neat, smooth circle like a bullet would make. Rather, a jagged hole, as if it might have been singed. Both live bullets and blank starter's cartridges were in the box with the pistols. The paper wad from a blank cartridge, if the gun was fired at close enough range, could penetrate Christy's skin.

His mind raced.

"I don't know, Christy," he said. "I'm afraid some of this is blood! I'll call an ambulance."

Adrenalin surged through him. The panic he'd initially felt receded. His rage rekindled. The party! This insolent girl! Her threats!

He locked the door leading to the entry hall with the flip of a latch. He scanned the carpet, finding a small, brownish mass. *Paper wadding from the blank that had struck Christy!* He went to his desk, music still blaring on the other side of the locked door.

A thought entered his mind. *Crime of opportunity.* The plan organized itself in seconds. *You're probably overlooking a dozen things!* Here, though, was a solution to everything. Such a chance would not present itself again.

With his back to a sobbing Christy, Damon grabbed the remaining pistol, checked that it was loaded, then turned, the pistol concealed from her view.

"The other gun is gone from the box," he said. "Was that the gun that shot you?"

"Y . . . y . . . yes," Christy sobbed. "Is an ambulance coming?"

Is the music loud enough?

"Soon," he said.

He raised the pistol, lined its barrel with the hole in Christy's blouse and pulled the trigger.

The horror on her face barely registered. His mind raced ahead. He retrieved the wadding, took a handkerchief from his pocket, and wiped the gun.

He opened the door a crack. He saw a portrait of chaos with a final knot of panicked teens fighting their way outside. The boy who'd shot at Christy lay prone, apparently unconscious. The other pistol rested where he'd dropped it, a girl knelt at his side.

No way to switch guns with the girl out there. He'd deal with that later. He returned the murder weapon to its box, tucking the container under his arm.

Back to the hallway. *Oh, God! The music! How could I have missed it? Volume controls for my stereo are in the office. Who turned the music down, and then up again? Sirens! No time!*

He retraced his steps. There, shrouded by darkness, slumped a figure in his leather chair. Hammond approached warily. He knew this girl. *Christy's friend. Melissa something. Also unconscious.* Another problem he'd deal with later . . . Then, a moment of genius. He held the pistol by its barrel and pressed it into this girl's hand.

Back to Christy, his body trembling. *No more loose ends.* He needed to be sure. Careful to avoid her spilled blood, he placed a finger to her carotid artery and found no pulse. The sirens louder now!

Quickly to his car. *No headlights. Bump along the fence line to a wire gate.* As he jerked at the wire loop holding the gatepost, he could see across this back field to Eighteenth Street, flashing blue and red lights closing fast.

Damon drove without headlights along a rectangular section road route that would return him to Highway 70. Encountering no traffic, he stopped short of the turnoff at Eighteenth and pulled into the Phillips Sixty-Six Truck Stop.

"Hello, Mr. Hammond," said an attendant, who hurried to greet his customer. "What can I do for you?"

"Needs a fill-up. Take a look at the oil. I'm just getting in from Santa Fe. Sometimes it uses oil on the highway."

Damon forced himself on a slow walk to the station's men's

room. He scrubbed his hands, then carefully inspected his skin and clothing for any sign of blood. He took several deep breaths. Staring at a mirror, he practiced an expression appropriate for learning his niece had been shot to death.

= = = ¦¦ = = =

July 2009
The Reunion
Saturday

Damon Hammond extended a shaky hand across his desk and pointed at the antique revolver.

"Put on those latex gloves before you touch it," he warned.

"Why would I touch it?" Darrel asked.

"Because you'll put it either in Buddy Boyd's house or his car. Someplace you know the police will look."

"Why will the police—"

Hammond coughed, a wet, phlegmy outburst. "This gun has been sealed in a plastic evidence bag since Christy died . . ." He pointed to the entry hall. ". . . forty-three years ago. My research . . ." He nodded to his laptop. ". . . shows Mr. Boyd's fingerprints should still be identifiable."

"So?" Darrel asked. What in hell did Hammond want this time?

"So, about an hour ago, I took it from its evidence bag—wearing gloves. I stood on the porch and fired a shot through a front window. The slug is imbedded somewhere over there."

Darrel inspected the wall Hammond had indicated. He didn't see anything, but a .22 slug would leave only a small hole. The slug might even be lodged in a couch or chair.

"I understand there's a reunion function this evening," Hammond continued. "After the restaurant scene yesterday, Mr. Boyd surely will not attend. So, he will most likely be alone, without anyone to offer an alibi. I'll call the police, and report that someone tried to kill me—fired a shot through the window."

"Why do you still have that damn gun?" Darrel said. "Are you telling me you have all the other stuff, too?"

"Any evidence of my niece's murder is well-hidden."

"Fuck. You, of all people, should know what kind of trouble there'd be if you're found with that stuff, no matter how old it is."

"A case resolved forty years ago? Findings neither questioned nor appealed? No one cares anymore."

"If the gun turns up again, you don't think they'll go looking?"

"You recovered that box for me in 1996." Hammond removed a handkerchief from his jacket pocket and wiped his lips. "They moved evidence storage from the courthouse basement to the new police station, what, 2002? Everyone will think that evidence box was either destroyed with other old files or lost in the move."

"What about the gun . . ."

"Who can connect that gun to Christy's death anymore? As far as anyone knows, it's just a gun."

"A pretty distinctive gun."

Hammond dismissed him with a wave. He pushed the pistol toward Darrel.

"Why do you even care about Buddy Boyd after all these years?" Darrel asked. "Why not just leave him alone?"

Hammond merely glared at him.

Darrel took a steadying breath. "I won't do it."

Hammond's glare remained unwavering.

"Mr. Hammond, I've done everything you've ever asked of me. I won't do this."

"Then you're of little use. Don't be expecting good news concerning that farm loan."

= = = ¦¦ = = =

Damon's next call went to Melissa Painter.

"Mrs. Painter, I need you at my house within the hour... No, you don't need to know why... I don't care. You WILL be here. I have a simple errand for you. I will broach no argument."

He outlined his plan and reminded Melissa that Buddy's weren't the only fingerprints still existent.

Darrel's question lingered. Why bother Buddy Boyd? Because, Damon reminded himself, twenty years ago, Boyd hired a man to investigate Christy's death. We can't have that. This time, we'll scare him away for good.

= = = ¦¦ = = =

A plan formed as Darrel left Hammond. Daylight waned. People were finishing dinner, getting ready for the reunion dance. Hammond was right. Buddy would likely be alone this evening. Darrel could slip away from the crowded gym, drive to Hammond's house and return within fifteen or twenty minutes. If anyone asked, he'd say he stepped out for a smoke.

= = = ¦¦ = = =

Damon still seethed when he snapped shut his cell phone. So much for Darrel. He would put the fear of God into Melissa when she arrived. He entered the narrow enclosure behind his bookcase. He found three sexually compromising photographs of Melissa with men not her husband, including one of Darrel. Two copies of police arrest reports. One for drug possession. One for driving under the influence.

He arranged the photos next to the revolver.

He tucked the second gun under the sheaf of papers on his desk. If he handed her a loaded gun, he needed a deterrent lest she do something foolish.

As he pushed out of his chair, a wave of nausea swept over him. He steadied himself after hacking through a series of deep coughs. He decided to rest until Melissa arrived.

= = = ¦¦ = = =

Melissa drank. She took pills. She'd attempted a Denver rehabilitation clinic several years earlier under the guise of a trip to Europe. But the cure didn't take. Doctors called her a *functional addict*. She got along okay. Hammond hadn't demanded anything of her for years. As he'd aged, his enthusiasm for sex had diminished. She'd even dared to hope he was done with her.

His call fractured that illusion.

As darkness settled, she parked by Hammond's carriage house. Finding the rear door locked, she walked around front and crossed through the unlit entry hall where she found him asleep on the couch.

She nearly called his name, but a single, daring thought arrested her. She could get a knife from the kitchen . . . no. No, she couldn't. Awful as he was, she just couldn't.

She waited a long moment. Details of his face were obscured

in shadow. The office desk lamp's glare beckoned. There, on the desk, washed in the narrow pool of light, rested a gun. She glanced over her shoulder to the gloom of the living room, then stepped closer. She couldn't make herself do it with a knife, but a gun? A gun offered distance. And distance was less . . . *No. Not even that.*

Then, she found the photos and arrest reports.

Melissa studied the pistol. It sure looked like the same gun Christy had shown her when they were kids. A plastic bag, its top jagged, where it had been torn open, rested nearby. Printing on the bag: *Christy Hammond/deceased. Hezekiah "Buddy" Boyd. Case No. 663101.* And a carton containing latex gloves.

So that's what he wanted. She thought of the fingerprints Hammond had hung over her head for all these years. Obviously, Hammond planned to implicate Buddy in some crime. *So why couldn't I do the same thing? I could take those arrest reports and photos and be free!*

Melissa crept to the door.

Hammond hadn't stirred.

She tugged on a pair of latex gloves, then took a deep breath.

He's an evil, evil man. I know I'm not the only one.

She shot Damon Hammond in the temple as he slept.

= = = ¦ ¦ = = =

Even the flush of adrenaline couldn't calm her panic. Melissa feared all kinds of complications if she planted the gun at Buddy's. She almost chickened out and threw it from her car window. But things just fell into place. She first thought of his car. *Unless, of course, it was locked. If he wasn't home, maybe the house? If his house was locked? A flowerpot on the porch, like he'd tried to hide it.*

Turned out, his car was gone. The door wasn't locked. She put it in the vanity under his bathroom sink.

= = = ¦ ¦ = = =

Darrel smiled when he found Hammond's front door dark and unlocked. He ducked inside and registered the desk lamp's glare spilling through the open office door.

Darrel would tell him he'd reconsidered. And when Hammond handed him the gun . . .

No, he's not here. Okay, that old bastard must be upstairs. Even better. But where's the gun? The latex gloves are here. What did he do with the gun?

He scanned the desk. *A pile of papers, a wood box. A newspaper with something . . .* He lifted the paper and there it was. *First, gloves.* Darrel identified the antique pistol as a top-break model. He flipped the barrel halfway down, careful not to open it so far that its extractor would dump the bullets on the Persian rug beneath his feet.

As he searched for a staircase, he found a couch and the sleeping form of Damon Hammond. Darrel didn't hesitate. He placed the barrel a couple of inches from the old man's chest, then fired.

"Asshole," he muttered.

chapter twenty-four

July 2009
The Reunion
Saturday Evening

Now that all these old friends had spent nearly three days together, Cullen observed that some of the pretense of amiability had worn off. From a distance, high school classmates were tolerable. Time had dimmed the reality of how annoying so many of them had really been. By Saturday evening, old cliques were re-established. Pretending everyone had mellowed and matured to the point that everyone gave a damn about everyone else became more difficult.

A geriatric rock band played sloppy *Turtles, Beatles* and *Lovin' Spoonful* covers. Crepe paper, ribbon and twinkling strings of mini-lights hung from the high ceiling. Thank goodness Darrel was keeping his distance. Lori looked ravishing. Weard appeared resplendent in his kilt. Shelby was off somewhere with Corinne, he supposed. He found her as she walked toward them and marveled at how beautiful she remained.

When she reached their table, she seemed a little out of breath.

"You were gone for a while," Cullen said. "Everything okay?"

"Fine. I was just . . . you know . . . mingling."

Weard leaned to Cullen's ear. "Would you mind if I borrow the car for a minute, man?"

"Um . . . do you have a license?"

"Of course. I'm an excellent driver."

"Well . . . I suppose so. Why do you need the car?"

"When I put on my kilt tonight, I forgot underwear. I'll need it for the dancing. All that twirling and stuff. I promise I'll be right back."

= = = ¦¦ = = =

How long, Darrel wondered, before someone finds Hammond's body? He lived alone. He had people who kept the place functioning for him, but they probably wouldn't be there until Monday.

Darrel chose a table far apart from Cullen, his girlfriend with the hooters, that goofball Weard Ward and Shelby Blaine.

Melissa had been bouncing everywhere all evening. She'd been particularly bubbly—probably drunk. Watching her flit from table to table, he wished he could tell her that despicable old man was finally gone. During high school, Melissa had been one of those girls they'd called *easy*. She liked alcohol, she liked grass and she liked sex. As two who had remained Arthur-bound these many years, Darrel and Melissa shared an on-and-off affair. While the physical aspect of their relationship had been dormant for some time, an emotional connection remained.

Through their relationship, they'd become aware that the threads connecting them included those in Damon Hammond's web. Darrel didn't know details of Hammond's hold on Melissa. He didn't think she knew what the old man had on him. They'd commiserated more than once, though, about a shared hatred, even disclosing an occasional fantasy of killing him.

Darrel didn't dare say anything tonight, though.

As she navigated to his outpost, Melissa laughed loudly and called goodbyes.

"How are you this wonderful evening?" she asked, pushing her chair close to his, placing her hand on his thigh.

"I'm okay. You certainly seem happy."

Checking carefully both left and right, she leaned close and whispered, "We're free. The old bastard's dead."

Darrel could not disguise his shock. *They couldn't possibly have found Hammond's body already. Could they?*

He squeezed her arm. "How did you know?"

Melissa whispered with a self-satisfied smirk, "Because I shot him. In the head."

"You . . . what? You shot him? When?"

"On my way here. Don't worry, though. They'll think Buddy did it."

She told him about the call, about Hammond's plan to frame Buddy, her finding Hammond asleep, about concluding Buddy's prints were on the pistol.

". . . then I put it under the bathroom sink at Buddy's house."

Darrel checked again to be sure no one could hear them. "That's impossible!"

"No. I really did . . ."

"Then why was the gun still on his desk when I was there a little while ago?"

"You were there?"

"Yes. Hammond must have called me before he called you. He ordered me to hide the gun at Buddy's so the police would think he'd tried to shoot Hammond. I told him no. Then I started thinking how I could get away with killing him. So, I snuck over there when everyone was dancing. I found him on his couch in the dark. I figured he was asleep. I got the gun, and I shot him in the heart."

Melissa's confusion as she tried to process this account was evident, as was the fear of realization when her mouth dropped open and her face drained of color.

"Oh, my God," she whispered. "Oh, my God!"

"What?"

"There were two guns."

"Two—"

"Damon had two antique pistols he kept in a box. Someone gave them to him, and they were identical. Christy showed me."

"Oh, shit!"

"This is bad, isn't it?"

"Yeah. If the police find the gun at Buddy's house and do a ballistics comparison, only one of the bullets will match."

"Oh, my God!" Melissa repeated, her whisper desperate. "What do we do?"

Darrel rubbed a hand across his face. The band attempted *A Hard Day's Night* and mangled the first chord combination.

"Why did you take the gun to Buddy's?"

"Because Hammond said—"

"Hammond was dead."

"I still had to make it look like Buddy shot him."

"All that matters," Darrel said, "is Buddy's prints. Where they find the gun won't make any difference."

"Oh, fuck. I didn't think of that."

Darrel clasped both her hands.

"Okay. Okay, you shot him in the head?"

She nodded.

"Let me think. A .22 caliber bullet would bounce all around

in his skull and get bent up. I shot him in the chest, a lot of soft tissue. We'll have to hope they'll use that bullet for a ballistics comparison. If we can get the gun from Buddy's house before police serve a search warrant, then they'll find the pistol I left at Hammond's house. And it will match the chest bullet."

"Be sure and wipe off that second gun," Melissa said.

"Of course."

= = = ¦ ¦ = = =

What if Buddy's there? What could I say? What excuse could I find to go inside and then to the bathroom?

Anxiety crawled over Darrel's skin as he turned onto Buddy's street and saw a police cruiser. Even if they'd found Hammond, no way they could get a search warrant this quickly. So . . . maybe Buddy or Cullen already found the gun and reported it. Only one way to be sure. He held his breath as he drove back to Hammond's house. *No cops. Everything dark. Okay. The cops have the wrong gun. I can get the gun I left beside Hammond, and . . . switch them at the evidence room? Could I? I still have keys . . .* Dangerous, but desperation moved mountains.

This time, Darrel parked along the section road on the opposite side of Hammond's property. He would approach the back way.

He tested the back door. Unlocked. He first grabbed gloves from the office desk, then stood over Hammond's body. Looking closely, he saw a neat entry wound at the temple.

He thought he'd left the gun below Hammond's head. Now it rested near the dead man's feet. *Must have accidently kicked it.*

Darrel pocketed the gun, then walked one more time through the office and living room to make sure he hadn't overlooked anything else.

= = = ¦¦ = = =

Sunday Afternoon
July 2009

Darrel waved to Mavis Zigenfoose, who sometimes filled in as receptionist at the police department during off hours and weekends.

"Hello, Darrel," Mavis called. "What can we do for you?"

"Just a social call," Darrel said. "I've got to leave a message for Jared."

Darrel didn't break stride as he spoke to Mavis. He walked right through a swinging gate that separated the civilian world from office cubicles, interrogation rooms and holding cells beyond the reception counter.

"Officer Cantwell's on vacation through Wednesday," Mavis called after Darrel.

"I know. But this is something I really want him to see, so I thought I'd leave it on his desk..." His voice trailed off. His pounding heart belied the breezy bravado he'd used to bull his way past Mavis. He paused, attempting a calming breath as he surveyed a handful of office cubicles.

He couldn't see anyone's head above the cubicle dividers, though he heard clacking of a computer keyboard coming from somewhere nearby. He marched straight toward Cantwell's desk. Cantwell had been Darrel's partner when Darrel retired three years earlier. They still occasionally saw each other. They'd hunted deer in the Hondo Valley last fall, and Darrel had taken a photo of Jared and his buck.

Darrel felt the weight of the pistol in the pocket of his sport coat. He took another deep breath, then called, "Hello?"

The scowling face of Homer Ridley popped up a few rows away. *Another break.* He'd have had a more difficult time if one of the younger officers was here.

"Hey, Darrel. Haven't seen you in weeks."

Darrel waved. "Yeah, I keep myself busy. I was downtown and wanted to leave something for Jared." He displayed the photo. "Um . . . do you mind if I run to the bathroom? I must've eaten something at the dance last night that didn't agree with me. I got the runs like crazy."

"More like you drank something . . ." Homer laughed.

Darrel nodded and hurried to the hallway behind the last row of desks. He checked that Homer's back was turned. He opened the bathroom door, then let it swing closed while he fast-walked to a second hallway branching to the left. He stopped at a door labeled *Evidence Locker*.

This, he thought, is where everything could fall apart.

He held his breath as he withdrew a key ring from his trouser pocket. He inserted a heavy, institutional key inscribed with ARTHUR POLICE, DO NOT COPY, then exhaled his relief to find they'd not changed the lock.

Shutting the door behind him, Darrel used his key again to open a heavy wire mesh entrance labeled, AUTHORIZED ADMITTANCE ONLY: ALL PERSONNEL MUST SIGN IN. The attendant's desk sat empty at this weekend hour. On a long shelf behind that desk he spotted three boxes, one marked HAMMOND.

Darrel put a glove on his right hand. He reached into the box, rummaged around until he felt a pistol in a ziplock bag. He carefully opened the bag and switched the guns. He hurried past rows of boxes and items stacked along metal shelves. Way in back, where the oldest evidence records were kept, he randomly chose a box, broke its taped seal, and shoved the pistol containing Buddy Boyd's fingerprints inside. Reluctantly, he also deposited his evidence room keys there as well.

As he retraced his steps, the clatter of Homer's keyboard suggested he'd gotten away with it. He silently swung open the bathroom door, chose a stall, stripped most paper off the roll, and flushed it down the toilet.

Darrel made a noisy show of shoving back through the door, stopping at Homer's desk long enough to say, "I wouldn't advise you go in there any time soon."

Homer laughed.

"And, by the way, I used most of the paper in the first stall."

He'd gotten about halfway to the lobby when Aggie Smoot nailed him.

= = = ¦ ¦ = = =

May 1969

Following the fight and Buddy's departure, Cullen kept his distance, not only from Shelby and Darrel, but pretty much everyone else, as well. Cullen's defense of Buddy made him a socially toxic commodity. Carol went out of her way to convince everyone her involvement with Cullen had been a horrid mistake, which she would under no circumstance repeat. He didn't even consider asking anyone to the senior prom or party.

Several guys with whom he normally hung around expressed sympathy for his plight, as well as guarded admiration of his willingness to stand up—for that brief, shining moment before he was knocked down—against Darrel and his gang.

Until prom night, though, Cullen's only significant human contact came at the hands, and various body parts, of Melissa Stanton.

Cullen and Melissa shared a relationship from birth. They entered the world three days apart at Arthur County General. They were cradle mates for almost forty-eight hours back when mothers were hospitalized for several days as they recovered from childbirth.

They attended kindergarten and elementary school together. Their parents were members of the Methodist Church and, at least through eighth grade, they were both sentenced to attend MYF each Sunday evening.

Anything personal regarding this relationship, though, went by the wayside somewhere around fifth or sixth grade when the juvenile social strata took shape and Melissa ascended to a higher rung.

By high school, Melissa and Christy Hammond were best friends. They topped almost every Arthur teenage boy's list of personal fantasies. Rumor had it some of those fantasies had been fulfilled—both at the same time.

Cullen thought that bit of gossip crossed to the realm of urban legend until an evening ten days before graduation when he took the Mercury for a drive to escape Lawrence Welk. Cullen's mom and dad were big fans. With everything else falling down around him,

Cullen thought one more polka might push him over the edge.

He avoided the main drag, cruising quietly along neighborhood streets with windows lowered to admit a sweet evening warmth. He fought a compulsion to turn toward Shelby's street. More than likely, Doug's car would be there. He would be inside, given a hero's welcome by Shelby's father as the sterling young man who'd saved Shelby from Cullen.

To avoid her house, he chose a dirt road bordering the development's back boundary. On one side of this road a monotonous parade of alleyway entrances and cinderblock fences rolled past. The opposite side featured a barbed-wire fence, its four strands wrapped taut around rough-hewn posts.

Cullen had just made a turn heading towards town when light stabbed from an alley, announcing an oncoming car. Cullen slowed, then slewed the Mercury left as a small sedan bounded from the alley, making a sliding, skidding attempt at a turn that left its passenger side hard against the barbed-wire.

Cullen heard gears grind into reverse. Spinning wheels gouged ruts into soft sand.

Cullen parked and walked to the other car. He approached the driver side window and bent to look inside.

"Hey, Cullen," Melissa slurred. "I'm stuck."

"Hi, Melissa. Um . . . let me see if I can maybe push you. But don't give it so much gas. We've got to rock it and get it out of the ruts you've already dug, okay? I'll push from the front. Put it in reverse, give it a little gas and then let up. After it rocks forward, I'll push again, and you goose it."

"Okay. I can do that."

"Be sure it's in reverse. Don't run me over."

She made an exaggerated A-OK sign with her fingers. "Gotcha."

The car broke free in a matter of minutes. Cullen returned to the passenger window.

"Thanks, Cullen ol' Cullen," she said.

"Um . . . are you all right?"

She put her head back and took a deep breath. "Probably not. I had just an itty bit to drink."

"Then you should park your car. Let me drive you home. You don't want to get stopped two weeks before graduation."

"Nope, I don't. Okay. Follow me. I'll park."

"Be careful. Go slow."

Melissa guided her car to a spot along a curb around a corner. Cullen stopped behind her. He opened his door to help her, but she was already walking toward him.

"Move so I can skootch in," she said.

He obeyed. She slid across the bench seat, stopping about halfway to the passenger door.

"Okay," he said. "I'll get you home."

"Nope. Don't wanna go home. Let's go for a ride."

"Gee, I'm not sure you should be—"

"Oh, c'mon, Cullen," she said, her voice husky with suggestion. "I know you're one of the really white-bread kids. But you're gonna sit there and tell me you don't want to go somewhere and . . . talk?"

"I thought . . . I thought you and Darrel were going together."

"Well, Darrel's not here, is he? You telling me you and Carol didn't have someplace? So, let's go. I wanna talk."

Cullen's mind raced. He recalled Chief Jackson's admonition in the principal's office. *Between now and graduation there will be no more incidents, or there will be some arrests. You two will keep as far away from each other as you can.*

So, screw Darrel.

"Um . . .okay," Cullen said. The Mercury took them to the windmill.

As they drove, Melissa drew a metal flask from her purse and drank. She offered it to Cullen. He considered the flask. Melissa nodded encouragement. He threw a short burst of fire down his throat.

Cullen gasped.

Melissa reclaimed the flask and laughed. "Scotch. Kind of an acquired taste."

He gasped again. "Yeah? I'm not sure why anyone would want to acquire it."

"You're funny, Cullen." She slid close, putting her arm around his shoulders.

Being careful of the fence posts, Cullen eased the Mercury toward the windmill. As he killed the ignition, Melissa recruited him into a long, wet kiss. Tentatively, his free hand explored her breast, first from outside her shirt, then—meeting no objections, undoing two buttons—inside her bra.

She leaned away from him, cheering him on with her smile. He undid the remaining buttons, slipped her shirt off her shoulders, then reached behind her and fumbled with the clasp of her bra. When he'd struggled for a moment, she smirked and said, "Why, Cullen Molloy, are you trying to undress me?"

"*Trying* being the operative word. Apparently, I could use a little help."

Melissa sat straight, contorted her hands behind her, and the bra disappeared.

Cullen savored the view of his third set of live-and-in-person breasts. He quickly concluded that, regardless of size or shape, all were fascinating. He bent to kiss one, then the other, lingering with his tongue. Melissa shuddered, pushed him momentarily away so she could wriggle out of her shorts and underwear. She leaned against the passenger side door, making no effort at concealment.

He stared with dry-mouthed disbelief.

"You know what we need?" Melissa said, the slur more pronounced. "We need some grass. I've got some grass in my purse."

Cullen was still trying to get his mind around the details peeking through soft brown fur at the meeting of her legs when the word *grass* echoed through his head. Melissa produced a thin, hand-rolled-looking thing.

"You mind?"

"Um . . . no. Go ahead . . . if you want."

She pushed the Mercury's cigarette lighter. Cullen doubted that lighter had ever been used before. When she touched the glowing coil to the joint, an acrid odor wafted about them.

"Uh, oh . . . um . . . I've gotta roll down some windows."

He scrambled outside, working at the hand cranks as he made a complete circuit, then slid back behind the wheel. The sliver of his mind occupied with how to get smoke smell out of upholstery quickly surrendered to the rest of his brain as it processed a nude Melissa Stanton sucking on a doobie.

She coughed a rough cough, then offered it to him.

"Um . . . no thanks. But you . . . you go right ahead. I'll just . . . you know . . . watch."

She laughed again.

"You've never done drugs, have you, Cullen?"

"No. Not . . . actually. No."

"I like drugs. Did you know, even after all that time our

parents made us spend at church, I didn't believe in God until I tried LSD?"

"LSD? Jesus, where would you get LSD?"

"Not from Jesus, that's for sure. I've got my sources. But that's a secret. Will you keep my secrets, Cullen?"

"Um . . . okay."

She pitched the last remnants of the joint out her window, then slid across the seat to him. Her kiss held a stench of burning marijuana, but Melissa's hand on his crotch made him willing to overlook the taste. She tugged at his jeans with practiced hands. The zipper and snap proved no obstacle.

Still kissing him, she grasped him, mumbled, "Mmmmmmm," then leaned against the door, again offering full disclosure.

"Are you going to fuck me, Cullen?" she said, her voice sultry.

Somewhere among the myriad carnal possibilities spread before him, Cullen had one of those non sequitur moments as he considered that word—sultry. The word had previously populated his vocabulary as a vague adjective, confined to the written page, only nebulously conceptual in its meaning.

This was no longer true. Now, he knew *exactly* what sultry meant.

The language lesson ended abruptly as Melissa ran a suggestive finger from her neck on a line between her breasts along a path to her belly button and beyond.

"Um . . . I don't . . . I don't have anything."

Melissa reached to the floorboard for her purse. This time she produced a square cellophane packet. She waved it at him.

"Okay . . . Melissa . . . I . . . I don't think I can. I mean, I certainly could. But I don't think I . . ."

Melissa put away the condom. "You know, I didn't think you

would. I don't know why I thought that. I'm not being insulting or critical or anything. You don't strike me as . . . well, I don't know. It's kind of sweet, really."

She kissed him again.

"So just do this."

She guided his right hand. She helped him find his way inside with his fingers. He marveled at how her wetness allowed such a smooth entry. She clamped one hand tightly about his wrist and demonstrated the motion she wanted. When he'd found the rhythm, she settled back.

Cullen fed on the details of her body as she rocked with a slight quiver that wandered through her. Then, despite all the details now open to his inspection, he found he could not take his gaze from her face—her eyes closed tight, mouth forming a small 'o,' expelling breaths in faster and faster bursts.

Finally, her whole being tensed. She arched her back, pushing her pelvis hard against his hand. She grabbed his wrist with an iron grip, holding his hand firm and still against her as she quivered. She emitted a low, otherworldly moan before collapsing back into the seat.

The Mercury and everything around it settled into a deathly silence, which lasted until Cullen said, "So . . . that was okay?"

Melissa laughed, then added, "Your turn."

He did not protest as she pushed him against the driver's side door, wriggled his jeans and underwear below his knees, and took him with her mouth.

The sensations were mind-bending.

Always before, with both Shelby and Carol, he'd simply gone home to finish alone under a blanket of guilt.

That was nothing like this.

He wavered somewhere between writhing to escape the torture of Melissa's tongue, and fearing she would stop. When he finally peaked, the waves of climax seemed interminable. He went on and on as Melissa finished him with her hand. His feelings wavered between elation and abject shame. He chose elation as the better alternative.

"So . . ." she said as she grinned, "I'm guessing that was okay, too?"

He finally glanced down at himself.

She winked. "I've got some Kleenex in my purse."

= = = ¦ ¦ = = =

During their return trip, Melissa didn't speak, just sipped quietly from her flask. As the roadway transitioned from dirt to pavement, she directed him to stop, then issued orders.

"Okay, Cullen, take the back way to my house. Don't go near the drag."

Cullen thought of a half-dozen responses, ranging from hurt, to amusement, to anger, even ridicule, before settling on no response at all. He took the back streets as requested. When the Mercury glided to a stop, he still hadn't decided what to say.

Melissa stood among the unattainable elite. As a sophomore, she dated seniors. This year, before she'd entered a steady relationship with Darrel, she bragged about dating college boys. So, on this strangest of evenings, Cullen had scaled the equivalent of a sexual Mount Everest.

He didn't feel good about it.

Melissa put it all in perspective when he started to get out of the car so he could open her door.

"Don't bother, Cullen. I don't know you well enough to kiss you good night. And, please, have the courtesy not to tell anyone. You're not exactly someone I want people to know I went out with. And who knows what Darrel might do if he found out?"

She weaved her way along the sidewalk.

Melissa and Cullen didn't speak again for another twenty years.

= = = ¦ ¦ = = =

July 2009
Tuesday Morning

"We're getting a different attorney. We don't have to tell you a fucking thing," said Darrel.

Darrel and Melissa occupied metal folding chairs on one side of a war surplus steel desk in a courthouse basement office. They faced Cullen, whose wooden chair groaned when it swiveled.

Grey filing cabinets lined the walls of a compact space. Only one of three bulbs in a ceiling light fixture burned, and an opaque glass window comprising the top half of a heavy oak door didn't help thanks to a poorly lighted outside hallway.

Cullen had asked Clifton Gladly for a space to confer with his clients. This was the best Gladly would do.

"You are absolutely right, Darrel," Cullen said. "Even though one of the reasons I called you here is to tell you this case isn't going anywhere, you both should hire separate counsel."

"Not going anywhere?" Melissa asked with a tremor in her voice. "What does that mean?"

"Their witness is shaky. They've changed their minds too

many times about who they should charge with murder. Their chain of evidence is completely screwed up, and I don't think they'll like the results of an autopsy report. So, as long as you don't confess to anything, I don't think either of you have a lot to worry about."

"Okay. Good. C'mon Melissa, let's go."

"Not so fast, Darrel." Cullen's tone took on a touch of menace. "I still have questions I want answered."

"And I wanna fuck Miss October. But we don't always get what we want, do we?"

Darrel stood, motioning for Melissa to do the same.

"Let me remind both of you," Cullen said, "that you have each admitted to shooting Hammond."

Darrel kicked his chair against the wall. Placing both hands atop the desk, he leaned into Cullen's face. "Whatever we told you was said in confidence. You told us you can't—"

"I'm not supposed to. But I will."

Their stares locked for a long moment. When Cullen did not waver, Darrel slammed his fist onto the desk, turned, righted his folding chair, and sat.

"Cullen, you wouldn't . . ." Fear etched Melissa's face as her eyes welled with tears.

"You'd get disbarred," Darrel said. "Fined. Maybe even go to jail."

"Yes, to all three. Consider this, though, Darrel. I don't practice law actively any more, and I don't really miss it. As for fines, well, I can afford them. Yes, I might go to jail. But not for thirty years. And not for murder."

"What do you want to know?" Melissa asked.

"Obviously, Hammond blackmailed both of you. I know why

he'd want a semi-corrupt cop in his pocket. But why you, Melissa?"

Melissa's expression crumbled. She covered her face with her hands and began to sob. "Because he was . . . he was afraid I'd seen something."

"The night Christy was shot?" Cullen suggested.

She nodded.

Darrel gaped at Melissa.

Cullen waited. Eventually, her sobs subsided. Cullen passed a handkerchief across the desk. "Tell me," he said.

Melissa took a steadying breath. "I was drunk. Way drunk, and Christy was mad at me. See, I was supposed to turn down the stereo when Christy opened that office door to confront Buddy—so everyone would hear. Turn down the music, then turn it back up. But I was so wasted, Christy thought I'd screw it up. She really yelled at me. I could barely focus, so I sat in a big old chair right by the stereo, staring at the volume knob, trying not to pass out. I turned the music down, heard a bang, and turned it back up. That's all I remember."

She gasped for breath against her sobs.

"When the police came, I was still out of it. They took me to jail, I guess. I didn't really recall anything until I woke up at home the next day."

"Did the police ever interview you?"

"Only once. When I said I hadn't seen or heard any of it, they left me alone."

"What happened next?" Cullen prodded.

"A couple of days later, Hammond had my parents bring me to his office downtown. He told them he'd found some things of Christy's, and since I was one of her best friends, he wanted to pass them along to me. When we got there, he told my dad he'd like to talk with me alone for a minute. Like it was some kind of, I don't know, some kind of spiritual thing—struggling with Christy's death and all. Anyway, my dad agreed. When we were alone, though, Hammond told me . . . he told me . . ." She sobbed again.

Cullen tried to muster sympathy for the woman but couldn't. "Please, Melissa, go on."

"He told me I was the one who killed Christy."

"What?" Darrel demanded. "That's crazy . . ."

"He said he saw everything from the back door to his office. He said Christy closed the front door after Buddy shot her with the blank, we were both laughing. I was holding the other gun. I said something about, 'I'll shoot you again,' and I shot her with a real bullet. I kept laughing, and I passed out."

"Do you think that's true?" Cullen asked.

"I . . . I don't think so . . . anymore. But I did for a long time."

With a nod, Cullen urged her to continue.

"Hammond said he had the gun with my fingerprints. He said he would keep it from the police and wouldn't tell anyone. He said everybody thought Buddy killed her, so if we just kept quiet, it would all go away."

"*He* didn't go away, though, did he?" Cullen said.

"No. I got picked up for a DUI a couple of months later. The cop who arrested me didn't take me to jail. He took me to Hammond. Again, Hammond told me he'd fix it. Then he started quizzing me about what I'd seen and heard."

"When did you finally tell him" Cullen asked.

"Tell him what?" Darrel demanded.

Both Cullen and Melissa ignored him.

"Not for a couple of years. Boy, what a stupid mistake that was."

Cullen shifted his weight. The old chair creaked beneath him.

"I kept getting into trouble, and Hammond always seemed to know. He kept getting me off the hook . . ."

"Did he . . . did he force you to . . ." Darrel asked with a note of sympathy Cullen wouldn't have suspected possible.

"Not when I was still a kid. That part didn't come until years later."

"What did you remember that scared him so much?" Cullen asked, guiding her back to the night of Christy's death.

"For the longest time, I thought it was a dream. I was on the chair in a dark corner. I was asleep. Then something woke me, and I saw a man kneeling over Christy. That's all."

She tried to look away from him. Cullen wouldn't let her.

"So, you knew all along," he said. "Buddy didn't kill Christy."

Melissa nodded and said in a near whisper, "I . . . I think so."

"That mother fucker . . ." growled Darrel.

"Don't act like it's such a surprise, Darrel," Cullen said. "You're not *that* stupid. You had to have a pretty good idea Hammond killed Christy. Especially after he panicked when the private investigator appeared and had you steal old evidence from police storage."

Darrel regarded Cullen with cold, dull eyes. "Yeah," he said. "I figured it out."

"Despite all that has been done to him, the both of you were more than willing to let Buddy face that same nightmare again by framing him for Hammond's death."

Darrel said nothing. Melissa sobbed. Her soft gasps filled the silence for several moments before Darrel asked, "So what are you gonna do, Cullen?"

Cullen stood.

"Please, Cullen," Melissa begged. "You've always been nice to me. That night out at the windmill when we were seniors? I've never forgotten. You were, so gentle, so—"

Darrel regarded Melissa with disbelief. "What the fuck are you talking about? What night? What windmill? That's when we were going together."

"I'm sure she'll tell you all about it later, Darrel," Cullen said. "As to what I'll do? I don't know. I guess that depends on what charges Clifton Gladly brings. I promise you one thing, though. I will not allow Shelby or Buddy or Weard to be jailed. If it comes to that, I'll trade the two of you for them in a heartbeat."

Cullen stepped around the desk. He flipped off the light on his way out, leaving Darrel and Melissa alone in the dark.

chapter twenty-five

July 2009
Tuesday Afternoon

"Shelby!" Corinne said, rushing to hug her. "Where have you been? I've been so worried. I couldn't find you after the dance. Then you didn't answer your phone all day yesterday. I called your motel. I couldn't imagine you would have just left... especially with the rumors!"

"Rumors?" Shelby asked. She gently extricated herself from Corinne's grasp as Corinne acknowledged the others.

"Hello, Cullen." She nodded a greeting to Buddy, Weard and Lori. "Yes, Damon Hammond is dead! Would you believe it? Some people are saying he was murdered! Shot in his own home."

"Um... yeah," Cullen said. "We heard something about that."

"Thank you for coming over," Shelby told Corinne.

"I was so relieved to hear from you. And I was worried when you said it was urgent."

"It is," Shelby said. "We... um... all of us... need you to make a phone call."

Corinne stepped back.

"A phone call?" Her voice dripped suspicion.

"Yes," Cullen said. "Just a phone call. Two-three minutes tops."

"None of you folks have a phone?" Corinne pointed to the land line next to the couch.

"We can't use this phone," Buddy told her.

"Okay, let's stop this right here. Shelby, what's going on? Where have you been for two days? You've gotten yourself in trouble again, haven't you?"

"Well, yes."

"What?"

"I was sort of arrested," Shelby said.

"Arrested for what?"

"Um . . . technically, I would have to say, murder . . ." Corinne's jaw dropped as Shelby quickly added, ". . . but I got unarrested, I think. Anyway, none of us had to stay in jail . . . for very long."

"None of us?"

"Buddy and Weard were picked up, too," Cullen said.

"Hi, Corinne," Weard said. He offered a morose little wave.

"For murder?"

"Not me, man," Weard said. "I'm the only one who didn't shoot him. I hope you're not carrying a carrot, though. I can't consort with anyone who possesses long, stiff vegetables. It was a condition of my release."

Corinne opened her mouth as if to ask Weard a question, then seemed to think better of it. Instead, she told Cullen, "I will not be a party to homicide. We should pray."

"Well, the homicide, if that's what it was, is over and done with."

"Isn't there some . . . whatchamacallit after the fact? I see it on TV all the time." When nobody answered, she said "Shelby, you tell me the truth! Did you shoot Mr. Hammond?"

Before Cullen could intercede, Shelby answered. "Not on purpose. You know me better than that."

"Corinne," Cullen said, "I know we're asking a lot. We just need someone to make a phone call. An anonymous phone call."

"To whom?"

"That would be the police."

"The police! Well, of course. Who else would it be? What am I supposed to say to the police?"

"Here. I've got it written down." Cullen withdrew a folded sheet of paper from his hip pocket that read, *A secret compartment behind Damon Hammond's home office bookshelf contains stolen police evidence.*

"Just read it and hang up."

= = = ¦ ¦ = = =

"Don't anyone tell Billy Bob," Corinne said. "He would just have a cow."

Finding a pay phone took a while. All the booths they'd remembered from childhood were long gone. Finally, they located one at Wal-Mart, way off at the far end of the home and garden department.

Glancing nervously about, Corinne hurried from the car where Cullen and Lori waited. As she reached for the receiver, though, she detected something gooey.

"Ewwwww." She trotted back to Cullen and Lori.

"I'm not picking that thing up. It's filthy."

Cullen handed her a pair of latex gloves. "Use these."

"What about my ear? I could get ticks or lice or something."

"Hold the receiver a little ways away," Lori suggested.

Scowling her objection, Corinne snapped on the gloves and strode back to the phone. She lifted the receiver with two fingers, struggled to get the other gloved hand into her slacks pocket where she'd put her quarter. She looked at the coin, then jumped away, leaving the receiver dangling.

"What's wrong now?" Cullen asked.

"I touched this quarter before I put these gloves on. It'll have my fingerprints."

"Wipe it off with your blouse," Lori said.

"Will that work? Aren't you supposed to use, like, Pledge or something?"

"I don't think they'll sort through all the change in all the pay phones just to—"

"There's only one pay phone in this whole blessed town!" Corinne snapped. "This is the first place they'll look!"

Cullen rummaged through his pocket. "Here," he said. "Use this one. This way, they'll think it was me."

Corinne returned to the phone and dialed.

"Neeeyeeeelo," answered a woman. "Y'all have reached the Arthur Police Department. Can I hep' ya?"

Corinne looked at her script. "A secret compartment behind . . ."

"Corinne? Corinne Snodgrass? Is that you? Are you all right, hon?"

Shit, thought Corinne, when did Mavis Zigenfoose go to work for the police department?

"No," Corinne said, dropping her voice an octave. "No, this isn't . . . A secret compartment behind . . ."

"Do you have a head cold, Corinne? You sound awful, hon. You should be home in bed."

"Dammit, Mavis, this is an anonymous phone call. So, don't you be guessing at things you don't know for sure."

"Um . . . okay, Corinne. You aren't being held hostage or anything, are you? You got someone listening there, so you can't say what you need to say?"

"No, I'm not being held hostage. I've got an anonymous tip for the police, and I wish you'd let me get on with it."

"Oh, all right. But you'd tell me if you were in trouble, wouldn't you, hon? I could give you a code word—"

"Mavis, I'm fine."

"Okay, let me get a pencil so I can write this down. This is pretty exciting. I just answer the phone a couple mornings a week . . . all right, y'all go ahead."

"A secret compartment behind . . ."

"Hang on, hon. Let me catch up here . . . okay, go ahead on."

". . . behind Damon Hammond's home office bookshelf . . . You got that?"

"I do."

". . . contains stolen police evidence."

"Police . . . evi . . . dence . . . All righty. Anything else?"

"Only that you need to remember this call is anonymous. I told you so right from the start. As a city employee you're ethically bound to honor that, regardless of who you might or might not think this is. You go speculating about anonymous calls, people will find out and no one will call anymore."

"Oh, don't worry, Corinne. You can count on me. I'll get this to one of the fellas first thing. Now you go home and get some rest. And say hi to Billy Bob."

Corinne stripped off her gloves, put them in the trash can beside the phone, then returned to the car.

"That took longer than I expected," Cullen said. "Did everything go okay?"

Corinne clicked her seatbelt closed. "Mavis Zigenfoose. That woman will talk your ear off."

= = = ¦¦ = = =

May 1969

The senior prom took place Saturday night before Wednesday's graduation ceremonies.

Cullen stayed home. He'd given a lot of thought to his clandestine encounter with Melissa. On one hand, the experience had been painfully erotic. But he could not help comparing that night with his earlier adventures, and those comparisons brought him back to Shelby.

Melissa's blunt sexuality stood in stark contrast to the awkward, gentle exploration he'd shared with Shelby. His dalliances with Carol were more perfunctory, someplace between these other two extremes. Ultimately much of the same wilderness had been explored. But these events had little in common.

A realization there might be other girls willing to accompany him on a conquest of this foreign and exotic land offered some emotional encouragement, some small respite to the longing he felt for Shelby. But Shelby, not Melissa, commanded his thoughts sometime past midnight—wishing he could sleep—when the telephone extension next to his bed trilled softly.

Cullen reacted quickly before the phone could ring again. He offered a tentative, "Hello?"

A brief interval of silence divided the moment as both Cullen and his caller waited for the click of another extension being picked up. When it didn't happen, Cullen repeated, "Hello?"

He heard a sigh.

"Cullen," the magical voice whispered, "I need to talk with you. But not on the phone. Can you . . . can you meet me at the park?"

Cullen's heart raced. He didn't hesitate. "Center field. Give me fifteen minutes."

= = = ¦¦ = = =

Elks Park occupied a two-block square patch of grass and trees bordering the Eastern State University Campus. It featured sandy, rutted base paths and the dandelion-infested outfield of Arthur's little league baseball diamond, which glowed under a set of yellow-hued mercury vapor lights most summer evenings.

The park had been long-deserted when Cullen arrived there at a little past one a.m. Starting the Mercury would certainly waken his father, so he walked, avoiding the lights of an occasional passing car driven by prom-goers still celebrating during the early morning hours.

Elks Park sat roughly at a halfway point between the separate housing developments where Shelby and Cullen lived—about a mile walk for each of them. Street lights cast enough illumination to provide visibility along the park borders, but the park's core appeared black on this moonless night.

Cullen passed through the first-base dugout. He slipped through darkness, stopping when he reached the center field fence. He waited a moment, hoping something or someone hadn't intervened to change Shelby's mind. Shadowy figures of trees, benches and picnic tables took form. He feared he was alone. On top of everything else, this disappointment would be too much to bear.

"Cullen?"

Her voice drifted from a bench at the base of a spindly pine standing as a contradiction to this arid, windswept place.

She took form as he approached the bench.

She stood. Shadows veiled her face, so he could not read from her expression what this summons might be about. When she sat, Cullen joined her, maintaining a careful space between them.

Now he could see uncertainty, the anxious set of her mouth.

"Thank you for coming," Shelby said. "I was afraid you'd say no."

"I . . . I knew you wouldn't have called if it wasn't . . . important."

She nodded, leading to another awkward void.

"So . . . how was the prom?" he asked.

"Okay." She fumbled with her hands. "I . . . I hoped I'd see you there."

Cullen offered a sarcastic little snort he immediately regretted. "I don't think anyone would have gone with me, given my current status. It's better for everyone if I just keep out of sight."

He felt her hand on his forearm. Then she touched the place on his cheek still yellowed with the remnants of bruising and swelling.

"Are you . . . are you okay? They said your ribs were—"

"Not broken. Only bruised. I wish you wouldn't have been there to see me get my ass kicked that way. Doesn't make me feel very . . . macho, I guess."

"Oh, Cullen, I was so proud of you. And so mad at Darrel and . . . everyone else. I still can't believe you did it. Why you, of all people?"

"I could see what they were doing. I remembered junior high. Buddy stood up for us when he didn't have to. I hated seeing him bullied and provoked when those cowards knew he couldn't fight."

Shelby took both his hands in hers.

"Cullen, what happened to us?"

"God, Shelby, I wish I knew. I was kind of a jerk when you got home from the hospital. I know that. But I never . . . I never stopped . . ."

"Me, neither," she whispered.

Cullen heard the wheels of a distant car thrumming over pavement, an exchange of soft coos between two mourning doves somewhere above them, and a soft flutter of wings.

"So, what's the deal with you and Doug?"

"Oh . . . God, Cullen. I don't know. He's . . . he's been great. We've had a lot of fun. He treats me well. And . . . and . . ."

"Your dad likes him?"

"My dad tolerates him. My mom likes him. She thinks he's funny. She likes how he treats me."

"Does he love you?"

He heard her sharp intake of breath, then her slow exhale. "Yes. Or anyway, he thinks he does. He tells me all the time."

"What do you tell him?"

"Mostly I . . . I avoid the subject."

"But you care for him, you like him a lot." A statement, not a question.

"Well . . . yes, I do."

"So please, Shelby, why are we here? Why did you sneak out of your house following your senior prom to see me?"

"Because I'm worried about you, Cullen." She returned her hand to his cheek and drew his face toward her. "I hate how you've just disappeared, how you're avoiding everyone. All because you had the courage to—"

"I don't *want* to see anyone, Shelby. I don't care anymore what anyone here thinks. A little more than two weeks, and I will be done with this place and these people forever."

Shelby withdrew her hands. "So, you're doing the summer session at New Mexico State?"

"Yeah, I leave two weeks from Sunday."

"You'll be home weekends, to visit?"

"No. My dad won't let me take a car. He'll drive me there, and I'll stay in the dorm. He says I need to spend this summer focusing on college, instead of running around doing other stuff."

Shelby nodded and lowered her gaze. Cullen put his hand under her chin, lifting her face to his.

"Shelby, I wish you would kiss me."

"You don't know how much I wish I could. But Doug . . . he's done nothing to deserve this. We're going to the senior party graduation night. He's making a big deal of it. Spent a lot of money . . ."

"I don't care about Doug. I don't care what you do to him."

She frowned.

"You said you don't love him, Shelby. Tell me the truth, right now. Do you love me?"

Shelby's eyes glistened. She turned away. "I can't do this to Doug."

Cullen grabbed her shoulders. When she wouldn't face him, he experienced a rage he barely controlled. "Just . . . just leave me alone, okay?"

He stomped away, back through the centerfield gate, back through the dugout, across the pavement before he dared turn.

Hoping . . .

He found only darkness.

= = = ¦¦ = = =

June 1969

Cullen spent the week following graduation packing his stuff, deciding what remnants of Arthur to include. A blue steamer trunk—a graduation present—lay open on his bedroom floor next to a cardboard box. The trunk contained record albums, a baseball glove, some books, a camera.

The box held stuff that didn't make the cut.

Items had been switched back and forth all week as he'd look at a particular book or record or photograph and feel the power of memories binding him to this place he was so determined to leave. He surprised himself at those things—and those people—he thought he could let go of, that somehow nagged and sniggled their way into the blue trunk.

On his final night, he thought he had everything sorted. He took one last look through the cardboard box and found pictures he'd rejected out of hand. These photos, long consigned to a dresser drawer, were of Shelby, one a painfully beautiful studio portrait taken soon after surgery had rid her of her glasses.

That's when the trouble began, he thought to himself.

Cullen felt a jab of pain, then refused to linger over her picture. As he shuffled through the box's contents one last time, he flipped the portrait face down. Metal tabs holding the cardboard backing into its frame had become worn and broken, and the cardboard slipped enough for Cullen to see a second, smaller photo behind the portrait.

This black and white picture had been taken with somebody's Kodak Brownie. Cullen and Shelby stood together, ultimate nerds, clad in their junior high band uniforms, saxophones dangling from clips at their chests. Both wore glasses—Cullen the black-rimmed Buddy Holly frames he hated, Shelby the thick lenses that magnified her eyes beyond all proportion. Cullen had his arm draped around her shoulders. Her glittering smile shouted her happiness.

Cullen stared at this photo. Shelby had done all she could to hide any pre-surgery pictures. Why had she preserved this one? Why had it remained concealed in the back of this frame?

He flipped over the photo and found a message written there.

Cullen, whatever happens, I never want either of us to forget that you thought I was pretty when no one else did. I love this picture. Someday, when you find it, I hope you do, too.

Cullen's careful resolve crumbled. He checked his watch. Nine o'clock Saturday night. No way she'd be home. But he used the bedroom extension and dialed anyway, determined to hang up if her father answered.

Shelby said, "Hello?" on the second ring.

A surprised Cullen didn't say anything for a moment.

"Doug?" she asked, and he knew this was a mistake.

"No, Shelby. It's me." He tensed, anticipating a curt response.

Instead, she said, "Cullen!" Her tone conveyed warmth and relief. "I didn't think you'd call before you left. I was giving you another hour before I—"

"Um . . . I didn't think you wanted to . . . what about Doug?"

"He's been calling. The day after the senior party, I told him I needed a break. I told him we were both getting ready to leave for college, we would be meeting a lot of other people, and, well, while I cared about him, I . . . I just didn't want to be . . . he's really hurt."

"Oh . . ." Cullen fell silent again, but his spirit soared.

"I was hoping we could talk," Shelby said.

"Sure. I could come by—"

"No, that won't work . . . my dad . . . can you meet me late? Midnight, maybe? The park again?"

"Yes, absolutely, I'll—"

He was interrupted with the click of another phone extension, followed by a brief silence. And then, "Shelby?"

"Mom, I'm on the phone," Shelby said.

"Oh, I'm sorry."

"Hello, Mrs. Blaine."

"Cullen? It's nice to hear from you. I thought you were leaving."

"Yes, ma'am. Tomorrow. I called Shelby to say goodbye."

"She misses you, you know. Remember what I told you the last time we talked."

"Mother!" Shelby said, but there was a giggle underneath.

"I've missed her, too. And I do remember. You know what else? Mrs. Blaine, you have a lovely daughter."

Shelby's mother laughed, the sound wistful. "Oh, Cullen, when I was your age, I knew someone just like you. If I don't see you before you leave, you behave yourself in Las Cruces, okay?"

"Yes, ma'am."

The extension clicked again.

"Sorry," Shelby said.

"That's okay. I like your mother. Um . . . do you think she

heard about us meeting tonight?"

"She knows I had to see you before you go."

= = = ¦ ¦ = = =

Shelby emerged through shadows at the center field gate a minute after midnight.

"You got here early," she said.

"I . . . I didn't want to be late."

She sat at the opposite end of the bench. His mind raced, reading all kinds of things into the space separating them.

She folded her hands.

"Are you all right?" Cullen asked.

"I . . . no, Cullen. No. I'm not. I feel bad about Doug. I almost gave in and went out with him tonight—before you called. I wound up telling him I was sick."

Cullen felt hollow. Suddenly the air seemed cold, raising a wave of goose bumps over his arms. "Shelby, if Doug's who you want, you should—"

She looked at him sharply. "Don't you care?"

"My God, Shelby, I've never cared about anything more. I want to be with you. These last months have been agony. I hoped tonight meant we can be together again."

"But we can't, can we? You're leaving. When will I see you?"

"My parents . . .. Maybe . . . maybe I could get a bus ticket to come home for a weekend without them knowing."

"Cullen, I feel like I've lost this whole year apart from you. I don't know why. And now it's gone."

She slid across the bench. They shared a hungry kiss.

They walked hand-in-hand through shadows of the town

that had molded them, each fated to take a separate path. They fantasized a life together. Their imaginations built a house in the mountains by a stream with horses and dogs and cats, where the rest of the world wouldn't matter. As the night surrendered to dawn and the mockingbirds crowed, Cullen waved from across the street as Shelby slipped into her house.

chapter twenty-six

July 1969

"Molloy, phone's for you—a girl."

The Resident Assistant at Conley Hall tapped at Cullen's open door. The outside temperature was one hundred and nine degrees. Most doors facing the walkway stood open. Conley Hall, not air conditioned, consisted of a cinder block structure built like a two-story motel with rooms opening to outside sidewalks. The whine of dozens of electric fans stirred stifling air, producing an alien sort of hum which constructed a cone of white noise that routine sounds from the surrounding world couldn't penetrate.

Along with air conditioning, the rooms at Conley Hall lacked telephones, which was okay with Cullen because he didn't have anyone to call except Shelby. He couldn't afford the long-distance rates more than once a week. They set aside nine p.m. Sundays, trading off calling each other. Cullen could afford about ten minutes. When Shelby called, depending on how recently her father had gotten a phone bill, they could sometimes stretch their conversation to fifteen.

So, Shelby's call on a Tuesday afternoon caught Cullen by surprise. It had to be her, though. He didn't know any other girls.

If his mom was calling because of something wrong at home—well, no one would confuse Cullen's mom with a girl.

"Better hustle," the RA told him.

Cullen wore gym shorts. He pulled a t-shirt over his head, shoved his feet into a pair of flip-flops and trotted quickly along the sidewalk. If he accidently stepped out of one of the loose sandals and his bare foot made contact with the concrete surface, he could suffer a burn that would raise blisters.

Cullen hurried into the dorm office. Four pay phones lined one wall. The receiver of the third dangled from its cord. Had to be Shelby. They always used that phone number. He wiped sweat off his left ear with the tail of his t-shirt.

"Um . . . hello?"

"Oh, Cullen, good. I was afraid they wouldn't be able to find you. Did I take you from anything important?"

The warmth of her voice told him, whatever the message, everything was okay.

"No. I was just, you know, sweating."

The unrelenting heat had become a familiar topic of their conversations.

"Would you be too busy sweating this Saturday to take me to a movie or something?"

"Saturday?"

They'd talked about his plan to squirrel away enough money, buy a bus ticket and maybe sneak home for a weekend. That plan sort of fell apart, though, when they got to details like where he might stay.

"Gee, Shelby, I'd give anything to see you, but I haven't got enough cash saved for the ticket."

"What if I came there? Would you be able to make time during all your perspiring to see me?"

"You're coming here?"

"Yes. My mom and me. I told you my aunt lives in El Paso? My mom was saying the other day how much she missed her sister. So, I sort of suggested she should go visit. She said Daddy was too busy to get away, and I said well what about just a girl thing. We're driving over Saturday."

"Wow, El Paso," he said. "El Paso is only forty miles away."

= = = ¦¦ = = =

Cullen knew the exact distance to El Paso because he'd been there three times already this summer. Not El Paso, precisely. But he had to go through El Paso to reach Juarez, Mexico, the sprawling, exotic border town just across the Rio Grande.

Cullen's roommate, Mickey Florey, owned a car, and a male freshman rite of passage at NMSU involved driving south to downtown El Paso, and the Stanton Street Bridge pedestrian border crossing. In 1969, the passage required no documentation to enter Mexico, although you had to show U.S. border guards a driver's license to get back.

Once across, gringo pedestrians ran a gauntlet of urchins selling Chicklet gum, beggars who competed against each other for fewest remaining body parts, and hustlers who offered swift passage to bars, brothels, chapels, and live entertainment. Anywhere along the avenue a shopper could barter for clothing, boots, hats, jewelry, glassware or fine art executed on black velvet.

For NMSU students, the bars, brothels and entertainment were the main attractions. Juarez had no discernible drinking age, no R-rated exclusions. Anyone's money was good for whatever service might be offered.

To a kid raised in the Eastern New Mexico/West Texas Bible Belt, a glittering avenue populated by foreigners with little pretense of morality proved both fascinating and forbidding.

Arthur was a town shrouded in morality, steeped in morality, washed in the blood of morality, and never rinsed out. By all appearances, in Arthur, among its adult population, anyway, nobody drank, nobody fucked—unless absolutely necessary—nobody coveted their neighbor's anything, and everybody attended church on Sunday, unless you were a Baptist or a Church of Christer. Then, you attended services on Wednesday nights, too.

This community-wide devotion to a strict religious-based code of conduct for young folks, though, often produced a result opposite its desired effect. High school students who, through the course of human nature, fell prey to many of these mortal sins along the section roads, left home figuring they were already doomed to hell, so why not give serious depravity a shot?

When Florey organized their first Saturday night trip across the border, Cullen rode along mostly because he was trying to find his place among a new set of acquaintances and did not want to seem prudish or judgmental. He figured he could just watch.

Their crossing into Mexico proved a raucous assault on his senses, though, and Cullen lowered his guard. The five boys crowded into the first bar they encountered. When it came time to order, Cullen's companions seemed familiar with the nomenclature. *Whiskey Sour, Mojito, Manhattan, Sloe Gin Fizz.*

Cullen suffered a moment of panic. He'd intended to ask for beer, although he didn't care for it. With each preceding order, though, his lack of alcoholic sophistication became more painfully apparent. He could think of only two possibilities. One was *boilermaker,* a term he came across while reading some dark noir detective novel. The other *daiquiri,* which he couldn't spell, but he'd read somewhere once that daiquiri had been President Kennedy's favorite drink. And he and President Kennedy were both Democrats.

"Frozen or on the rocks?" a bored bartender asked him.

Another mistake. His drink was apparently more complicated than the others. Frozen sounded better than something with rocks, so he chose that, hoping the quiz had ended.

When a bluish drink arrived, heaped with finely shaved ice, Cullen lifted his glass and braced for the bite of the alcohol. His first gulp of Jack Daniels straight at a party he attended during the last half of his senior year—before being shunned because of the Darrel Jensen fight—tasted awful. As was Melissa's scotch. With his first tentative sip of this cold blue stuff, though, he found the rum smooth and mixers sweet.

Cullen decided he could develop a fondness for daiquiris.

They each had a couple of drinks. Thus fortified, they walked into the night to continue their adventure.

A little further along, a marquee hung over the sidewalk advertising GIRLS in flashing neon. The place's windows were covered with white paint and posters, featuring beautiful women wearing elaborate costumes of silk and feathers and come-hither expressions that, indeed, made the boys curious about coming hither.

They craned their necks at posters as they strolled. When Florey, the leader of their pack, passed the brightly lighted entryway, a man with slicked back hair and a tuxedo grabbed his arm.

"Prettiest girls in town," the man announced. "You come inside, now. You don't want to miss this show."

Florey appeared startled. "Um . . . I don't know—"

"What, you don't like girls?" the man asked, playing to Florey's companions who watched with uncertainty. "You like boys better? My cousin's got a place with boys."

"What? No. Of course, I like girls."

"Good. Then we fix you up."

The man whistled. Another man physically hauled Florey inside.

"You guys going in?" the first man asked. "Or do *you* like boys better?"

They sat near a stage where two women stood with indifference, bathed by blue light.

Their host raised his hand, snapped his fingers, and a waitress wearing bikini bottoms and tassels covering the nipples of her small, golden breasts, appeared with a tray. She placed a beer before each boy, tassels dangling, and demanded about twice what they'd paid for their drinks at the first bar. The man who'd escorted them stood close, arms folded across his chest, ensuring payment.

A juke box thumped to life with the trombone slide leading into David Rose's *The Stripper.* Looking a little bored, these women removed each other's clothing and simulated various sex acts for the duration of the song. As the song ended and the juke box clicked through the process of finding its next selection, Cullen felt a presence behind him. He turned and found himself eye-level with the tassels.

A little startled, he leaned away. She stepped closer, squeezing her small breasts together and shaking her tassels at him.

"You want to dance with me?" she asked, offering a suggestive wink.

His cohorts watched with open-mouthed apprehension.

"Um . . . no, I don't . . . um . . . I don't . . . dance."

Her face collapsed, and she sounded wounded. "You don't like me?"

"Oh, I like you . . . fine."

"You don't like girls . . .?"

Cullen could see where this was headed. By now, though, he understood the ploy. "I like girls a lot, but, well, I really don't have any more money."

That got everyone's attention. Cullen and his troops were quickly back on the sidewalk.

= = = ¦ ¦ = = =

"Mom says we can stop in Las Cruces for a late lunch Saturday," Shelby said on her next call. "If you had a car, I could stay with you for the afternoon and you could drive me to my aunt's house in El Paso later."

Cullen's mind raced. A car. A car. Where could he . . .Florey would be gone this weekend. Florey lived in Phoenix. He'd asked Cullen to drive him to the El Paso airport.

"I think," Cullen said, "that I do have a car."

= = = ¦ ¦ = = =

Cullen planned a brotherly sort of hug, the kind where huggers lean from a distance and the only real body contact is neck up. Shelby would have none of it. She bounded to him, clamped her arms around Cullen's neck and kissed him. In deference to her mother, Cullen felt relief that no tongues were involved.

A few seconds into this embrace, Cullen heard another car door open.

Mrs. Blaine said, "Hello, Cullen. It's . . . um . . . nice to see you. And the polite thing, Shelby, would be to let go of Cullen at least long enough to say hello."

Shelby broke the kiss, stepped away a little so Cullen could see her roll her eyes. She said politely, "Hello, Cullen."

Cullen grinned and, without taking his gaze from Shelby, said, "Hi, Mrs. Blaine. Thanks for bringing Shelby."

Shelby pulled him into another hug as her mother said, "Okay, let's get out of this heat and have something to eat."

Cullen had researched nearby restaurants and chose VIP's Big Boy a few blocks off campus on Valley Drive. Compared with anything Arthur had to offer, this chain restaurant featuring a statue of a fat kid holding a burger high on a tray in one hand amounted to fine dining.

"Are you sure, Cullen?" Mrs. Blaine asked. "We could go to something a little more . . . formal? I'm buying."

"I'm not sure what else there is," Cullen confessed. "I don't get off campus much. There's a pay phone. I could check the yellow pages."

"No, that's all right. This will do."

"So, what are your plans for the afternoon, Cullen?" Mrs. Blaine asked after she abandoned her burger and dabbed her lips with a napkin.

"Well, I thought I'd show Shelby the campus. Then I thought we'd see a movie and have dinner. Then we'll drive to El Paso through the valley instead of the Interstate. It . . . um . . . takes a little longer. The drive's pretty, though. There's pecan orchards, the river . . ."

"So, you'll be getting to El Paso when?"

"Oh, mother," Shelby said. "We don't know, okay? We just want to spend some time together."

"Can I have at least an estimated time of arrival?"

"One a.m.," Shelby said.

"How about eleven?"

Shelby sighed in protest.

"Look," Mrs. Blaine said, "I get that you're both eighteen now. I understand the rules are different and Cullen lives in a dorm—"

"Mother, please."

For a moment, the clatter of plates and silverware around them supplanted their conversation.

"What are the rules about having girls at your dorm room, Cullen?"

"Um . . . we have to check in at the front desk, and the door has to stay open."

"Do you plan on following the rules?"

"Mother!"

"I'm guessing," Mrs. Blaine said, "the dorm will be a part of a campus tour."

"So why do you just assume—" Shelby protested.

"Because I was eighteen and in love once," her mother said. "You two have been through a lot over the past six years. You grew up together. You've alternately broken each other's hearts. Now you've been apart for several weeks and both of you are heading into the world. Neither of you knows what, or who, you'll find there. So, for now, please, be patient and don't . . . don't . . . well, just don't."

Shelby started to protest, but Cullen squeezed her hand.

"Mrs. Blaine," he said, "you told me not too long ago to hang in there. I did. Nothing is more important than Shelby. I won't do anything to hurt her or disrespect her or . . . I won't, okay?"

Mrs. Blaine half stood, leaned across the table separating

them and kissed his forehead. "Thank you, Cullen," she said. "Do your best."

= = = ¦¦ = = =

"So, will the tour include your dorm room?" Shelby asked, displaying her shoulder bag. "Or will I have to change clothes in a public restroom somewhere?"

Mrs. Blaine had dropped them at the Campus Union Building and gone on her way.

"I guess eventually we have to," Cullen said. "My roommate's car is parked there, and I left the keys in my room. But we really do need to kind of behave."

"I have to change clothes with the door open?"

"No . . . I'm sure we can . . . you can change in the bathroom. I think. I'll tell the guys next door they have to stay out."

"Guys next door?"

"Two dorm rooms share one connecting bathroom. It's a real pain."

They left Shelby's bag in a book locker at the CUB and took a walk through the sprawling campus. Nineteen-Thirties-era buildings, stately two-and three-story affairs made of beige brick, mocked Spanish architecture with roofs of red Mexican barrel tiles.

Broad concrete walkways crisscrossed a campus dotted with expanses of green lawn. In the quiet of a summer Saturday afternoon, a steady tick of impact water sprinklers, moving through their graceful arcs, provided a rhythm to their arm-in-arm stroll.

"My English class is here," Cullen said, pointing at a set of stone steps leading to a pair of heavy doors. "My teacher is pretty interesting. His name is Medoff. He writes plays. He's letting us read his new one. It's pretty . . . sexy. Not like high school English."

Cullen explained that English and history classes he had three days a week were at opposite ends of the campus. "So, I practically have to run from one to the other, and I'm all sweaty for history."

"Speaking of sweaty," Shelby said, "I will need to take a shower before I change clothes."

"Um . . . yeah. I want to shower, too . . ."

"I don't suppose they'll let us take one together, will they?"

Cullen laughed.

"No, I think I could get expelled if we did. Even though it might be worth it."

"So, what do we do?"

Cullen thought for a moment. "Okay. I'll take a shower first while you wait at the office. Then we'll get permission for you to shower after me. I'll talk to the RA. He's a pretty good guy."

= = = ¦¦ = = =

"You and your girlfriend want to take a shower?" the resident assistant asked incredulously. His feet were propped on his desk as he stared at a television set bolted to the wall.

"Well, yeah, but not, like, together," Cullen said.

The RA took a quick glance from the television and, seeing Shelby, did a double take. "What, are you crazy? If you don't want to take a shower with her, I'll certainly volunteer."

"What? No, I mean . . ." Cullen stammered.

Shelby laughed.

"I'd be happy to shower with her," Cullen said. "But not . . . I mean, I would take a shower with her if it wasn't against the rules . . ."

"I'm not offering to shower with anyone," Shelby said. "I just want to stop being all sweaty, so I can change clothes before we see the movie."

"Can we figure out something so she can take a shower?" Cullen asked. "Please?"

"You sure you want to shower in a bathroom shared by four guys?" the RA asked Shelby. "Sometimes those bathrooms can be a little . . . toxic, if you know what I mean."

Shelby looked at Cullen.

Cullen shrugged and conceded, "He could be right."

The RA ran his finger across a glass covering a rooming diagram on his desk.

"Since it's summer session, we've got some empty rooms. Four down from you, first floor, Molloy. I'll give you a key to Thirty-five. There's no towels or stuff. Let her use yours. If you're in there, keep the front door open."

"Thank you," Shelby said as Cullen accepted the key.

They took the long sidewalk, passing half a dozen doors standing ajar as residents tried to cope with the swelter.

The last open door stood adjacent to Cullen's room. Cullen and Florey shared their bathroom with Quint Fisher, who sat shirtless, and Art Carpenter, who lay atop one of the two beds with a plastic bag of ice draped across his forehead.

Cullen acknowledged them with a nod, motioning Shelby to follow. As he unlocked his door, Art and Quint stared from their doorway. Art said, "She's a girl."

"Nothing gets by you, does it, Art?"

Shelby smiled and offered a discreet wave.

"What's she doing here?" Quint asked.

"She's my girlfriend. She's going to take a shower."

"She can't."

"Yes, she can. We cleared it with the RA. He gave us a key to an empty room. She's going to shower there while I shower here."

"You can't."

"Why?"

"Our shower's full," Art said. "Of ice."

"Why?"

"We got beer. We want to keep it cold," he whispered.

Cullen checked. Sure, enough, they'd piled two feet of crushed ice inside the shower stall.

Shelby peeked over his shoulder. "I suppose you could climb in over the top, but then you'd freeze your ankles."

Cullen sighed. "Did you leave the front door open?"

Shelby asked, "Can you grab some towels?"

= = = ¦ ¦ = = =

They walked from the movie theater a couple of miles off campus three hours later. Shelby wore a light blue blouse and a white skirt. Her hair spilled over her shoulders. Silver bracelets decorated with turquoise adorned each wrist, along with several plain silver bands that jingled a little when she moved.

"So, what now?" she asked, slipping her hand into his.

"We're going to a great Mexican restaurant."

"Are you sure you can afford this? We don't have to do anything fancy."

The truth would have been, no. He would deny Shelby

nothing tonight, though. He'd skip a few meals next week.

"This place isn't expensive. It's . . . well, you'll see."

Cullen made a short drive east from Las Cruces' Main Street, then turned onto a narrow lane lined with single story adobe structures at least a hundred years old. He slowed to a crawl, squeezing between a raised sidewalk and an oncoming car. He negotiated another turn, entering a plaza the size of a small city block and surfaced with brick. At the plaza's center sat a gazebo, painted with the red, white and green of the Mexican flag, where a mariachi band made a raucous, happy noise.

People sat on benches along the perimeter, watching a handful of men and women as they danced. The men wore cowboy hats, pressed jeans, and polished boots. Their long-sleeved shirts had pearl snaps buttoned to the collar. Their bolo ties were clasped with silver and turquoise. The women wore bright flowing, swirling dresses colored in reds and yellows and oranges, which mimicked the clouds painted by the setting sun behind them.

Twin majestic towers of St. Genevieve's Catholic Church presided over the north end of the plaza. The church took on a neon glow in the rich, low light of sunset.

Cullen parked near the church.

"My God, Cullen, it's beautiful!" Shelby told him as she spun herself in a series of slow circles.

"You remember Mr. Howard's history class?" Cullen asked her. "About the Gadsden Purchase? This is it. Before the Gadsden Purchase, this was Mexico."

Holding hands, they walked through a plaza framed by shops carved from single continuous structures. A few ornate doors, closed and decorated with elaborate ironwork, indicated entrances to private residences. As dusk prevailed, miniature white lights twinkled through elms and cottonwoods whose roots bumped the plaza's brick surface into irregular mounds.

Cullen steered them to an adobe building that spread over much of the adjoining block. Its exterior walls were covered with stucco painted a bright white. Ceiling beams protruded about a foot, forming a row of round, blunt logs a foot or so below the roof.

Around the corner, the restaurant's entrance displayed a pair of heavy, elaborately carved doors. Painted on the wall was a picture of a parchment scroll with a careful script:

> ***La Posta***
> *This is the original La Posta, the only station that remains standing on the Butterfield Trail. For more than a century, these old adobe walls have withstood the attack of elements and men and have sheltered such personalities as Billy the Kid, Kit Carson and Pancho Villa. Now Mesilla sleeps, but La Posta still offers its traditional hospitality and fine food to all who wander here.*

Cullen tugged at the door's weight and ushered Shelby inside. The cave-like entrance corridor seemed a little forbidding with its low ceiling. A jewelry shop to one side of this corridor and an art gallery on the other were both closed. Wall sconces along the walkway were not adequate to chase the shadows.

That walkway, though, opened onto a brightly-lighted room with a high ceiling. Just past its entrance sat an aquarium, featuring shiny silver fish with tiny mouths and sharp protruding teeth. A sign identified them as piranhas and warned patrons to protect their fingers.

"Piranhas?" Shelby wondered aloud as she gazed at the fishes' lethal smiles.

The fish held their attention for only a moment as a jagged squawk issued from a set of floor-to-ceiling cages, containing a fake tree and a half-dozen exotic birds, including parrots, Macaws and Mynas. Another sign warned visitors their digits were in peril should they try and pet the pretty birds.

Shelby peered with fascination at a green parrot sitting on a swing a couple of feet above her. The parrot returned her gaze, cocking its head from side to side while cracking a peanut with its talons.

"Hello," said Shelby.

The bird dropped the peanut, gave a shrill whistle, and answered, "Hi, there, cutie!"

Shelby giggled. Her face glowed when she turned to face Cullen's smile.

"Two for dinner?"

The question came from over Cullen's shoulder.

A hostess escorted them to one of several small rooms that collectively served as a dining area. This room featured the same low ceiling as the entrance corridor and included a kiva style fireplace in one corner. Exposed vigas—rough log beams—and a thatch of sticks and smaller logs resting atop them formed its ceiling.

"How did you find this place?" Shelby asked.

"My dad brought me here when he drove me down. This restaurant opened in the late thirties when my parents went to school here. Dad says my mom got her recipe for enchiladas from this place. Flat, layered cheese enchiladas, not the rolled-up kind."

"Is that what you're ordering?" Shelby asked.

"Yep, I have to," he said. "Red enchiladas served with an egg on top."

Shelby ordered rellenos, made with world-famous Hatch chilis grown just north of Las Cruces.

Three mariachis, a guitar, a fiddle and a bass, stopped at their table to sing *Adios, Mi Corazon,* a song based on a poem called *A Border Affair* written in 1907 by Charles Badger Clark about a cowboy who wandered into Mexico and met a girl with whom he fell in love.

Spanish is the loving tongue,
Soft as music, light as spray
'Twas a girl I learned it from
Living down Sonora way.
I don't look much like a lover,
Yet I say her love-words over
Often when I'm all alone
Mi amore, mi Corazon

Shelby reached across the table, covering his hand with hers. "Cullen," she said, "what if our lives could always be like this?"

After their meal, they retraced their previous path, pausing to talk with the birds again. Cullen wrapped his arm around Shelby's shoulders, and she slipped hers around his waist as they walked to the car.

"I guess it's time to go to El Paso," Cullen said as he held the door for her.

"I guess. But, God, I don't want to. Let's take the long way, okay?"

chapter twenty-seven

Wednesday
July 2009

"So, what's it going to be, Clifton?" asked Cullen. "Who will you charge with what?"

They faced each other across Gladly's desk. Cullen and Lori occupied the leather armchairs. Chief Burke sat on a couch behind them.

Elbows on his desk, Gladly considered Cullen's question longer than he should have. "Attempted murder for Jensen, Painter and Blaine," he finally said, challenging Cullen with a frown.

Cullen laughed. "What about Buddy Boyd?"

"Undecided. But we had the fingerprints, so he's not off the hook."

"*Had* being the operative word," Cullen said. "Chief Burke's crew let Buddy's fingerprints escape, remember?"

"The prints *were* there. Our lab people saw them, matched them. Police officials confirmed it. We'll get affidavits . . .and ballistic tests match the gun with the two intact bullets taken from Hammond's body."

"I'm thinking," Cullen responded, "that the disappearance of fingerprints calls chain of evidence into serious question.

Obviously, someone you can't identify disturbed the evidence while it was in police custody. You can't even prove the gun you have is the same gun Buddy turned over to you."

Gladly didn't answer.

"That leaves Weard Ward," Cullen said.

"Second degree assault."

Cullen patted the leather on his chair's armrest. "Technically, I don't think you can assault a dead person."

"We're a little vague on time-of-death. Hammond could still have been alive when Ward shoved that carrot up his nose."

"Please, Clifton, can we be realistic here?"

"Hey, count your blessings. Chief Burke over there thought was should charge Ward with sodomy."

Cullen and Lori laughed aloud. Even Gladly seemed to be fighting a smile.

Finally, Gladly said, "Okay, what do you think your clients deserve?"

"It's not a matter of what they deserve. It's a matter of what you can prove. And, in my humble opinion, that would be nothing."

"They shot the man, Cullen! All three of them!"

"Do you have any physical proof of their presence?" Cullen asked. "Any physical proof of who fired the first shot? Was that first shot Hammond's foot, his chest, or his head? Which suspect—if any—shot him where, for that matter?"

"We have a witness . . ."

"Not to the shooting."

"We have a witness to the order they came and went. And muzzle flashes."

"You have a witness whom everyone in town knows is a conspiracy freak. She's reported so many 'crimes' over the years,

Chief Burke's police force has stopped taking her calls. She's reported everything from terrorist cells to alien invasions."

"There was only one report about aliens," Burke corrected from behind him.

"Yes." Cullen said. "It was a bunch of high school kids driving through town on their way to Roswell for some sort of space nut convention."

"I can't," Gladly said, sounding more than a little deflated, "just let them off scot free."

"Okay, we go to trial, then. This thing will be so entertaining, I'll bet I can sell it to Court TV. Maybe even get a book deal out of it. You and the Arthur Police Department will be famous, Clifton. Of course, not in a good way." He paused. When Gladly began to speak again, Cullen interrupted. "We haven't even discussed your biggest problem, have we?"

"What's that?"

"Come on, Clifton. What about those inconvenient rules of discovery? You'll have to admit it eventually, anyway. Tell him, Lori."

"I'm guessing," Lori said, "your autopsy report will show that, at the time Mr. Hammond suffered the three gunshot wounds, he was already dead."

Gladly tossed a malevolent glare at Burke.

"Why are you looking at me?" Burke complained. "I didn't tell 'em. And we've got 'em now! I'll arrest 'em right here."

"Chief Burke has a point, you know," Gladly said. "The autopsy *does* show Damon Hammond died of a heart attack. All the shootings were post mortem. It's hard to know for sure about the carrot because, well, because the coroner says he has very little forensic experience with nasal assault."

Gladly lifted a letter opener and studied it. "To an experienced investigator, the lack of blood at the crime scene would show Hammond's heart was not beating when he was shot. So, my question is, if you or your clients hadn't been at the crime scene, Mr. Molloy and Ms. Summerlin, how would you know he was already dead?"

Cullen shrugged. "A good guess."

"More likely," Burke said, "you broke into Hammond's place. You searched his office, you found a hidden room. Then you had Corinne Snodgrass call the police department, so we'd go and find whatever *you* might have put there."

"It is difficult," Gladly pointed out, "to make an anonymous phone call in such a small town."

"Who said it was Corinne?" Cullen asked.

"Mavis Zigenfoose," Burke snapped.

"Did Mavis record the call?"

"No. Corinne was smart enough not to use the emergency line."

"Is Mavis some sort of voice recognition expert?"

"She knows what Corinne Snodgrass sounds like. She talks to her at church every week."

"Did Corinne identify herself?"

"NO!" Burke yelled. "She didn't have to!"

Cullen returned his attention to Gladly. "Any physical proof *we* might have been there?"

Gladly didn't answer.

"How about Aggie Smoot? Did she see anyone?"

"Haven't heard from her," Gladly said. "I think she's mad at us."

"Again," Cullen said, "I believe you've got a problem with proof. But, tell me about this secret room? What was there?

Whatever was there, has it been carefully inventoried and stored? So, in case charges are brought against me or Lori, or any of my clients, I can examine those records in detail, and talk in open court about what I find? Or what somebody might have photographed there?"

Cullen glanced over his shoulder at Burke, whose face practically glowed with rage.

Another silence intervened before Gladly spoke again.

"Cullen, those people shot him. Regardless of whether he was already dead, at least two of them did so with intent to kill him."

"Damon Hammond made a lot of people's lives miserable over a lot of years," Cullen replied. "I don't condone murder. I think I can understand, though, how someone might finally be pushed too far. I think most folks around here will treat Damon Hammond's passing as a relief rather than a tragedy."

"Regardless," Gladly said, "Hammond was a prominent citizen. How can we just let it go?"

"Lie," said Lori.

"I beg your pardon?"

"I don't know about you personally, Mr. Gladly, but there are a lot of people in this little town who have no problem manipulating the truth. As a former police officer, I'm appalled at what I've seen here. Just make something up."

"What would you suggest?" Gladly said.

"How about suicide?" said Cullen. "Cremate the body and tell everyone he committed suicide."

"He suffered three gunshot wounds!" Gladly protested.

Cullen shrugged. "So, he was a lousy shot."

= = = ¦ ¦ = = =

Wednesday, 2009

"Well, I must say, Cullen Molloy, that was pretty slick."

Lori and Cullen stood over open suitcases, taking a last look to see who might have forgotten what. Lori put her arms around his neck with a little too much distance separating them.

"What was pretty slick?" Cullen asked.

"You got them off the hook. All of them."

He laughed. "*We* got them off the hook. I hate to think of what mistakes I would have made without you. And, I think Darrel isn't out of the woods yet. They can get rid of most of the stuff from that secret room, but I left a note with Gladly suggesting theft of evidence should be vigorously investigated."

"Or what?"

"I left it to his imagination."

Her smile dissolved. She bit her lower lip, then asked softly, "So, who are you going home with? Shelby, or me?"

Cullen pulled her close and kissed her, mimicking Augustus McCrae. "*Lori darlin*, I love you. Yes, yes, I know I love her too, but . . . all week, you've allowed Shelby and me our odd relationship. Your understanding makes me love you that much more."

Lori hugged him. "We need to say goodbye. They're waiting."

= = = ¦ ¦ = = =

"And that's why you left?" Buddy asked as five friends shared the table in his mother's kitchen one last time.

"Not one of my finer moments," Cullen said. "Immature and self-pitying as it might sound, though, I was crushed when Shelby told me. I found myself right back in high school, imagining how I'd have felt if I'd known. I guess I used it as an excuse to do something I'd needed to do my whole life. I had to get as far away from Arthur—and these fucking straight lines everybody pretends they live by—as I could. The two of you sort of forced a choice I never would have made otherwise. I can't tell you how good it was for me."

"Everyone needs to raise some hell, man." Weard offered a sagacious nod. "For me, it was Cambodia. That was a real trip."

"Cambodia?" Shelby asked.

"I'm not supposed to talk about it."

A lingering silence punctuated the moment until Buddy cleared his throat, then said with a wavering voice, "Cullen, when Shelby and I . . . when we . . . it didn't . . ." He stopped.

". . . didn't mean anything?" Shelby completed his sentence.

"Oh, Shelby, no. I don't . . . I can't . . ."

"It's all right. The whole thing confused me for the longest time. The blunt truth, though, is it *didn't* mean anything. I was just like you. I didn't do it because I loved you or wanted to spend my life with you. I suffered a teenage crush, seasoned with budding hormones. You accommodated me. Then events overwhelmed us all."

"Your miscarriage," Buddy whispered hoarsely. "I nearly killed you, Shelby."

"What, are you determined to live under a guilty cloud? Cullen told me that thing you said about who we are being the sum total of people who've influenced our lives? Well, I like who I am. You made an important contribution."

Lori put a hand on Shelby's shoulder. "I find the four of you remarkable," she said. "I've known for a long time Cullen is a special person. Remarkable people, it seems, surround themselves with remarkable friends. I . . . I understand why he loves you, Shelby. And why you love him. I don't understand how the two of you can be so reluctant to—"

"Oh," Shelby sighed, "I do love him. But I don't think either of us really wants to screw that up with the reality of living together. If I'm completely honest with myself, my commitment to independence has only deepened with age. Lori, I know you look at me and see a lonely woman with too many cats. During my weaker moments," she continued, grinning at Cullen, "I do indulge myself with fantasies of a life together. The thing about real, ongoing physical intimacy, though, is it eventually gets down to morning breath and snoring and farting and the impossibility of disguising those fifteen extra pounds when you're naked. Cullen and I never have to face all that. When we see each other, we surf along this perpetual state of limerence, where we are on our best behavior, shining like new pennies."

"Wow," Cullen said. "You fart? I . . . I'm not sure I can deal with that."

"God, me neither," Buddy said. "I'm having a hard-enough time knowing you snore."

"No sweat for me, Shelby," said Weard. "Cut one right now if you want to."

"What about you, Cullen?" Lori insisted. "How can you love someone and not want . . . more."

"Several times in my life," Cullen said, "I was desperate for more. The only way it would have happened, though, is if we'd married when we were young. Let me tell you about being married to me when I was young. I was selfish, moody, petulant. I brought my frustrations with work home and visited them upon my poor wife. I thought marriage offered some sort of guarantee of security and commitment. I knew nothing of how to work at a relationship. My wife got the worst of me."

When both Shelby and Lori started to voice a protest, Cullen raised a hand. "I know, I know. One person is never solely responsible for the failure of a relationship. But it's who I was. I would have been the same with Shelby and killed this connection between us. I hope I'm not that person any more. I hope now, the people I love get the best of me."

Again, Lori expressed her amazement. "This bond that has carried you through all these years, and through so much turmoil. Buddy, I looked you up. Did you know Google says you're worth half a billion dollars?"

"Yeah, well, Google's full of shit."

Cullen laughed. "He has to say that because of the IRS."

"Oh, come on, Cullen," Buddy said. "You know how it is. It may look like a lot on paper, but there's not much real liquidity there."

"Yeah," Cullen said. "He scrapes by on a hundred million or so."

Although Lori knew she shouldn't raise the next question, she did anyway.

"So, Buddy and Shelby, there's not even a remote consideration the two of *you* might—"

"Oh, no," Shelby said. "Buddy's secretly in love with LuAnn, his executive assistant."

"What?" Buddy said. "Wait a minute. I never said—"

"Exactly," said Cullen. "You never said. But everyone who works for you knows you've conducted this affair forever. Something else you should understand. LuAnn deeply respects Hezakiah Boyd. But she's in love with Buddy. The worst thing you could do is let Buddy somehow slip away."

"I nearly did that," Buddy said, his tone reflecting the depth of that revelation.

"It's all right," Cullen said. "She adores you. More importantly, she adored you before you were loaded."

Lori experienced a eureka moment. "Oh, I get it. The whole Buddy-Hezekiah thing. It's a part of punishing yourself with guilt over killing Christy. You can't take the final step into an emotional commitment, because you secretly regard Buddy as a horrible person."

Slowly, Buddy's smile bloomed. "Lori, I think you just saved me about a hundred thousand dollars in psychiatric bills. You're right, Shelby, I do love LuAnn. I'm going to go home and tell her so."

He added, "I still have one guilty shadow hanging over me, though. That's Charles LaVelle. I'm suffering some skepticism about his death while driving home from his investigation here being an accident. I'll have someone look into it. Darrel Jensen may have more to answer for."

Shelby put an arm around Weard's shoulder. "Okay, Billy, I guess that leaves you and me."

"No, man," Weard said with a startled expression. "I'm already married. Maybe even twice. The first one got pissed and said, *I banish thee* three times. But I didn't stay in-country long enough to pin down their divorce laws. I'm not supposed to talk about it."

"You've got two wives?" The upward lilt of Lori's voice conveyed her astonishment.

"I already told you, man. The CIA, they fucked me up."

"Ah, well," Shelby said as she laughed, "alone again, naturally."

Their collective chuckles dissolved to another silence, which Shelby deflected with a question.

"Okay, guys, can someone explain to me, if Hammond killed

Christy, why did he hate Buddy so much?"

The others deferred to the former police detective. "My guess is that, at first, he did it as part of his act to be sure Buddy took the blame. Later, he got scared when he thought Buddy hired someone to reopen the investigation. Beyond that, though, Hammond was clearly a psychopath—calculating and unfeeling. One characteristic of psychopaths is their ability to believe their own lies."

"Whatever his reason," Buddy said, "Hammond certainly had me believing in my guilt." He paused. "So, what happens to us now? I've only gotten a glimpse of the effect all this has had, but I can't hide anymore. Certainly not from the four of you. We need to stay in touch—not just say we're going to. We kid ourselves, thinking we've got plenty of time. Then we turn around and it's forty years later. This includes you, too, Weard. You've got to stop being this mysterious vagabond who drops into one of our lives ever half-dozen years or so."

"I need some advance notice, man," Weard said. "It's not like I don't have things to do."

"Fair enough," Buddy said. "A year from today. My place, Desolation Sound. I'll buy a sailboat. Cullen will teach us to sail."

He offered a quizzical look.

"I'm sure Lori and I can clear our calendar," Cullen said.

"I'll just have to schedule my nipple reconstruction surgery around it," Lori agreed.

"Um . . . okay," Buddy said. "I'm sure there must be more to that story, but I've always been reluctant to ask people about their . . . um . . . nipples."

"Call me," Shelby told him. "I'll give you the background."

"Will you be there?" Cullen asked Shelby.

"Sure. Can I bring a date?"

"Not if we have put on some kind of mask to cover the way we feel about each other," Cullen said. Glancing at Lori, he added, "It takes a pretty special person to understand this thing about you and me."

"Good point," Shelby said. "I'll be careful."

"That leaves you, Weard," Buddy said. "Can you work us into your plans?"

"Um . . . let's see. What's today? Wednesday? I could probably finish in the Ukraine by Monday and catch a red-eye . . . yeah, I'll be there."

"The Ukraine?" Cullen asked.

"I can't talk about it."

"Well," Cullen said with reluctance, "I guess Lori and I've got a plane to catch. We'd better get going. Buddy, do you need a ride to Lubbock?"

"No. I'll drive Weard to Santa Rosa, then fly out of Albuquerque."

"The Blue Hole, man," Weard said. "I'm telling you, it's a fraud."

"Will you at least stay long enough to be sure he doesn't drown?" Shelby asked.

Buddy promised he would. He kissed Shelby and hugged Cullen.

"I love you both." His voice cracked with emotion. "Anything you need, anything you want, either of you. You, too, Lori. You know . . . you know . . ."

"Yes," Cullen said, "we do."

"And you'll explain some things to LuAnn when you get home?" Shelby prodded.

"I will, right after I spread my mother's ashes in the most beautiful place I know."

They helped close the house, then waved as Buddy and Weard drove away.

= = = ¦¦ = = =

Bags packed, they found Shelby in the motel lobby.

She nodded, smiling sadly. Cullen went to her.

"Cullen, I don't know how to thank you."

He kissed her. "Be happy. It's the best thing you can do for both of us."

Shelby kissed him again and smiled that enigmatic smile, laughing with her eyes. "Just remember, we'll always have Juarez."

Cullen grinned, raised her chin with his hand and answered with his best Humphrey Bogart impression, "Here's looking at you, kid."

Shelby kissed him, waved to Lori and walked to her car.

"Juarez?" Lori asked, watching her go.

"It's a thing we say. We both like *Casablanca*."

"Juarez? The Mexican drug cartels? Murder capital of the world?"

"Same one."

"You're not telling me you took that poor girl to Juarez."

"Yes. Yes, I did. But the world was very different in 1969."

epilogue

August 1969

Cullen had never been happier as Shelby slid across the seat and leaned close to him. He couldn't help remembering that first night four years ago, her glasses, the pink Nash. He started the car as she kissed his cheek.

Highway 28, the pre-Interstate two-lane route connecting Las Cruces with El Paso, wound south past Old Mesilla, following the Rio Grande River through cool green orchards of pecan trees and fields of alfalfa, beans and cotton. Some of the valley's beauty was lost to darkness, though a full moon gave enough light that Shelby seemed mesmerized, her head resting on Cullen's shoulder.

"You want to stop for a minute?" he asked presently.

Ahead, Highway 28 crossed the wide river bed via a flat little bridge with suspect-looking side railings. Instead of crossing, Cullen turned on to a dirt road which ran along the north bank of the river. "This is the levee road. Last time the guys drove to Juarez, I noticed this turnoff."

"Okay."

They drove less than a mile to a copse of cottonwoods and a spot wide enough for Cullen to park among them. The river bed below was flat, a silver ribbon of water running along an aimless, twisting rut through its center.

"This is it?" Shelby asked. "The mighty Rio Grande?"

"Yeah. They tell me that at times the river really rips through here. Fills all the way across. But they built a dam a long time ago. Now, they kind of turn the river on and off. Um . . . is there anything I can do to ease your disappointment?"

"Kiss me."

Which ignited the spark.

Soon their hands were exploring. After one particularly long entanglement of lips, arms and other stuff, Shelby came up for air. "Didn't you make some sort of promise to my mother?"

"Oh, yeah. I wasn't talking about this. When I made the promise, I was talking about, you know, that other thing."

Shelby organized herself a little. "Right. That other thing. You've still got . . . you mean you and Carol didn't . . ."

"No. We did some stuff. But not the other thing."

Shelby touched his face and kissed him. "This will be a night we can remember all our lives. I guess I wouldn't want to get it all confused with that other thing, either."

Cullen backed Florey's car from the trees, retracing their path.

They crossed the bridge to Highway 28, then continued south through villages with names like Santo Tomas and San Miguel until modern civilization finally reclaimed them.

Highway 28 became McNutt Road, New Mexico became Texas and Paisano Drive. The river ran below them. A steep hillside on the opposite bank was dotted with the light of dozens of glowing fires.

"What's that?" Shelby asked.

"Juarez. The poorest part. If we were driving past in daylight, you'd see all the shacks made of scrap lumber or even cardboard."

They rounded the mountain, and with a burst of light, El Paso and Juarez sprawled before them.

"That's Juarez?" Shelby marveled at the gaudy display.

"Yeah. The border crossing is just ahead. You'll start seeing signs."

"Could we go there? Just for a little while? I'd love to see Mexico, all the things you've talked about in your letters."

"Well . . . we'd have to walk."

"Could we? Please?"

= = = ¦¦ = = =

Shelby clung to Cullen's arm as the bridge descended into the raucous swirl of sounds, color and smells along Avenida Lerdo. Before Cullen could stop her, she gave a dollar to a doe-eyed little girl—who hobbled suspiciously and had one arm bound by a sling—in exchange for a box of gum.

"No, don't . . ." he began, but he spoke too late. The semi-maimed, orphan Chicklet zombies descended en masse. Cullen and Shelby ran to escape.

They crossed an invisible barrier the urchins could not seem to penetrate, arriving at the province of semi-mutilated adults who, sensing weakness, limped, hopped, scooted and crutched alongside them, making their pleas, offering valuable merchandise—elongated pennies with the complete Lord's Prayer inscribed over Abraham Lincoln's face, or No. 2 pencils, or coupon books for things related to GIRLS.

"Quick, over here," Cullen said.

They ducked through an open doorway. Again, the portal represented some magical force field that rendered the halt and the lame powerless to enter.

"Wow," Shelby said, "that was . . .bizarre."

"My fault. I should have warned you."

Only now did they study their surroundings.

Shelby confronted a room of empty tables facing a low stage lighted by a single bulb behind a circular disk—like the ones they sold at Woolworth's to light artificial Christmas trees—rotating from red to green to blue to yellow to white. Three bored forty-something women clad in bikinis sat smoking cigarettes at a long bar.

"Uh, oh," Cullen said as one of the women stood, adjusted her boobs with both hands, and sashayed towards them. "Um . . . let's try someplace else."

He took Shelby's arm. They darted back onto the sidewalk.

"Was that . . .?"

"Yes," Cullen said.

Having escaped their pursuers, Shelby inhaled the scene around them. Rich aromas of food booths assailed her. They strolled past shops where salesmen urged them inside with flattery concerning Shelby's beauty and Cullen's good fortune.

As they reached the next bar, one where employees did not remove their clothes, Cullen smiled. "Have you ever tasted a daiquiri?"

She tasted two.

Once on the sidewalk again, a man wearing a white shirt and thin black tie approached. He introduced himself as Armando, while pointing to a store front across the street, tucked between a sidewalk restaurant and a magazine stand featuring periodicals devoted to masked Mexican wrestlers. Painted on a whited-out window in black letters, the word *CHAPEL*, situated above a neon sign flashing, *Modelo—Cerveza Especiale*.

"My cousin's the judge," Armando told them. "You wanna get married?"

Cullen laughed and urged Shelby onward.

"You don't want to marry this beautiful creature?" Armando seemed astounded. "What's wrong with you?"

Shelby grinned. "Yeah, Cullen. What's wrong with you?"

Having learned not to engage the sidewalk hustlers, Cullen put his arm around Shelby and moved on.

With cat-like quickness, Armando once more loomed in front of them. "Okay. So maybe you're already married. You wanna get divorced? We got a special tonight . . ."

Armando's pitch trailed off at the next stall as a wrinkled woman, her hair bound in a red, white and green scarf, plucked at Cullen's sleeve. "You need some nice jewelry for this pretty girl. Let me show you."

Like most of the shops, many of the items were gaudy and cheap. But the aged señora reached under a serape draped about her shoulders.

She withdrew a necklace—a thin silver chain from which hung a delicate, perfectly sculpted, silver rose, not quite the size of a dime. At the middle of its open petals glinted a tiny diamond.

Shelby gave a gasp of delight.

"How much?" Cullen asked.

"Oh, Cullen, no. I didn't bring much money. You can't afford—"

"Thirty dollars." The woman grinned, stretching the deep wrinkles. "She likes it, I can tell. The rose is beautiful, like her. See the silver against her skin?"

The woman draped the chain so the rose lay against Shelby's arm.

"I could pay ten dollars," Cullen said.

"Oh, no. This is not like what the others sell on the street. This is fine workmanship. I gave you my bargain price already. But, since she is such a pretty girl and you are so much in love, I do twenty-five."

Cullen adopted a regretful expression. "The rose *is* beautiful. I am short of funds, though. All I *have* is fifteen dollars. Would you take my last peso?"

The woman waved a dismissive hand, turning her attention to straightening the other merchandise.

"Come on, Shelby."

They passed five paces when the old lady called after them, "Okay, okay. A *vieja* like me shouldn't stand in the way of true love. Fifteen dollars."

They retraced their steps. Cullen asked the woman, "Can you change a twenty?"

She cackled a dry laugh. She clasped the chain around Shelby's neck and said to her, "This one's a scoundrel. You be careful, okay?"

= = = ¦¦ = = =

They walked another hour, neither willing to abandon this night. But with each step, Shelby weighed the extension of their time together against her mother's capacity for worry.

Finally, she said, "Cullen, we need to go."

He nodded. Retracing their path, Cullen stopped abruptly, turning her to face him. He cupped her face with his hands, then kissed her.

With a nod toward the other side of the street, he said, "We could, you know."

"Could what?" Shelby followed his gesture toward the word CHAPEL painted with black letters on a whited-out window.

"No one would have to know. We could just . . . do it."

"Oh, Cullen, how could we? You're here. I'm going to Colorado. How would we . . . what would we . . ."

Cullen's grin told her he was kidding . . .maybe.

"I guess I wouldn't want you to get married in a chapel with a neon beer sign in the window," he said. "But it's a thought, isn't it?"

Shelby laughed.

"Don't worry, Cullen," she said. "We're eighteen years old. We have all the time in the world."

ACKNOWLEDGMENTS

First and foremost, thanks to Nancy for her unwavering belief and support.

Thanks also to my editor, Laura Taylor, who shepherded and encouraged this book from its earliest moments.

Two writers' groups have shaped my education as I've attempted to learn this craft—
The Southern California Writers' Conference, where I found Laura and Acorn Publishing, and
The Writers' Hotel.

Scott Wolven and Shanna McNair have offered so much valuable insight.

I must add clarification regarding the gunfight at the haunted house. The young woman who originated that scheme and perpetrated the shooting is nothing like Christy Hammond. She was a smart and beautiful girl who formulated a plan I have long admired. No one was injured. This is the second time I have borrowed this scene for literary purposes, the first as a short story published many years ago in New Mexico Magazine.

Finally, thanks to Shelby and all other childhood friends who created the memories that spark an old man's imagination. Remember guys, if anyone asks, it's fiction.

Made in the USA
Monee, IL
03 September 2019